An Ordinary Hero

An Ordinary Hero

Debra Feldman

Debra Feldman

To Jeff —
All good things in life!

Mystery and Suspense Press
New York Lincoln Shanghai

An Ordinary Hero

Mystery and Suspense Press
an imprint of iUniverse, Inc.

For information address:
iUniverse, Inc.
2021 Pine Lake Road, Suite 100
Lincoln, NE 68512
www.iuniverse.com

ISBN: 0-595-28862-6 (pbk)
ISBN: 0-595-74904-6 (cloth)

Printed in the United States of America

This book is dedicated to my mom and dad, and to the men and women who served our country in Vietnam—a place where those in charge should have known better, but somehow didn't.

Special thanks to:
A man who'd like to be known as just Joe, Rick Renshaw and Marc Leepson—a bunch of extraordinary guys who fought for their country in Vietnam and got to come home alive.

Acknowledgments to the following ordinary heroes and their contributions to this book:
Johanna, Rick, Patrice, and Victoria for their total honesty
Vivian Kane M.D., F.A.C.E.P., Dr. Mona Sigal
The Massachusetts Police
Sergeant Justin Smith, US Marine Corp.
Sergeant Patrick Kelley, Sergeant Gerald Patten, US Army
Staff Sergeant William Kanute, US Army
Staff Sergeant David Pratt, US Army
Sergeant Sean Moser, US Army
And to all of those who offered information and support, but preferred to remain nameless.

An excerpt from: *The Book of Life— Dictionary of Time*

Anti-Time (an•ti'•time), proper n. Any moment before a specific Reweaver's own time, or a time where it is possible for a Reweaver to overlap their own life.

Overlap (o•ver•lap'), proper n. Emotional Time travel to the past. Naturally occurring phenomenon, long thought to be a myth or old wives tale, implemented by Time to correct outcomes of events.—**See** UNLIVE, v.t. *1. to undo or annul (past life, etc.). 2. to live so as to undo the consequences of.*

Prior memory (pri•or mem•or•y), proper n. Once Time and its Reweavers have cause outcomes to change, a memory from a previous outcome that no longer exists.

Red Tattoo (red tat•too), proper n. The pale red circular mark that Time places on the upper left arm (deltoid) of any Time-piece or other Reweaver.

Reweaver (re•weav'•er), proper n. Overlap missionary. Marked by Time with a pale red broken circle; also known as the Red Tattoo.

Second memory (sec'•ond mem'•or•y), proper n. Though not personally experienced, a memory of a changed outcome.

Time-piece (time'•piece), proper n. First, or primary, Reweaver, of any particular Overlap tale, transported to the very beginning. **See also** REWEAVER, n.

It was a moment in history, a time of war, when a series of seemingly inconsequential events led up to a mission going sour. The mission was covert, meaning there are no records. There were few survivors. Of those who did survive, some have taken their own lives, the others refuse to talk. They have their reasons. It is doubtful we will ever know the true facts of this mission or why it was worth the loss of so many lives. This novel is a fictitious explanation of the events that led up to, and away from, that moment.

PROLOGUE

▼

Time is a fragile, invisible fabric, woven from predetermined events, written into the Book of Life. There is no way to erase or alter them. Outcomes, however, are permitted to take random twists and turns and are the result of choices made after an event occurs. Time sits as sole judge and jury over whether an outcome is satisfactory.

Although Time travel is possible, it is not the voluntary act it was long thought to be. The process, called Overlap, is Time transporting a traveler's emotions into Anti-Time—a Time before their own, sometimes to Overlap their own lives. Travelers, known as Reweavers, bring the future into the past to offer answers and interfere with outcomes without actually interfering, but it is not themselves who must ultimately be satisfied by what remains, it is Time.

Who will Time select to be a Reweaver? Those who possess courage in spite of overwhelming obstacles; with an unshakable sense of obligation to protect; who will find the truth when it seems impossible; a willingness to sacrifice themselves without regard for rewarded; with the ability to attach themselves to others in ways that are more binding than blood? It is all of that, together with opportunity and being the one person who will instinctively, if purely accidentally, know, do, and say, that which is necessary to help those whose lives would otherwise be destroyed. They effect nothing…and everything.

This is one such story, the telling of which is a story in itself, about ordinary people, performing extraordinary deeds, which turn them into ordinary heroes. They can be nothing less.

CHAPTER 1

▼

BROOKLINE, MA—2010
CLOSURE

It is almost 8:00 AM on a typical fall Sunday in New England. The streets are practically deserted and today's weather is pleasant. The sky is a clear blue and today's temperature will reach 68 degrees—perfect sweater weather. There is a light breeze and the brisk nights set the trees ablaze with bright, crayon-colored leaves—orange, yellow, copper, and red.

The Pie Lady II, a dessert store in Brookline, Massachusetts, is closed for the day. Blinds are drawn, the front door is locked and a sign, in the picture window, asks customers to please return on Monday. Connie and Emily are out back, working at the kitchen's roll-out counter. The big industrial oven is preheating and two pots are simmering on the stove. The smell of blueberries and Bing cherries, each bubbling away in a syrup made from their own juice, Karo syrup, lemon juice, and a little lemon zest, fills the kitchen. Connie pulls out two rolling pins, while Emily prepares their work surface with a light sprinkle of flour.

The Pie Lady became an enormous success; because Connie never used anything but the finest ingredients, ensuring that her pies and cakes were always fabulous. Today, following SOP (Army talk for *standard operating procedure*), only the best will be used for the people who made life, as they now know it, possible.

An Anniversary, of sorts, is planned for later in the day and everyone is bringing their culinary specialty to Connie's house. Connie's and Emily's specialty is pies, and they still have much left to do before the party. As usual, there will be way too much food, but…so what. Before Connie left the house this morning, she put a huge roast into the oven, which is cooking as we speak. Her best baby-sitter volunteered to keep an eye on things and intervene. "The roast could decide to set itself on fire," he insisted. Connie was certain that by the time she returned home, the nearly done roast would have been ignored all day and the baby-sitter would be napping in his favorite spot.

Tonight's gathering marks the fourteenth year they celebrate being together. It also marks the first day of the life they all know. Yesterday, on Emily's sixteenth birthday, that new life was officially set in stone. It is the life that should have been theirs from the beginning, but wasn't; because people sometimes act like fools, do foolish things, then keep painful secrets. That silence altered the outcome of everyone's future.

The key to the future they wanted was sharing secrets. Everyone, but Emily, attended the School of Hard Knocks to learn that an unused key has no value. Emily learned from a legend and a story and everyone else's mistakes.

Over the years, Connie told the legend and story so often that Emily could recite them verbatim. And that was pretty much the point. Initially, Connie needed to remind her of several tiny details, insisting that none of these particular details was insignificant enough to be left out. Eventually, Connie simply listened. As the day of Emily's sixteenth birthday approached, it was essential she know the legend and story forward and backward.

In the life that was, everyone did a rather fine job of screwing things up. Time's messengers—the Reweavers, Overlapped their own lives to lead everyone down an alternate path. Everyone has waited fourteen long years to hear the entire story and see proof that Overlap is real. Today, they'll finally have it. It will look like only so much very old paper, but it is a harsh reminder that the details of their life could have been different, and once upon a Time, in another life, they were.

Yes, today is a typical, early fall, New England day. Yesterday? A girl, named Emily, celebrated her sixteenth birthday with her grandparents, in a small New England town, then traveled thru Time.

Connie and Emily each roll out the pie crust in front of them, while an awkward silence hangs heavily in the air. Connie's silence destroyed the future she wanted so badly, but she promised long ago to change her ways and tell the whole story, as many times as it took, to mend the past.

"CeeCee, tell the story again," Emily requested, without looking up.

"You've heard it so many times, you can tell it to me."

"I know, but I like when you tell it. Please? You promised. Remember?"

Did she remember? Could she ever forget? Connie's mind replayed the story. It begins by saying: *one member of our family, close to all, traveled backward in Time to the very beginning. Without the power to change events, a legend and a story as her only weapons, she altered the outcome of all of our lives.*

She is the young traveler who, today, has made it possible for them to celebrate the life they share on this very special Anniversary. That's Anniversary with a capital 'A'.

CHAPTER 2

▼

BROOKLINE, MA—2005

Popi's old file cabinets were made of real wood, had beautiful carving on the sides and eight huge drawers. Emily wanted them, but not for filing. She turned down the new dresser her parents promised, insisting that the most expensive dresser in the world didn't compare to Popi's cabinets.

The problem was, they spent over three decades in Popi's office and every drawer was overstuffed with old files. The contents of the folders were too old for anyone to care about or want any more, but Popi maintained that some held very sensitive information. One never knew the horrible things people were capable of doing with such documents. Emily could have the cabinets, but there was a caveat. She had to destroy every last paper in every one of the eight drawers.

No problem, she thought, *I'll borrow dad's shredder*. But there were paper clips and staples that needed to be removed first and the small shredder could handle only five sheets at a time. Even working methodically, dis-assembly-line fashion, destroying the documents was an enormous project. She started at 7:00 AM and didn't finish until 9:00 PM that night. "Should have had a bon-fire!" She berated herself, when she was nearly done. "At least that would have been fun."

Stuck way in the back of the last drawer, behind the metal slider, was the last old folder. There wasn't anything especially unusual about it, but she had to work so hard, just to get it out of the drawer, she investigated its contents—ancient photographs and yellowing sheets of paper. Instead of destroying them, she folded the papers, then stuck them and the pictures into a back pocket of her jeans. She planned to ask Popi about them later, but, with one thing and another, she forgot.

At nearly ten o'clock that evening, Emily complained of a funny ringing in her ears and a queasy belly. She figured the old dust in the drawers aggravated her allergies. Popi made her lie down on the sofa, immediately, and covered her with one of CeeCee's afghans. Before going to the kitchen to brew one of his home remedies, which was mostly hot water and lemon, he recommended that, if Emily found herself drifting-off, she should go with it. She worked hard all day and deserved the rest, but allergies were not Emily's problem.

Her head began to feel foggy. She felt pulled by a force from within her that was constricting her heart, distancing her from the reality she knew. All she remembered was Popi's last instruction, *just go with it*, and that's exactly what she did.

CHAPTER 3

▼

PETERBOROUGH, NH— 1938

According to the sun's position in the sky, it was mid-morning. The ringing in Emily's ears and queasiness were both gone. She was walking down an unpaved country road, lined on both sides with huge, ancient trees and gravel crunched under her shoes. Well back from the trees were houses, each with a wide front porch. One particular yard caught her eye. A young boy, about her age, was sitting on a tree swing, as if he were waiting for someone.

The familiar setting was the opening scene of her recurring dream. In a moment, she expected the sound of her own voice to wake her up and the boy would vanish until next time. She stopped at the fence around the yard, as usual, and called to him.

"What cha doin'?"

"Waiting," he answered. "My friend, Connie, is inside, probably for the rest of the day, if I know her. Her mom made some new dresses and Connie has to stand still while the hems get pinned. She can never stand still and can't come out to play until all the pinning is done."

From inside the house next door came the sound of an impatient female voice. "Constance Yellowfeather, if you don't stand still, you're going to grow out of these dresses before I can hem them."

"Yep," the boy said a bit dejected, "gonna take all day."

The dream never advanced this far; because this was no dream. The myth of Overlap was every bit as real as CeeCee always said it was. There really was a Time-piece, who went back to the very beginning and told the legend and story for the first time. Emily was that Time-piece.

"I'm Emily," she introduced herself.

"Well, today, I'm Ethan-bored-stiff-waitin'-outside-while-Connie-gets-dresses-hemmed-Craig. But that's too formal. You can just call me Ethan." Emily laughed, which made Ethan feel a little better. "Can you skip stones?"

"Sure," Emily assured him.

"Really!" He was surprised and skeptical. "Most girls don't know how. Connie's practically a guy and she'll never get the hang of it. There's a great spot, called the lake in the stream. It's huge and perfect for skipping. Wanna go?"

"Fine by me." Emily accepted the invitation, glad for an opportunity to do a little show-and-tell where no one else was likely to overhear or interrupt.

When they arrived at the widest place in the stream pool, Ethan picked up a handful of stones, kept some for himself and gave the rest to Emily. Knowing her time with him was limited and the importance of choosing the right stones, she selected others that were more suitable. Electing not to waste time taking turns, she skipped four in a row. Each one hopped twelve times.

Ethan let out a low whistle. "That's really something! Who taught you to do that?"

"My Popi."

"Yeah? Does he live around here and more important than that," he was grinning from ear-to-ear, "would he teach *me?*"

"Well, he lives around here, but he can't teach you."

Ethan slowly nodded, terribly disappointed. "I understand. It's a family secret." Then he brightened. "What if I offered him something in exchange?" Ethan offered hopefully. "What's your Popi's name?"

"I believe he said that today his name is Ethan-bored-stiff-waitin'-outside-while-Connie-gets-dresses-hemmed-Craig." Ethan looked at her suspiciously. "You see, it's not a secret, just physically impossible for you to teach yourself something, *before* you know how to do it—if you follow me."

"You're one of those crazy lunatics, aren't you? Escaped from a special hospital."

"An escaped lunatic, hanging around, skipping stones…with you?"

Ethan gave it a second. "I suppose not, but I don't know what an escaped lunatic might do, especially one who says they think I'm their Popi."

"No. No. I didn't mean to say I think that," Emily assured him, and he looked a little relieved. Maybe she wasn't a crazy lunatic after all. "What I meant to say was, you *are* my Popi." She skipped another stone, made it hop fifteen times and knew she had Ethan's undivided. "There's proof, if you can stand to hear it. It's pretty grizzly and scary." Ethan's nod said to proceed. "Ever seen anything like this?" Emily pushed up her sleeve to expose the light red birthmark on her left upper arm.

"The Red Tattoo? Never saw one, but I heard stories."

Connie's dad, Horace Yellowfeather, told him and Connie tales of Overlap—people from the future who help and protect people who came before them in Time.

"Then you know that I'm here to Reweave this moment. If I'm successful, you and I can fix our future."

"How old are you? Ten?" Emily nodded. "And I'm ten. Two ten-year-olds can't fix something as big as the future, can they?"

Emily shrugged. "If we couldn't, I wouldn't be here. Our story says: *the stones of the Time-piece jumping on water begin the saga of the end at the beginning.* The letter "T", in the broken circle, marks me as the Time-piece and the very beginning was when we skipped the stones. We made them hop on the water."

"But what's the value of skipping stones?"

"I didn't say I understood it. All I said was that we had to do it. You invited me and I said yes. Making them hop was a means to an end. I got your attention, didn't I?"

Ethan nodded. Did she ever! How cool would it be when his friends saw him skip the same stone twelve or more times—with one toss!

"If we can change the outcome of events, maybe we can prevent the first tear, in the fabric of Time, from happening. Then, if the others can close up the remaining holes…," Emily's voice trailed off.

"And if they can't?" Ethan's mind spun out of control.

"Let's just say that nothing in life should carry so high a price. Nothing." Emily's solemn words belonged to someone with experience beyond her tender years. She skipped her last stone and rubbed her hands together to brushed the sand from them.

"Well, what *is* the price?"

Emily silently stared at the water remembering Popi's by-words. *Never take anyone's word for anything.* Ethan would only believe the answer, if he figured it out on his own.

"Changing the future sounds like an awfully big task," he persisted. "You look pretty calm about the whole thing."

"Now who sounds like the escaped mental patient? You said it yourself, I'm ten, born in 1994. And this is what," Emily did some quick math, "1938? The whole thing starts with me, which means I'm the beginning. How can that be? Shouldn't I be the end? CeeCee says I'm the beginning because in the future it happened when I traveled and by then it had *already* happened.

"Time brought my emotions here to reweave the holes in Time. Well, great!" Emily threw her arms up. "Now what? Our lives are so screwed-up, it's supposed to take four of us to fix it. What if one of us makes things worse? What if it's me? All I have are words—a legend and a story. No reasonable person would believe either one and everything hinges on you believing anyway." Tears of frustration welled in Emily's eyes. She reached around to her back pocket, where she always kept tissues, in case her allergies made her nose run.

"Wait a minute!" Emily held her breath and reached into the opposite pocket. Fortuitously stuck in her pocket, the photographs and papers, from the file, had traveled with her. She had hard evidence, but would it convince Ethan she really wasn't some nut-case with a wild story? If not, the Red Tattoo was just a birthmark.

"Popi calls me Nosy Watkins, and I guess I am. He knew I'd check the Jane Doe file. That's why he made me clean out his cabinets by myself. But what do we do with it?"

She handed everything to Ethan. He examined the pictures—gruesome images of a nearly naked woman. They featured an assortment of fresh injuries, several stitches and a hose in her right side and enough blood to make him uncomfortable. There were bruises, in varying shades of green and yellow, and scars on her back. One or two were still kind of purple, but the rest were white. Ethan knew that meant they were old. He cut his knee open, on a rock, once, sliding into home plate. He spent the balance of the summer watching the injury heal and the scar change the many colors from purple until, more than a year later, it was finally white. He read the graphic descriptions of the injuries and his eyes grew wide as saucers. On the top of the page, in block letters, was printed the name Jane Doe.

"Do you know who did this?" His voice, almost a whisper, was tinged with genuine concern. "Where did you get these? They're awful."

"I found them, when I destroyed Popi's files."

"If your Popi thinks *I* did this, I didn't. I swear. Honestly, I could never hurt anyone! And I never even met any lady named Jane Doe."

"Of course you didn't do it, and, I already said, you *are* my Popi. Jane Doe is just the name you put on the file, so no one would open it and accidentally learn who the woman really was. Her real name is on the back of that last sheet, at the very bottom, in tiny letters. It goes sideways up the page."

Ethan looked at it quickly. "This says 'Constance Yellowfeather'."

"That, it does." She absently skipped another stone.

"You *are* an escaped mental patient." Emily shook her head. "Connie's nine," he vehemently protested. "This woman is a grown-up with…" He was too embarrassed to say the word for the female anatomy, so he made a curving gesture, out and away from his chest, then back again, "you know, she has…," and he made the curving gesture again.

"Are you trying to say 'she has breasts'?" Ethan blushed, but nodded. "That's 'cause the pictures weren't taken until 1965. She needed emergency medical attention that night. Somehow, Pop-op and his friend Carl knew to bring her to you. You were the doctor."

"And this stuff," he gently waved the papers and pictures, "came from one of *my* files?"

"That's right."

"News flash—there's no money for college, let alone medical school. If you know so much, you'd know that."

"I know there's no money *yet*," Emily corrected him. "Look at that name again."

Ethan did. "Still says: 'Constance Yellowfeather'."

"Read it out loud. You're missing something."

Ethan began, "Constance Yellowfeather…," he finally saw the small plus sign, followed by three letters and a superscript number. "That's how I write my initials—EMC^2. The squared is kind of cool, instead of those goofy Roman numerals, which are so square. Hey, that's kinda funny—I'm squared, not square."

"Yeah, whenever someone tells Popi that he's so old he's square, he says, 'I'm not square, I'm *squared*. Besides, it's all relative.' Then he writes his initials, like that, on a piece of paper, gives it to them, and adds 'Go to the library and look it up, Einstein'. He thinks it's big-time funny."

"Einstein? You mean the scientist with the hair?" Ethan used his hands to show Einstein's wild hair-do.

"That's the one."

"I don't get it."

"Give it a few years," Emily giggled, "you will."

Emily taught Ethan to select the special skipping stones. "Half the trick is choosing the right ones." Then she demonstrated the technique, which Ethan practiced and practiced, until he finally got the hang of it. In his precise moment of victory, he saw an unmistakable flash of light in Emily's eyes. He ignored it.

"Now you can show me, so that when I come here, I can show you, and get your undivided. It's a nice little circle of events." She finished by explaining how to save the money for college and medical school—the extra jobs (before and after school), the years of hard work and sacrificing anything extra, and how he would have to convince his father to allow him to even try saving the money. "Papa Simon will offer you a deal for college. Whatever it is, take it."

"If I worked all day, every day, I could never earn enough money for College and Medical School."

"You could, if you invest the money and it grows. Put it in a mutual fund called The Investment Company of America. The dividends and interest will turn the money you earn into the money you need. You're not twenty-one, so Papa Simon will need to open the account for you."

"What's a mutual fund?"

"A group of stocks or bonds that are held by a company. In this case, the Investment Company of America. By buying into the fund you won't need to build a portfolio of your own. You can own a share of *their* portfolio."

"You are nuts!" He was shocked. "The stock market completely crashed not so long ago. Men committed suicide, jumped out of windows, or shot themselves, over the money they lost." Ethan shook his head "I'll never convince my dad to trust my future to it."

"But you have to!" Emily was emphatic. "Otherwise, you can't help CeeCee."

"All of this *is* real." Ethan finally looked as though he believed her.

Emily's relief was audible. "What changed your mind?"

"Everyone around here calls Dad Sy, 'cause they think he likes it, but he doesn't. He hates it. They even rhyme it with other words, call him Sly Guy Sy, and he hates that worse. My dad isn't sly. He's a nice man and even if some prankster from school put you up to this and you guys made up everything, you'd never know to call him Simon. Besides, only Connie's dad and I ever call her CeeCee."

"The second *Cee* is for Canter," Emily volunteered, "Grandma Ruth's maiden name."

"Did Connie tell you that?" Emily nodded. "We're best friends and I almost had to pry it out of her," Ethan offered. "She says it's hard enough to explain being a Native American with blue eyes and blond hair; without also trying to explain being half Jewish on top of it. Her dad's got a great answer for that one. He says they're Jewish Indians, from one of the lost tribes. 'The Shmohawks'." Emily and Ethan said it together, laughing. "Why am I laughing?" He asked.

"Cause it's funny!" Emily offered.

"Not that funny. I've got a little Shmohawk in the mix myself." Then Ethan turned serious. "Mostly, it was those pictures. They're color. Is this the future of photography?"

"Color photographs isn't the half of it." Emily got excited. "One day, there'll be special cameras that make instant home movies you can watch right on your TV."

"What's a TV?"

"Never mind." Emily laughed at herself. "I forgot where I was for second. Let's just say that all that stuff is in the future."

Ethan had been pacing and mumbling, not really listening, trying to get a handle on a detail needling his brain. *If she wasn't born until 1994, there must be two generations between her and me.*

"Emily," Ethan hesitated voicing his speculation. "This thing you do today, it doesn't protect only CeeCee, does it? It protects your Pop-op and his child *and* you. Is that right?" Emotion brought a lump to Emily's throat. All she could do was nod. "Your Pop-op, is he…my child?"

Emily could hardly believe that Ethan figured it out on his own. She nodded again. This time, the tears spilled over the flood gates and ran down her cheeks.

Ethan draped an arm around her shoulders. It was an action far beyond his own tender years, but he couldn't help himself. He wanted to protect her. "I'll find a way to convince dad. I will!" It sounded more like Ethan was trying to convince himself. "I never had a friend like Connie before. She's my…," he hesitated, but realized he wasn't admitting anything Emily didn't already know. "She's my girlfriend. I'll find your Pop-op's friend Carl and I won't let anything bad happen to any of you. I promise."

"Overlap is just a concept to me. Can you explain how it works? It might help one day, if I know."

"Overlap isn't accidental and you can't volunteer or choose to go. Time chooses you, marks you, so the holes in the fabric of Time know where to attach themselves. While the holes become the same size as your emotions, you see your mission in a recurring dream, kind of a preview. When the Overlap is about to begin, there's an eerie kind of whistle that no one else can hear, which is the Wind of the Ages blowing thru the holes. Oh, there's a feverish queasy-in-your-belly feeling, like you're coming down with the flu and it feels like something squeezes your heart, separating the you on the inside from the one on the outside. When it's time to go, you go. There's no putting it off and no refusing. Not that I wouldn't have come. I'd do anything to help and that's probably *why* Time chose me.

"Your emotions pass into Anti-Time and, when your mission is complete, the whistle returns and Time lets go again. Somehow, your emotions and the correct outcome mend the holes. The whistle stops, the queasy fever goes away and you're home. At least, that's the myth. I only hope it's that easy."

"But if they're holes, couldn't someone who isn't the Reweaver, say, someone smaller, accidentally fall thru them?"

"You know how each piece of a jig-saw puzzle fits one specific hole in it? Well, each Reweaver is the perfect fit for one specific hole in Time. Even identical twins aren't totally identical, so only a marked twin could Overlap. The other twin could never go in their place. My emotions were the perfect fit for these holes, and how I ended up on Jones Road today.

"I'm this story's first Reweaver, its Time-piece. Today, I will accidentally cause something that needs to happen. Something that wouldn't have happened at all, if I hadn't come."

"Which is what?"

"Search me. Maybe it was giving you the Jane Doe file. It's the only one I didn't destroy. I planned to quiz Popi, I mean you, about it, but I forgot and that's how it was still in my pocket when I needed to show it to you here. I emptied the cabinets by myself, remember, so only I saw it or could take it. Having it showed you CeeCee's name, in your own writing. Without it, I'm just some girl with a vivid imagination. Plus, you never taught anyone, but me, how to make a stone skip like that. You effectively turned me into an anomaly who could cause that which *must* be."

"You're talking in riddles. What is *that which must be?*"

"Any event written into The Book of Life. No one can change or prevent them. Today's event, whatever it is, is written in that book. Hey, when you figure it out, let me know. In fact, tell me when I get back." She teased. "You have over sixty years to solve the puzzle.

"Our family has a legend and a story. Used together, they form our map and keep us from getting lost. They will be told and retold thru the years, until the legend's meaning is revealed. All I can do is answer questions and tell what I know, and what I know is that everything starts today with my stones jumping on water and later CeeCee choosing Jack will prove that Overlap is real."

"Wait a minute." Ethan couldn't believe it. He thought they were crazy about each other. "CeeCee chooses someone else!"

"Yes. It's the outcome of an event."

"So, let's change the event!"

"I need you to pay attention and remember what I tell you. We cannot! Whatever is meant to be, must be. It's important that she choose him. You don't have to like it, just pray the truth will change the final outcome."

The truth? Jealousy tore at Ethan's heart. Who gave a rat's ass for the truth when some stupid story warned him that Connie, his CeeCee, would choose some other guy? He'd lie thru his teeth if he had to. He had a quick conversation with himself. *Well, fine! If Connie wants to be with stupid Jack, maybe I should let her.* Then Ethan calmed down. *OK, so CeeCee chooses this guy, but maybe Emily's right and the truth will make her unchoose him. Get the details.*

"Who is this Jack? Why did she choose him?"

"I'm ten." Emily shrugged. "They don't tell me everything. No one says why, all they say is *Jack.*"

"And the truth can stop her from wanting to choose him?" The whole thing sounded ridiculous.

"You know," Emily's mind quickly flew over every detail anyone ever told her, "no one, including CeeCee, ever said she *wanted* to choose him, just that she *chose* him. Maybe that choice caused the first tear—it was a bad outcome.

"OK. Suppose you're right. How can you know that choosing this Jack isn't an event?"

"Because it was a deliberate act, not some chance occurrence, like Isaac Newton sitting under that tree when, BAMM!, an apple landed on his head. My time here is short, so I'm afraid you're on your own to figure that out too. It'll be an event that causes CeeCee to make a choice and she chooses Jack. Look at it from Time's perspective, it might make it easier."

"What?" Ethan was lost.

"From the look on your face, CeeCee's choice sounds like a life altering event, but an event made her do it, so it's an outcome, like you and CeeCee becoming friends. I'm sure that feels like an event too, but the only reason you met is because Papa Horace took the job at the chemical plant and moved the family to Peterborough. Only then did he buy the house next to yours, which allowed you and CeeCee to meet and *then* become friends. Everything, but taking the job, is a result of moving here, none of which would have happened if Papa Horace hadn't taken the job in the first place."

"Are you sure you're only ten?"

"Sometimes I wonder that myself."

"I don't see what any of that has to do with CeeCee choosing this Jack."

"OK." Emily went with an explanation a little closer to home. "Let's try this another way. Let's say you kiss her—"

"Yeah. Let's say that." Ethan interrupted, making them both laugh. He liked the idea of kissing CeeCee.

"Stop that!" She admonished with a smile. "Anyway, it's absolutely an event that requires some sort of response or choice. Probable outcomes—she sits there in shock; slaps your face; or kisses you back. Let's be optimistic and say she kisses you back."

"By all means, let's be optimistic." He began to smirk.

"On the surface, a small event caused a small outcome—a kiss given got a kiss back. But, fast-forward three days and you find out it didn't end there. She told her mom, your mom, all of her friends, and printed it in the local newspaper. Everyone in town starts talking about it and the kids at school tease you unmercifully. Nothing, beyond your kiss, would have happened on their own, which makes your kiss a tiny little event and everyone in town knowing about it a great big outcome. Get it now?"

"Yeah. I get it. And only a bad outcome can tear hole in Time, not a bad event or even a good one, like us kissing."

"Correct. This event is capable of producing an outcome that could go either way. The simple act of withholding the truth turns a desirable outcome into an undesirable one and tears our family's first hole in Time."

"You said that before, first hole, first Overlap. How many will there be all together?"

"Seven, including this one."

"This is hard," Ethan's brow knit together, "and complicated."

"Yeah," Emily agreed, "and no instruction book."

Emily told of the way things were, the balance of the story as she knew it. As she was done, the strange whistle and queasiness returned. She eagerly shoved up the left sleeve of her shirt. Her silent expression spoke volumes.

"What's wrong?"

"The circle...it didn't close all the way. I wasn't successful."

"Well, whatever else there is to say, say it! Whatever else there is to do, let's do it!"

"But I don't know anything else; they don't tell me everything. Besides...I hear the whistle. We're out of time." Downhearted, Emily stood. "We better get back. CeeCee could be looking for you by now and, if she is, you'd have to explain where you've been, and with whom. Think you could explain this?"

Ethan admitted that he could not.

Emily left Ethan where she found him, sitting on the tree swing. Just before she departed, he asked one final question. "Emily, these pictures and papers...*this* is the price of us being together, isn't it?"

She cast her eyes to the ground, but when she looked up again, her expression said that he was right.

"I can't allow that! It's unacceptable!"

"There's only way to bring the price down. I must be successful next time. And, in the meantime, you do *exactly* as I asked. Never waiver, not for a second. Remember, the truth can change CeeCee's choice, which, in turn, will change the outcome. And you can't tell her anything I told you...unless she asks. Even then, all you can do is answer her questions. Answers only, swear and promise."

Reluctantly, Ethan gave his word.

"You know that guy, Einstein, some of his last theories were about Time and how our lives in the past, present, and future may exist simultaneously. I believe those theories came from being directly involved in an Overlap. Maybe a visitor made him see that *it has become appallingly clear that our technology has surpassed our humanity*. That's a direct quote. The only remnant of humanity evident in our technology, those photos, is that Jack didn't actually kill CeeCee. Maybe you can help the Reweavers force our humanity to overtake our technology and keep her from being beaten in the first place.

"Do you quote everyone?"

She shrugged. "In our hour of need, they'll save us from ourselves, so that, in the moment of change, we can forget just how grateful we really are."

"OK, I'll bite," he smiled, "who said that?"

"You did." Her voice held a high degree of pride.

"Do you remember everything you're told?"

"I guess. So when I get back, tell me *everything*. OK?"

"Promise."

Ethan shoved Emily's gift into the back pocket of his pants. With great resolve and determination, he swore always to tell the truth, no matter the cost. Nothing would ever be as costly as CeeCee being nearly beaten to death. He also swore to convince everyone that he had to be a doctor. *He just had to.*

A little ways down Jones Road Emily turned around and called out, "See ya later!" She laughed at how silly it sounded, when he wouldn't see her for more than sixty years.

"See ya later!" Ethan called back, laughing for the same reason.

Connie came bouncing out her front porch door, just as Emily disappeared out of sight, around the curve in Jones Road. "What cha been doin' all day?" She asked, descending the steps.

"Nothing much." He looked at Connie as if seeing her for the first time.

"You OK?" She asked, sitting next to him on the swing. "You look kind of funny, like you saw a ghost or something."

"Me? Nah! Couldn't be better."

Ethan smiled, knowing that one day, his Connie would be the mother of his, as yet, unborn son and then, for the first time, he kissed her.

CHAPTER 4

▼

BROOKLINE, MA—2005

Emily returned to her own Time. When she opened her eyes, Popi was holding her in his strong arms, and she was hanging on for dear life. Her grip finally relaxed and they held each other in silence. He whispered in her ear. "The answer is: I became a doctor. It never would have happened without you."

"But, Popi, I failed." Tears of disappointment streamed down her cheeks.

Ethan kissed the side of her head. "So you'll try again."

"But I'm scared I'll fail again."

"Sweetheart, it's not brave, if you're not scared."

"Why does everyone keep saying that to me?"

"Because you're the bravest girl we've ever known." Popi pulled her closer. "You're my hero."

Telling the story should have been enough, but it wasn't. Emily misspoke one detail—a detail that her family slightly altered when they changed the story's rating from R to PG; because of Emily's tender years. Connie didn't just *choose* Jack, she married him, and *slightly prematurely*, gave birth to her only child.

Yesterday, Emily turned sixteen and traveled to the middle of the story, then to nearly the beginning, and told her tale three more times, but it was the R rated version, so telling it *was* enough.

CHAPTER 5

▼

JAFFREY, NH— AUGUST 31, 1947
IN THE BEGINNING .

It was 5:15 AM. Constance Makepeace was alone and lay in a dimly lit hospital room, awaiting the doctor's arrival. She was ready to deliver what would turn out to be her only child. She had been in labor for a little over two hours.

The first labor pain woke her at 3:00 AM. Knowing that it might be a while before her water broke, she got up and quietly got ready. She put the small suitcase, packed weeks before, near the front door, lest it be forgotten in their haste to leave for the hospital. Then, she brushed her teeth, had a quick shower and got dressed.

Connie's husband, Jack, specifically said not to wake him until the very last second, if her labor started during the night. At best, he would have a long day ahead of him, which included completing Connie's chores. He couldn't do that on no sleep. When you lived on a farm, there were always chores and they had to get done, whether you wanted to do them or not. Allowing Connie to lay in a hospital for a week was a luxury they could ill afford, but luxury or not, like it or not, that is what would happen. Her water broke while she was in the shower and at just past 4:30 she hesitantly woke him.

"Jack." She put her hand on his shoulder and shook him gently, "It's time."

He squinched-up his face, opened one eye and looked out the bedroom window. It was pitch black. "It's too early! Let me sleep." He groaned.

"Jack." She reluctantly touched his shoulder again. "The baby is coming."

"Fine!" He tossed off his covers, griping at her, as if she had some control over the situation. He threw on a flannel shirt and overalls, not bothering either to comb his hair or brush his teeth. "Come on!" He snapped. "I don't have all day."

They drove to the hospital in silence, not a word passing between them and arrived at 5:00 AM. Jack dropped her off at the curb, without so much as a kiss. It made little difference to him why Connie would be gone on this day and for the next six. The bottom line was the same. He could not play *farm manager* and skip out at noon, to spend the better part of the day and evening at Duffy's Tavern, drinking away most of what little money the farm earned. No, he and their farm-hand, Chris Wilson, would share the chores. Jack sped away, fishtailing down the road.

*   *   *   *

Dr. Weaver examined Connie to confirm she was properly dilated before moving her. From her advanced condition and the speedy progress of the labor, this would gratefully be a quick and easy delivery. Connie was transferred to a gurney and a nurse wheeled her into the delivery room. Matthew Martin Makepeace was delivered from his mother, at precisely 6:30 AM and Dr. Weaver smacked his bottom.

It would not be the last time someone smacked Matthew Makepeace, just to make him cry.

Although it was a swift and relatively easy labor, the baby was large, weighing-in at ten pounds, four ounces. He had a full head of strawberry blond hair, like his mother, large hands and feet, and a birthmark on his left arm. The doctor was tired, underpaid for his long hours, and like Jack, for him, this day got started way too early. He didn't question the unusual mark; because frankly, he didn't care. He sleepily noted it on the hospital form, along with the date, time of birth, and the infant's length and weight. The last task was taking the baby's foot print, then he was cleaned and placed, naked, into his mother's arms.

Connie cuddled him and spoke in softly hushed tones. "Hello, young man. I could hardly wait to meet you." The infant seemed captivated by the sound of her voice and looked as if he understood every word. He was happy to be held and hear in full the faintly familiar voice, heard muffled from inside the womb, for the last nine months.

She counted his fingers and toes, held him to her right breast where, without prompting, he began to suckle. For the briefest moment, Connie was completely happy and silently proclaimed that her son was perfect in every way. Then she saw the tiny Red Tattoo on his left arm. She touched it, brushed her thumb over it lightly several times. She wanted to rub it away, wish it away, will it away, but the mark remained. Connie gave a heavy sigh.

Whether others considered Overlap to be real or myth was immaterial to Connie Makepeace. Her newborn son had been marked by Time with the small, pale red, broken circle of the Reweaver. Legend held that each Reweaver was a tiny fragment of Time's fabric. Together, a legend's Reweavers would force that which was written, in The Book of Life, to come to pass. This was the way of Time. It was a fact.

Connie knew, all too well, the fate that awaited her son—endless, sleepless nights and heart-pounding nightmares, filled with paralyzing fear. One day, Matthew would begin to witness his mission in dreams. They would both prepare and frighten him. What he did with that fear, how he used it, when the moment came, would either save him or kill him. He was chosen because his instinct would instruct him how to preserve and repair Time, but would that instinct include preserving himself. Life with Jack was already hard. Now, for Connie and her son, it was also complicated and dangerous. The good news was that Time would always protect him. The bad new was, at what cost?

"I'm sorry my Matthew." Connie apologized. "My poor sweet baby, my special boy, the hero of someone else's life. I hoped you wouldn't have this task in front of you. I'm so sorry."

CHAPTER 6

▼

JAFFREY, NH—
1947–1965
NO LIFE SO PRECIOUS...

The Makepeace Farm was a run down chicken ranch that sold live and slaughtered chickens and fresh eggs. Jack Makepeace, an undereducated bull of a man, inherited the property from his father, a loveless soul who thought horses and children needed to be whipped regularly. Jack followed that example, but Connie always stepped-in and took the beating herself.

"Thems is your beatin's, boy," Jack said. As if Matthew needed reminding.

He tried protecting his mother, even before Jack's first blow found its mark. He would beg, tears in his eyes, "Please, what ever I did, I'm sorry! Tell me what it was and I won't ever do it again."

"This ain't for what you done," Jack sneered. "It's for what you might do, when I ain't lookin'."

Jack despised Connie for her willingness to take Matthew's pain, his black eyes, his welts, and made him stay in the room to watch. "Ya see, boy. Don't pay to care about no one. Never can tell when they's a smackin' in it, and they always is, ain't that right Connie?" Then, Jack would hit her even harder.

Begging made the beating worse and tears meant the business end of Jack's belt. By the time Matthew was six, he learned to give Jack what he demanded.

It was about then that Matthew started really helping on the farm, by tending the baby chicks in the incubator. Each day, he fed them, made sure they had plenty of water, and emptied their litter pan. He liked looking after things and was proud that the chicks thrived. He was even more proud that he helped the farm to be successful.

The farm also maintained two cows, which required milking twice a day and hay, corn and grain to keep them good milk producers. They needed to be let out for grazing in the morning and brought back in before nightfall. Their stalls needed cleaning—the shoveling of manure into the trough behind the stalls, that ran the length of the barn. The heavy manure was then pushed and shoved to the end of the trough, until it was finally shoved into the manure spreader at the side of the barn.

It was hard, dirty work, most of which was accomplished before Matthew began his home-school lessons with Connie. When Matthew was ten—big enough to do it alone, Jack let Chris Wilson go. He figured why pay someone, when you had a built in slave?

*   *   *   *

By the time Matthew was eleven, he was bigger and stronger than Connie. He figured his body could stand Jack's beatings better than hers and it became her turn to watch in silence. She often thought they should each run in a different direction; Jack couldn't possibly chase both of them. Neither of them had a prayer of really getting away. Jack would just beat whichever one he caught first, which would probably be Connie, and when he caught her, he would probably kill her.

Matthew stood stoic, vowing never to cry, no matter how hard the blow, which only made Jack strike harder. Matthew came to think of Jack as little more than a beast. Refusing to cry came to be a matter of honor. Although the exact moment he made the vow faded over time, he never forgot the vow itself. Jack Makepeace, and no one else for that matter, would ever make him cry again.

The following year, Matthew hit an incredible growth spurt. From a puny five-two, he hit six feet even—four inches taller than the old man. He wasn't sure he could take Jack in an all-out swinging match, but a good back-handed whack would send the guy flying.

Once, while trying to grab a chicken to slaughter it, the bird bit the back of Matthew's hand, really hard. Matthew yanked his hand away with a yowl, then gave the bird such a forceful back-handed smack that its head literally flew off in one direction, while the body ran around the coop in the opposite direction. It was at that point, Jack's beatings stopped. At least Matthew thought they did.

Matthew thoroughly cleaned the coops in late May or early June. One year he waited until mid-August and no matter how early in the day he began, the intense heat of late summer was positively excruciating. He promised himself that was a one time mistake.

Although the main coop's poop-pen was only a dug-out section of floor covered with chicken wire, it was a big coop with a big pen. Clearing away the dung seemed to take forever. The chicken waste was carried to the manure spreader one shovelful at a time, which was still less effort than shoveling it into a wheel-barrow, hauling it, and *then* shoveling it into the spreader.

It was hot, stinking work. By mid-morning, his manual labor mixed with the heat in the coops to cause his body to perspire and his pores to open. No matter how he swore to keep his shirt on, unbuttoning the front and rolling up the sleeves never provided enough relief. Before long, the shirt was hanging on a nail and his unprotected skin was on fire from the caustic fumes. The stench draped over his sweaty body like a heavy blanket of acid, causing his exposed skin to suffer what felt like the attack of a thousand microscopic bees. Bathing afterward was only more punishment. The stink so completely became a part of his skin and hair that he needed a scrub brush to remove it. By the time he was fit to associate with other humans, his skin was bright red and tingled like a sunburn.

The years passed and, despite Jack's laziness, their business increased. Each year there were more chickens. Each year cleaning the coops took longer and longer. Even with the monumental task of cleaning main coop behind him, there was the endless tide of chicken shit in the small coops to contend with. It wasn't a task he lingered over, like mowing hay, which was actually kind of fun. He was never finished with those coops soon enough.

Some of their land actually belonged to the Filmore Ski Tow. They worked it as tenant farmers, growing a field of hay that was never nearly enough to feed their cows, but some hay was better than none, so it was always worth doing. The Filmores took back the land during the winter months. All of the chickens were transferred to the large coop and the smaller coops, built on wooden sleds, were towed to a row of trees, out of the way of the ski run. Crowding the chickens made them nervous and lay fewer eggs, but the smaller coops had no heat. A nervous chicken still had value. One that froze to death didn't.

Ben Filmore usually hired Matthew as a ski instructor. The work was fun and it was one of the few times in the year he got paid for his work with cash.

*   *   *   *

As Matthew got older, Jack did progressively less, until he did nothing at all. Matthew and Connie took on all of the farm's responsibilities, becoming a great team. Connie looked after the house, took over the incubator and collected eggs. Matthew fed and slaughtered chickens, hauled grain and bails of hay, chopped cords of wood, and shoveled mountains of manure. He even went on ambush patrol with their twelve gauge shot gun. Someone had to kill the ground hogs that ate their hard work and Jack was too busy stewing his prunes down at Duffy's. And Matthew bartered with neighboring farms. He mowed and bailed hay; they paid in some of the bailed hay, chickens, and sacks of grain for the cows that produced the milk that helped him grow strong enough to do the work in the first place. Matthew saw it as a nice little circle of events.

So much muscle and strength were involved in completing Matthew's daily tasks, that he filled out a little more each day. By his fifteenth birthday, he weighed in at one-sixty, most of which was lean athletic muscle. When he was ready to begin tenth grade, Connie decided he needed the social interaction of a real High School. He quickly made friends, who encouraged him to take up after school sports. *The teams need you*, they pleaded, but Connie and the farm always needed him more. In his junior year, Connie's small side business, of home made pies, earned enough money to re-hire Chris Wilson. He did some of Matthew's morning chores and all of his afternoon chores. It gave Matthew the opportunity to try out and make first string for Basketball, Baseball and Football with his best buddy Carl.

By the time Matthew was seventeen, he was six-two, one-eighty, and still growing. Jack always seemed afraid of him, but everyone at school thought he was a quiet friendly kid that was just really big. Teachers referred to The Big Guy and everyone knew who they meant. He and Carl were even in height, but Matthew had the broadest shoulders.

Coach Evans, big on nick-names, didn't much like Big Guy. All of his guys were big. When Matthew Martin Makepeace joined the football squad, Coach took his three Ms and christened him Tre—Italian for three. After that, Connie was the only one who ever called him Matthew.

*   *   *   *

Jack had resumed beating Connie, but the long sleeves she wore, even on the hottest summer day, concealed his dirty-work. And he was bright enough to choose only the nights Tre was out of the house, at one after-school practice or another. He'd corner her in the kitchen, smack her around for a while, then add painful words. "Clean up this mess, ya hag," then he spilled her hard work onto the floor. "No one wants your old pies!"

Of course, cleaning up Jack's mess was only the beginning of Connie's evening chores. There was also the business of masking any visible bruises, so Tre wouldn't know. And then, still feeling the sting of Jack's hands, she had to remake the precious pies that paid for Tre to have some decent clothes and play after-school sports.

Word of mouth eventually had people traveling from other towns to buy Connie's pies and the money they earned allowed Tre a little time off from the farm, just to be a kid. Jack cursed Connie's success and for not simply handing the money over to him. He made excuses, "She don't respect me, else she'd give over that pie money, so I could treat myself the way a man like me deserves, 'stead of wastin' it on the boy."

Joy Evans, affectionately known as Mrs. Coach, sometimes came to watch practice games. Near the end of her sixth, and last, pregnancy, she waddled on into the gym and took a seat in the bleachers. Coach waved to her from center court, smiled warmly, cupped his hand around the side of his mouth and yelled to her, "Keep thinking boy! Think: full basketball team." Then, he flexed his arms like Charles Atlas and stomped around in a little circle.

Despite being uncomfortable and feeling very much like a beached whale, Joy laughed and yelled back to him, "Hey John, you want to come over here and bite my pregnant a—?"

He wagged a finger, making sure she didn't finish, his face expressing a reprimand that required no words. Everyone witnessing the exchange, including Tre, laughed with them. That interaction made him realized that he never once saw his mother or father laugh—not in nearly eighteen years. He remembered Connie's soft words and strained smiles, when he was very little and she tucked him in at night, but that was as close to a laugh as she ever got.

The whole town knew Coach had his heart set on a sixth boy, and that Joy was, not so secretly, hoping for a girl. Everyone else picked a side. One day, Principal Stone came over the loud speaker in the middle of the afternoon. "Coach Evans has canceled practice. He went to meet Mrs. Evans at the hospital. Let's all wish them the best of luck and hope for a nice healthy—" His last word, *baby*, was drowned out by the male students yelling BOY! and the female students yelling GIRL!

The day Joy delivered, most of the team headed for the hospital after school, for first looks at the team's latest addition. Carl pleaded an important paper needed finishing and he was Tre's ride. They headed straight home at the last bell. If Tre helped with Connie's evening chores, she could have a night off to relax. He was glad for the opportunity to surprise her with the two hours he usually gave Coach.

When he walked in the front door, two hours ahead of schedule, the house was both dark and silent. He turned on the living room lamp, calling into the darkness, "Mom! I'm home." Given the hour, he felt certain she would be there. The total silence was not only surprising, it was disturbing. Cautiously, he headed for the back of the house, calling to her again. He reached the kitchen and flipped on the overhead light.

Connie was in a heap, in the middle of the kitchen floor. She had a black eye, bloody lip and assorted bruises that would turn an ugly black and blue. Her visible injuries were bad enough, but the ones Tre couldn't see worried him more. He silently cursed himself for not knowing what, apparently, had been going on for quite a while. A childhood with Jack confirmed that a beating as severe as this was hardly the result of nearly a decade of abstinence.

Tre jumped for the phone, so enraged that he could have killed, but kept the angry tremor from his voice. "Hey, Carl, listen, can I borrow your wheels? I need to run an errand."

Carl didn't realize Tre's request was not also an invitation. "I'm there before I hang up."

He tried to say, *No, I only wanted to borrow the car,* but it was too late. Carl's family lived at the next farm over and, in under two minutes, Tre heard the slam of his car door. Friends since they were crawling, Carl headed straight for the kitchen and let himself in through the back door. Though he always suspected Jack was no Ward Cleaver, the scene, that could only be described as surreal, took a few seconds to sink in. He stood, transfixed, in the doorway, then rushed in and dropped to the floor next to Connie.

"Holy shit!! Is she still breathing?" Ever so carefully, Carl cupped the side of Connie's head in his hand. "Mrs. Makepeace, Connie, can you hear me?" She blinked and tried a feeble smile that made her lip start bleeding again. Relief. She was alive.

At six-two and one-eighty himself, Carl Summers was a tough opponent on the field. He was also every teams' first-aid maven and one of the gentlest people on earth. Tre noted it again as he handled Connie's broken and battered body. Carl planned to enlist after graduation. He was going to be a medic. In fact, that had become his nick-name. He knew things. He also the kind of people who could help Connie Makepeace and then keep quite about it. He made a quick phone call, then the boys wrapped her in a blanket and Tre carried her out to the car. They gently placed her on the back seat and Tre climbed in after, cradling his mother, as if she were the child and he the parent.

Seeing her like that, Tre remembered all the beatings she took in his place. Connie was not just his mother, she was his protector. *It was my turn to protect her, but I failed.* Tre pushed the thoughts aside. "I can't lose her. I won't lose her," he whispered. Matthew held Connie closer and began to rock. The strange little story she told, to entertain him and Carl on days when it was either too rainy or too cold to play outside, crawled into his mind and replayed itself. Sitting in the back seat, he tried, once again, to decipher the legend's cryptic messages. He began to wonder if the story or the telling of it was ever meant as entertainment. Was it really a warning to prepare both him and Carl for this moment? Carl started the car and they headed for Keene.

*   *   *   *

Connie was in bad shape. The doctor, Ethan Craig, deemed it out of the question for Tre to see the extent of her injuries or what it would take to patch her up. He was obviously too upset for the kind of visual. Ethan made Tre take a seat in the waiting room, with assurances that he and Carl would take care of her and that she would be fine. Tre could see her when she was cleaned-up.

"She's tough for such a little bird." Ethan remarked after inserting the tube in Connie's side and suturing the incision closed. His heart broke, looking at the beautiful woman lying on his examination table. "She defended herself with the arm. There's virtually no other way to break the ulna so close to her hand, without also breaking the radius. At least it didn't come through the skin." He showed Carl an X-ray. During his years in practice, he'd unfortunately seen worse. "This wasn't the first beating. It should be reported."

"Yeah?" Carl was informal. "Who were you planning to report it to and exactly what do you think they're gonna do about it? They'll call it a domestic squabble, tell you to patch her up, send her back, and butt the hell out. They'll wait until he kills her, then shake their heads. *Tsk, tsk, such a shame. Wish we had known. We might have prevented this.* They don't know; because they don't want to know and they do nothing; because it's easier than getting involved."

Unhappily, Ethan had to agree. They lived in rural New Hampshire where women and children were thought of more like property than people. Their small-town community was fully equipped with abusive men with nothing better to do than beat their wives and kids. The system the authorities used was *patch 'em up and send 'em back.* A lone physician could not buck the system.

Ethan's mind drifted back to when his family lived in Peterborough. Their new next-door neighbors were a family named Yellowfeather—half Native American; half Jewish. The daughter was a pretty little girl named Constance with a beautiful smile and her father's strawberry blond hair—unusual for Native Americans. The summer the Yellowfeathers moved in, Connie was six and he was seven and Ethan had a crush on her from the day they met. By the end of their first month as neighbors, they were best friends. By the time Ethan was a junior in High School, they were inseparable.

Connie grew to be a delicate beauty and Ethan tall and handsome. He was also really smart, and from the time he was ten years old, never talked about anything but becoming a doctor, how he couldn't be anything else. He just couldn't! But poor men can ill-afford to send their children to a good college and then medical school and Ethan's father was a poor man.

"It's a lofty goal, son, but I don't earn anywhere near that kind of money. We get by and the three of us have a pretty nice life." He looked around at their home and property. "Maybe mom and I can put together enough money for a technical school, but four years of college, and four more of Medical School? I'm sorry, Ethan, but we just don't have the money."

"I'll get a job, before or after school?" If nothing else, Ethan Craig was persistent.

"Ethan, please, don't set yourself up for disappointment. There are enough of those waiting for you around every corner. What kind of job? Who would you work for?"

"I'll take any job that will have me. Maybe I could sweep up for Mr. Barns in the market, stock shelves, stuff like that...or a paper route. If I start now, I know that by graduation, I'll have saved all the money I'll need. Please let me try, Pop."

"OK! OK! You try." Simon Craig gave it. "No harm learning the value of a dollar or how hard it really is to earn one. Tell you what, I'll start saving too. It wouldn't hurt me to put away a few cents.

"Saaaay!" Simon Craig was getting an idea. "How about if I talk to your mother about it. She sticks some pin money in her jar every week." He was liking this idea more and more. "Sure! The three of us could do this thing together." He started to pace back and forth, very proud of himself for thinking of a way to help his son reach his goal. "Yeah, it could be a family project. You," Simon stopped pacing and placed his hands on Ethan's shoulders, "could be our investment. Of course," he tapped his cheek with his index finger, as if thinking, "we'll eventually want a return on that investment. I think a grandchild will cover your debt quite nicely." He indicated the Yellowfeather's house next door with his thumb.

"Dad!" Came the embarrassed response. "I'm ten. She's nine."

"Some day you'll both be older and your mother and I are very patient. Like any good investment, one must wait to receive a worthwhile return." He extending his hand to seal their new business arrangement. Ethan went to accept, but was surprised when the hand was abruptly pulled back. Uh, oh! The proposal was going to have an addendum.

"For our project to be successful, you have to keep up your grades. Truth is, money is only half of it and the money won't mean a thing unless you have the grades to back it up. They slip and your job is history. You'll have to accept the future your mother and I can afford to give you." Simon spit onto his palm, like he saw the kids do, and once again offered his hand in a bargain with his son. "Is it a deal?"

Ethan jumped at the offer. He spit into his own palm and took his father's hand, feeling very grown up. "Deal, Pop! You're the best!" Ethan paused. "Dad, why do guys spit first? It's disgusting."

Their deal sealed in spit, Ethan and his father each made a face, then dragged their hand across the front of their own shirts and began to laugh. Helen Craig picked that moment to step out onto the front porch. "What's so funny, you two?"

They looked at each other, spit on their palms and extended them to Helen. She turned up her nose. "I'm not shaking those; you spit on them. It's disgusting."

They collapsed into convulsions of laughter and tears ran from the corners of their eyes. Each time they tried to explain, they laughed even harder.

"Fine, don't tell me!" She went back into the house shaking her head, letting the screen door slam behind her. "Men!"

Ethan and Connie spent every possible minute together. Connie shared Ethan's dream and knew that every penny earned was ear-marked for College and Med School. Evenings were happily spent listening to the radio and eating pop-corn or going for long walks and just talking. If only in the smallest way, Connie felt she was helping by not asking to go to movies or anywhere else that would cost Ethan the precious coins he was saving for their future. By Ethan's gradua-tion day, the Craigs had reached their goal. In September, Ethan was going to college. Connie was despondent over remaining behind until she also graduated.

"It's one year and I'll be back between now and then. I'm planning to spend the rest of my life with you. It's the truth. All you have to do is believe me." He insisted. "You do believe me?"

Connie gave no response, verbal or otherwise.

Ethan took her by the shoulders and, gripped by panic, forced her bowed head to look at him. "Connie, please say you believe me." She stared into the face of the man she had loved nearly all of her life and saw all she needed to see—tears. She threw her arms around his neck and held him to her. He felt her silent nod. "This is just what we need to do now. The second you get your diploma, we'll be married. I don't have money for a ring, but you're *my* girl. You'll *always* be my girl! Nothing and no one can change that. Not ever! Understand?"

Ethan didn't have the money to travel back and forth from Boston very often either, but he and Connie wrote nearly every day, Ethan returned late in Novem-ber, for the Thanksgiving holiday. Once they were reunited they acted like an old married couple and the night they borrowed Simon's car, they acted like a newly married couple. Before either of them knew it, they were in each other's arms naked, and, of course, it made the good-bye even harder for Connie. She wanted to beg Ethan to stay, but school was his future, their future. He had to go back. Being so near the end of the semester, Ethan could not afford to come home again until winter break. Two days before he was due to return, a letter arrived from Connie saying she couldn't wait forever. She had met and already married Jack Makepeace.

Ethan was heart-broken and jealous beyond words. What in the hell hap-pened? It was nineteen years later, and he still didn't have an answer. Suddenly and without any more reason than that, Connie simply couldn't wait. He loved Constance Yellowfeather nearly all of his life and now she was someone else's wife, would be the mother of someone else's children. Ethan kept his hurt to himself and wrote to Connie one last time, to wish her a good life.

Though Connie and Jack moved to the Makepeace farm in Jaffrey, Ethan had little incentive to return to Peterborough during the winter recess. He opted to remain in Boston, taking a temporary job as an orderly. The money wasn't great, but the job eliminated any chance of seeing Connie and Jack in a town where everyone knew everyone and everyone else's business.

After graduating from medical school, he took a residency in Boston, then opened a family practice in Keene. He'd lived there ever since—a shattered heart preempting his return to the place where he loved Constance Yellowfeather and there was nothing but memories of her and their time together.

Every now and then, Ethan heard about the star line-backers of the Jaffrey High School Football team, Connie's son Matthew and his best friend Carl Summers. He listened with more than a little extra interest, whenever their names were mentioned, but never made a comment, and, all the while, silently wished that Matthew Makepeace was his son instead of Jack's.

*   *   *   *

Ethan cut away Connie's blouse, not to overlook any injuries. He froze, pin-drop-silent, holding her broken left arm in his hands. He finally found his voice. "Does Tre know about this?" Carl was speechless, shaking his head. "You know what this means." It wasn't a question.

Ethan handed Carl a piece of paper with front and back body diagrams. They would chart the location of every mark on Connie—old scars with an 'O'; new injuries with an 'X'. Ethan scribbled notes, making comments to Carl as they went. Feeling certain that anyone who found the file must never know to whom it belonged, it was ultimately indexed with the name Jane Doe.

He tended to the worst of Connie's injuries first, then he applied ice to the black eye and stitched her cut lip. Ethan and Carl left Connie to rest. They found Tre worn out from worry, his head tipped back to the wall, fitfully dozing.

"Tre." Ethan leaned down, put his hand on the boy's shoulder and gave him a gentle shake. Tre woke with a start, grabbing Ethan's arm in reflex. "Son, it's over."

"Over? No!" He jumped from the seat. "You said she'd be OK! She isn't…," he was unable to finish the thought.

"She's sleeping, but she's going to need some looking after. Is there anyone at home to do that?"

"She has me." Tre was a little indignant. "We have each other."

"Of course, son."

It was the second time Ethan called him son. Tre thought it should make him uncomfortable, but it didn't.

Ethan admired Tre's commitment. "You can take care of the farm and fix her meals, but she'll still need someone to help her with bathing and such. You can't be *that* someone."

He looked at Ethan blankly. "I didn't think of that."

"Can you afford a nurse, or is there someone you can call?"

"I can ask my mom," Carl volunteered.

Tre didn't want to involve anyone else in their messy personal business, but Carl's mom, Fran, had always been a good friend to Connie. He was glad for the offer.

"I'll come see her in a few days, to remove the tube, close my incision, and make sure her progress is on track. In the meantime, any problems, she needs anything, anything at all, you call immediately."

"Thanks, but you already did so much. We'll be fine."

"And if you're not," Ethan displayed a folded piece of paper with his telephone number on it, "you'll already have this." He slipped it into Tre's shirt pocket. "Son, in this life, you can never have too many friends."

"Thank you, sir."

"It's Ethan." He extended his hand. Tre reluctantly took it and the instant their hands clasped, each man knew—*this is no ordinary guy.*

*   *   *   *

The boys and Connie returned to Jaffrey, her arm set in a plaster of Paris cast, a patch over her left eye, remnants of dried blood near the stitches on her now swollen lip, and the hose of a Pleur-evac machine inserted into her lung, and stitches to hold it in place. Tre and Carl tucked her in, elevating her chest and head with every pillow in the house, the Pleur-evac sitting on the floor next to her bed. Ethan also gave Connie something for pain and she was sleeping quietly, but she didn't look good. Carl felt her forehead. Fever. Ethan predicted it and advised that she not be left unattended.

"Stay with her, Carl."

Carl knew Tre's temper and tried to anticipate his next action. "Don't go do something stupid that'll land in jail or dead yourself."

Tre had something besides murdering his father in mind. "As long as this remains unchanged," Tre flashed the still broken circle of his birthmark, "I'm marked for someone else's future. Remember?"

Carl learned all about Tre's mark, when they were boys—what it meant and what it was going to mean down the road. When Jack wasn't around, Connie baked pies and told and retold her story. *Someday, one Reweaver will go back to the beginning of our lives together and share responsibility for everyone who comes afterward.* He tossed the car keys and Tre snatched them out of the air. Carl sat in the chair next to Connie's bed.

"I remember, but there's no need to tempt fate. You already pulled that shit the day those assholes came down to the quarry. You can't expect to keep getting away with that kind of stunt. Don't forget, even Superman has Kryptonite."

"Yeah, yeah!" Tre dismissed him as he left the room.

Carl took Connie's hand, all the while praying she would be all right. "I'm right here Connie, you're not alone."

Tre went to his room, grabbed something from the back of his dresser and headed for Duffy's Tavern.

CHAPTER 7

▼

JAFFREY, NH—1965
TOTAL SEPARATION

Jack was in a back booth, piss-drunk, with his tongue half-way down the throat of a bleach blond tart. Neither of them saw or heard Tre enter. He grabbed the woman by the arm and yanked her from the booth.

"Say! What gives?" She protested, in her loudest, whiny voice, trying to wrench her arm from Tre's grasp.

"Make yourself scarce." Without even looking at her, Tre used her arm to shove her in the direction of the bar. The woman stomped her foot, but getting no reaction, turned on her heel and left in a huff.

Jack sat up and gave his son a grey-toothed smile. The first smile ever, in Tre's recollection. "Come to join me?" Jack winked watching his life sized Barbie-doll disappear around a corner.

Tre took a seat opposite Jack. "I'm not here to socialize."

"Fine," Jack's simpering smile disappeared. "Your business, then get lost."

"You don't give me orders any more, old man. She barely weighs a hundred pounds. How long has this been going on?"

"What do ya expect? I can't get no sleep. She wakes me up screamin' every fuckin' night. I got important things to do."

"She's your wife. Nothing's more important than that! And a beating is no cure for nightmares. If you hear me having one, you gonna beat me too? Try it," Tre's tone was menacingly harsh. "Oh, please," he prodded, "try it."

Jack ignored most of what Tre said. "So, I got a little sloppy. She ain't dead…is she?" His voice was tinged with a bit of concern.

"No thanks to you."

Relieved, Jack's sarcasm returned. "I suppose you got her all cleaned up, nice and purty."

"There's no nice and purty, you asshole. You gave her a black eye, broke her arm and three of her ribs. One of them punctured a lung. She needed a doctor. He sent her home attached to some machine."

"You stupid or something! That doctor could report it, involve the Police. I'll smack you where you sit, boy!" Jack spit out the words. He forgot both Tre's size and strength, rose from the seat, and lifted his right arm to strike.

Tre grabbed it mid-swing and bent it backward, throwing Jack off balance and made him yell. "You're done smacking me!"

"You owe me respect," Jack snarled, rubbing his arm.

"I owe you nothing. Don't think, for one minute, I've forgotten the years of beatings. Come near either one of us again and I'll kill you."

"You and the hag are worthless trash to anyone but me," Jack snorted. "Who's gonna take you in?"

"No, no," Tre corrected him. "Who's gonna take *you* in?"

"That ain't fair; it's *my* house!" Jack was practically whining. "Where will I go, what will I do?"

"I couldn't care less."

"But the farm is how I earn my money."

"*You* earning money," Tre let go of a bitter laugh. "Mother and I earn every penny the farm brings in. You sleep 'til noon, then piss away what little money we do make. We might as well flush it down the toilet."

"But it ain't fair!" Jack protested again. "You can't take my home and give me nothing."

Tre's eyes narrowed. "I'm way ahead of you." He slid out of the booth, reached a hand in to where Jack was sitting, grabbed the front of his shirt, and lifted him several inches above of the seat. Jack struggled to get free as Tre brought them nose-to-nose. "I'll keep silent about tonight's foray into the wonderful world of wife-beating, but, tomorrow, you and I go to the lawyer's where you will file for divorce and sign over title to the farm. Take your clothes, the car, your little chicky, if you want, but never talk to me about fair again. You have two choices, permanently disappear on your own, or I'll do it for you. Either way. But if you leave it up to me, unlike mother," the image of a beaten and crumpled Connie flashed in Tre's head, "there won't be enough of *you* left to find. Get me?"

Jack knew better than to answer. Tre threw him into the wall at the side of the booth and the back of his head hit the stucco, hard. Tre reached into his pant pocket and tossed what he grabbed from his dresser drawer onto the table—half of his skiing money.

"You can consider that," Tre cocked his head toward the rolled-up bills, "and the car, your in-full divorce settlement."

Jack was nearly a nightly customer at Duffy's, had been for years and knew all of the regulars. As Tre exited, he considered very carefully that none of them came to his rescue or even turned around. He touched the now tender spot at the back of his head, then checked his fingers. Blood. He snapped-up the bills.

Jack asked himself where Tre got so much money, then decided he didn't care. It was his money now. Without the ball and chain, he was free to do whatever he wanted. To hell with Connie. To hell with her and the boy, they didn't know a good thing when they had it. He told himself that he hated the farm anyway—too much work, too much stink. If Connie and the boy wanted the headache and the backache so badly, so be it. "Let them have the shack. Who needs the pennies the farm earns?"

Plus, there was always some dame willing to pay, when she was getting a man with an active cock. He thought of how busy he was in their little back-water town, even married, and he never paid a dime. Bleach blond, Annie, made decent money waitressing. He assured himself she'd be damn glad to have a prize catch like Jack Makepeace move in with her. Besides, Tre was big and really strong. A threat from him was as good as a fact and Jack figured gone was a hell of a lot better than dead. He could fix Connie when Tre wasn't around to protect her. Right now, he had three hundred dollars, no wife, no son, and no obligations.

*   *   *   *

The next day, Connie and Jack's divorce began to process and the title to the farm was transferred to Tre. Although property usually appreciates in value, the Makepeace Farm was run-down when Jack inherited it and, nearly nineteen years later, the place was nineteen years older, nineteen years more run-down and worth a whole lot less. Jack never made the first repair that wasn't absolutely essential.

Tre and Carl completed every project that Jack had put on indefinite hold, working all summer long and thru to December. Surprisingly, the foundation and cellar were in good condition, but the roof, outside walls, and entire interior required extensive repairs and all of the small chicken coops needed to be rebuilt. Once the kitchen and bath were updated, it was actually a nice little farm, but Connie couldn't manage it alone, even with Chris Wilson's help. The life was too hard, too precarious and Tre had other plans. He decided to rent it.

By the time the renovation was complete, Connie's broken body was mended. The half inch scar on her face and the one on her side would be the only lasting reminders of life with Jack.

The day finally came when Connie was moving out and the new tenants were moving in. The rental of the farm would net sufficient income to provide her a place to be safe and, with Jack out of the picture, never beaten again. Tre located a sweet little apartment, in Keene, with a store front directly below. Best of all, the entire building was rent-to-own. If everything worked out, Connie would be set.

One phase of her life was over, but what should replace it? Renting the farm was one thing, knowing what Connie should do with herself afterward was quite another. Mother and son talked it over. Her years baking pies gave them an idea—turn her small business into a real business. Instead of being thought of as *that pie lady over in Jaffrey*, she could become the owner and operator of *The Pie Lady—a dessert store*. Fine pies and cakes, baked fresh, daily.

Once Connie was settled, and her business was off to a rousing start, Tre broke the news that he and Carl enlisted and both requested Vietnam. In ten days, they would board a Greyhound bus, bound for Boston, then a government charted Blue Bird that would take them to Fort Dix. They already had their tickets.

Tre and Connie sat on the new sofa in her living room. "But Vietnam, Matthew," she objected. "You and Carl…you're still boys."

"No, mom." he corrected her gently, "We're men."

"Yes," Connie hesitantly agreed. "I suppose you are."

"They need us. We *will* come home, alive. Honestly!"

Connie put her arms around him and pulled him close. "Do more than just stay alive, Matthew. Come home one piece."

CHAPTER 8

▼

FT. DIX, NJ— JANUARY, 1966
BASIC

The trip to Ft Dix was on the Army's dime and Uncle Sam was happy to foot the bill. What were a couple of bus tickets against two big, strapping, young men, who volunteered for 'Nam. No one in their right mind *wanted* to go.

The first leg, from Jaffrey to Boston, took about two hours. Carl and Tre played cards most of the way. There wasn't much to say and nothing else to do. They were headed for a war, and platitudes like *War is hell!*, live on; because the fact of the matter is—war *is* hell.

There was a two hour lay-over between buses, exactly enough time to grab a burger and a show in The Combat Zone—a short walk from the bus station. For once, the New England weather cooperated. The air was frigid, but at least there wasn't snow, up to here, or a down-pour of freezing rain to wade thru. They wouldn't be able to *enjoy* anyone they found interesting, if only in the most carnal sort of way, but naked women were at least nice to look at. The reputation of Basic was anything *but* nice, and there was eight weeks of that to look forward to. Might as well get in some fun and a few laughs, while they could.

*   *   *   *

They pulled into camp around mid-night. Those already in residence, except the Drill Sergeant who greeted them, were long asleep. All the sleep the new recruits got was done sitting up on the bus, their heads dangling to one side or the other, in a seat that was a size too small. Their in-charge herded them here and there, first for uniforms—five sets of everything, plus a pair boots, then for bedding and a pillow. It was hustle-hustle, then stand in a line that didn't move the first inch for forty-five minutes. They call it *Drill Sergeant mind control*—men that tired will gladly do anything, if the promised reward is a bed.

The first week of camp was mostly a rerun of the night they arrived—more hurry-up and wait. Mornings started at 6:00 AM and they were in formation twenty minutes later. Two-by-two, and still half asleep, they ran a mile in dry beach-like sand. Feet sink down a long way, when you're a big man to begin with, you're wearing heavy Army boots, and gravity is working against you. At first, the run was punishing. Tre's thighs burned as he yanked them up to get his big feet out of the sand. By the end of the first week, the challenge was exhilarating. It became his private test—how fast could he run and, once they were in, how quickly could he pull his feet out of the sand? After the run, it was two-by-two to the mess hall. Whatever soldiers say about regular Army chow is true. Looks and tastes like sh-- on a shingle, but the food at Camp wasn't bad, there was just never nearly enough of it. Every item was portion controlled, so Tre and Carl were served the same quantity as men five inches shorter and forty pounds lighter.

A kindred spirit appeared in the guise of a guy called Poopsie—an inch taller than the two of them, when Basic started, and thirty pounds heavier. Although his height maxed-out at six-three, Tre and Carl, each six-two, were still growing. The three of them were perpetually hungry, so if a stomach growled, it was most likely one of theirs. Portions at the Enlisted Man's Club would have been sufficient, but the place was off limits, unless you were invited. That happened only once—a Sergeant took pity on them.

*   *   *   *

Poopsie knew nearly everything about military procedure—how it worked and how to get around it. When it came to figuring strategies and preparing for the next day's training, he knew it all. He was also a true and loyal friend—a welcome addition to any platoon. He was actually a really sweet kid, considering he was a true Army brat, had attended a military High School, and his dad was a Colonel. Neither the school nor his dad was able to change his sweet disposition or his nick-name.

"How is it going to sound when I introduce you to my colleagues. It's Private Poopsie now, which is already bad enough," the Colonel complained. "What happens when you get promotions? Someday you'll be a Captain. I can't introduce my son as Captain Poopsie. It makes you sound like a cartoon!" The Colonel shook his head in dismay. "It's just not dignified. It's just not military. This whole Poopsie business," he blustered, for the umpty-umpth time, his face beet red, shaking an index finger in the direction of the kitchen, "is all your mother's fault!"

Poopsie good-naturedly laughed-off his father's tantrum. "You're right, sir. It is all mother's fault." Then he put the blame where it truly belonged. "If she hadn't allowed you to name me Abernathy, she never would have given me a nick-name like Poopsie. I'll go have a word with her about it right now."

Of course, Colonel Tilson (he was Captain Tilson when his son was born) realized, too late, that his son would be interacting with boys whose nick-names were Bobby, Tommy and Andy. What did he expect other children to call Abernathy? Abe? Nate? Those made him sound like a little old man. Wanda Tilson said that she would come up with something, and so she did.

The Pajama Game was her favorite Broadway play. A scene in a smoke filled nightclub—Hernando's Hide-Away (Oley), to be exact—featured a disembodied voice calling for their beloved, Poopsie. Well, Abernathy wasn't exactly his mother's beloved, but she love him more than anything and that was close enough for Wanda Tilson. Abernathy indeed! She called a family meeting to announce her decision.

"Are you insane?!" The Colonel couldn't stress his displeasure enough. "It's, it's...," words momentarily failed him, while his face turned bright red, "...that ridiculous name from that play we saw. Isn't it?"

"Yes, it is. But Sweetheart," her voice was even and held no malice, neither real nor contrived, "I'm not the one who had to name him Abernathy. I wanted Peter, but that was just too plain and the initials sent the wrong message."

Oh, no, the Colonel silently chastised himself. Peter was too ordinary for his child and, yes, P.M. Tilson—the night-owl? Absolutely not! It simply had to be Abernathy, Abernathy Montrose Tilson—A.M. Tilson. His first born son would be all Army, and needed a name with authority, to carry him thru the military with everyone's respect. The Colonel got the *all Army* part right, but it turned out that the kid liked to sleep past noon and now people were going to be calling him Poopsie, for god sake!

"Do you have a better idea?" Wanda smiled sweetly at her husband. The Colonel dropped his chin to his chest and shook his head, completely disgusted with himself for having made such a fuss over his son's name. "Didn't think so." She kissed his cheek. "Fine," she patted his shoulder twice, "Poopsie it is."

As the time for his son to enter High School drew closer, Abernathy's nick-name was the least of Colonel Tilson's worries. All The Command talked about was how imminent an all-out war in Vietnam was. The Colonel worried that his son would be sent into combat to fight a war that the good guys wouldn't be allowed to win, against an enemy that saw guerrilla warfare as *de rigueur* and whose tactics you couldn't discuss in front of the gentler sex. The conflict had all of the ear-marks of another Korea, or worse.

A weak name like Poopsie might lead others to believe that he was weak. The Colonel knew from first-hand experience, a weak soldier was the same as a dead soldier, and that simply wouldn't do—not for his son, not for his little Poopsie. The Colonel was all Army himself and loved every bit of soldiering; except the potential it had for costing him the life of his only child.

When the Brass talked strategy, it was always about the numbers, what per cent would be lost, the number of casualties they could live with. But Poopsie was not a number, or a per cent—he was a son, and the Colonel and Wanda Tilson could never endure his death. As it turned out, the Colonel needn't have worried about his son dying in a jungle, somewhere in South East Asia. During Poopsie's third tour in 'Nam, he earned a new nick-name—The Ear Collector.

*   *   *   *

Thanks to their size and demeanor and the fact that they were a bit older than the others, Tre and Carl were made Platoon Guides. Four Squad Leaders reported directly to them. Although the Army encouraged its men to write home, it was hardly mandatory, except if you lived in barracks two or three and Tre and Carl were your Platoon Guides. Those men wrote to someone every day.

"It won't kill you to scribble a couple quick lines to remind people in the real world that you're still alive. Someday, you'll be glad you did it."

Tre and Carl each collected forty letters every day. It was no coincidence that their mail run paralleled the appearance of Poopsie and the outside food trucks, at the Ft. Dix PX—just about 7:00 PM. The skiing money that Connie insisted Tre put away, or the half of it that was left, came in mighty handy.

It takes a lot of exercise to become strong enough to perform the duties of a soldier. They had to run a mile in six and a half minutes; took forced marches of twenty miles with full packs; scurried across a thirty foot length of monkey bars; bayonet and pugil stick training; hand to hand combat; the famous obstacle course; and more push-ups and pull-ups than can be counted. If you did too few, the Drill Sergeant whipped out his invisible crystal ball and, amazingly, always saw KP in your future. Tre could do limitless push ups and pull ups. Perhaps that's why he never learned to cook, but then again, he reminded everyone, no one ever got Ptomaine because of him either. He made avoiding KP sound so magnanimous, as if he were doing everyone a favor.

Tre could do endless lengths of monkey bars too. "Who let the great white ape out of his cage to do tricks?" The Drill Sergeant would demand. "Ya mind giving us a break? Fine, you're the best! We all give you the big salaam." He and the other men dropped to their knees, arms extended over-head, and bowed three times—ala the Three Stooges. "Salami! Salami! Bologna!" They chanted. "Now swing on down Monkey-boy and save the show-boating for the contest at the end of Camp."

Beginning with week two came the addition of six weeks of 'how to' classes— jumping from choppers, executing a proper grenade throw, but mostly how to use the lethal assortment of weapons available in-country—M-16; grenade launchers; M-60 rapid-fire machine guns; and the M-79 (the blooper). They broke them down, put them back together, cleaned them, and, of course, fired them. But no matter what else they learned, discipline was drilled into their heads as the key to being a good soldier.

"You can bet your month's wages that the guy giving orders knows a little something you don't," the Sergeant advised, "and whatever it is, that thing that you don't know, it's crucial to choosing a course of action. Your job, as a soldier, is to follow your orders to the letter and not waste time asking questions. When you're about to take a ridge, no one wants your opinion. Your hesitation could get an entire Company killed. The field of battle is no democracy. It's the purest form of dictatorship you'll ever find."

Pugil stick training was, by far, Tre's favorite; because he was really good at it. The sticks looked like kayak paddles, whose ends were heavily padded. Soldiers were pitted against members of their own Company, just like bayonet training, but with choreographed moves and no pointy weapons. The padding was so thick that the worse damage you could inflict was a third-degree embarrassment.

Ft. Dix held pugil stick contests between platoons, to find a single champion. The platoon champs were three white guys, Tre among them, and a big black kid, named Isaiah Jefferson—also an ex-football player. Isaiah used his cool head and his fast jab to defeat his first two opponents. Then it was down to him and Tre.

Isaiah was fast and plenty strong, but so was Tre and Tre had a secret weapon—experience getting whipped, and not with anything as nicely padded as a pugil stick. He also learned to control his temper, after the chicken-biting-and-backhand-beheading incident and took Isaiah's fast jab with a smile. He won the match and was crowned Pugil Stick Camp Champ. (Try saying that three times, fast.)

Ft. Dix mirrored the rest of the U.S. in 1965, black or white—not black and white. There were cliques of whites and militant blacks and friends were seldom, if ever, made across racial lines. Isaiah walked back to his friends who encircled him. Tre followed. He made his way thru a sea of unfriendly black faces who were ready to take him apart, if he showed any sign of gloating.

The militants usually scared the crap out of the white guys, but they never met a white guy like Tre. When he reached Isaiah, he extended his hand. "We'll get plastered some night," he offered, "and I'll tell you how I won that match, not that knowing would have helped." He looked around at Isaiah's friends. "It's a secret weapon, guys. I'd tell all of you, but…then I'd have to kill you."

Isaiah laughed at Tre's joke and accepted his hand. "Make it soon. Basic's almost over."

It might have turned into a confrontation, but Tre's graciousness was totally disarming and bridged the gap between blacks and whites. The camaraderie carried over once they were in 'Nam and, every now and then, he'd run into Isaiah or another man who attended the match. They'd call to him, *Say, hey, brothah,* which some of their more militant friends didn't understand.

"How can you call that honkie brothah? He's whiter than white, with damn yellow hair!"

But the brothah always had his back. "Underneath the white skin and the yellow hair, he's a brothah. Mess with *that* brothah and you'll be messin' with *this* brothah."

The night Isaiah and Tre got toasted, it was on Shooters with beer chasers.

"OK, so what's this unstoppable secret weapon?" Isaiah asked once they each had on quite a buzz.

Tre swore Isaiah to silence then gave him the blow by blow of life with Jack—no pun intended. "The secret, my man, is the same three that get you to Carnegie Hall. Practice. Practice. Practice." Tre pointed to the scar on his cheek, then removed his shirt, revealing an especially grizzly scar on his back. The years that passed never diminish the memory of the particularly punishing blows that put them there.

"Guess you didn't get those from any pugil stick."

"Belt. Metal tip on the strap end." Tre pointed to his cheek again. "Belt buckle broke the skin on my back in two places and the prong went in about half an inch." He demonstrated Jack's form, slowly pulling an invisible belt from his belt loops, swung it over-head, then brought it down with a whip-crack sound.

Isaiah winced, asking himself: how could any father do to his son what was done to Tre by his? He couldn't help thinking that a man who already survived so much, had to go on and do something extraordinary with his life. As Tre put his shirt back on, Isaiah noticed the light red mark on his arm. He wondered how it went unnoticed until that moment. Basic had nothing but gang showers and pick-up games of basketball were teams of shirts vs. skins. Tre was usually a skin.

As a kid, Isaiah heard tales of Red Tattoos and the extraordinary things the ordinary people, who had them, did. Until he saw the fabled mark in the flesh, he didn't believe they were real or that any of the outlandish stories were true. Although he didn't know why, Isaiah suddenly felt that he owed Tre. It was an odd, unsettling feeling for guys who were practically strangers. But if the need arose, Isaiah would protect this man and his family.

"After growing up with that, and never flinching, I could stand there all day and take anything you dished out with that little padded stick." Tre was so smashed, his words slurred together. "You didn't stand a chance, ya pussy."

"That's *brothah* pussy, to you."

"Whatever you say."

They staggered back to barracks two, barely holding each other up and each man quietly passed-out on the floor next to his bunk.

*   *   *   *

Basic's eighth week comprehensive competition was comprised of five physical training events, each worth 100 points. Over the years, only a handful of guys had earned perfect scores, but anything over three hundred meant a rewarded.

Five hundred points meant a one week pass and that your name was etched onto a plaque that would remain at Ft. Dix forever.

Tre was a big man, six-three by the time Basic was over, but amazingly agile. The first four events of their competition had been pure agility and Tre earned 100 points in each one. He felt sure the last event would be at least part agility. If it was the grenade throw, he was a shoe-in for a perfect score. The last event was announced to groans. The two-man carry—pure strength, a forty yard dash, carrying the man closest to you in height and weight. For Tre, that was Poopsie and, even after eight weeks of Basic, he still outweighed Tre by thirty pounds.

Poopsie hopped up on Tre's back. On your marks, get set, go! Tre swore at him for the entire forty feet. "You big fat pig! It's your fault, if I miss the record! Ever consider a diet?"

Tre had no effect on Poopsie's self esteem. He just yelled back. "I thought you were strong. Is that as fast as you can go? Giddy-yap horsy!"

Turnabout is fair play, so when positions reversed, Tre had more barbs for his friend. "Come on turtle, the idea is to finish the race today!"

Tre earned only a three-day pass and his name would not appear on the plaque. He decided it was all Poopsie's fault and that his friend owed him fame and a four-day vacation at the place of his choosing.

By the end of Basic, they were more like weapons than men—strong, tough, fearless, able to travel endless miles wearing full packs without stopping, go days without food, 24 hours without rest, even sleep standing up…if they had to. They were, in fact, the quintessential lean, mean, fighting machines.

CHAPTER 9

▼

IN-COUNTRY—
APRIL, 1966

PFCs Matthew Makepeace, Carl Summers, Abernathy Tilson, and Isaiah Jefferson boarded a plane bound for Long-Binh airport together. Each carried little more than their issued clothing. A man who was treated like an outcast, Lloyd Cummings, past them in the aisle and took a seat in the back. Once they landed, they traveled by truck, with fifteen other guys, from the airport to Xuan Loc in the Bien-Hoa Province.

Xuan Loc wasn't just another flattened hill with a number. It was a real village, where Vietnamese families had lived for generations. The Army's compound was on the edge of that village. Once your honeymoon was over and the Army decided where they needed you, you were reassigned. The four boys were lucky, Xuan Loc was where Uncle Sam wanted all of them.

Men on the short list—thirty days and counting, to leave Vietnam, were assigned to show new guys the ropes. Tre, Carl, Isaiah, and Poopsie were assigned to Sergeant Ryan Harris, nearing the end of his second tour. On their way to The Enlisted Man's Club, a monkey scurried across the roof of the Officer's Mess. "You can take that as a good omen, if you like. Monkeys never come into the compound." Harris joined them for a few beers, made sure they were assigned quarters, then escorted them to the weapons room, to select their new best friend and make sure they got the right ammo for it.

"You can have whatever weapon you want, but I recommend the over-and-under. It's a combo weapon, M-16 on top, M-79 grenade launcher on the bottom. M-16's not reliable and jams too often to trust as a solo. You might find yourselves needing the backup. It's heavier, but ultimately, you'll be glad you were lugging around the extra weight…if only for the peace of mind. Over here, there's no such thing as too much fire-power.

"And take a P-38 while you're at it. It was originally made for German officers in World War II." He picked up the gun and examined it with the awe of a soldier who understood its true usefulness. "There isn't much ammo around for these things and it'll cost you an extra half-hour every day to keep it free of rust, but it will never let you down, especially if you're about to be captured. Use it when you see fit."

"I don't understand. Why the sidearm?" Tre asked. "It's not that kind of war?"

"If Charlie gets that close, the P-38's not for him. Not for the enemy. It's for you." Harris laid the weapon back on the counter and looked Tre in the eye. "It's *that* kind of war."

For a moment, Harris silently berated himself over having added that last bit, but decided it was better that they knew going in, than to find out later and the hard way. That was day one.

*   *   *   *

Initially, they stayed in a rear area of the city. It was pretty safe, similar to Long Binh, Saigon, and Da Nang, in that respect. The only real hazard seemed to be rockets, but you could hear them coming and dive for cover. Rockets could do plenty of damage, but mostly they blew dirt and things into the air and made a big mess.

It took about a week to get acclimated to being in-country; the weather, the heat and humidity, but mostly the smell. It defied description and that particular smell was everywhere.

"Is it always this fucking hot?" Poopsie mopped his forehead.

"Nah! Sometimes it's hotter," Harris laughed. "Don't worry, you'll get used to it."

"Ugh! What *is* that smell?" Carl uselessly waved a hand under his nose.

"Fish sauce. The locals put it on everything. You'll get used to that too."

"Don't count on it!" Carl griped.

The walls of hooches were lined with small reminders of home—pictures of family or girlfriends stuck on lockers and posters of rock bands—The Doors;

Jimi Hendrix; that Easy Rider poster of Peter Fonda riding a motorcycle, sans helmet. Fonda wasn't too popular among the blacks, they preferred James Brown. The name Fonda would eventually become unpopular with everyone serving in Vietnam.

*   *   *   *

The Vietnamese language was too complicated for GI ears to make a distinction between a friend from the South and a foe from the North. But North or South, the words for 'I surrender' were exactly the same. Chu hoi.

Grateful locals sometimes said it, when offering food to men being transported from one place to another, or those making a mail or ammo run. Even with their hands palms up, to show that they held no weapon, the offering usually received something less than a warm reception. Sometimes, a local got the benefit of the doubt, which got your Squad some fresh fruit. Sometimes, when the weapon of choice was a hidden bomb, the benefit of the doubt got them killed. Add in the prospect of deserters from the South working for the North and every day was a crap shoot.

In times of war, men make few friends. Guys get killed every day and the mind can stand only so much loss and making friends with the locals was too chancy. What if you let down your guard on the very day the Cong strapped a body-bomb to someone you knew? What if you let them get close on the wrong day; because they looked as innocent as they were?

The end result was that GIs mistrusted everyone equally, or just about as far as they could throw them. Even a lone Vietnamese youngster could cause thirty men with rifles to pop out of a truck, and point them directly at the child's head. When you can't tell who your friends are, everyone's the enemy. The question was always life or death, so the answer was always lock and load. A wise man once said: *If one of us has to be miserable, better it be you.* In times of war, especially guerrilla war, that phrase becomes: *If one of us has to die, better it isn't me.*

*   *   *   *

Tre was artillery, sent out on three month stints to bomb-flattened hills, that had numbers instead of names. The Army blasted everything into splinters, defoliating huge portions of jungle, completely changing the landscape. Living quarters were corrugated conduit, with generators, for electricity. You could never tell how long your fuel would last; a bad generator drank gas like cheep wine—fast and by the gallon. Once dug in, the overall ambiance was 'Early Filth', but, for three months, it was also home.

Tre's squad destroyed any remaining vegetation, careful to also destroy any remnants of underground cities, then set up *the Berm*—perimeters with observation towers. It supported our guys and the South Vietnamese infantry with artillery and was built from two rows of concertina wire—slinky-type coils with razor blades in place of barbs. The blades were meant to slice-up anyone trying to get into camp, but sometimes they didn't. Each time our guys built a better mouse trap, Charlie raised a better mouse. Collections of ornamental bells and tin cans soon decorated the wire, to warn of intruders, and the noisier the better. The enemy might be clever enough to get into camp unhurt, but he still had to face Claymore mines to get out. They were filled with ball bearings to ripped the hell out of anyone trying to get past them.

During the day, Tre's Squad laid traps and sometimes stayed until the enemy actually came. They ventured out just far enough to make their presence felt and tell the North Vietnamese and the Cong that they were unwelcome. Another of the Squad's jobs, ambush patrol, put Tre in mind of the ground hogs back home, except that these varmints shot back.

During his time away, there were no haircuts, and, unless it rained, no shaving, showers, or clean clothes either. His food supply, C-rations and LERPs (long range patrol rations), always ran out about half way thru a stint. The men could carry in only so much and it was too dangerous to try and chopper in more. They were forced to rely on the friendlies, South Vietnamese soldiers stationed with them, to acquire food on their behalf. They ended up eating what the locals ate: rice and fish wrapped in grape leaves. No one ever got fat eating rice and fish.

When there wasn't enough food to fill everyone's belly, for some, the answer was *chewing beetle-nut*. Similar in use to chewing tobacco, the hard piece of chaw was put between the cheek and gum and sucked on. Beetle-nut came from a locally grown plant that made teeth black and had a stimulating effect, similar to speed. Oh, the soldiers were still hungry, just so high they didn't care. After three months out, a man ended up about twenty pounds down, smelled like the locals and felt twice as bad; because he knew there was another life, a better life, but he also knew what it was like to be a part of the land. With luck on his side, and fear to keep a constant flow of adrenaline, sounds became sharper, smells more distinct, and he stayed alive.

GIs tried to train the South Vietnamese to take over and protect their own land, but Vietnamization was just another losing battle. Farmers for generations, the Vietnamese made poor warriors.

*   *   *   *

Poopsie was infantry, one of many who routinely went out on patrol. During their third tour in 'Nam, he became the Leadman on night patrols. The Cavalry would have called him the Scout. In the service they call it *taking Point*. He would silently slip forward before the rest of the men and, if there was a problem, dash back to warn them.

It was on one such mission, while Poopsie was still one of the many at the rear, that Corey Black, slithered into the night. Ten minutes later, something made the hairs on the back of Poopsie's neck stand straight up. Sergeant Greg Smiley, accustomed to the vibes Tilson picked up like radar, had the Company proceeded down the Ho Chi Min Trail with more than the customary caution. Suddenly and without a word, Poopsie pulled Smiley off the road and every man behind them followed suit. The men dug-in and wordlessly waited for the all clear that never came.

Poopsie and Smiley took Point together and silently melted into the darkness, finally arriving at Black's last known position, some two thousand yards ahead. They found him with his arms pulled backward, bound around a tree, his body strapped to that tree with barbed wire. His pants and undershorts were pulled down around his bound ankles. His head hung down, chin on his chest and blood was everywhere.

When Poopsie drew close, and lifted Black's face, he saw the cause of the unnatural silence. His cock and balls had been cut off and shoved into his mouth. He was still breathing. The Cong had left him there, gruesomely gagged, to bleed to death.

They stepped away and Smiley began to puke. Poopsie's mind raced, flying back to his first day in-country and Sergeant Harris' words. Bits and pieces formed an order of their own, and echoed in his head. *Take a P-38 while you're at it. Use it when you see fit. It will never let you down. Not for the enemy. It's that kind of war.* Poopsie's P-38 sat in its holster, mostly unused. He fired it once to kill a snake. Without another thought or hesitation, he pulled out the sidearm and mercifully shot Black in the heart. For PFC Corey Black, the war was finally over. For Abernathy Montrose Tilson, who'd been in-country nearly three years, the war was just beginning. He would never forget Black's look of sheer terror, the tears in his eyes, or the blood. So much blood.

As of that night, Poopsie vowed to fix every Cong he could, in Corey's name, by assuming Black's place. On his first night mission, instead of waiting out of

sight, Poopsie sat smack in the middle of the Ho Chi Min Trail—shirtless, ban-
danna around his head, brazenly smoking a joint, that he scored from a druggy,
and twanging out chords on an air guitar, not looking like much of a threat. The
enemy silently approached, but Poopsie smelled him coming.

Charlie's inevitable question, snide as ever. "Chu hoi?"

Poopsie looked up blankly, as if he were the flipped-out druggy he pretended
to be. The enemy came closer still. Closer. Poopsie smiled a vicious, menacing
grin, then sliced the man in half with a machete he acquired from one of the
locals. He finished the job by slicing him up like bologna. The coup de gras was
taking the man's ears as a souvenir. Covered in enemy blood, he leaned the
sliced-up man against a tree and waited in the bush for the North Vietnamese.

It was a dramatic scare tactic meant to make the enemy turn tail and run. Each
mission produced a new trophy—another pair of ears and gossip spread quickly.
Poopsie dried the ears and made necklaces, periodically hanging one around a
victim's neck, to confirm the gossip was true. Everyone, on both sides, soon
learned the tale of The Ear Collector.

Father Tilson, The Colonel, need not have worried about the death of his son.
He needed to worry about his son's life instead.

*   *   *   *

Carl Summers was a medic, assigned to the same Company as Poopsie and
took the same patrols. Carl patched up the wounded, saving whatever lives and
limbs were possible to save. There was always too much blood and even carrying
eighty pounds of extra gear on his back, he never had nearly enough supplies.

Carl was on the Ho Chi Min the night Corey Black was found. In the weeks
that followed, he watched helplessly as Greg Smiley lost his mind, and Poopsie
turned into someone already dead inside or, at the very least, dying. Carl wished
for the knowledge and opportunity to help Poopsie and anyone else who ended
up like him. He wondered how many unfortunate bastards would lose their souls
in Vietnam, then fail to resume *normal* lives back home.

Theirs was a world where men killed other men, fighting a fight that belonged
to someone else. It was a world where a man got fragged for pissing-off another
man. It was easy enough. In the midst of a fire-fight, you toss a grenade into a
hooch, or fire straight at the man you wanted to 'get', knowing full well the
blame could be assigned to an enemy sniper. How the hell would any of them
return to a world where a tough decision was soup or salad?

*   *   *   *

Isaiah spent five tours, mostly in the hanger, mostly with his head stuck inside the front end of a chopper, trying to make sure our guys were as safe in the air as they were on the ground. The strains of Jimi Hendrix blasted into the air, while he tried to fix the unfixable, scavenging good engines from destroyed choppers and putting them into ones that would fly—Hueys, Black Hawks, Medivacs, Cobra gun-ships. The Cobra was thought of as the most feared weapon the U.S. had in Vietnam. It was gratifying to know that Charlie shit bricks when he heard one coming. Another Cobra in the air—another brick was shat.

*   *   *   *

Lloyd was with Special Forces, involved in countless Covert-Ops, most of which sustained heavy losses. Men died all around him or were seriously wounded. He walked away. Those facts earned him a bad rep and a tag—piece of shit. The bad rep nearly cost him his life. Many soldiers, not-so-silently, questioned his allegiance and whether or not he was a Pointman. He was a suspect, and prior to the conclusion of two very particular missions, he remained a suspect.

No one, however, suspected that he was involved in a state-side Covert-Op—an operation that began in the weeks before he left for Vietnam and became the life he would live for the rest of his life. Lloyd was not a gambler by nature, but in this case, there was no alternative. Gamble and he might lose; refuse and it was a sure thing. One false step, one wrong word, breathe too loud, and it would all be over—and not in a good way.

CHAPTER 10

▼

OAHU, HAWAII— APRIL, 1968

Tre and Carl deplaned at Honolulu. The warmth from the tarmac felt good under their feet. A soft breeze greeted them, as their taxi entered the city.

Their reservation was at the Ilikai Hotel—tenth floor, a great view of the beach, two queen size beds, and a bath with limitless hot water. Tre wanted a real haircut, so they agreed to meet in the hotel bar. While Carl waited, he investigated the nearby activities. The man at the desk handed him the same flyer he gave to hundreds of servicemen. Feeling nearly human, Tre exited the elevator and found Carl in the bar, already enjoying an ice-cold beer. Carl caught the waitress's attention, alerting her to bring over the second beer he ordered, when he'd ordered his own.

"Nice looking waitress," Carl commented.

"Not my type," Tre dismisses her without a second glance.

"She's pretty, she's female. What other type is there?"

"Tonight, my type is a round-eyed girl. Blue, green, brown, hazel, I don't really care, just as long as they're round."

"Then have I got a place for you! Round-eyed girls, as far as the eye can see."

"Where?" Tre was skeptical.

"A USO dance." Carl waved the flyer in Tre's face. "Come on. Let's go."

"A little on the hokey side." Tre peered over his frosty mug.

"Hokey, yes, but it says here that there'll be dancing, round-eyed girls, liquor, round-eyed girls, food, round-eyed girls, Bob Hope, and round-eyed girls. OK, no Bob Hope, but definitely round-eyed girls. Anyway, it's our first night and we don't know a soul. I'm all ears, if you have a better idea."

"The USO? The hell, you say! What a fabulous idea!" Tre clinked glasses with Carl. "The USO it is!"

The USO was a short taxi ride to a building near the Royal Palace. The music was loud. Some of the men were in uniform, while others, like Tre and Carl, were merely guys on leave—their uniforms hanging in a hotel closet. A friendly blond-haired girl, with a big magic marker and stick-on name tags, greeted them.

"What's your name, soldier?" Her voice was welcoming.

"Name tag? I don't think so," Tre's answer was aloof. "I wear enough of those already." He jingled his dog tags for her.

"Oh, dear!" Her concern was genuine. "Just everyone wears one. See!" She proudly displayed her own tag—it said *Amy*. "Otherwise, how will anyone know your name? Come on," she said, a little too perky for Tre's liking, "what's your name, soldier?"

"How do you know I'm not Navy?"

"It's a gift, I guess," she smiled guilelessly.

"Tre," he relented, not withholding his exasperation.

"It's very unusual." She ignored his tone, wrote his name on the paper tag and stuck it to the front of his shirt. "There! Now you're all set. Enjoy the evening."

"Former cheerleader, Amy?" He asked.

"Captain of the squad, two years running." She smiled proudly, then paused giving him a skeptical look. "How did you know that?"

"It's a gift, I guess." He gave her his best rah-rah smile.

"Oh!" She smiled her biggest cheerleader grin, as if she understood, then she really did. "Oh, you're just teasing me."

"Yeah," Tre said, without much enthusiasm.

"Go on." She waved him off and moved on to Carl. "What's your name, soldier?"

Your turn for a little too much cheerfulness, Tre thought, *coming here was your bonehead idea*. But Carl seemed to like the little cheerleader. In fact, Carl always liked the cheerleaders. "They're my dream come true, act happy, even when they're not and…they're so flexible!" He hoped this little, Amy, person was no different.

Tre homed in on the bar and ordered a scotch-rocks. The woman to his right was chatting with another GI. The guy finished his drink and excused himself to the men's room. Tre wasted no time engaging her in conversation; after all, she was a round-eyed girl. They exchanged first names and he asked her to dance. She felt so good in his arms, better than he thought she would. She was a little bit of a thing compared to him, but they fit together nicely and she was his for the rest of the evening.

They held hands, went for a walk on the beach, and he kissed her. He breathed in the smell of her—Dove soap and Molly. They sat on the sand and he told her things about himself, his mother, his childhood. When he got to the parts that were difficult to talk about, she instinctively wrapped a protective arm around his broad shoulders and just listened. The gesture said everything: she was the one. She knew everything and didn't run the other way.

*   *   *   *

Tre spent every day of his leave with Molly. Some days, the only reason he got dressed, was to bring her back to his room to get undressed again. Being together felt so right, so easy. He liked how easy it was. Nothing in his life had ever been this easy. Everything up to that moment was hard, beyond hard.

They had moments of completeness, when they finished each other's sentences and moments of complete silence, because words were unnecessary. There was much heavy sighing when they cuddled and nothing but each other when they made love.

The first time they were naked together, they made each other laugh. Molly was sitting on the end of Tre's bed, in her bra and panties. He was already erect when he removed his pants. She swallowed hard, when he faced her. "Oh, my!" She strained to get the words out. "Is that for *me*?"

"Yeah," he looked a little shy and embarrassed. "It's your first time and you're so, you know…," he groped around for the right descriptor, "…so little. Look at you! Look at me!"

"You worry too much." She assured, flashing her most wicked, bad-girl smile.

He came over to the bed and stood directly in front of her, leaned down and kissed her. "Are you sure?" He made no effort to conceal his concern. She reached up, put her arms around his neck and pulled him down on top of her. He kissed her neck and rolled them both over to undo her bra. Molly sat up on his belly and removed the lace garment.

"The signs are very clear," she said.

"Yeah? What signs?"

"The ones that say: slippery when wet."

They dissolved into laughter, and then into each other.

Later, as they lay on their sides, nesting like spoons, Tre whispered, "Molly."

"I'm sleeping." Her voice was groggy, and she dismissed him with the wave of a droopy hand. "Stop poking me."

"I'm not—" He started to defend himself, then laughed when he realized she meant his erection was pressing into her. "Molly." He whispered again, pulling her closer. His hand slid down her warm naked body, to the delicious place between her legs and found her ready for him. He slid it back up her silky skin and began teasing a nipple. She half-heartedly slapped his fingers. "Come on!" He pretended to whine. "It's no fun having a puppy, if you can't play with it."

"Is that what I am? A puppy for you to play with?" She pretended to be hurt, but her eyes were still shut and she snuggled backward into him.

"I'm sorry, Molly." His voice husky with desire. "Let me make it up to you."

"You really want to make it up to me?"

"Yes, please."

Molly opened her eyes and rolled over to face him. "You've been quite naughty." Her brow knit together, as she considered his penance. "If you want to make up, you'll have to kiss me *everywhere*." She emphasized the last word.

"Not *every* everywhere!" A hand leapt to his heart, in mock horror.

"Yes!" Her most commanding voice assured him. "*Every* everywhere!" She wrapped herself around him, then rolled onto her back, pulling him with her, to enjoy his weight on top of her.

He rested on his elbows wondering how he was lucky enough to find her so easily, let alone at all. He couldn't believe that he hadn't know her his entire life. "Well, when you're right you're right. I was bad. I'll never learn my lesson, if I'm not properly punished. If I have to kiss you everywhere, then…," he gave a heavy sigh, smiling at her wonderful choice of punishment, "…I guess I have to."

*   *   *   *

Oahu, May 1968

The five mornings immediately following Tre and Carl's departure, Molly got to the bathroom just in time to throw-up. She was chronically nauseous, chronically exhausted, and although she was in bed every night by 9:30, it did little good.

Heaven only knew what kind of strange viruses were common in Vietnam and she was afraid she caught a serious illness from Tre or Carl. She visited a local doctor who gave her a thorough exam. He ran a battery of test and, three days later, called her with the results.

"Congratulations Mrs. Houser, you're pregnant."

Molly was so excited. Tre's baby. She didn't want to distract him from the war with this kind of news, but she was sure he would be as excited as she was. She went to speak with the NCO (Non-Commissioned Officer) in charge of the Reception Station on Oahu, a shabby little office on Leilani Boulevard. He was less than delighted with the visit and treated her with the contempt of someone who'd been waiting too long to have the stick removed from his butt.

"We met here while he was on R&R," she explained, thinking it would help.

"How romantic," his sarcasm was not lost on Molly. "Lady, do you have any idea how many guys were transported here for R&R."

"His name is Tre."

"Sounds like a nick-name. I've got no way of looking up a guy by his first name, let alone a nick-name. I need a last name. I need his full given name."

"I have a picture." She pulled the photo out of her purse and showed it to him. "That's his friend, Carl."

"Very nice." He hardly gave it a glance.

"Don't you have pictures *I* could look at?"

"What do you think this is, a police station and I have a room full of mug books out back?" Unfortunately, that's exactly what Molly thought. "Tens of thousands of men have already gone to 'Nam. Most of them passed thru Hawaii once or twice. They don't send me snap-shots and I don't know any of them by their first names. I'll tell you again, I need his full given name. I need his rank. I need his serial number. I need dog tags. I need something. You've got nothing. I can't help you."

"There has to be something you can do!" She insisted. "Please! It's so impor-tant that I find him."

"Oh, all right!" He finally stopped writing, slapped his pencil down on the desk, and looked up, condescending to offer her some help. "Type a generic let-ter, including a way to be contacted. Say that…you're looking for a soldier who goes by the name of Tre and that it could be a nick-name. Send it to the editors of Post Newspapers and Base or Fort Newsletters, and ask them to print your let-ter." He handed her a list of Boot Camps. "I'd start with these. A lot of Drill Ser-geants stay put for a while, one of them might remember your guy. No guarantee, mind you, but it's probably your best bet." He picked up his pencil and bent his head back down to his paperwork, hoping she would just go away.

"Thank you. Thank you very much. Good-bye." A smidgen of hope tinged her voice.

"Yeah, yeah, yeah," he dismissed her with a few waves of his hand. "You're welcome. Good-bye!"

Molly left feeling down-hearted. The help, such as it was, offered only the tiniest glimmer of hope. For the process to work, the editors actually had to print her letter and Tre or someone who knew him would have to read it and contact her. There was no way to ensure that any of those things would happen, let alone all of them. The NCO might be a thin lipped jerk, but he was also right. It did look pretty hopeless.

It never occurred to Molly that she'd have trouble finding Tre. She assumed she'd just see him again when he returned for his next R&R. He said he'd return, and she believed him. But that was six months away and she'd be showing by then. The USO might not take kindly to her getting pregnant on their watch. She could lie and say they got married, but then she'd have to produce some sort of document to prove it and she didn't have one. She might never find Tre, if the USO sent her home. Her only real hope was staying where she was. If they threw her out, without a job and a place to live, she could not afford to stay in Hawaii, on her own and pregnant. Her parents would never support her so far from home, but they'd be happy to have her *at home*, despite her predicament.

Plan B, her father always said—always gotta have a Plan B. Molly loved Tre, like she never loved anyone, and he was her baby's father. She would keep her mouth shut and her belly in, for as long as possible. She would wait to hear from the Boot Camps and hope for the best. If the USO sent her home, well, there was always Plan B—keep looking for Tre and, in the meantime, apply to colleges near home.

Her mom would be willing to help take care of the baby, and she could become a...a lab technician. Yes, being a lab technician was a good job, and with luck, she could be a lab tech in a hospital. Babies often needed doctors just when you could least afford them. At least there would be health care. Her decision was made. Although it would likely be a lonely life, even with her baby, it was a very possible and not too horrible Plan B.

*   *   *   *

Oahu, September 1968

Tre returned to Honolulu as planned. His first night back, he visited the USO. It was a whole new group of girls and not a one of them knew Molly. One suggested that he speak to the office manager. Next morning, Tre spoke to the unpleasant man in charge of the girls.

"I'm looking for a girl named Molly, about so tall," he used his hand to indicate where the top of her head came to on him, "blue eyes, brown hair."

The man pretended to look thru his records, knowing full-well that he wasn't giving out any information about that stupid girl. "I have no record of anyone named Molly."

"She was here six months ago. Her room-mate was a perky little blond, named Amy. Used to be a cheerleader." Tre thought the information would be helpful in jogging the man's memory.

The man pretended to look again. "Sorry, I have nothing. No Molly. No Amy." He'd be damned if he was going to tell this guy anything. And what would he say. *Oh her? Yeah, I remember her. Got herself knocked-up. Didn't even get the guy's last name.* Shit! She probably slept with dozens of them and, at that rate, the father could have been anyone. What if this guy wasn't *the* guy? Or worse, what if he was, but didn't want the girl if there was a kid in the bargain. He didn't need a confrontation and he certainly didn't want this over-grown soldier to kill the messenger. He was too old to barn-wrestle with a guy half his age and at least twice his strength. It was just easier to plead ignorance.

"She probably got home-sick and left."

"No. She wouldn't do that!" Tre protested. "I promised I'd be back and she promised she'd be here!" Tre barked at the man, making him jump. "Even if she went home, you'd still have a record of her, an address, some way I could find her."

"Well, look, I'm pretty new here myself," he lied. "The last manager didn't keep such good records. It's a real shame, but I have nothing on your friends."

"People don't just disappear!" Tre yelled at the man, banging both of his huge hands on the desk, making him jump again. "This isn't the middle of the war or the DMZ, you asshole!"

Tre stormed out of the office letting the door bang behind him. Without the USO's help, that was the end. There was nowhere else to go and no one else to ask. Molly was simply gone.

CHAPTER 11

▼

CAMBODIA— NOVEMBER, 1968

The small convoy of trucks seemed to be taking the indirect route. It was a covert night mission, code named Fred Astair.

There wasn't much conversation between the shot-gun and driver of the last truck. Each had volunteered for numerous missions, but neither had even met the other before. The trucks stopped. The drifting timbre of a conversation, taking place up ahead, made its way back to them. The driver and shot-gun turned to each other, stunned.

"Open the door as quietly as you can and get out," the driver instructed. "Don't waste time looking around for me and don't look back. Just run like hell. I'm right behind you. Go! Now!"

The shot-gun knew better than to ask questions. The passenger-side door opened without a sound and he dropped noiselessly to the unpaved road. The driver slid over to the open door and did the same, swung the door closed and quietly latched it. Half crouched, they slipped into the brush. A sudden spray of automatic gun-fire was all the motivation they needed to bolt through the dense foliage, jump over dead and fallen trees, and crash past palm fronds that smacked them in the face.

His heart pounding, the sound of blood pulsing in his ears, the driver stopped to catch his breath. He was very much alone. Ignoring his own advice, he took a quick look around and called in a low voice. "Hey, man, where are you?" He tried again and got a reply, but instead of his partner, it was Charlie staring him in the face, grinning like an evil devil. The blast of his weapon nearly sliced the driver in half. Charlie pulled off the driver's boots, tied the laces together, slung his rifle over one shoulder, the boots over the other, and walked back to the road humming.

*   *   *   *

The shot-gun came-to in the dark, a pain in his head and another in his side. He lay on a dirt floor with his face smashed up against something. The slightest movement sent a pain rolling around his skull. It was a relief to black-out from it.

When he came-to again, there was a bit more light. It was impossible to tell how long he'd been there. He got into a seated position and saw bamboo spears sticking up from the dirt floor—everywhere, but where he landed. He was hurt pretty badly, but missing the spears—punji sticks tipped with feces, to be specific, was practically a miracle. They were capable of inflicting a wound that could have turned septic and killed him. As it was, the jungle heat and moisture in the pit mixed with the excrement to create a stench that made him gag.

His head continued to ache. Examination of the pain in his side, revealed a giant abrasion over a wide swath of dark blue and purple. The right side of his neck felt as if it had been cut with something. He touched the tender line. Dried blood. He tried to remember who he was. He failed. He tried again. All he accomplished was making his head throb.

Parts of his shirt were shredded in the fall and the lettering above the right breast pocket was meaningless. The left leg of his trousers also was shredded and the skin beneath was badly scraped and bloody. The garments, made of dark material, somehow seemed official. Was he some sort of an official? He didn't know. He had no memory from before waking up in the pit. He checked the cargo pockets of his pants and found some candy bars. He ate one. Hungry as he was, somehow he knew more food could wait, escaping the pit could not.

He looked up. It was as if his fall had hardly disturbed the pit's camouflage. The lack of any human sounds made him think no one knew he was there, but someone was bound to check, eventually. He fell asleep, trying to put together a plan of escape. The pit, about eight feet deep, was hotter and brighter, the stench worse, when next he awoke.

Bamboo poles and strong wire reinforced the sides, to prevent them from caving in, but there was no place to get a foot-hold. He pulled and tugged, until three poles loosened and finally came free. He used them to dig up a few punji sticks. Slow, tedious work, but binding the sticks and poles together with the wire made a usable a ladder. At nightfall, he climbed out and stumbled noisily, trying to get his bearings. *Quiet, you must be quiet.* He literally willed it to happen.

B-52s had removed whole chunks of the jungle's thick canopy. Just ahead was one such break. A flash of a childhood memory guided him in using the North Star. With no idea where he was, or from which direction he came, he had less idea which way to head now. He chose South. *But if I remember how to use the North star, why can't I remember my name?*

His lips were badly parched and something inside him said that without water, soon, he would die. He pulled fruit from the trees. It wasn't water, but some fluid was better than none at all. He walked all night and finished the last of the candy bars. A familiar smell drifted toward him—a foul odor that made his nostrils flare. Lurking in his subconscious was the knowledge that the bad smell was a good thing. He headed toward it.

A small village came into view, just beyond another break in the trees. The foul odor was coming from there. As he stumbled into the village, a woman emerged from one of the dwellings, with an infant strapped to her back. He smiled at her and collapsed.

The village sat close to the Cambodian border and the woman knew enough to keep him well hidden. When he came-to, she was bathing him with cool, wet cloths. He was burning up with fever, his head spinning and his skin felt as if it were on fire. He was naked, except for the bandage on his side, and another on his leg. There was some awful smelling goo under them.

She wrapped him in the family's only quilt and had already laundered what was left of his tattered clothing. The garments, now dry, lay neatly folded on a stool. He tried to thank her. She recognized his face as American, but spoke no English and did not understand. Charlie and Joe were the only American names she knew. GI Joe was a friend who called the enemy Charlie.

"Joe?" She pointed to the uniform, hopefully.

What was she asking? Joe? It was so familiar. Fever and pain muddled his reasoning. Aw hell! Joe was as good a name as any. "Yes," he said, then drifted in and out of feverish dreams.

Over the course of the next few days, he roused a few times when it was light. The woman and infant were always missing, but, likewise, a jug of water and a cup were always in their place. When they returned at dark, the woman gave him food—covered in sauce, the source of the foul-smelling, good thing.

His only concept was dark and light and the days slipped by. In the light he was alone. In the dark, the woman and her child were there—a sad woman and a happy baby. She was kind and Joe was grateful. The woman tried, unsuccessfully, to teach him some Vietnamese. But even without language in common, the baby liked Joe and laughed when they played together on the floor of the hooch. Every now and then, the woman smiled too and didn't look quite so sad. Little-by-little, his body healed and his strength returned, but not his memory.

During the light, after he was better, when she went away, she left the child with Joe, which was no small relief. Working was easier and at the end of the day, her back ached a little less.

This had been her husband's village, but he was killed during a bombing raid, while she was pregnant. Her own village was many weeks journey from this place and if she and the infant were to make that pilgrimage, they would need help. They had none. There was also no way to be certain that any of her family were still alive, or, if they were, that they were still in the same village. So she stayed where she was, working the nearby rice paddies to earn her living.

Joe would not leave the place, with the safe smell, until it was absolutely necessary.

*   *   *   *

A South Vietnamese Company was scouting just over the Cambodian border. If there were men to be rescued, or returned, they would try. They came upon the mangled, shoeless driver and, considering what was left of him and his uniform, it was amazing they recognized him as an American. Something shiny lay near his body. The leader picked it up. A dog-tag. Another lay a few feet away. It was possible that neither tag belonged to the dead man, but there was no other body and no one to ask. The leader and his men could not read English, so both tags were hung around the dead man's neck. It was not the leader's problem. He would let the Americans figure it out. They built a litter and carried the body to the nearest American compound.

CHAPTER 12

▼

CAMBODIA— NOVEMBER, 1968
THE FOLLOWING NIGHT

It was pitch black and William was walking a dirt road, illuminated by nothing but starlight, again. A large group of men, dressed and armed for combat, was moving-out ahead of him, again. They would not notice a Sergeant Major, wearing full battle fatigues, slip into their ranks. They would think he was one of them, just another soldier. They always did.

It was William's recurring dream which, lately, came nearly every time he closed his eyes. It was like a silent movie—action and movement, without sound. In another few minutes, his heart pounding in his chest, adrenaline coursing through his veins, he would awaken, drenched in sweat, yet not altogether sure why.

The two men, directly ahead of him, had their usual exchange, but rather than struggling to read their lips, their words struck like sledge hammers. One faceless voice said, "Awful lot of trouble for boots and C-rations."

"Yeah, somethin' stinks," another voice continued. "Shit, let the gooks keep 'em."

William's memory caught up with him, came into focus, and confirmed that the faceless men were right. Every man on the mission, except those pulled to take a ridge, was lost. What was so damned important about that ridge? Down, just behind it, with a hole in his leg and a bamboo spear in his side, was future Senator Lloyd E. Cummings, the son of a Lifer. A Lifer no one liked, including Lloyd.

*   *   *   *

The Vietnam era held special fascination for William. He memorized the details of many of its missions and the fables attached to them. After the Freedom of Information Act passed, many became public; mostly regarding stuff that wasn't supposed to have happened—like that remains of MIAs were suddenly found and returned to the U.S. from countries where they were never supposed to have been. Less common, but just as real, were tales of Americans who worked both sides of the war—GIs who mysteriously dropped from sight, then used their uniforms to act as Pointmen on behalf of the enemy.

William's nightmare was of one such Army Pointman, responsible for the slaughter of hundreds of innocent boys, trying to kill Colonel Cummings' son. Rumor was that the kid was his father's whole life—always had to know where his son was, what hill, what detail. It gave everyone the false impression that if anything happened to the kid, say he died in-country, it would have been as good as killing the old man. Some believed that was why the Colonel retired shortly after his son nearly lost his life, twice, in as many days—he couldn't function under the stress of not knowing his son was OK every second. It was a nice little smoke screen.

There were nearly thirty attempts to make sure Lloyd Cummings ended up dead—two of them overt, both ending in total disaster, and neither one successful. The first overt attempt came the night he rode shot-gun in the lead truck of a convoy. They were ambushed. Lloyd was badly injured and stranded. Next night, another mission tried to get back those same trucks. They were also ambushed. The Cong wasted all but the four who separated from the others to pack Lloyd out of Cambodia. That act miraculously saved his life as well as theirs.

The initial theory was that Lloyd was a Pointman, therefore, it was no coincidence he survived so many disasters. But when he was hauled back into Xuan Loc, shot and half dead, those rumors died a quick death, replaced by people saying he led a charmed life. Cummings and the men who saved him knew better. Their hunt for tangible and legitimate evidence, however, proved fruitless.

Over the years, Lloyd's rescue was distorted into a tale over which William was often questioned and teased throughout his own tour in the Army. "Hey,

Houser. You related to *The* Houser—magical, mystery man that single-handedly saved Senator Cummings? Came out of nowhere and then, BANG!!!, disappeared into the jungle with the other Super-heroes. Ooh-eee-ooh!" They always made that eerie sound associated with unexplained Sci-Fi events, followed by the theme for the Twilight Zone.

Only Cummings knew how many were in his rescue party and from his first debriefing, the story remained the same. It took the muscle and war savvy of four men to get him out alive; and the two medics, one of which was Houser, to keep him that way. No one could confirm or deny the special assignment to find Cummings in the first place, or what little of the story he told. Whenever pressed for names, it was always: *Sergeant Major Houser and the Super-heroes*. The Army couldn't persuade him to say more and the press never drew him out.

Washington disavowed any knowledge of Houser. He had no Army records, no Basic had trained him, and no one at any Army medical facility ever laid eyes on him. His only confirmed sighting was the night he and three others rescued Cummings, after which, all four disappeared into the Vietnamese landscape. They were like reverse Pointmen who never came forward to claim the hefty reward, that was privately offered, or their medals for bravery. Most assumed they either never existed, or subsequently died. Why else wouldn't they claim all of that money? Why else indeed?

With the single exception of Lloyd Cummings, all who participated in two particular missions either died during, or vanished afterward. The Army was too busy drowning in the Mei Lei massacre to expend much effort investigating. All available hands were in the business of covering their own asses, while finding a scapegoat for the slaughter of civilians. But it remained indisputable—the only way the Cong could have been up the same soldier's ass so often, and with such deadly accuracy, was with help from someone on the inside. Even with a bounty on his head for the duration of the war, and long afterward, the Army never found the traitor.

William knew the whole Lloyd Cummings story, cover-to-cover, and now knew that *he* was the leader of the rescue party that saved him. William was Sergeant Major Houser.

*   *   *   *

Lloyd's four paragraph public story:

All of Lloyd's young life he was called Army brat, though he lived every day of that life in one place, in a house that had been in his mother's family for generations. There was nothing remotely military about him, except voluntarily serving five tours in Vietnam.

Rather than painting the town red with his friends, Lloyd spent his graduation night with his brother, Junior. They had dinner in the fanciest restaurant in town, then hit the beach for a walk. Around 10:30, they called it a night. It was only by coming home early that Lloyd and Junior saved their mother's life.

During his second tour of duty, a convoy, for which he was riding shot-gun, was ambushed. Miraculously, he emerged from the jungle alive. The balance of that story was that Lloyd was a big man, six-foot-three, and given the extent of his injuries, it would have been impossible for him to return to Xuan Loc without the help of at least two other people, who had access to a truck.

Lloyd's fifth tour concluded with the first U.S. troop withdrawals, after which he became the man who went to Washington to design landmark legislation protecting abused women and children. He used his war record to get himself elected and his family's money to set up safe houses across the country. Then set about redefining the boundaries of the phrase *restraining order*. He was instrumental in broadening its scope from preventing not only any sort of physical contact, but any contact whatsoever. It eventually came to include telephone, the mail, fax and e-mail.

Lloyd's more detailed, private story:

Lloyd's father had beaten his wife for years and the M.D.s at Walter Reed kept the details of those beatings under lock and key. The night of Lloyd's High School graduation, in a drunken rage, Colonel Cummings beat his wife to within an inch of her life and sent her crashing down a flight of stairs. He nearly killed her.

The Army cited the brutal beating of Jean Cummings to persuade the Colonel to retire. He promised to go quietly and they promised not to press charges for the beating.

Lloyd and his brother, Junior, were walking the beach, about half an hour's stroll North of Cummings Point, where they came upon a girl having a bon-fire. She told the brothers a fantastic tale, warning that their mother was in danger. If they didn't leave immediately, it would be too late. The boys left, but only to prove that the girl was a crank. They found their mother not five feet from the front door, in a pool of blood. The worst of it was a concussion and a ruptured spleen. Without emergency surgery, she would have bled to death from internal injuries. Upon admittance to Walter Reed, it was discovered that all of Jean Cummings' previous medical records had gone missing.

While in-country, death stalked Lloyd Cummings and everyone near him. Well, nearly everyone.

Lloyd decided to release a public version of the private story. He enlisted the help of Juliet Cohen, Jean Cummings oldest and dearest friend. She spoke to an eager, young, cub reporter, stating that Jean's injuries were the result of a break-in, but that she would make a full recovery.

The reporter and the local paper she worked for, saw it as a terrific human interest piece. The story's headline: **Army Kids Save Mom After Home Break-in,** was followed by an article that stated nothing was stolen from the home and the perpetrators were not apprehended. It appeared in print only once, buried on page twelve of the evening edition.

On further consideration, Lloyd didn't want to leave that paper, or any other, with the resources to dig around and find the truth. He sent Juliet to purchase the reporters notes, paying dearly for the guarantee that no additional articles would ever be written.

"Jean and the boys don't want a fuss made over them." she explained. "Yes, the boys are heroes, but please, allow them to be quiet heroes and leave it within the family. Mrs. Cummings would rather not be made into a public spectacle when she comes home."

*   *   *   *

Lloyd enlisted before graduation, and already had his reporting date. The Army had honored his request for Vietnam. Why not? It was great PR. A Colonel's kid, one of their own, elected to serve in-country. The rest of the private story was that Lloyd spirited his mother and younger brother out of Virginia, far away from Cummings Point, and into a new life with new names, where the Colonel would never find them. That night began Lloyd's career of helping women with nowhere else to turn.

The Colonel went berserk upon discovery that Jean not only checked out of the hospital AMA (against medical advice), but that she and Junior disappeared, and Lloyd had arranged it. Father and son duked-it-out in the living room, where the Colonel smashed lamps, furniture, and anything else he could get his hands on, including his eldest son. That night, Lloyd took a room in town and never spoke to this father again. Lloyd left for Basic without the Colonel ever learning that anyone, besides Lloyd, knew the whereabouts of Jean and Junior.

Once Lloyd was in Washington, he worked tirelessly to pass unpopular legislation, that saved the lives of battered women and children. Isaac Newton said that every action has an equal and opposite reaction, so the opposition looked under every rock for the spark of Lloyd's zeal. Jean's medical records and the reporters notes had long since vanished. Nothing remained to connect either Lloyd or, his long missing brother, to any sort of personal agenda.

The Army never would have forgiven Lloyd for taking a new identity and going MIA *before* he shipped out, but he shouldn't have cared. After the events that took place before he left for Basic, figuring he'd be safe from his father, half a world away, was terribly short sighted. Hindsight and Time revealed outcomes that were much farther reaching. Jean's family, the Saunders, were the actual owners of the house where the Cummings family lived and didn't allow the Colonel to remain in it alone. With Jean and Junior missing, Lloyd gone off to war, and no home, the Colonel had no family and no reason to retire as planned. All he had was uncontrolled anger and an appetite for revenge.

*   *   *   *

William was among a collection of volunteers—Privates, PFCs and a few Sergeants, on a doomed retrieval mission. The fear-factor was high and the conversation almost non-existent. As the march continued, William mentally verified his tools—a weapon, full canteen, ammo, the contents of his medic's pack, poncho, flack jacket, and helmet. He felt in his pocket for his precious gifts.

Once at the staging area, William identified one of the Sergeants in charge. It tore at him that all but three of these men would be lost, but, in the future, they were already dead. There was nothing, whatsoever, he could do about it. Born was born. Dead was dead. If he died in this jungle, he would not return to his own Time—he would stay dead. His guides said that only he and three very specific men had a mission. He approached the Sergeant knowing that he would get whatever, and whoever, he wanted. He outranked everyone.

"I'll need three men to move with me, Sergeant." His tone was friendly, but matter-of-fact.

"Yes sir, Sergeant Major," he did not salute. "Which men?"

All eyes were riveted on the Sergeant Major, awaiting his response. William surveyed the group for the three, now familiar, faces. They were close to the front of the pack, each half a head taller than the others. "You, you, and you. We move east."

The three men each noted the quickest flash of light in the Sergeant Major's eyes, looked at each other, but said nothing. They waited for their Sergeant to release them.

"Those are my three best men, sir," the Sergeant objected.

"I'm afraid they're my men now, Sergeant."

"Yes, sir." The Sergeant turned his head and called their names. "Tilson. Summers. Makepeace. Front and center."

They hustled forward and replied in unison, also not saluting, "Yes, sir."

"I didn't get your name, sir."

"Houser—special assignment." William extended his hand.

It was completely unmilitary, but the Sergeant accepted the hand anyway. "I'm Baker." Then he turned to dismiss his men. "All right, you three go with Houser. Do your best to stay alive.

"The rest of you listen up," he addressed those remaining under his command. "Charlie captured our trucks and we have word they're parked on the other side of that field, down there. They were ambushed and we could be too, so keep your heads down, talking to a minimum and your eyes and ears open. Hold your fire until you hear the signal. Everyone's been assigned their leader—Wentworth, Mayhue, Connor, Fitz, or me. Gentlemen...," the Sergeant elongated the word, then made a forward aching motion with his weapon, finally pointing it in the direction of the field to their North, "...let's rock and roll."

The men broke into five groups, each a silent sea of olive drab, that moved toward the field of low brush. The three under William's command headed East with him, into a stand of trees. When the men reached the open field, they got into low crawl—on their bellies, weapons across their arms at the elbows, and slithered, with their faces in the dirt, like four legged snakes. William and his detachment were crouched in the overgrowth, making their way to a low spot, some three hundred yards away.

The sudden sound of gunfire, mortars, and machine guns, came from everywhere at once. The men in the field were surrounded—caught in an ambush. Makepeace started to scramble out of the relative safety of their position, but William grabbed his ammo belt and dragged him back.

"Exactly where are you going?" William's lips formed a tight line in his face.

"I can't sit here and hide like a coward." Tre struggled to release himself. "I can't do nothing and just leave them."

"You're not doing nothing. You're doing your job and your orders come from me. You see that ridge?" The Sergeant Major pointed off into the distance. "*That's* your destination."

"But the men, they'll die."

The moments were ticking by and William still had to accomplish his mission. He grabbed Tre by the front of his shirt and put his own face into that of the very young soldier. They stood eye-to-eye, the same size, the same build. He chose his words carefully, as he considered that part of the future that was unchangeable. "They're already dead and if the three of you don't get your asses over that ridge, you'll die with them and you won't have helped anyone."

"But, I gotta get...," Tre's voice trailed off as he feebly tried to pull away again.

William's grip tightened and his face turned to stone. He shook Tre until he was forced to look at him. "There's nothing to get. You have your orders." From an ancient memory, someone else's words left his lips. "Orders can keep you alive, soldier. If you listen you live. If you don't, the only thing you **get** is dead."

Tre saw the unmistakable, lightening quick, flash of light in the Sergeant Majors eyes.

"Remember that! All of you. Understand?" They remained in stunned silence as Tre's head and eyes drifted in the direction of the field, which, by then, had to be a sea of crimson. William's voice was a bit softer, but more demanding as he tugged hard to make Tre look back at him. "Do you understand?" Tre and the others nodded. "Good!" William released his grip to prepare his own weapon. "Now, all of you, lock and load...and let's move."

The smell of blood was thick in the air and, soon, it would mix with the pungent smell of rotting underbrush, the aroma of wild palms, tropical moss, mold, and humid soil, to transform itself into the heavy odor of death. The Sergeant Major was right—the other men were dead. It made no sense—an enormous waste and nothing to show for it, not even the stupid supplies. All Tre wanted to know was: *what genius Brasshole put together this mission?*

Tre decided they would be lucky if any of them lived to tell about this night and questioned if it would ever be safe to do so. As they headed for the ridge, just beyond the trees, that a pale red circle marked him for a purpose hidden in his nightmares was clearer than ever, and either Carl and Poopsie were part of that purpose or the luckiest sons-of-bitches he ever met.

The four men made their way to the far side of the ridge and discovered their *special assignment*, to get out an injured man. William started treating his injuries, but once Tre ascertained the man's identity, he and Carl and Poopsie stepped back, their weapons still in their hands, ready to leave.

"There a problem?" William looked up innocently. The pale, drawn-faced, soldiers were silent. He addressed Carl. "Get shot in both arms on your way thru the jungle, Summers?"

Carl's answer was indignant. "No, sir."

"You're a medic." William gestured at the medical supplies on his back "Why carry that crap around if you don't intend to use it? Put down your weapon, open your bag and get busy."

Carl took the direct order and helped dress the injured soldier's wounds, but could look neither at Tre nor Poopsie.

After a long silence, Tre found his voice. "This was our special assignment? We're risking our lives to save this piece of shit? Colonel Cummings kid?"

William smiled at the fury in Tre's eyes, never taking his own off the face of his patient. "You're not really a *piece of shit*, are you, Cummings?" His voice reflected mock disbelief. "Tell me you've got more going for you than your Mommy's money and your Daddy's reputation." William carefully and gently removed Lloyd's helmet, then lightly slapped his face as he began to slip out of consciousness. He'd lost a lot of blood and was suffering from exposure. "Stay with me, Cummings."

Lloyd's eyes fluttered open, his response weak, "Yes, sir."

William held Lloyd's face in his hand as he checked his pupils, then gently examined the spear and bullet wounds. Infection. "You allergic to penicillin?"

"No, sir." Cummings' eyes closed again.

William slapped his face again. "No one dies on my watch. Do not go gentle into that good-night."

"Rage. Rage against the dying of the light." Tre and Lloyd simultaneously finished the quote, Tre's voice flat and without inflection; Lloyd's strained. They momentarily locked eyes.

William smiled.

"Don't even go there," Tre snapped. "Our common ground begins and ends with knowing that quote."

"Really?" William tossed Lloyd's helmet to Tre who, from reflex, just caught it. "Whose picture is tucked inside *your* helmet?"

Inside Lloyd's helmet was a photograph—himself with one arm around a petite woman, the other around a young boy. Tre gave it a quick glance, noting the writing in the margin.

"This kid's going to do great things, save a few lives along the way, like his idols, if we don't lose him first." William scanned their faces. "Weren't all of *your* idols heroes? Audie Murphy, Sergeant York—two of the most decorated soldiers in WW I and WW II. They just did their job, never waited around for thanks or acknowledgment. Don't you see yourselves as silent heroes with a few medals on your dress uniforms?" The three didn't respond, but inwardly acknowledged that the Sergeant Major had their number. "That's what I thought. This kid thinks he's Superman, except that on this particular day, in this particular jungle, he found Kryptonite. So, what are you gonna do, fellas? Walk away, or stick it in a lead box before it kills him?

"Here!" William tossed Lloyd's gun and radio to Poopsie. "Check 'em."

"Dead and empty." Poopsie brandished the two useless objects in his hands. "So?"

"So, this kid stayed on the wire and under fire, until that thing wore out," William indicated the radio, "and he was out of ammo. Took a hit in the side and one in the leg for his trouble." William cut away the compression bandage, Lloyd had used to stem the flow of blood from his thigh. The center was wet and crimson, edged in dried blood. "Do you suppose he ended up here while out for a midnight stroll?" William felt as if he were talking to three brick walls. "He was part of the first ambushed mission. Look, I don't care if your only option in the Army is to follow orders. No one ordered you to take this shit patrol. It was strictly volunteer. You *all* volunteered. Why?" William scanned their faces again, but they offered no answer.

"I need a fresh bandage for the leg and something to tie it on with." Without missing a beat, William leaned his right shoulder toward Carl, offering the sleeve of his shirt. "Cut close to the armhole, then lose the cuff and tear the sleeve into strips."

"No!" Tre barked before Carl even reached for his scissors. William threw Tre a stone stare, until he stooped down and offered the left sleeve of his own shirt. "Use mine, it's cleaner."

Carl removed the sleeve and unveiled the pale red birthmark on Tre's arm. William didn't stop to acknowledge the mark and spoke to no one in particular, "Say, this isn't your first tour. Ever consider becoming a lifer?"

"Not in a million years," Tre answered for everyone and practically spit the last word, "sir."

Tre told himself no one would become a Lifer after living thru this. He rose, giving Poopsie a nod to begin building the litter necessary to get Cummings out of the jungle. How did the Sergeant Major know about the photo in Cummings' helmet, or that this wasn't a first tour for any of them? And why make the very same Superman reference Carl made the night Tre had words with Jack? Tre hated questions he couldn't answer.

CHAPTER 13

▼

VIETNAM—1968
THE SAME NIGHT—AT THE REAR

Benny Walker, a skinny, pimple-faced, radio operator, sat alone in the Colonel's command bunker. It was a slow night and he was listening to a tape recorded letter from his pen-pal, Robin Greene. Her friendly voice chattered on and on about College life and how awful the meal plan food was. He wondered how good she would think it tasted if she were stuck in the Infantry, like his friend Larry, and had eaten only Army chow or nothing at all for almost a year.

Benny knew Robin because she answered an ad asking kids from home to become pen-pals with guys serving in Vietnam. His parents bought the precious recorder, without telling him in advance, and he received it a week after arriving in-country. He couldn't have been more surprised, when he opened the package. His family's letter was stuck inside the machine and Robin's first letter was in an unopened, padded, mailing envelope, addressed to his parents' home, in Wisconsin.

"Hi, son!" His dad's voice came from the recorder. "Hi, sweetheart." It was his mom. "Hi, Benny!" His kid sister's voice floated into the air. "You're supposed to tape over our letter and send your news back to us." His mother's voice jumped back in. "The salesman said we can use the same tape many, many times before it has to be replaced. I put in an extra package of batteries, for when these wear-out.

"I went behind your back and signed you up for a pen-pal." His mother sheepishly admitted. "Please don't be mad. I know I should have asked you first, but I was afraid you'd say no, without even giving the idea a chance. The envelope is the first letter from your pen-pal. It's a girl, named Robin Greene. Don't worry, we haven't listened to it. We may be butinskys, but lucky for you, we aren't nosy as well."

There was laughter in the background.

"Say! Leave us out of that." His father objected. "You're the family butinsky."

"Yeah!" His sister added, laughing. "We're just along for the ride."

"Stop clowning around." His mom reprimanded. "I wrote Robin's name and address on the empty envelope. Please use it, honey. It could be fun and, even if it isn't, maybe corresponding with a stranger will take your mind off of the war for a few minutes."

The letter continued with tid-bits from their currently hassled life, how much they missed him, along with instructions to get enough rest, eat enough food, and stay as safe as possible.

Benny absently ran a hand over his closely cropped hair, then rubbed his cheek, glad Robin couldn't see his terrible crew-cut or his bad skin. To date, they hadn't exchanged photographs and neither one had the first idea what the other looked like. As always, Robin ended by asking him to take extra good care of himself and to try and return home unhurt. This time, she also asked if they could meet, when his tour was over.

"We've been doing the recorded letter thing for almost a year now and by the time you get this one you'll be about due to come home. What did you call it? Oh, yeah—you're on the short list. It would be so great to meet face to face. Do you think we could—you know, after you visit with your folks? Anyway, gotta go study. Write back soon. Bye." The tape ended.

By the time he got around to answering Robin's tape, so many days had passed, that she was more than right. This night was the last of his tour and, tomorrow, he would begin the journey home. By this day next week, he hoped to be sitting in his parents' living room, where they would all be watching something on TV. He chuckled picturing his dad in his usual spot—the recliner, and his mom and sister on either side of him—on the sofa, shoes off, their crossed legs up on the coffee table. As the evening passed, somehow the three of them would automatically cross their legs the other way, in unison. It never failed to crack-up his dad.

Benny was stuck in a rear area that didn't see much action, which meant that his tape would be as ho-hum as Robin's, but in the middle of a war, no news was the only kind anyone wanted from the front. Of course, Benny was stationed at the back of the front, but still...

He didn't have much to report, since his last letter, except that he really was coming home. Maybe he'd take Robin up on her offer to get together. He was acting as company clerk, no one would say 'boo' if his route home included the town where Robin attended university. She had such a sweet voice, always had something cheerful to say and sent great care packages—things only someone who really was nice would do.

"Hi ya, Robin. Benny here. Gee, it was really terrific of you to send the care package. You can't believe how crazy everyone went—like it was Christmas or something. The rolls of T-P were a huge hit and I can't even begin to describe the feeding frenzy when we got a whiff of the chocolate. The food here isn't bad, but getting something homemade, well, I can't tell you how great it was. Needless to say, we made short order of the brownies. Everyone sends their thanks."

Robin knew the brownies were only OK and made from a mix (so, not *exactly* homemade), but it was something personal she could do for Benny and she wasn't *exactly* a gourmet cook. Sending the toilet paper was her roommate's idea.

"Get the two-ply, quilted, kind, with little flowers on it." Marcy suggested. "My friend's brother said it's the best thing you can get from home...besides food. Can you imagine, guys in the field use leaves, when they run out of T-P." Both girls shuddered at the thought.

"Nothing much going on here. Just the usual—" His radio burst into life, interrupting his dictation.

"Fire Base Sierra Echo X-ray, this is Ginger Rogers!" The panicked voice shouted. "We are surrounded! Request immediate extraction!" The rat-a-tat of rapid fire weapons was audible over the wire. "Repeat, request immediate extraction!"

"Colonel!" Benny yelled, jumping out of his chair, knocking it over backward, and bolting for the door. He spotted the Colonel returning from a leisurely stroll around the compound. He cupped his hand around the side of his mouth and yelled again. "Colonel! It's Ginger Rogers, sir. There's trouble!"

The Colonel dropped his cigarette to the dirt, ground it out with the toe of his boot and came to the radio at a walk. He snatched up the handset and barked into it. "Ginger Rogers, this is Fire Base Sierra Echo X-ray. Who do I have?"

"Sergeant Phil Baker. There's VC everywhere! Request immediate extraction!"

"That's a negative, Sergeant. Request for extraction denied. Your unit must retrieve or destroy Fred Astair's cargo. I repeat, retrieve or destroy, at all cost."

"We cannot reach that destination. We're being over-run! It's like they were waiting for us; like they knew we were coming. We're out-manned and out-gunned. Most of my men are down. My radio operator is dead and my medic's been hit. I repeat, request immediate extraction!"

"You have your orders. I don't care how you do it, but get those men in there and do the job you were sent to do." There was no reply. "Ginger Rogers, come in!" Silence. "Ginger Rogers! Do you read me?"

The non-stop hail of gunfire continued to be audible over the still live radio, but there was no answer from the Sergeant, named Phil Baker. The Colonel threw down the handset and stormed out of his quarters, letting the door bang behind him.

The persistent sound of the distant battle pierced Benny's eardrums, then came a sudden loud blast, then nothing. He stood in shock, reliving the unbeliev-ably barbarous episode that was over in a matter of seconds.

The Colonel took his usual evening constitutional. It put him away from the command bunker, though his men were on a top priority, take no prisoners, mis-sion. (The second mission to end in total disaster in as many days.) When Benny shouted that the men were on the wire and in trouble, rather than making a mad dash for the radio, the Colonel wasted valuable seconds crushing out his cigarette, and maintained his leisurely pace. He made no offer to pull the men out or even let them retreat. In fact, though the mission and its men were clearly doomed, he ordered them to stay. Had he intentionally abandon his own men? Did he want them to die?

The voice of the now dead Sergeant echoed inside Benny's head. *It's like they were waiting for us; like they knew we were coming.* He covered his ears with his hands, trying to make it stop, but the Sergeant kept asking for the lives of his men, kept repeating the Army's three magic words—the ones that meant losses were too high; the situation no win; hopeless. *Request immediate extraction.*

Benny tried, unsuccessfully, to deny what happened, wished he was wrong, but knew that he wasn't. As the mental instant replay came to an end, Benny Walker, just barely nineteen years old, sank to his knees on the floor.

The tape recorder clicked off.

CHAPTER 14

▼

XUAN LOC, VIETNAM— 1968

LATER THAT NIGHT

When it was over, four rather large targets returned to Xuan Loc, their cargo in-toe, their special assignment complete, and except for Cummings injuries, not a scratch on any of them.

Tre showered, washing the stink of the jungle from his skin and tried, but failed, to wash the memory of what happened in the field out of his head. He shaved, dressed, grabbed his helmet, as defense against the in-coming that had been entering the compound all day, and went looking for Houser. He found him at The Enlisted Man's, sitting by himself, on a stool, at the bar. He was nursing a Scotch. Tre took the empty stool next to him, ordered a Boiler-maker, rested his arms on the bar, and clasped his hands together.

"You know something about Cummings the rest of us don't?" The question was not presented PFC-to-Sergeant Major, or even soldier-to-soldier, but man-to-man.

"I know he's not a bad guy, doesn't matter that he's got an asshole for a father."

Tre looked at Houser, raised an eyebrow, his tone a bit superior. "The asshole doesn't fall too far from the tree."

"He has a mother too." William raised his glass in a salute to Cummings' mom. "Maybe he didn't fall too far from *her* tree."

Tre considered his own family tree. The Makepeace side sure wasn't much to brag about. The Yellowfeather side was a totally different story.

"How did you know that he wears his mother's picture?"

"Saw it when I removed his helmet." William detested the lie, but how would he explain knowing it was there? Tre bore Time's mark, but did he fully comprehend its meaning. William spent nearly two decades researching it and never found the first bit of usable information. Then, the least likely source obliged him with a thorough explanation. He barely understood it himself. He decided not to take the chance that Tre knew even less.

"So, whose picture *is* tucked inside your helmet, asshole?"

Tre chuckled, removing the pictures from his helmet, sitting on the bar. He passed them to William who gave them the once-over. He recognized one photo immediately.

"Who's this?" He held up the unfamiliar image for identification.

"*My* mother." Both men laughed out loud. "She's getting married soon. Army gave me Compassionate Leave to attend the wedding." Tre silently chastised himself for divulging something so intimate, then shrugged it off asking, *what difference does it make that the guy knows about mother's wedding?*

"Gee, she's beautiful." William carefully checked the other photo. "And who's this lovely lady?"

"Just someone from the past. A USO volunteer."

Tre's glib response made her sound unimportant, but if that were true, why carry her photo with his mother's—in a place that kept it close to him whenever he faced battle...and death. William wondered for so long, whether he and his mother were abandoned that, now, with the opportunity to ask, he just had to know.

"Gonna see her again?" He hoped he sounded friendly instead of nosy.

"I tried, but it looks like she was transferred or went home, along with every single person that might have known her. I hoped to get her address from the USO, but that was a dead end. I never even knew her last name. She was just...Molly." He kicked himself over the name Molly knew—his nick-name. "For all I know, Molly is short for something and, if you want to find someone, it's nearly impossible to do it with a nick-name. If I ever see her again, believe me, it will be one hell of a coincidence."

"Do you believe in coincidence?"

Tre sipped at his drink and gave a one-word answer. "No."

So he did come back and went looking and he gave it a lot of thought. William was glad to know it. He thought to himself—*Yep, 'Just Molly' went home pregnant and unable to find you. The USO was so embarrassed that they sent her whole group packing. Then they basically destroyed any records they had on any of them. She returned from Hawaii with three souvenirs—a memory of a wonderful guy (whose real name and last name she didn't know either), a photograph and, a few months later, me.*

"She's fabulous. Great smile, great legs." William returned the pictures the way he received them, Connie's photo on top.

Tre nodded and returned them to their place of honor in his helmet without looking at them again, recalling the face and body that he couldn't get out of his head.

"Well, I hope you find her."

"Yeah, me too." Tre thought the bitterness in his voice made him sound just as pathetic as he felt. *You're a grown man, mooning over a girl*, he berated himself, *even if the girl is Molly.*

"Say!" William tried not to sound too much like a know-it-all. "Maybe her group was relocated." *Yeah, back to Boston.* "I move around a lot and have a great memory for faces. Give me your home address. I find anything, I'll let you know."

"You'd be wasting your time."

"It's my time, besides, you never know." Again, that instant flash of light in his eyes. Tre noted that his voice carried the optimistic tone of someone who already knew the answers to questions for a test that hadn't yet been written.

Tre allowed an awkward silence, then changed the subject. "I don't know how you pulled it off, but you saved the lot of us."

"I saved only Cummings. I just got the rest of us out alive. None of us was supposed to die in that particular jungle on that particular day."

"Yeah?" Tre's one-word question spoke volumes.

"Yeah." So did William's answer.

"And you know this because…"

"Because if we were supposed to die, we would have," William filled in the blank.

"You some sort of a fatalist?"

"Not exactly." William tapped his own left deltoid, indicating he saw the mark and knew its meaning. The only answer for such a question was the truth, although the truth didn't provide much of an answer.

Tre nodded. So the guy knew the drill, but Tre wanted no part of discussing it. He preferred his nightmares remain just that—his nightmares. Reviewing them with strangers, especially if they were repeated among the men, would make him seem like a child and a fool. This rat's nest was no place for children. It was a place where fools got themselves or others killed and Tre was not willing to die before the circle on his arm had the opportunity to close.

"Still…we owe you."

"Fine. You save me next time and we'll call it even." Then William reached across himself, extending his right hand. There was another inexplicable flash of light in his eyes.

Soldiers came and went, or got careless and got killed, making men who were careful for themselves, and others, a commodity that was in very short supply. Tre liked this man; he was smart and kept his head under fire, so he blew-off the unnerving flashes and carefully considered the proposed bargain—save this man next time. Tre got the distinct impression there was either going to be a next time or that, somehow, there had already been one.

"So, then it's a deal?" William asked.

Suddenly and without explanation, Tre absolutely knew that he would come out of this horrid stink-hole alive. "Deal!" As their grips locked to shake hands, Tre felt a disturbing intimacy. But was it intuition or some cosmic connection? He decided it didn't matter.

"I'll never forget you," William offered.

There was the briefest pause, as each man committed the other's face to memory.

"I'll never forget you either," Tre answered.

They finished that drink, and one more, in silence. The eerie whistle in William's ears returned and he got up to leave. Cummings was alive. The past was preserved. But he was nearly out of time and there was still the matter of interfering with the future without really interfering. Cummings was now the key, but how to create a scenario where he could talk to Tre and the others? William rested his hand on Tre's shoulder and gave him one last thing to think about.

"You guys have bugs up your noses about Cummings, and that's fine, but talk to him. I have. He's in pretty rough shape and sleeping, but he is conscious. Go give him a nudge. He'll be receptive to a conversation. Like it or not, you men are hooked together for life. Don't judge him by the sins of his father."

William felt Tre's back go stiff as he considered how different his own life would be, if others judged him by the life Jack Makepeace led. The thought was revolting.

"Get your friends and just talk to Cummings. Say you'll think about it."

"Maybe."

"I'll take that as a yes." William left the bar and headed for the compound PX.

CHAPTER 15

▼

BOSTON, MA—1996
MY POP-OP

Now that Tre was back in the states for good, his nightmares came with cruel regularity. It was the same two that periodically terrorized him since he was a teenager, always bringing with them the type of fear that filled him on the night he found his mother beaten to within an inch of her life. He was a soldier, albeit a retired one and it was unacceptable for a soldier to be terrified of anything.

Tonight, Tre nodded off for less than an hour. He awoke in a sweat, screaming bloody blue murder. God! When would it stop! He decided that the nights he opted to stay awake were preferable to those when he let himself fall asleep. In the end, he always wished he hadn't and tonight was one of those nights.

In the nightmares, he was always running. From something. Toward something. First, down a seemingly endless stretch of beach, his feet sinking like lead into soft sand. Next, down a city street, mostly shrouded in darkness. The running wasn't exhilarating, like his morning runs. Rather, each step brought him closer to the most intense fear of his life. He felt an unknown terror, and sensed a danger closing in—on him, on Molly, on his mother. But what…or was it who?

He would awaken, yelling, with breathing so hard and labored that his lungs felt as if they would burst, his mind full of questions for which there were no answers. The images were as if from another life—a life he had no part of. In any life, Molly and his mother were the only women he ever loved. And there they both were, so vivid, invading his sleep like vapors, scaring him to death, nearly breaking his heart, which continued hammering in his chest long after the nightmares were over.

They made him think of the service, especially in The 'Nam. Why was it always The 'Nam? Why couldn't he get the memories of that fucking war out of his head—things he did and said and that were said to him? Back then, he was scared 24-7, but the fear became a welcome ally. The constant flow of adrenaline heightened his senses and kept him alive for five tours. This. This was different. This fear practically paralyzed him.

Tre needed fresh air to clear his head. It was late, but Boston was a busy city where people were out and about 'til all hours, using all mode of transportation. A middle-aged man riding a bicycle in the middle of the night would hardly get a second glance. He stuck his key into the pocket of his shorts, not bothering to change from the clothes he fell asleep in, locked the door behind him, jumped on his bike, and headed in the direction of Kenmore Square.

Isn't there a game tonight? Boston against Philly? Maybe I can loose myself in the after-game crowd, forget about every other thing, and feel like any other fan having a beer. But the game had gone into extra innings, and Kenmore was nearly deserted. There wasn't yet a crowd in which to get lost and having a drink companioned only by his thoughts, well, he'd had just about enough of those for one night.

Tre decided to head up Brookline Avenue, then go around the Jamaica Way, maybe even have a dip in the pond near Olmsted Park. He tried very hard not to stare at the kids, with hair in every color of the rainbow and pierced everything. Just ahead, a familiar looking man was standing at the curb, waiting for the crosswalk light to change. He was reading the newspaper held in one hand and sipped at the cup of coffee held in the other. During the day, Brookline Avenue was crowded with all manner of vehicles to watch out for. With the lateness of the hour, the man paid no attention to the few on-coming cars.

From the corner of his eye, Tre caught sight of an erratically driven sports car. The same set of wheels was cruising Kenmore Square with a pair of teenagers in the front seat playing *rev-em-up,* at every stop light. The driver inched the car forward and back before flooring-it, each time a light turned green. God damn motor-heads!

Knowing teenagers well enough to expect them to do stupid things, Tre pedaled hard and quick, until he was far to the right and well ahead of the hot-rod.

Suddenly, it was barreling down the street, weaving out of control, the driver and his front seat passenger wrestling over control of the steering wheel. Stupid!

The crosswalk light changed and the pedestrian stepped into the street, his face still buried in the newspaper, the hot-rod headed right for him. Tre heard a strange, unsettling, whistle and a sudden flush made him break out in a sweat, as he desperately tried to reach the pedestrian before the car did. He came along side the man. Grabbed his arm. Pulled him down and backward, out of harm's way. The pedestrian rolled to the ground and out the end of the crosswalk. His paper and drink flew into the air, showering him in newsprint and latte, as Tre's bike turned directly into the path of the on-coming car.

The front bumper of the speeding car rammed into Tre's leg, which, combined with the force of the impact and the angle of his approach to the crosswalk, sent him flying, back first, into the windshield, followed closely by his bicycle. He and the bike rolled up and over the car's roof, as the driver hit the gas, instead of the breaks. It plowed directly into a utility pole. The accelerated forward motion sent Tre and the bicycle sliding down the back end of the car and off the trunk. He scraped over another five feet of pavement, on his shoulder, before finally coming to a stop in the middle of the street.

Tre's twisted wreck of a bike landed next to him, and something went skittering toward the gutter, unnoticed. The object landed at the curb on the opposite side of the street, directly under a sign that read: STREET SWEEPING 1ST AND 3RD MONDAYS.

It was over in a matter of seconds.

*   *   *   *

The pedestrian ran to the bicyclist and took a mental inventory of injuries. The car's impact broke his lower left leg; the shattered windshield caused some superficial cuts and bruises on his back; scraping over the pavement produced a giant strawberry on his shoulder; and a trickle of blood ran from his nose.

"Jesus, mister! What the hell were you thinking, except that you probably saved my life?"

"You save me next time…we'll call it even." The man drifted into unconsciousness.

The pedestrian grabbed the bicyclist by the front of his shirt. "No one dies on my watch!" No response. "Hear me, god damn it!" Words like a salve. Words of hope. His prayer when things were beyond his control. "Do not go gentle into that good-night." No response, certainly not the one he wanted. "Shit! Where's an ambulance when you need one?" Then he ran toward his original destination, where an Ambulance with two EMTs was parked at the ER of Boston Memorial Hospital. He heaved a sigh of relief.

The pedestrian, Boston Memorial's ER attending, and the two EMTs rushed back to the street with a gurney, a back board and a cervical collar, and got the bicyclist onto the stretcher.

The car was a wreck and someone had been hurt, from all outward appearances, seriously so, but they all knew it could have been worse. "This guy's one lucky son-of-a-bitch." One EMT remarked. The EMTs returned for the occupants of the car.

Once in the Trauma Room, the ER attending got a better look at his patient. He was solid and rock hard—easily the same height and build as the doctor, but even at six-four and two-ten himself, the injured man was bulkier, without being fatter. A quick guess put his age at somewhere in his forties, his weight between two-twenty and two-thirty.

He examined the patient's face and head. Except for a possibly broken nose and an old scar on the man's left cheek, there were surprisingly no visible injuries or obvious swelling. The man's pupils were responsive, but he remained unconscious. The doctor continued assessing the situation and barking out orders—a ventilator and breathing tube, X-rays for his neck, chest, pelvis, and broken left leg and CAT scans: head, neck, chest, abdomen, and pelvis. Several IV tubes were hooked up and a tube drained the patient's stomach through his nose.

The patient was assigned to Dr. Eric Walters, head of Neurology, and although he was not due to come on duty for another six hours, Walters picked that moment to walk into the Trauma Room, with his nurse—his wife Beth. He quickly relieved the ER doctor of his patient, who carefully watched him examine the man's face, leg, bloody nose, and bruised left shoulder. He thought it odd that he knew all of the patient's injuries without consulting his chart.

Walters gave the trauma nurses new orders. "No CAT scans. X-ray for the leg only. He's breathing on his own and it isn't labored, so he won't need the ventilator." Then talking to Beth, "I want to know about anyone looking for him, claiming to be family or friend. No one sees *him*, until I see *them*."

"But doctor…," one of the Trauma Nurses started to protest the new orders.

"But nothing." He turned back to Beth. "He's to be carefully monitored and not left alone. I want a schedule of who's with him—naps, potty breaks, meals, the works. No one else gets in—no exceptions."

"Eric, even the ICU has rules," Beth reminded him.

"Yes, of course." Beth was right, but Eric knew what must be done. "Then we'll have to try and bend the rules."

The ER doctor was checking the man for ID. "Eric, other than this key, he's John Doe."

"How's your bed-side manner?" Eric figured there was nothing to lose. "This guy doesn't need anything special, just let him know, in even the smallest way, that you're there."

"And he can't be unattended, not even for a second?"

"Correct."

"Why not?" The ER doctor's question was calm, but pressing. "What's that? I can't hear you." His firm, even tone elicited nothing but more silence. "Eric, some John Doe just maybe saved my life on the street. We don't know where he came from, then you waltz into the ER, as if on cue, order a 'round-the-clock watch, want him isolated from visitors, and end up requesting my services as a baby-sitter. This isn't even your shift. You're obviously bent on protecting him from something. Do *you* know this man?"

"Not exactly." Eric needed the doctor's cooperation and not just for baby-sitting. "It's a long story."

"I've always preferred unabridged versions to Cliff Notes."

"Join me for a walk?" Eric asked.

The ER doctor turned to the senior resident. "You're in charge for the next fifteen. Page me, if all hell breaks loose."

The bicyclist was admitted to intensive care. Beth took the first watch while Eric and the ER doctor disappeared for a private discussion and a little scavenger hunt.

The tow truck arrived and the Police were on their way.

THINGS CHANGE

CHAPTER 16

▼

XUAN LOC, VIETNAM— 1968

AFTER DRINKS WITH HOUSER

Something bothered Tre most of the night and he had both of his recurring nightmares, to prove it. His awoke, dripping in sweat, his heart racing. Hard to tell if it was the visions or the hot stinking place. Gratefully, he did not cry out and awaken the entire hooch.

With full morning came curiosity. Tre examined the pictures that resided in his helmet. He touched the familiar faces, as if they were alive rather than replicas created from chemicals on paper. Connie's picture was three years old, touched a million times, after what seemed like a million days and a million successful patrols. Molly's photo was maybe six months old, taken on nearly the last evening of a two week R&R, on the island of Oahu. She was with Tre and Carl at a patio table, under the stars, in the nightclub of the Ilikai. Carl asked their waitress to take a picture, then had copies made. It was meant to be a momento of a really fun and funny night that they laughed about for days afterward.

The evening's entertainment was a fireworks display, the sound of which took Tre and Carl by surprise. Before Molly knew it, they each grabbed an arm and dragged her under the table yelling, "In-coming!" At first, she thought they were joking and laughed, then it became obvious, she was the only one at the Ilikai. The boys were somewhere that lives were at stake. Each blast produced another cry. "In-coming! Get down!"

Molly had to do something quick, but what? She grabbed both boys by the front of their shirts, one in each hand, and shook them for all she was worth. "Guys! Guys! It's fireworks! Fi-re-works!" She said it in syllables. "Come on! They're fun, we like them. Fireworks!"

Finally, Carl gave a sign he was back. "Fireworks." He repeated and Molly eagerly agreed. Carl instantly understood what happened and reached for Tre, still screaming at the top of his lungs. He grabbed Tre's arm and tried, once more, to shake him back to reality. "Tre, man, it's not in-coming! We're OK! We're in Hawaii! It's not in-coming!"

Tre stopped yelling, his eyes cleared and he returned from wherever the sound of the sky-rockets took him. He scanned the periphery, from their hiding place under the table. A sea of motionless legs had gathered around their table and curious eyes were beginning to peer in at them. He, also, realized what happened and looked from Molly to Carl, feigning innocence to cover his embarrassment. "Think anyone noticed?"

They collapsed into uncontrolled seizures of laughter. Although the rest of the evening proceeded without further incident, there was a fair amount of spontaneous giggling from Molly and intermittent chuckling from himself and Carl. Molly was so tired that, around eleven, she put her head on Tre's shoulder and promptly fell asleep. The picture wasn't taken until well past midnight, but even with Molly unconscious, Carl knew it would make for a great souvenir.

The Sergeant Major's words dallied in Tre's head, *She has a great smile and great legs.* His mouth dropped. Molly wasn't smiling nor were her legs in the picture. Tre now had a question in need of an answer. Never a good thing.

He went looking for the Sergeant Major, but he was nowhere to be found. When Tre asked after him, at the clerk's office, he was advised there was no Sergeant Major Houser.

"Check again!" Tre demanded of the overworked and hassled man.

"Look," the clerk snapped, "I already checked. Three times! I got no Houser, not the Sergeant Major variety or any other kind. You want one so bad, go make him yourself!"

Something, fundamental, warned Tre that perhaps he shared too much and involved the wrong man. He forced a smile, gave an *I guess I got the wrong name* kind of shrug, left the office, and went to round-up his friends.

He found Carl and Poopsie at The Enlisted Man's, seated at a table, in a deep huddle. It took a world of convincing to get them to even consider speaking with Lloyd Cummings. They each saw that first flash of light in Houser's eyes and it gave them The Willies. They did their good deed. Cummings was alive. They wanted nothing more to do with the whole business. Practically pleading, Tre's voice got a little loud when he mentioned Cummings by name.

From the far side of the Club came a drunken voice. "You friends with that piece-of-shit, Cummings?" The same table produced another voice. "Who ever dragged his sorry ass out of the jungle needs to get shot. Fuckin' waste-of-space-Army-brat, can't be trusted." Still a third voice, with bad grammar, slurred his own interjection. "Yeah, don't need no guy can't protect hisself."

Carl quickly advise everyone to keep their cool, but the drunks left their own table and, fueled by liquid courage, came over to make sure trouble got started. Four men came up behind a still seated Tre and one shoved his chest into the hard edge of the table.

"Hey, asshole." Tre tried to ignore him, but the drunk persisted, shoving him again.

"Go sleep it off." Carl advised, hoping to avoiding a confrontation.

"Shove it, dick-weed. Our beef's with Cummings and his asshole friend, here."

The man grabbed a handful of Tre's shirt collar and yanked him backward, sending him and the wooden chair, he was sitting in, tumbling over. The flimsy chair smashed into kindling and Tre rolled directly into another drunk, bowling him over like a ten-pin. Their original target out of reach, a third man lunged for Carl and Poopsie, making them jump backward, out of their seats. The equally flimsy table gave way under the soldier's weight, and crashed to the floor. The man sprung back up, dazed and weaving, but ready to do battle with whoever was handy.

At that precise moment, Isaiah Jefferson appeared. The odds were improving; four men to four drunken men. Isaiah extended a hand to help Tre up from the floor. "You OK brothah?" Tre indicated that he was fine and Isaiah addressed the drunks in *militant speak.* "Do not be tellin' me you was messin' with the brothah!"

"This ain't your fight, Nigger! And he ain't no brother." One of the drunks piped up. "He's a Injun. A fuckin' half-breed, Heeb-Injun, ya moron."

"You don't know nothin' about the brothah and calling me Nigger, just made it my fight. You offend *all* of the brothahs when you disrespect *any* of the brothahs. And, it's *an Indian.*" Isaiah corrected the drunk's grammar. "Come my brothahs." Isaiah swept in his arms, to include Carl and Poopsie, his voice calm and almost ministerly. "These honkie infidels must learn, once and for all, that they can't be messin' with none of the brothahs."

What had all the earmarks of becoming a full fledged brawl turned into the simple ejection of waste matter (the drunks) and the removal of a few pieces of broken furniture.

As they exited the Club, Isaiah turned to Tre, "You aren't seriously a yellow-haired, blue-eyed, Jewish, Indian, my brothah?"

Tre made several tsk, tsk sounds. "That's yellow-haired, blue-eyed, Jewish, *Native American*...from one of the lost tribes."

"That tribe got a name?"

Tre struggled to keep a straight face. "The Shmohawks."

CHAPTER 17

▼

XUAN LOC, VIETNAM— 1968

EMILY

Isaiah accompanied Tre, Carl, and Poopsie to visit Lloyd Cummings. Unbeknownst to any of them, that single act irrevocably intertwined his life with theirs. The four men let Lloyd tell his story without interruption.

"My brother and I had big plans for my graduation night—just the two of us, a big night on the town—my treat. After dinner, even all dressed up, we kicked off our shoes to walk the beach. A little ways up from the pier, a girl was having a bon-fire. She greeted us, like she was expecting us, and the way she looked at us, it was…," Lloyd shook his head searching a proper explanation, "…it was almost as if she knew us, really well, only we didn't know her. I'm sure of it. She insisted we join her celebration of a major birthday. It wasn't much of a party; just the girl, and she was dressed in one of those girl-volunteer, hospital outfits."

"You mean a candy-striper?" Carl asked.

"Yeah. She had a folder full of medical records with our mother's name on them. One with a picture fastened to it. A giant bruise covered nearly her whole thigh."

"Any chance it was someone else?" Carl asked.

"None. Mom has this funny shaped birth mark on her leg. Sure, the old man always had a stick up his butt, about one thing or another, but I never dreamt he was hurting her." Lloyd shook his head with self loathing. "I can only guess he was selective about when and where he hit her."

"Only when no one was around and only where it didn't show." Tre could relate.

"Exactly," Lloyd confirmed. "I asked where she got the folder. Can you imagine, she just walked into Walter Reed and took it. I guess, with the outfit and all, no one even questioned her. She offered to trade us for it. I do her a favor, she'd throw it in the fire. I agreed, but I couldn't let her burn it. She hands the thing to Junior and says: *then you'll need to put these in a safe place until you find a lawyer you can trust.* I don't get it. The kid was twelve. Why give it to him?"

"You enlisted and wouldn't need it," Tre supplied.

"Well, yeah, but she couldn't have known that. She told this fantastic tale and, next thing, she's claiming to be from the future, saying: *please listen, or we'll all regret it.* At what seemed near the end, mid-sentence, she got up to leave—something about a whistle caller her and making another stop. It was ridiculous. The only sound on that beach was waves. When we offered to douse the fire, she just took-off. She got about ten yards down the beach, turned around and yelled a farewell we didn't understand. That was the last we saw of her.

"It was the weekend and our last brothers-night-out for a good long time. As long as we were together, who cared if the girl turned out to be a practical joker and the whole thing ended up being a wild goose chase? It'd be an adventure we could laugh about in twenty years. Meantime, in a military family, you listen to every warning, no matter the source, so we hustled back to the house. As we rounded the corner of our block, the old man's car was screeching out of the driveway. It tore-off down the street, like the police were chasing it.

"I parked, we ran inside and everything was exactly as the girl described. If we hadn't found our mother when we did, she would have bled to death from a ruptured spleen. We bundled her into the car and rushed to Walter Reed, then wrote down everything we could remember, but the legend part reads like riddles and the story, it was so wild…" Lloyd's voice trailed off. "Who would believe it? And who knew there'd be a quiz later?"

"What did the girl want from you?" Carl asked.

"Two things—remember some lines from Dylan Thomas and protect the Pop-op. And why, you might ask; because according to her, they would find me and be my way out. I never forgot her words, but I also didn't understand what they meant…until now. Our trucks made exactly one stop and I got out to take a leak. Short moments later, I heard someone yelling—get out; stand over there; is this everyone; stuff like that. Either someone saw me step away, or said I did, 'cause the whole area was sprayed with rounds. That's when I started running like hell. I was so scared, I didn't even know I was hit until I fell. That's when I caught the bamboo thru my side. My radio was half busted. It wouldn't receive, but I kept sending, just in case. After the battery went dead, there was nothing to do but bleed and think. Soon, a faint echo of the girl's voice was saying: 'hang on, hang on' and reciting the Dylan Thomas. Once she was there, I couldn't get rid of her. The only reason I'm alive is because I had one too many beers with dinner and my radio was hanging from my shoulder. Ordinarily, I'd have left it in the truck.

"Say, why did you leave the others anyway? I'm sure they needed every man to recover the beacons."

"Hold up. They told us it was supplies," Carl said. It was almost a question.

"Fred Astair's mission was to set up hi-tech beacons along the Cambodian border, to monitor comings and goings." Lloyd shook his head, in disbelief. "Very hard to believe they spared four guys to go look for *me*."

"Not they. Houser pulled us on his own," Tre said, "and he wasn't *looking*, he knew exactly where you were."

"How is that possible? I wasn't sure where I was."

"Don't know, but Tre's right," Poopsie verified. "He had a confirmed destination."

"What else can you tell us?" Tre asked.

"Only that it was a really bad idea for half the guys on a Special-Ops mission to be volunteers and since you finished the poem," he indicated Tre, "you must be the Pop-op. But what's a Pop-op?"

"Usually granddad." Tre shook his head. "What did the kid look like?"

"I'd say you've been busy, if you have to ask?" Lloyd and Tre smiled at each other for the first time since meeting. "She had light hair, kind of dark blond and I guess you'd say she was pretty. Shit! It was three years ago, there was no moon and only a tiny, little bon-fire. Believe me, I was more concerned with those medical records than the girl." He thought for another second. "Oh, she had a mark on her arm, looked like a tattoo. It was supposed to convince us, but I never saw anything like it before."

"Was it red?" Tre's voice was solemn. Lloyd nodded. "Where did she have to go?"

"It's too long ago. I don't remember."

"Try," Tre insisted. "It's no piece-o'-cake, but—"

"Ooh!" He pointed at Tre. "That's it, but not cake. Something about helping someone learn to bake a pie?" Lloyd said it like a question, then corrected himself shaking his head. "No, that can't be right. It sounds even more stupid when you say it out loud."

Tre and Carl locked eyes. "Maybe not so stupid." Tre quickly unbuttoned the cuff of his left sleeve and pushed it up his arm. "Did the girl's mark look like this?"

"Yeah, but there was a number or a letter inside the circle. Are all you guys in some sort of club?" Lloyd tried to make light of it.

"What do you mean *all you guys*? It's just the girl and me."

"And Houser," Lloyd said.

"Houser had this mark?" Tre could hardly believe it. "You're positive?"

"Yeah. What is it?"

Tre saw no point in delaying the inevitable. "Sign of the Reweaver."

"Like in Overlap? Isn't that a myth?" Lloyd surveyed the others.

"Not to someone who bears this mark," Tre's answer was tight. "What else did the girl tell you?"

"A crazy story wrapped around a fairy tale," Lloyd was sarcastic, "then she stuffed that enigma into a riddle. But, you know, fantastic as it all was…Houser knew every detail, from the girl and the poem, right down to the three of you. He warned that until it's all over, I should only ever say that Houser and the Super-heroes saved me; because it would be safer. We need to find him and ask questions."

"There's no Houser to ask. He disappeared," Tre snapped his fingers, "right into thin air."

"He was here last n—," Lloyd started to contradict.

"And the Army never heard of him," Tre interrupted. "If that's right and he had this mark, there's no one to find. Not yet anyway."

"Not yet? What the hell is that supposed to mean?" Lloyd demanded.

"Hey, this sounds like a spy novel," Isaiah quipped brightly.

Lloyd blew-off the entire idea.

"Isaiah's right," Tre corrected. "There is a spy."

"Who?" Lloyd was exasperated. "You can't blame every failed mission you can't explain on an imaginary Pointman?"

"This one's not so imaginary and he had access to your specific whereabouts," Tre defended.

"You make it sound like a plot," Lloyd strenuously objected.

"And you think it isn't?" Tre challenged.

"It was two missions. Two. It's a coincidence!"

"It's not two…and you know it. It's not even the first time you were sent to Cambodia. They gave you three days of jump school last time, then threw you out of a plane. How many were with you? How many were lost?" Lloyd suspected Tre already had a body count, or he wouldn't have asked. "Tragedy's like some sort of divining rod where you're concerned, Cummings. It's found you wherever you went, on all three tours. I checked. There's only one way such misfortune stalks one particular soldier for so long, and it isn't coincidence. Someone moving troops around wants it that way. Anyone high ranking enough for that probably attended West Point."

"Point Men are sworn to protect," Lloyd objected. "Besides, it's conspiracy and treason, espionage, aiding the enemy, and any number of other crimes against the government. All punishable with prison."

"That's true," Tre's tone turned arrogant, "but not if you don't get caught. Think for a moment. Mission names come from a list. I know it, you know it, everyone knows it. Are Fred Astair and Ginger Rogers anywhere on that list? No, but the names are linked and so were those missions. The only common thread, you, survived twice, by accident. The in-charge had to have received your signal to know where to send us, so he knew you were alive. Why not assign any of Ginger's men to get you? Who leaves a live soldier stranded in the field? Someone who wants him dead.

"How many of your missions have gone sour?" Lloyd suspected Tre already knew that too. "One more and, you should excuse the expression, but it'd be a dead-give-away to whoever is after you. That's not the case with us—no priors to send up red flags and, you're the only one who knows who we are. If Houser's suggestion was really a warning, then someone is ready to kill all of us. If we never come forward, to identify ourselves, now they actually need you alive, to do it for us. Funny enough, now you're safe. If we all keep our traps shut, so are the rest of us," Tre concluded.

"But why, in god's name, would anyone want me dead?" He demanded.

"Why probably depends on who," Carl's grim tone took everyone by surprise. "Maybe we need to ask *who* in god's name would want you dead?"

"But I'm nobody. My very particular death serves no useful purpose!" Lloyd vehemently protested.

"That you know of," Carl interrupted Lloyd's rant.

Lloyd whipped his head around, indignant eyes flashing at Carl. "Who would it benefit? Who?" He demanded, scanning the others. "I'll tell you who. No one!"

"Then maybe you need to ask the other way around," Carl offered logic. "Who would it hurt?"

Lloyd knew all too well who would suffer if his demise.

"Houser denied saving anyone but Cummings, and maybe I'll give him that," Tre admitted. "He didn't exactly *save* us, but he did *spare* us. Without him, we would have gone into the field to die with the others, leaving Lloyd to die precisely where he fell. We survived, so he survived. I doubt that was part of the plan.

"If Houser is who he appears to be, then Ginger's ambush was an event that couldn't be changed, or he would have tried. All Houser could do was preserve the past. In English, that means keep the four of us alive. No doubt, the in-charge will want the Brass to see Fred and Ginger as just two more failed missions tacked onto the back of a very long list. Houser's warning could mean there's a way to get to the bottom of this with no one stopping us—we keep quiet about it. My gut says not to let this go. Maybe that's the whole of it." They all fell into stunned silence.

*   *   *   *

"Cummings is right when he said the girl's legend is clues. Her story is supposed to be the Rosetta Stone that explains it, but it isn't. I should know; they belong to *my* family," Tre finally admitted.

"Maybe your family's too close to the legend to use the story to decode the clues," Isaiah suggested. "We could examine them line-by-line. Maybe the four of us are far enough removed to see what your family never could."

Everyone agreed that it was at least worth a try. Lloyd finished telling the remaining details of the girl's story and Tre repeated his family legend, in its entirety.

"The family legend reads like this: *One member of our family, close to all, traveled backward in Time to the very beginning. Without the power to change events, the legend and story as her only weapons, she was able to alter the outcome of all of our lives. The stones of the Time-piece jumping on water begin the saga of the end at the beginning, while CeeCee choosing Jack proves Overlap. The father knew a story would pass from daughter to daughter and brothers, from mother to son, from son to the five, from a brother to the son, and from all to the one. Papa Horace first heard it from the sweet daughter of a medicine man, who went back in Time to first tell the tale. Silence protects five big men from danger offering money. Even as they search, the three continue to defend, while four serves and five serves the partner of the company.*

Do all to befriend the fish-keepers. They find the pusher from the Points hiding in building five. Their wives will save them, son will save mother, and son and the son will save each other by repassing the words of the mother to secure a future that already happened.

"Jesus Christ! No wonder you can't figure it out. Where did it come from, I mean, originally?" Isaiah asked.

"Search me. I got it from my mother."

"How about the girl?" Isaiah turned to Lloyd. "Did she say where she got it?"

"I forgot this, but yeah." Lloyd's memory of the night on the beach refreshed itself. "She said someone named CeeCee told her. She said it so off-hand, like I *knew* this CeeCee, but I don't."

Tre looked at Carl. "How could—?" Carl looked away; the shock and hurt on Tre's face was too painful. "Carl," Tre persisted, "if you know something, now is the time to speak up."

On a night, that seemed to have been in another life, Carl promised Ethan Craig that he would keep Connie's secret. Now, there was no way to keep his word. "I'm sorry, man. Looks like she never wanted you to know and it wasn't my place to out her. It's a mark like yours. I think she traveled the night you left me with her."

"Who *is* this CeeCee?" Lloyd asked.

"My *mother*." Tre was so stunned, his eyes lost their focus and the other men became a blur. "Almost no one calls her that any more, but it's her nick-name, from when she was little."

"Seems like you and Beach-girl are connected through your mother, Make-peace. Where did she get the story?" Isaiah was still seeking the true origins.

"I always assumed it was her father, but the legend clearly says *Papa Horace first heard it from the sweet daughter of a medicine man.* If he told my mother, it would be considered a passing and mentioned with the others."

"Aw, for Christ sake!" Poopsie protested. "The sweet daughter of a medicine man? Please say you're kidding!"

"Why? It's a clue that needs translation."

"Into what?" Poopsie demanded. "OK. I give. What turns a daughter into a *sweet* daughter?"

"If she were kind, it could be said that she's sweet," Isaiah suggested.

"Sugar is sweet," Carl offered. "Or, how about candy?"

"Thank you, Webster and Roget," Poopsie's tone was sarcastic. "And this helps us exactly how? It tells us nothing."

"Substitute sweet for candy," Lloyd suggested, "and that could make Beach-girl the *sweet* daughter? After all, she was a *candy*-striper." It made sense to him.

"Even if she's the right girl, *sweet daughter* comes from the legend. That makes it a clue, with a meaning that's still unclear," Tre corrected Lloyd's reasoning. "Yes, the story mentions her outfit and that it got her into Walter Reed's records, but the outfit's not a clue, so there's nothing about it *to* decipher. According to the girl, the birthday itself was major. I'm thinking that's what turned her into a sweet daughter."

"Turning twenty-one is pretty major," Isaiah proposed. "You're finally legal. You can drink and vote, though hopefully not at the same time." Everyone laughed.

"Very funny, but still wrong," Carl corrected him. "Candy-stripers are high school girls. She wouldn't still be a candy-striper, if she were turning twenty-one."

Lloyd shook his head dispirited, then immediately brightened. "What if she were turning sixteen—*sweet sixteen*? That's pretty major for a girl, a daughter, and they're really only sweet sixteen on the actual birthday. It's the right age for how old she looked. After we find her, knowing the day she becomes the sweet daughter will tell us *when* she travels.

"She also had to go help bake the pie she mentioned, but maybe she saw Tre's Papa Horace too. If she did, everything fits." Lloyd was proud of his theory. "But what's with the medicine man? How did the Indians get involved?"

"That's *Native Americans*." The others simultaneously corrected him, then laughed at the singularity of their timing.

"Pardon me! You don't have to jump all over a guy."

"Native American culture believes that a medicine man is simply one who cures," Tre explained. "Houser had the medicine for you. A cure, if you're inclined to look at it that way."

"If Houser really is a Reweaver," Carl continued, "then a clock was ticking. Time needed someone in place, who wouldn't miss a beat, even under the pressure of everything going on around us. He had to be more than a medic. Maybe a doctor, whose specialty is keeping his head while working in the place most likely for all hell to break loose. The ER. If we factor in medicine man, that might translate to doctor of Native American descent, which also attaches him to Tre. Or…I could be wrong."

"None of us knows what gospel is," Tre conceded. "Any interpretation that sounds wrong, probably is, so speak up. The passings are as good a place as any to start, then we'll work our way thru the legend, OK?" Heads bobbed in agreement. "From *daughter to brothers* sounds like Beach-girl telling Lloyd and Junior, *from mother to son*, my mother telling me, and *from son to the five*, me telling us."

"But the legend doesn't say who told the mother," Isaiah noted. "It's Overlap, so could both daughters and the mother all be the same girl?"

"The first one to tell of an Overlap is always the Time-piece. If daughter to daughter were the same girl telling herself, and that girl were my mother, then that'd make her the Time-piece, but she isn't. Remember, Carl said her mark is like mine."

"Suppose only one daughter and the mother are the same person? Connie was a daughter before she was your mother. You know what I mean—passed to her as a daughter, not passed on until she was a mother." More of Carl's simple logic.

"Could be!" Tre got excited by how the details were falling into place. "Also, by the Time Papa Horace heard it, *the father* already knew, so the father and Papa Horace are different people too. Why say he knew if you don't say 'til later who told him. There must be a reason that the father was the first to hear it, even though neither he nor Papa Horace ever repeated it. Next, if we agree that I'm the one called *son*, and the next passing is from *a brother* to *the son*, then *the son* is someone other than me. Plus, there are only two guys who are brothers and know the story." Tre rushed thru the rest of his summary. "Lloyd and Junior. Nothing else fits. The rest of us are only-children."

"Junior cannot be involved in this!" Lloyd strenuously objected.

"Why not? Because you say so?" Tre lost his infamous short temper. "Everyone who knows about this is involved, right up to here," Tre indicated his chin, "that includes Junior, all of us, and anyone we tell. Participation isn't optional and there's no fucking instruction book. We can't even be sure that anything we do won't make things worse, but try conjuring up the consequences if we do nothing."

"But Junior is...," Lloyd's unfinished thought trailed off as he thought about how necessary it was to keep his mother and brother hidden away.

"He's what?" Tre's face reddened with anger. "Out with it!"

Lloyd refused to elaborate. "He can't be pulled any further into this, that's all." He didn't care that his lack of explanation made him appear obstinate.

"You want to exclude Junior? Fine!" Tre conceded, his tone off-hand. "You be the brother that finds and tells the son. The legend only says *a* brother, it doesn't say which one."

"Me?" Lloyd's head was spinning. "I couldn't!"

"Well, the next passing is from a brother and if the brother isn't gonna be you, then the only brother left is Junior," Tre concluded. "No one wants to involve more people than absolutely necessary, but if Junior is the brother, well then, damn it, he's the brother. You don't have to like it, but you do have to accept it."

Lloyd shook his head in dismay. He was so careful, immediately put his mother and Junior beyond the old man's reach, made them safe. It was obvious that Junior wasn't any safer than the rest of them. Maybe his mother wasn't either. He had to admit, if only to himself, that Junior was involved right up to his chin, exactly like Tre said. For the first time, Lloyd realized that Junior's future, maybe even his life, depended upon the help of these men. For his mother and brother to stay safe and alive, he had to take them into his confidence.

*   *   *   *

There was still the rest of the legend to interpret. Tre picked a place to continue.

"Maybe *offering money* means there's going to be a reward for saving you. I guess we'll know that soon enough, and the *danger* attached to the money could mean that identifying ourselves, would put us in jeopardy, like Houser implied. Keeping our names *silent* prevents that. It's a plausible interpretation if you factor in that we're all supposed to be dead right now. Well, what do you think?" Everyone agreed, it sounded logical. "Besides, like Cummings said, he's mostly a nobody-very-important, like the rest of us. Frankly, we could all disappear and no one besides our families would notice. So who'd believe that someone *among* the rank was trying to kill him, and us for saving him? Except maybe the bastard that did this," Tre quickly added. "And before any of you go getting high minded and think we need to come forward anyway, please consider that by not know who this Brasshole is, we might reveal ourselves to the very one who's looking for us."

"OK, OK," Lloyd conceded, "but Houser said I *should* use his name? How is that safe?"

"If he said to use his name, then he's a wild card, a distraction, not real in this Time," Tre confirmed. "Batting around his name keeps *whoever* spinning their wheels looking for someone other than us. Anyone interested in permanently shutting us up can look all they want, if the only name they have is Houser's. No one can find a man who doesn't exist and they can't kill who they can't find. If they find us, well…," Tre didn't finish the thought. "Let's not forget that I'm marked too and the only one who hasn't traveled yet. If I do my job right, hopefully this nightmare will end."

Tre needed to convey and the enormity of their situation and dispel any skepticism. "Look, Houser knew things, but *how* did he know." Tre turned to Lloyd. "How did he know exactly where you were?" He turned to the others. "He had three hundred men to choose from, why pick the three biggest targets? And why the Dylan Thomas? It isn't exactly mainstream. How did he know Lloyd wears his mom's picture in his helmet or that his mission was volunteer? He knew for the same reason he knew everyone in the field was dead; because as far as he was concerned, this story...our story, was so much very old news. It makes sense that our little Junior told him because he *is the brother*...and Houser and *the son* are one in the same."

"Shit!" Lloyd was obviously kicking himself. "I thought it was funny that Houser was sitting right here when I woke up last night, like he knew the exact moment my eyes would open. And he kept saying I'd be fine; like he knew that too. We've all seen minor injuries turn septic and you only have to look at these to know they're badly infected. Houser gave me some sort of an injection when we were in the jungle and another last night, then handed over a plastic bag and some needles. He said give everything to Carl with instructions to administer one injection for six more days and keep the bag refrigerated. I asked how he was so sure Carl would come. He said, *because it already happened*. I didn't connect the dots till just now, but Jesus, Beach-girl said that at least twice and it's in the legend—it already happened."

The others digested that last bombshell while Lloyd continued. "She also made a big point of how the five men in the legend were brave, like some guy named Ben thought a girl named Gwyneth was brave."

"And Ben and Gwyneth are...?" Isaiah asked.

"No one we know, but if you believe everything else, then they're actors she saw in movie, called Bounce, released in the year 2001. She said she watched it on a D-V-D that five big men gave to her. D-V-D's some sort of theater movie for the home. You stick the thing in a special player and watch it on your TV. Anyway, there's a scene where this Ben tells Gwyneth that she's brave. Gwyneth corrects him, saying she was so scared. The scene pretty much ends when Ben says, 'it's *not* brave...if you're *not* scared'. At the end of the film, Gwyneth reverses things and says the same line to Ben."

"Oh. The little story about Ben and Gwyneth...," Isaiah touched his hand to his heart and pretended to wipe away a tear, "...it makes me feel all warm and fuzzy inside." They all laughed. "Isn't it just barely possible she mentioned the turn-around in the movie because things reverse at the end of this story," Isaiah suggested. "You know, she thinks you guys are brave, you think she's brave." There were skeptical looks all around. "Or not. It was just a thought."

"Where's the bag and needles?" Lloyd put them into Carl's outstretched hands. He took a moment and rolled his eyes. "Didn't you even look at these?"

"What? No! Why?"

"During the fourteen weeks training at Fort Sam Houston, I never saw this once," he held up the bag of drug mix, "and I doubt they were hiding it. From Houser's instructions and asking about allergy to penicillin, it's probably penicillin's cousin. These," he held up one of the disposable needles, "are fairly pedestrian, but a month's pay says that no one ever heard of," he read the label on the bag, "Ceftriaxone; because it hasn't been developed yet. There's icing on this cake, if anyone's interested." Carl looked from face to face. "Boston Memorial Hospital is printed across the side of this label. I doubt the Army is doing business with them this week."

"You guys are stuck in the middle of some seriously fucked-up shit." Isaiah offered his evaluation, thinking he was along strictly as a sounding board.

"The story says, 'Silence protects *five* big men'," Tre said.

"Yeah, Houser plus the four of you. No?" Isaiah asked.

"No. Houser's name will be known, not silent, and when I ran into him at The Enlisted Man's, he said *you men are hooked together for life*. He was the one out in jungle, he had the medicine, but he didn't say 'we're hooked together'. He never included himself."

"So who are you saying *is* the fifth man?" Isaiah eyed Tre, who eyed him back. "I don't like that look and I definitely don't like where this is going."

"You asked a question, you got an answer. Every question has one. There's nothing says you're required to like the one you get. Next time, if you don't want to know, don't ask, OK?" Tre gave a wry smile. "Look, Houser said, *get your friends and just talk to Cummings*. No one specifically invited you, yet here you are and we're *friends*.

"Overlap stories are told to their Reweavers from the time they're children. Let's include Beach-girl in that sentence. We might think of ourselves as tall, but we're not children. To most children big and tall are the same, so if you were trying to hide us from adults, while, at the same time, pointing us out to a child then *we* are five big men. Carl and I are each six-four. Poopsie, you're what, six-three?" Poopsie nodded. "Cummings?"

"Six-three, at last count," he admitted.

"Isaiah might be the runt at six-two, but—"

"Hey! I'm sitting right here and I *can* hear you." Isaiah's voice was tinged with indignity, that he would ever be characterized as diminutive. "I'll have you know that, in my family—"

"Yeah, yeah, yeah," Tre dismissed him with a wave. "I already heard all about how it is in your family. They think you're big, which is exactly my point. Protecting us tonight means you accidentally protected Cummings and you 'came with', as a *friend*, so now, you're involved. Those drunks will eventually sober-up and if they remember anything at all about tonight and talk to the wrong somebody, *that* somebody could put you together with us and Cummings and get the five of us killed. Our lives are as twisted together as braided rope and tonight, my brothah, you became the last of the five the strands."

"Shit! When am I gonna learn to mind my own damn business?" Isaiah shook his head. "Let no good dead go unpunished!"

"I second that, and gentlemen, when we're done here, this conversation never happened. Oh, and Cummings, after everything that's already happened and what probably will happen down the road," Tre poked the air with his index finger, punctuating each word, "you just better do something fucking amazing with your life."

They were in the midst of an unfolding legend and, together, they *were* that legend. Each man let the news sink-in.

Poopsie was silent throughout the entire discussion, but hanging on every word. He knew that they might be stationed together, but this night could end up being their only opportunity to say everything that needed saying. In the middle of a war (declared or otherwise), anything could happen. He was not about to allow their meeting to end until they were really finished.

"Suppose you're right about what we covered so far. We aren't done and if we don't finish, we have the same nothing we had when we started. What about the fish-keepers and the rest of it?" All eyes turned to him. "Unless we're talking tropical fish here, something's wrong with your legend; there's no fish in the Army. Fish would be Navy. Besides, both beacon missions were covert and too far inland to involve them, but if someone saw Naval personnel somewhere, anywhere, just say so and I'll shut up."

While they concluded that both missions were strictly Army, Tre objected. "But, I'm telling you, that's the clue!" He looked to his oldest friend in the world for reconfirmation. "Carl?" Carl nodded. "Cummings?" Lloyd conceded it was what Beach-girl recited.

Poopsie's tight-lipped expression confirmed otherwise. "Yeah, and I'm telling all of you, there's no fish in the Army! None! Not anywhere! Is that clear enough?"

Unlike Lloyd, who avoided all contact with the armed forces until he enlisted, Poopsie spent his entire life living and breathing the Army thru his dad. He knew roughly everything there was to know about all things military. If there were fish in the Army, Poopsie Tilson would know about them and where to find them. But it was a fact, there *were* no fish in the Army. The word, however, poked at him, transporting him to a day long ago.

He was maybe eight years old, and the Tilson men spent nearly the entire day using Poopsie's plastic Army men to recreate one of the Colonel's battles, from the Korean War. His mind leapt backward to their mostly insignificant conversation, and was swept-away in a tide of old memories.

"That Sergeant, (the Colonel meant himself, when he was younger and lower ranking), didn't follow orders, but his actions saved his men and won the battle. In such an instance, he could either lose his Sergeant's stripes or receive a commendation—depends on how the Brass feel about what he did. Either way, though, commended or condemned, the incident will follow him for the rest of his career."

Poopsie asked how and the Colonel explained.

"The mission was written up as a win for the good guys and the soldier received a commendation, which was added to his personal fiche. If he'd lost his Sergeant's stripes, that would have been a black mark on his personal record instead. And if the incident had been chronicled as a botched mission, it would live among that stinking fish in the Pentagon, forever."

"Even though we won?" Poopsie couldn't believe it.

"Yeah," the Colonel was loathe to admit, "even though we won."

Not only did the Colonel always referred to a mission gone sour as *that stinking fish in the Pentagon*, he was the only one Poopsie ever heard call the fiche *fish*—stinking or otherwise. His mind snapped back to the present with answers to their questions.

"Holy crap!" Poopsie exclaimed excitedly. "The fish-keepers don't keep *fish*, they keep fiche. Microfiche. Every U.S. serviceman has fiche, all of us, even the one that's after Cummings. It's kept at the Records Center out in St. Louis. Every mission is written up on it and stored in the only building five there is, the one in D.C., the Pentagon.

"If we're to understand that the fish-keepers actually find our man, then the mission records we need must name names, otherwise we'd be completely screwed. Each record will have to be reviewed, one-by-one, in a fiche reader. And that's the good news. The bad news is the records are off limits to us. We'll need to persuade the fish-keeper in D.C. to find them for us. Then we'll need the fish-keeper out in St. Louis to pull the personal file of anyone noted and somehow connect them to Lloyd.

"It's going to be hard enough to persuade just one of them to cooperate. I can't imagine how we'll convince both of them. Those guys are usually civilian pencil pushers who live and die by the book. In case you hadn't guessed, helping servicemen ain't in the book. But, if those are our clues, and we believe..." he searched his friend's faces. "We do believe all this, don't we?" Four heads silently bobbed. "Then we find them and convince them."

Getting into the Pentagon to snoop was just the beginning. The way Poopsie explained the government's record keeping system, years and years might pass before they found anything. Even then, they still had to identify and locate the person who orchestrated the sabotage, confirm that they were some sort of pusher, and make a connection between them and Lloyd. It wasn't going to be simple; not even as simple as finding a needle in a hay-stack. Their collective futures depended upon two men, they didn't know yet, willingly and successfully finding twin needles, in two different hay-stacks, half a country away from each other. The bonus? The Army would demand the kind of proof that was irrefutable.

*   *   *   *

"Before we get too far afield, let's get back to the legend," Poopsie suggested. "I never heard anyone but the Colonel refer to the government's fiche as *fish*. It's very specific. Something probably only I would think of. Isaiah isn't so big, but—"

"Hey!" Isaiah objected again, wagging a finger at them. "You guys better stop saying that, or you're going to hurt my feeling."

"Your *feeling*?" Tre asked, over a chorus of nervous laughter.

Isaiah shrugged. "Why use more than one at a time?"

"As I was saying," Poopsie eyeballed them into silence, "the fact remains that he isn't really *all* that big, yet his family thinks of him that way. Tre and Lloyd were so familiar with the Dylan Thomas that they both finished the quote. Someone please convince me it's another happy accident that Carl is a medic, who could not only identify the medicine, but give Cummings injections without anyone else knowing about them." He shook his head, unconvinced. "Why are you a medic anyway, Summers? No one actually likes carrying eighty pounds of extra crap on their back every time they go out on patrol?"

"It was Ethan." Carl looked at Tre. "Turns out he's good friends with Coach and offered to give a crash-course in first-aid to one man on the team, so someone, who knew something, would always be around when an injury happened. I thought Coach picked me, but it was Ethan. You know how Coach is with the nick-names so, naturally, mine became 'medic'. I casually mentioned to Ethan that I was going to enlist and he was all over me. Must have said, *You should really be a medic*, about a thousand times."

"Who the hell is Ethan?" It was a collective question.

"The man my mother is marrying in a few months." Tre could hardly believe it. "Ethan's involved in this?"

"Fabulous!" Poopsie rolled his eyes. "Add in that Lloyd and Junior heard *Tre's* family history from some girl on a beach and that the five of us were each assigned to Xuan Loc, and you've got an awful lot of coincidence. Logic says— this much coincidence isn't logical. My point is, and the fact remains, Tre's family never could figure out their own legend; because it *can't* be figured out by them. It needs *us*, each sticking in our two cents to translate some part of it."

All heads, but Tre's, shook in denial. He had his whole life to get used to the idea that something beyond his control was in control his life. It was the life he expected. It was a life his friends wanted no part of. He understood how unsettling and *un*expected these developments were for them and calculated their shock-value.

"Poopsie's right," Tre finally said. "All Time is, is events and outcomes. The legend appears to be just a list of them and the one we're in charge of is getting Junior together with Houser. If we don't, we don't get the outcome we need or want."

"But how? It's impossible!" Lloyd dismissed Tre's notion in utter frustrated. "First we have to find Houser and we haven't got the first clue where he is."

"Maybe the first clue is exactly what we've got. Can we can agree that medicine man is the equivalent of a doctor of Native American descent?" Heads bobbed. "Carl's gut says he came from an ER, so we stick Junior in the one where Houser got the medicine…Boston Memorial. All those in favor?" Hands reluctantly raised. "So, it's decided. Junior waits at Boston Memorial for Houser to show up. Only problem, neither the legend nor the story say when that is and Junior can't just hang around, without attracting undue notice. That is, unless he belongs there, as a doctor himself. That's going take years of study and an awful lot of smarts, on top of which, he has to figure out a way to hook up with Houser as a good friend, so his story will be believed. I sure hope he's up to it."

"Oh, no!" Lloyd went pale and his voice dropped to almost a whisper.

"What do you mean, *oh, no*?" Isaiah demanded, jumping out of his chair. He had reached the end of his tether. For him, it was enough, and enough was way past too much. "You mean to say there's more? Uh, uh! No way!" He was unnerved and emphatic. "There simply can't *be* more!"

Carl and Tre each put a reassuring hand on one of Isaiah's shoulders. They held him steady while Lloyd told what was left to know.

"Remember I said the girl yelled a farewell we didn't understand? Well, I think I do now, and it explains the legend's numbers. She said, *Good-bye, Doc. Good-bye, Senator. Be sure to tell the five I said, you're welcome. See ya later!* If her good-bye was accurate and Junior becomes a doctor, that means my future is somewhere in Congress. State or U.S., it's always been called *serving* in Congress. It makes me number four."

"Lloyd might be on to something," Carl agreed. "What if Houser choosing Poopsie, Tre and me started the numbering process. That would make us *the three* who defend."

"Defend who?" Isaiah didn't follow.

"Not who, what," Carl answered. "We defend the only thing worth defending. The country. And we stay in the service. Next addition was Lloyd, number four, serving somewhere in Congress. Last one in was Isaiah—number five, serving the partner of the company." He looked at the others. "What, like a secretary? But which partner, in what company? We don't have time for more scavenger hunts."

Isaiah grew up in Silver Springs, Maryland, so close to D.C. that it was practically a suburb. He slowly sank back in his chair, a stunned look on his face.

"What's wrong with you?" Carl asked.

"Pick a state, any state, and ask another name for the CIA. There are two possible answers. Ask the same question in D.C. and there's only one answer. *The Company.* They have only one partner I know of. Show of hands for the FBI being my future employer and D.C. the city where I go next?"

Tre's mind raced. "This legend seems scrupulously word specific, even making a distinction between *son* and *the son*. Anyone else catch that our clue wasn't, *five big men protect each other for a while*? That confirms what Houser said—we're attached for life and we've been warned. The only way out of this stink-hole alive is together. In plain language, none of us leaves if anyone stays and none of us stays if anyone leaves. The five of us travel as a unit, or not at all, and keep each other's backs until it's over…whenever that is. And when Isaiah goes to D.C., we all go with him—to find that Pusher; because the legend says we will. Agreed?"

Each man resolved to maintain his part of their bargain.

*   *   *   *

"Can we get back to the true origins of this legend?" Poopsie gave the others a moment to do just that. "We already said it six ways, without actually saying it out loud. The five of us wrote it and gave ourselves clues that only we could unravel." His friends protested the conclusion, but he quickly regained the speaker's floor. "Consider the fish and the partner of the company," he instructed, "and it's the only conclusion that makes sense. I wish there was some other explanation…*any* other explanation, but there isn't and we all know it. If we really stick together for life, write this story ourselves, and our translations are correct, which, by the way, I believe they are, then, someday, we'll be telling this story to *the one*—the sweet daughter. She's the last passing." Poopsie looked at Lloyd. "Did she give her name, so we're sure we have the right girl when we finally meet her; because we're gonna. Remember how she said, *see ya later*."

"Emily. She said her name was Emily."

"So everything depends on her," Tre advised.

"But didn't she pass on the same story as the others?" Lloyd didn't understand.

"Yes, but only the legend is a list of events, Overlap is circles of them. Without the girl, our circle would have a missing piece and remain open. She took the story all the way back to the beginning and got all the circles started," Tre clarified. "Remove her from the equation and three of us would have died in that field, leaving you to die exactly where you landed. Surely, you couldn't have returned to Xuan Loc under your own steam. Fortunately, we had her, so none of us died. Now we can write the story, Junior becomes a doctor, giving him a way to find Houser, he tells Houser about us, gives him the bag of medicine for you, tells him where to find you, all so we can write the story. That's our circle. Get it now?"

Lloyd finally got it. *Everyone* finally got it.

"It appears critical for each of us to be present in the future. If any of us die before Emily turns sixteen, this future we've been told already happened, will vanish." Tre snapped his fingers. "Just like that. Houser protected us, but now were on our own, with only the legend and story to guide us. We know what we know, but we don't know everything and that's dangerous. Remember, death is an event. Nothing can undo it. If Houser had died here…" Tre shook his head, not finishing the thought. "He didn't just protect us, he preserved his own life as well."

Their meeting over, the four left Lloyd to rest. On their way out of the infirmary, Carl's voice was so low that no one but Tre heard him. "Tre, that mark runs in families, doesn't it? Do you suppose—"

"Probably." Tre's abrupt answer meant the discussion was over. Houser recited the very words Molly said to him the day he left Hawaii. Like Poopsie and the *fish*, it was very specific and something only he would know. The clerks words swirled around in Tre's mind: *I got no Houser, not the Sergeant Major variety or any other kind. You want one so bad, go make him yourself.* If he was right about Houser's pedigree, then *Beach-girl* was who he thought she was, and, some day, Beach-girl would be *his girl*. Unfortunately, that meant he really was *son* and son's destiny was to save mother. But save her when and from what…or whom? Tre's chest tightened.

* * * *

The next day, while making a deposit at the Bank of America, Isaiah literally bumped into his next door neighbor from home, Craig Boatman, whose number was called three months before Isaiah enlisted. Right before Craig left for basic, Isaiah casually joked: *Hey, if I'm ever in 'Nam, I'll be sure to look you up.* They both laughed. It would never happen.

"Watch where you're going, asshole!" Isaiah and Craig each barked, before they realized who the other man was. Sudden smiles replaced stone stares and a warm embrace with slaps on the back apologized for harsh words.

"I'll be a son-of-a-bitch!" Craig couldn't believe he ran into his good friend. "You were high in the lottery. What did you do, butt-head, enlist?" Isaiah's embarrassed smirk said Craig was correct. "You do know that you're a schmuck?"

Between the two of them, only Isaiah appreciated how correct Craig was. Would some other guy have been the fifth man, if he hadn't enlisted? It was pointless conjecture. He was the fifth man, which was why not even his mother's pleas could keep him from enlisting.

"Yeah, I know."

"Well…" Craig shrugged, "…long as you know."

Isaiah was rattled and looking for any excuse to go get wasted. Running into an old friend was all the excuse he needed. He and Craig called their respective jobs to say they bumped into an old friend and were not coming in.

The men working in the hanger were on high alert, pulling eighteen-hour shifts, with the next day off. Isaiah's additional day off wasn't on the schedule, so someone came looking for him, although he was too drunk to remember who. The guy said something about a Huey making a funny noise that couldn't be duplicated on the ground. He had to go up with the crew. Isaiah was so toasted that making the trip right then would have been a colossal waste of time, and a really fine buzz with an old friend. Since the chopper wasn't a danger to fly, he bagged. It could wait until he was sober.

Three days later, when he walked into the work area, three black boxes were stuck over in a corner. They looked burnt or rusty, but, upon closer inspection, they were coated with dried blood, that of the door-gunner of the Huey he was asked to repair. The chopper, itself, parked nearby, had a hole in its side, where it was hit by a rocket. Although the pilot and co-pilot were unhurt and able to land the thing, the rocket hit the door-gunner just below the shoulders. It cut him in half, killing him instantly.

A powerful feeling come over Isaiah. Bumping into Craig Boatman was no accident. He hadn't seen Craig once, not in all of the time he was in 'Nam, but on that particular day, he literally collided into the one guy in the entire world for whom he'd blow-off work and with whom he'd spontaneously go get drunk. Too drunk, in fact, to *go* to work.

The legend's nearly indecipherable and bewildering clues kept wrapping around each other, until Isaiah's otherwise lucid and reasoning mind shattered into a million tiny shards of mirror. As each piece reflected bits of other nearby fragments, only one thing remained certain. If he hadn't heard Emily's story, he wouldn't have been so upset that he'd accept any excuse to ditch work and go get drunk instead. He most definitely would've reported to the hanger and been up in the chopper when it was hit. He'd have been right next to the door-gunner, listening for that stupid noise, and been killed right along with him.

Had Emily, one way or another, preserved each of their lives, made sure that the people she loved remained among the living? Why was he included? Was he one of them? If so, what was his part? To be the author of their circle in Time? Find a way to thank Emily so she'd *know* she did not fail—give her a reason to say 'you're welcome'. If he could do that, then he was right. There would be a turn-around at the end of their story, just like the D-V-D story.

Isaiah had so many questions, not one single answer, but he was resigned to one fact. No matter his actual place in the line-up; first, second, third, fourth, or fifth—even as the runt, standing at only six-two, he really was one of the five big men in the ancient tale.

CHAPTER 18

▼

COMING HOME—
AUGUST 2, 1969

As the weeks became months, Poopsie completely lost his grip on any sort of life beyond the battlefield. Although the patrols for which he acted as Leadman suffered no losses, those close to him could not ignore the hollow look reflected in his eyes—the one that said he was losing his mind and his soul. Any other man could have requested and received a discharge, but Poopsie was not any other man. His future was mapped out, their task still lay ahead of them and he gave his word. He would not even ask for medical leave. They all stayed, or they all left. And they were all staying until it was over. But in his current condition, he was of little use to anyone, including himself.

Carl was the only medical personnel they dared consult on the subject of finding an answer for Poopsie. Treatment at the Peaceful Center was their only viable option. It was the one location, they were fairly certain, Poopsie was safe on his own.

As a medic with several years of combat experience and extensive knowledge of Ethan's facility, Carl recommended the Center to the Army's Psychiatrist as the best treatment alternative. It met all of the Army's criteria and was successfully treating assorted military personnel. The Army decided that Poopsie should be given a chance to pull himself together and treat the invisible wounds, which had scarred his all too human heart. He was given six months Convalescent Leave.

*   *   *   *

The five friends each completed three tours of active duty, and each was eligible for reassignment. While they were secure in the knowledge that Poopsie would get the care he so badly needed, their only safety was in staying together. Poopsie would not go home alone. Each man requested state-side duty for the same six months, to work as drill Sergeants at Ft. Dix.

They traveled to Boston via Germany, parting company at Logan Airport. Poopsie's next stop was Manchester, New Hampshire, then South to Dunbarton by car. There, he would spend three days, with his god-mother, his mother's sister, Cynthia, in the quiet serenity of small town New England. Dunbarton was a town with plenty of nothing-very-exciting, someone who loved him, and where the most exotic thing was a small general store in the center of town. It was a good place to begin the healing.

Tre, Carl, Isaiah and Lloyd traveled on to Ft. Dix, catching the next flight, Military stand-by, to the place where it all began. And Jaffrey, while not exactly next door, was only a short plane ride away. Their plan, at the end of the six months, was for Poopsie to be well, so each could request additional tours in Vietnam—the one place they were all safe.

*   *   *   *

A psychiatrist named Dorothea Miles joined the clinic some six months earlier. She had already begun a residency in Pediatrics, but learned of Ethan Craig's work while she was still in Med School. She wanted very badly to be a part of it, to help in the shaping of it, to help the soldiers who were otherwise considered lost causes. Everyone has reasons. Dorothea kept hers to herself.

Ethan interviewed her himself and found her to be serious and enthusiastic and young. Every year during High School, she took college courses at the Community College near her home. She compounded that by accelerating her undergraduate studies, and topped it off by finishing medical school early. Graduating so early, she was nearly a child herself.

When the winter snows were heavy, she instructed patients and caregivers to play outside in it—throw it up in the air and twirl around in the shower of flakes; flop backward into giant drifts making angles and butterflies; build snowmen and igloos; have piggy-back races in it, but strictly forbade snowball fights. Among the other gifts she brought to Jaffrey were intelligence, patience, humor, an inner child and she often let it run amuck, a contagious laugh, huge brown eyes that always seemed to sparkle. Ethan was sure that, along with her superior medical talents, those eyes and that laugh could drag anyone back from the edge.

Dorothea was in charge of the new *Mommies* and gave them the eye-opener—their first lecture on becoming a new Mommy. "These men are the worst cases, which is why you and they are here. Some of them are catatonic and those that are not, can't hold onto a simple train of thought. Sharp sounds jolt them or send them diving for cover. Their minds are still somewhere in the battlefield, desperately trying to get home. Your *babies* saw and did things that defy description. Memories of those sights and sounds, torture them and have transformed them into people you no longer know—beings completely without innocence, humor, or remorse. They have become what even they cannot stand.

"Together, we will *erase* them," she told the Mommies. "To do that, you must behave toward these men as though they are infants, beings who never existed until the day they arrived at our door. Each man has been assigned to a mother, his own when possible. Others of you are wives, making last ditch efforts at bringing home living husbands. We will do everything possible to make that happen for you, but know it is a complicated process.

"Your baby is your sole responsibility. You will begin from the beginning, treat him as a baby, speaking to him in your sweetest Mommy tones, prepare his bath and bathe him like an infant, choose his toys and encourage him to play with them, prepare his food and feed him like the infant we say he is. Remind him daily exactly how precious he is to you. Hug him, caress his face, tousle his hair, choose his clothes for the day, take him for walks, hold his hand, tuck him in at night, sing to him, read to him, and kiss him good-night on the cheek or forehead. Hold him close and rock him when he is sad or frustrated, making as much loving, physical, contact as you can.

"Wives, I cannot stress this strongly enough, there is to be no sexual contact of any kind." Some nervous laughter escaped a few. "All joking aside, sex is for men. Contrary to all outward appearances, the men in our care are infants and infants do not have sex. I know that I am being blunt and may sound harsh or prudish, but any adult treatment will undo every good thing that may have been accomplished up to that point. I know that I am young, but I assure you that I am not naive as well. Adult behavior will not go unnoticed, but neither will someone pull you aside for a quiet discussion and a reprimand. I have learned that one infringement only begets others, so forgiveness and clemency are not options. They don't work in this program. Your things will be packed and you will leave the program immediately. It's as simple as that.

"Those of you who are mothers know that Mommies fall in love with their babies and that sons love their mothers in a way that is almost unexplainable. Oedipus was not the only son ever to have oedipal feelings. Wives who have been sent packing returned to their homes alone, while the successful Mommy took her place in every way. The infant loved her with the soul of his being. Although he knew another Mommy gave him breath, his new Mommy gave him back his life. He ended up loving her like he never loved another human being. Of course, our babies are men, so what they came to feel was not baby love, it was man love. I hope I have been clear, without also being brutal.

"The Peaceful Center is your last hope, your soldier's last hope, the true last ditch. You are here; because nothing else has worked. Your job is to put the nightmare of this war behind your baby and give him a clean slate on which to write the rest of his life. He doesn't care any more. You will help him care again and hold him when he finally can cry. He fought for us, saw other men die for us. We must not fail him."

Dorothea kept her usual case load to that of being a guide for men who did not need to be erased or require a *Mommy's* care. Sometimes, there was no other option and no other Mommy available. It didn't happen often, but it did happen. Her most recent baby had two brothers, no wife, a mother who died several years before, and father's, as it turned out, did not make good Mommies the second time around. Her baby graduated the program on August 1, 1969 and went home to his family to beginning a new life—his Air Force uniform carefully packed away and safely out of sight. Perhaps, someday, he would be able to look at it again, but that day was, most assuredly, a long way off. And if it never happened? For him, the war was over. He didn't have to look at the uniform ever again.

Of course, Dorothea was exactly right. She became the woman that in all of his life he always loved. He wrote to her every week, for the rest of his life. And when he married, Dorothea attended the wedding, but not as a guest. Along with his father, she walked him down the isle and gave him to his new bride.

Today, Dorothea would become the guide for the next man in. The next man in was Poopsie Tilson.

Poopsie was actually better off than the men who desperately needed to be erased, although it would have been difficult to convince anyone serving with him of that. After determining that it wasn't necessary for Poopsie's mother to become his Mommy again, Dorothea became his guide, caregiver, and doctor. She greeted him at the door when he arrived.

"Welcome to the Peaceful Center." All Poopsie saw were her eyes. "Let's get you settled." She took him by the hand, as she would a small child, and led him up the stairs to his quarters. "Your room is all ready: fresh sheets; an empty closet; a chest of drawers; and an absolutely dreamy, down pillow you can mash into a shape that fits perfectly under your head." Dorothea stayed in the room while Poopsie unpacked. "Some of your records arrived. I see that you come from a military family."

He nodded. "This place is my last hope of remaining in the service. I just have to stay in,…for myself," he quickly added, without elaborating. "I just need to work my body, maybe whack logs in half."

"You already failed at being your own doctor, that's why you're here. I'm your doctor now and I'll say what's best. We're going to turn you into an old softy. Your job is to look after the baby chicks."

"But they're so…so little!" He made a space between his thumb and forefinger. "And I'm a big guy." He puffed up his chest to illustrate his point. "What if I hurt them? Isn't there something bigger to do, like shovel stuff or carry stuff?"

"You're used to taking orders, right?" She stared at Poopsie, waiting for a nod. He paused, staring back and got lost in her big brown eyes for a second, which was just about a second too long. He finally nodded. "Well, for now, consider me your in-charge. I give the orders. You, sir, are to report to the incubator at 0-600 hours, where you will feed, clean, and play with the baby chicks. And those will remain your orders, until I say differently. Have I made myself clear?"

Poopsie sat on the end of his bed, stared into Dorothea's beautiful eyes and nodded again. If she said play with the baby chicks, he'd do it. In fact, if she had said jump off the roof, he would have done that.

The weeks passed and Poopsie began looking forward to each day. Every morning and evening he tended to his babies and they chirped happily when they saw him draw near. As he stuck his huge hands into the incubator to put in food, change the water, or clean the litter tray, they jumped all over him with excitement. Each chick peeped in his face like a child crying, *look at me, look at me*. He didn't even mind when they hopped onto his big arms and, in their excitement, took a poop. He just laughed, shook them off and told them they were disgusting.

Poopsie had been at the Peaceful Center for about a month when the balance of his records arrived. Dorothea read them and filed them. The man described in the records was clearly a different man from the one in her care. His mind was in much better shape and he was definitely on the mend, or so she thought.

The supply of fire wood was getting low and a bon-fire was planned for that evening. The man usually assigned to the task had a high fever, a bad sore throat, and was sent to bed. Dorothea asked Poopsie to assume the other man's chores, until he was back on his feet.

"Finally something big to do!" He displayed a playful grin, then went out back to chop the cord of wood, delivered earlier that morning. The rhythmic sounds of chopping soon changed into something that resembled hacking. Dorothea went to investigate.

All around the chopping stump were toothpick-size slivers of wood. Poopsie had dropped the head of the ax to the ground, was leaning on the handle, swaying slightly. "Chu hoi? It's too late for chu hoi, mother-fucker!" He yelled at the stump and spit it.

Dorothea made a running jump at Poopsie's back, and climbed on, piggy-back style. If he noticed she was there, he gave no indication. With her legs around his middle, she hauled herself up until her arms were around his neck and her lips were near his ear.

"You can stop now. You killed all the Charlies. They're dead and you took their ears," she spoke gently. "You're home. There's no need for chu hoi. No more chu hoi," she repeated.

Poopsie stopped yelling. His mind finally cleared, and he saw the defenseless tree stump for what it was. He started hyperventilating and got light headed. He let go of the ax handle and it fell to the ground with a light thud. Dorothea quickly jumped down, helped him sit on the stump, then knelt between his knees. She took his face in her hands, tried to make him look at her, but it was clear he saw someone else, in some distant place, far from Jaffrey, New Hampshire.

"Ohmigod! I'm sorry. I'm so sorry!" He said to the *someone else*, turned his head, wretched twice, and threw up. He dropped his chin to his chest, beating the heals of his hands against his temples.

Dorothea stopped him, crooked a finger under his chin and lifted it back up. "Who are you talking to, Poopsie?" He didn't respond. She took him into her arms and his head nestled comfortably into the curve of her neck. She tenderly stroked his head. "What have you done that you're so sorry?" Her voice was gentle and soothing.

"I killed him." He held her tightly. "I had to. They'll hate me. I hate myself. We're in big trouble and they could Court Martial me. Then, I'll be out. It'll be worse if I'm out."

"They call you The Ear Collector, don't they." She felt him nod that it was true. "That's what you were doing just now, capturing Charlie and collecting another set of ears."

He pulled away, wondering how she knew that. Had she seen what he saw?

"It's over. Do you understand?" She drew him back into her embrace.

Poopsie slowly shook his head. "It may never be over."

"You and I will get to the bottom of this, but, for now, there's no more chu hoi and no more cutting off ears. We'll break you of this, like we would nail biting."

"But this isn't like nail biting!" He protested, pulling away again.

"Poopsie, people bite their nails because something makes them start and then they can't figure out how to stop. That's exactly what's going on with you. Something made you start. We'll find a way to make you stop." Dorothea took Poopsie back into her arms and rocked him. "It'll be a good long time before you whack anything else." Poopsie buried his face into her shoulder, and tried to cry, but couldn't. Dorothea knew they were too far along in the program to start from zero and send for his mother. "It's back to the incubator and the baby chicks for you, mister. They seem to just love you."

A little more than two months into the program, it was Tre's turn to fly in on a weekend pass. Connie and Ethan decided to meet him there and were already at the clinic, when his taxi pulled up. Connie was with Poopsie playing with the baby chicks, and Ethan was with Dorothea being filled-in on Poopsie's progress. Tre went straight to her office and interrupted.

"You guys ready for me?"

"Tre! Come on in and meet Dorothea." Ethan made the introductions, "This is my son, Matthew. Everyone, except his mother, calls him Tre. And this is the not so world famous, but extremely talented, surgeon of the mind, Dr. Dorothea Miles. We stole her from Pediatrics," he announced proudly.

Dorothea and Tre shook hands and the three of them took seats. Tre leaned forward, elbows on his knees, anxious for any good news. "How's our baby?"

"We've made some real progress since he murdered the tree stump last month." Tre gave her a quizzical look. "He was in-country," Dorothea tapped the side of her head to indicate it was all in Poopsie's mind, "and for some reason, he needs to go back there. Why, in God's name, I can't tell you. I was hoping he'd open up that part of himself, but he's afraid. And I'm afraid that puts us at a stalemate. The Army gave us six months to get him back to active. I'm not usually a pessimist, but unless I have some real answers, real soon, he might never be fit to return to duty and that fact might be his final straw."

Dorothea would never breach a patient confidence, but she needed answers and Poopsie's display at the chopping stump had been anything but private. She described the episode.

"He was reliving something and whatever he saw or did made him the way he is now. I couldn't sort it out and he either wouldn't or couldn't explain. He's in some sort of trouble—afraid of a Court Martial. But, to whom was he apologizing? Who did he kill? And why in the world won't he talk about it? He's in terrible pain and I can't help him if I don't know what he's dealing with. His records don't answer my questions." She sighed heavily. "It's a jumble of a tragedy, maybe several tragedies, but however many it is, it's one too many for Poopsie."

Tre retold what happened the night Poopsie and his Sergeant, Greg Smiley, found Corey Black; how Greg couldn't live with the vision and ultimately took his own life.

"Charlie chopped off Black's *Johnson and the boys*, then shoved them into his mouth, like a gag, to muffle any screams. What was Poopsie supposed to do, let the poor bastard finish bleeding to death? There's such a thing as dignity in the field, so he shot him in the heart. So far, no one's said a word—not the Army; not Black's family. Given the situation, my take is, the Army looked the other way. Of course, there's always the possibility that they think Charlie shot Black. His weapons can use our ammo.

"The Japs tortured and hacked-up our guys the same way in World War II. Charlie is a student of history. He fights like a Jap and kills like one. We'd do well to follow that lead, but the government doesn't want the bad press. If we went public with what's happening to our guys, explained how they die, no one would give a shit what we did to the North or the damn VC."

"So that's why he did it." Dorothea mumbled, half stunned.

*   *   *   *

Dorothea's mind returned to a night shortly before her Med School gradua-tion. She was visiting her parents for the weekend and offered to answer the door-bell when it rang. Standing on their front porch were two solemn-faced officers, in full dress uniforms. She screamed. Her parents ran to see what happened. If she lived to be ten thousand, she'd never forget the older officer's words.

Sergeant Gregory James Smiley died in the line of duty. On behalf of the President of the United States and a grateful nation, the secretary of the Army thanks you for his ultimate sacrifice and we offer our most heart-felt regrets.

Dorothea stepped back toward the wall. She leaned against it for support, while her parents cried in each other's arms. She slowly sank to the floor, stunned beyond anything she could have imagined. And the two officers, they offered their heart-felt regrets.

Her parents were barely functioning, so Dorothea was left to make arrange-ments for Greg's funeral. She opted for a private service in their home town. No point burying him in Arlington, where none of them could visit the grave, and less point in a military funeral. Why have guns salute him, when guns had killed him.

There was no covering up the fact that Greg was shot in the head, so it ended up being a closed casket. The funeral director, Charles Menlow, was an older man and had seen every manner of death-by-devices. He was not a coroner or a medical examiner, but he knew a self-inflicted wound when he saw one. He pulled Dorothea aside.

"They bring that nightmare into our homes every night. No photograph or film footage could possibly convey, to us, what it's like for the boys over there. Perhaps it was too much and your brother ended the war the only way he could. I hear that, one day, you're going to be a doctor. Maybe you can be the kind that helps soldiers like him," he gave a sideways nod in the direction of Greg's casket, "but *before* it's too late. Perhaps I was wrong to tell you, but I though you deserved to know."

No, she didn't think Mr. Menlow was wrong. In fact, she was glad for the information, but whom would it help, when she didn't know why? Now, she knew. Greg saw something, the same something Poopsie Tilson had seen—a thing so terrible it caused one man to take his own life and the other to nearly lose his mind.

*   *   *   *

Dorothea explained that Greg Smiley was her brother, that she married young, just a month before entering college. By her senior year of undergrad, it was obvious the marriage wasn't going to work. Her ex didn't mind that she got an education, as long as she ended up being June Cleaver. She aspired to be a female Ben Casey. They divorced. Although the marriage was short-lived, all of her important college records were in the name of Miles, so she kept the name.

Her brother's death, at his own hand, made her question Pediatrics as her true calling, when Mental Health was where she could do the most good. There were plenty of excellent baby doctors, but who would be doctor to the poor-babies—soldiers whose minds and souls were lost in war? It seemed as if this war was never going to end and every day there were more and more poor-babies with no one to help them. Warehousing them in institutions wasn't good enough or what they deserved for the sacrifice they made.

Greg didn't leave a note, so until that moment, there was only the lingering question that refused to go away: *why?* The horrors of war make men do horrible things, sometimes to themselves. Greg was a decent guy whose mind couldn't take the reality of another man mutilated for the glory of war. Dorothea finally had an answer and some closure. She would share that answer with her parents to offer them the same closure.

Even before Greg's death, Dorothea gave seriously consideration to working with shell-shocked soldiers, whose minds had shut down and would otherwise be lost to the society they helped preserve. What about the survivors of wars before Vietnam? The scars on their minds were every bit as real, every bit as deep and they needed help every bit as much.

The professors said her theory was too simple for a problem as complex as a damaged mind. They discouraged her pursuit of psychiatry and recommended she remain in pediatrics. She didn't understand what difference it made that a theory was simple, as long as it worked. Except for the bad memories, the men needing treatment acted like babies. What if she could start them from the beginning again? What if she applied what she'd learned about raising well adjusted babies to accomplish it? What if the process also destroyed their bad memories? What if?

She basically shelved the idea, but held on to the theory. In her last year of Med School, Dr. Ethan Craig was a visiting lecturer at Boston University's School of Medicine. The Peaceful Center was well established by then, but it was mostly a rest-home. Ethan took only those patients who, given enough quite peacefulness, would recover, to a certain degree, on their own. Dorothea's *baby program* would give nearly every man at least the hope of, one day, being whole again. Thinking Ethan might take her seriously, she approached him.

They spoke at length, over coffee. Their conversation felt exactly like an interview, until nothing happened afterward. It appeared that Ethan wasn't interested. Disappointed, Dorothea began her internship in Pediatrics. One night, six months into it, the phone rang. A female voice with a slight Texas twang answered and the caller asked to speak to Dorothea.

"Just a sec," came the stiff reply. "It's a man, for you," the female voice added into space.

Dorothea accepted the receiver, weariness etched in her voice. "This is Dorothea Miles."

"And this is Ethan Craig," he identified himself. "Everything is in place. All we need is you."

He quickly explained having spent the previous six months putting every thought she presented into action. He resisted calling sooner; wanting to avoid raising false hopes, in case the zoning board wouldn't go along with the plan. In the eleventh hour, though, the town of Jaffrey approved it; considering the Center would not only provide a valuable service, but receive Government funding, bringing desperately needed income into their town.

"You'll be in charge of the new Mommies. Would you like the position?"

"Would I like the position?"

"Didn't I just ask that?" He made her laugh. "Well, would you?"

Did she want it? Only more than anything in her life.

Texas-twang snatched back the phone. "Who ever this is, you deserve an award! You succeeded at doing what no man has done before. You made her speechless. She's sitting here like one of those stupid toy dogs, her head bobbing up and down." There was silence from Ethan's end of the line. "Are you still there?" Texas-twang asked, a bit annoyed.

"Yes, I'm here," Ethan answered evenly.

"Good. So are you coming to get her or what? She does nothing but study and poop around. I'll be glad to get rid of her."

People said Dorothea she talked too much and should consider, instead, listening to the people who already knew what they were doing. But every day after Ethan's fateful phone call she reminded herself—*my big mouth made this happen.* From the day she arrived at The Peaceful Center, Dorothea talked the new Mommies green.

*   *   *   *

"On top of everything else," Tre continued, "and because of things you're better off not knowing, we're safest together and in 'Nam." He gave Ethan a side-long look. "It's safer for everyone else as well. Our friend Poopsie is an integral part of that *we*. Of course, the down-side is: we're in 'Nam."

"What's going on, Tre?" Dorothea donned her no-nonsense face. "Carl, Lloyd, Isaiah, and now you...all very protective of Poopsie, and that's really great, but I can't help him without answers or an explanation, and none of you seem willing to part with those. I'll tell you, like I told each of them, in the field of psychiatry, the silent treatment doesn't work. The purpose in having each of you come here was to talk about it, so why *won't* any of you talk about it?"

Tre's own words, on the night the five learned who they were, came back to haunt him. *No one wants to involve more people than absolutely necessary,* but they needed Poopsie and Poopsie needed Dr. Miles and she was no good to him with her hands tied.

"Getting you to understand will require a whole lot more than talk. It will require your unquestioning belief. So I'll explain, but only if you agree to just accept what I say, and never repeat this to another living soul...doctor-patient confidentiality."

"I'm Poopsie's doctor, Tre. My confidentiality is with him, not you."

Tre gave it a second and turned to Ethan. "Dad, I'm feeling really stressed, like I might flip-out any minute. I might just crack, if I don't see a doctor right away." Tre looked directly at Dorothea. "Can you recommend a really good one?"

Ethan had no choice. "Dorothea, will you?"

She reluctantly agreed and Tre escorted Ethan from the room, reaffirming that the information wasn't safe to know.

Tre closed the door securely, came back to where Dorothea was sitting and leaned against the front of her desk. His knuckles went white as his grip tightened around the edge of the desk. He carefully measured his words. "In 1968, three hundred Army volunteers crossed the border into Cambodia."

"The Army wasn't in Cambodia in 1968," Dorothea's tone said that she didn't believe him.

"Precisely. And of the three hundred that went in, exactly three walked out, Carl, me, and our friend Poopsie only..." he looked at the floor for a second then back at her, "…only no one was supposed to." He let his words hang in the air. "Do you understand what I just said?"

Dorothea's mouth fell open and her head silently bobbed.

"That mission effectively joined the five of us at the hip."

"But how—"

Tre held up his hands like a crossing guard. "Everything else is need to know and you don't need to know." He shook his head. "You don't want to know. You've met the five of us. Ever seen such big targets?" It was a rhetorical question. "You'd think we'd each be as easy to hit as the side of a barn, but, except for Lloyd, on the night that bound us together, death and bullets stalk us, but they never touch us. Other men fall or die, we walk away. I'm not complaining, I'm just saying. Top that off with finding Corey Black and the facts behind Greg's suicide, and Poopsie's carrying around an awful lot of guilt. So, you were almost right, except that it was *two* too many tragedies for Poopsie.

"Each of us has spent the last three years witnessing the worst of man's inhumanity to man—guys charred into crispy critters by napalm or hit by white phosphorous. That stuff burns right through you, from the inside out, while you're still alive. The only way to stop it, is to cut it out. Picture yourself as the closest person to a man that's been hit and you have a machete. Imagine carving away chunks of his face, his body, on the off chance you can save his life. Imagine the sound track and news real of *that* running thru your head. Now, suppose you're also lugging around the ghosts of Corey Black and your brother. Who would you become? What would your mind be like? I've done three tours, seen and survived a lot of shit, but being the one that found Corey Black…," Tre shook his head, "…even I can't imagine.

"Cutting off Charlie's ears, then hacking him to pieces, is simple. That it's only a small fraction of what's going on makes everything look like a jumble, but maybe that's good. Everyone is hidden by Poopsie's brand of insanity. None of us is safe on his own and we're sitting ducks, if we get separated. It was plenty risky sending him here, when the closest the rest of us can be is Dix. Every day we pray that near enough is good enough. Poopsie cannot get booted, not over Corey Black or from falling to pieces trying to hold himself together. He cannot! I can't make it any clearer than that." Tre's voice was firm.

Dorothea resolved to find a way to save Poopsie's mind.

"You know what you *need* to know. Still want to know *why* we won't talk about it?" Dorothea nodded. "Every war has missions that go bad, when you're on foreign soil and yours is the side that's outnumbered. Hundreds of men go in. Few, if any, come out. It happens. There are losses in every battle and on both sides. Everyone expects it. This time, some Brasshole made sure of it. He gathered up good men and sent them to a place no one was supposed to be—men not less brave than us, not less important to their families. My own Sergeant, in fact."

There was deep bitterness in Tre's voice and the muscles in his face went tight, at the thought of Phil Baker. He called Phil's parents, when he returned to Ft. Dix, just to see what, if anything, they knew. They knew nothing. The government had said Phil was MIA. MIA. Except that Tre had nothing but the deepest respect for Phil and thought him to be a fine leader, he had nothing real to add. When he hung up the phone, he silently swore, yet again, that none of them would rest until they knew what happened to Phil and the others and why.

"Like you said, the U.S. wasn't in Cambodia in '68, so the Army can keep claiming they're MIA, only they're dead. There'll be no official records, no acknowledgment of any sacrifice, and there will be no mission to cross the border again to collect whatever's left of the bodies. We mean to find out why so many boys were intentionally sent to slaughter. For that, we need Poopsie; because when the dust settles, the five of us will be all that's left. Our silence, and now yours, is all that's keeping us alive…and *that's* why we won't talk about it."

*   *   *   *

Ethan returned to the office and Dorothea filled them in on Poopsie's progress beyond the tree stump incident. "He does all of his chores, helps change linens, does laundry, washes dishes, never gives an argument—"

"Stop right there." Tre commanded.

"What?" She was genuinely baffled.

"Poopsie would rather be covered in honey and set out for the ants than do laundry and wash dishes. I'm no fool. What have you done with the real Poopsie Tilson?"

Dorothea had been so certain she could help Poopsie, but she immediately questioned whether her were professors right? Was her theory too simple? Had her treatment changed Poopsie in a way that meant he'd never again be the man he once was? Her eyes met Tre's stare. Uncertainty. Vulnerability.

"That's it!" Tre pointed an accusatory finger. "You saw it, didn't you, dad? She captured him with those eyes. No argument, indeed." He crossed his arms in front of his chest, but smiled. "He's in love with you."

"Don't be ridiculous! I'm his doctor, for goodness sake!"

"My dear," Ethan rested a hand on her shoulder, "I suspect that goodness has nothing whatsoever to do with it."

▼

CHAPTER 19

WASHINGTON, D.C.—1972
LIFE AFTER VIETNAM

The five friends returned to Vietnam, remained until 1972, and ended up as part of the first troop withdrawal that same year. Being there for so long and involved in so many battles, each man moved up the ranks, returning to the U.S. as Master Sergeants, having earned numerous awards. Between them, it was nearly everything but the Gold Star.

*   *   *   *

By the end of U.S. occupation, Da Nang was forever under rocket attack and came to be known as Fire City. On the day five big men departed the air field there, the situation was exactly the same. Two hundred boarded a plane under extremely hostile conditions and, though they were leaving under heavy fire, none of them seemed to care. They were leaving. Going home.

Once aboard and safely in the air, there was little conversation and none at all from five particular guys. Each was deep in his own thoughts. They might be going home, but their lives were about to become more complicated and dangerous. The five had short visits with their families, then *got the hell out of Dodge*. Five big men and their wives moved to D.C. to begin new lives.

Tre, Carl and Poopsie remained in the service to hopefully determine the identity of the Pointman—the *who* that wanted Lloyd dead, and probably them as well. The service was going to be their career, but if they didn't want to spend those careers as enlisted men, they needed higher education and Officer Candidate School.

As much as he wanted to be number five, Poopsie was one of the three. Besides, his reputation as The Ear Collector, and time at the Peaceful Center, put the FBI well beyond his reach. He was, instead, inducted into the Honor Guard, where they were delighted to have such a decorated soldier in their midst. He also signed up for his first semester of college. His wife, Dorothea, left Jaffrey, shortly before the boys returned home, to take over a case at St. Elizabeth's. His post with the Guard allowed him to be with her in D.C. and remain on the Army's active list, while he furthered his education and took some well deserved state-side duty.

∗   ∗   ∗   ∗

Even after the USO booted Tre's wife, Molly, and her then roommate, Amy Peters, the women kept in regular contact. Amy was laid off from her job and felt pretty down about life in general. Molly invited her for an extended visit and she stayed with them in D.C. During that visit, Carl and Amy got reacquainted. Carl knew she was the girl for him, though the legend said their wives would save them and Amy hadn't done anything remotely similar to that. Within a few months, they were engaged and married in a small outdoor wedding held at the home of Amy's parents.

To celebrate their first year anniversary, everyone, in town or local, was invited to their place for a cookout. Carl was flipping burgers at the grill while everyone, but Amy, was playing either Frisbee or catch. Amy exited the kitchen's back door, carrying a Tupperware bowl full of potato salad, just as Carl tossed a grape in the air and caught it in his mouth.

"I hate when you do that. It's like having a food fight with yourself," Amy reprimanded.

"But it's fun. Watch." Carl tossed another grape, angled under it and caught it handily. When he looked back at Amy, in place of his usual Cheshire Cat grin, his mouth was agape. The grape had lodged in his air way. His hands flew to his throat.

"Oh, god! Oh, god!" Amy dropped the bowl to the ground. The impact sent potato salad flying in every direction. In a flash, she spun Carl around, grabbed him around the middle and punched her balled up fists into his diaphragm. Nothing. She summoned all her strength and punched again, groaning. "Agh!!"

The grape popped out and Carl was fine, but Amy was a mess. She was shaking like a leaf and dropped into the nearest chair. The others caught the tail end of the commotion and rushed over.

"What in Hell's going on over here!" Amy's dad demanded, trying very hard not to overstep his authority.

"Slight brush with death is all," Carl jibed, kneeling, "but Amy saved me." He shot a knowing look at his friends. Tears streamed down Amy's face and fear was still in her eyes. She grabbed him around the shoulders and clung as if life depended on it. He gently rocked them both, trying to calm her. "Baby, I'm fine. Really."

"You won't be, if ever scare me like that again!" Amy scolded, lightly beating a fist into his back. "Dr. Johanson says it's unhealthy to upset a woman when she's pregnant." It wasn't the way Amy wanted to make her announcement, but Carl hadn't exactly given her much choice. Eight and one half months later, Amy gave Carl a son. They named him Anthony, after Amy's dad; middle name of Charles after Carl's dad.

Carl became a psychiatric nurse. His OTJ (on-the-job) training was at St. Elizabeth's. His days were spent working directly with the loaner Psychiatrist, Dr. Dorothea Tilson. Upon graduation, a full-time position came available at St. E's. He took it. St. E's was part of Walter Reed Army Hospital, which meant Carl could remain on the Army's active roster, serve his country when needed, and basically have a regular job and a regular life.

*   *   *   *

The passage of time had made Tre obsolete. He had two choices—return to Ft. Sill for complete retraining—new equipment, weapons and strategies, or begin with something entirely new. Tre opted for new. He was accepted to college and began preparing for a totally new life in the hi-tech environment of Data Systems. He discovered that he was still an excellent student and had quite an aptitude for computers. He was reclassified, but would remain on the Army's active list. He landed a job at the Pentagon.

*   *   *   *

Michelle Drake, secretary to Henry Simpson, greeted Lloyd when he visited the law firm of Simpson & Donahue to arrange for Irwin Cohen's position. She sat in on their meeting taking notes. That morning, Simpson learned she'd taken the LSAT and passed with flying colors. Michelle attending Law School would cost the firm one of it's most over-worked and under-paid employees and personally cost Henry the most organized and efficient secretary he'd had in years. He was furious and shared his displeasure.

Simpson thought he laid down the law, basically forbidding Law School. As if Michelle were fool enough to leave her future in his hands. She had her own plans, wanted the life she wanted, but even with her savings, (the money earmarked for school to earn that life), she still needed at least a part-time job. Simpson & Donahue would never offer her that, nor, she realized, was it the place for a lone Jew, like Irwin Cohen, with no allies. In Lloyd's absence, he would either be forced out or eaten alive by the partners.

Although Lloyd arrived relying on a cane, he made a big point of being home on convalescent leave. Michelle thought it was too damn bad he would mend well enough to return to that horrid war. He was handsome and she appreciated his loyalty to Irwin.

As Lloyd was about to leave, she approached him, her bravado hiding big nerves. "If Mr. Cohen really comes on board here," she sounded blasé, but her heart felt as if it were tapping out a thousand beats per minute, "he'll need an associate who knows the ins and outs of this firm and doesn't think Jews have horns."

"I got that impression. You know someone like that, who's available?"

"You're looking at her. I was read the riot act for my performance on the LSAT. I don't think I'm long for my current position."

"You did that badly?"

"Henry only wishes. I start Law School in the fall and I could use a part-time job, if Mr. Cohen can get by with that. I've been here long enough to know where all the bodies are buried. You and your friend don't know it yet, but you need me."

"Irwin's work is very sensitive. You aren't even in school yet, but can I assume you're on board with the whole attorney-client privilege thing?"

"Does the big, brown bear sh—"

"Yes," Lloyd interrupted. "Daily." He smiled, envying Irwin the pleasure of this woman's company.

Michelle gave her two weeks notice and Henry fired her on the spot. She spent every day of that two weeks with Lloyd, after which, he and Michelle helped Irwin get his office in order. Irwin's contract, with Simpson & Donahue, stipulated that his assistant would be paid by the Saunders Foundation and, therefore, needn't be approved by the partners, beyond a background check.

Irwin and Michelle moved into their office space five days before Lloyd returned to Vietnam. Simpson and Donahue strenuously objected to the arrangement, but Lloyd reminded Henry that he fired Michelle for a job well done, and no severance. She wasn't independently wealthy, nor was she so devastated at being fired that she'd never work again. She needed a job and was free to work for whomever she chose.

Lloyd reiterated that he, alone, controlled the Saunders Foundation finances and would not be happy to hear that his attorney or that attorney's assistant were being harassed. He made assurances that several back-up firms were chomping at the bit to have any association, whatsoever, with the Foundation and its charities. And, even from as far away as Vietnam, he could make those alternate arrangements a reality, leaving both Simpson and Donahue to collect *zero* percent of Irwin's billable hours.

Lloyd asked Michelle to marry him, at the airport, before he boarded his plane. He gave her a two carat engagement ring and swore on all that was holy, he would return to her in the same condition as when he left. Something in his voice told her it was a prediction. They were married in a small ceremony, in the chapel at Ft. Dix, when he and the other soldiers were reassigned there.

*   *   *   *

During Isaiah Jefferson's stint as a Drill Sergeant his father became critically ill. Ralph Jefferson was running a high fever and had lost consciousness twice. He was rushed to the local hospital by ambulance and admitted without diagnosis. Isaiah's mother called, controlled panic colored her voice.

"They don't know what's wrong with your daddy. It's bad, baby. Can you come?"

Could he come? Nothing could keep him away. The Army gave him a weekend furlough and he rushed to his father's side. The soldiers begged him to take the train, but he rented a car, drove straight thru, and haphazardly parked in the hospital garage, across the street from the main building. He stood at a corner, impatiently, and repeatedly, pressing the crosswalk button.

Approximately five feet to his left, a bus stopped to let off passengers. Denise Williams, a beautiful woman with flawless mahogany skin, twisted her ankle descending the bus stairs. She cried out as she lost her grip on the handrail. Isaiah instinctively jumped toward the bus door. Denise fell forward and landed right in his arms, her lips mere centimeters from his.

An elderly man, in the process of having a heart attack, lost control of his car. At the precise moment Isaiah jumped toward the bus, the car jumped the curb, and took-out the cross walk light he had been pressing with such vigor.

Without actually meaning to, Denise had saved Isaiah's life, fulfilling the legend's prediction: *their wives will save them.* He spontaneously kissed her and asked her to marry him. Of course, she said no. He seated her on the bus stop bench, ran to the ER, got help for the poor man in the car, then personally carried Denise across the street, for some medical attention of her own. The hospital's proximity to the action meant the man in the car survived and Denise…well, Denise left the hospital on crutches.

Isaiah went to console his mother and visit his father, but not before wangling Denise's address and phone number from the emergency room nurse. That night, he bought flowers and groceries, then stopped by her apartment around dinner time. "Can't expect a girl to shop or cook on crutches." He smiled from the hallway, holding two overflowing brown paper bags. "I hope you're not a vegetarian. I got steak, potatoes, broccoli, salad fixings, and wine for tonight. The rest is for the next few days."

Against her better judgment, Denise let him in, whereupon Isaiah prepared a delicious meal. When they were finished, he did the dishes and left her kitchen cleaner than when he started. From that moment, Denise was his and, eventually, she said yes.

Isaiah's father? While his wife and son were with him, his fever spiked, then broke, and his mystery illness disappeared, still undiagnosed. He was held for an additional day's observation with no relapse, released the next day and given a clean bill of health.

Isaiah was number five. His destiny was serving the partner of the company and no one could fight destiny. Upon his return from Vietnam, he applied to the FBI. Making the grade meant school—classes; books; training in the field. His parents, afraid he was setting himself up for disappointment, tried unsuccessfully to persuade him along another path. Isaiah Jefferson was one of only a few black men accepted to the FBI that year.

CHAPTER 20

▼

WASHINGTON, D.C.—1972

When Tre reported to the Pentagon, every pound of his two-twenty was more like rock than muscle. In-country, his size and strength were assets and soldiers *wanted* to work side-by-side with him. Their hope was to be protected by whatever magical barrier was protecting him—and they often were.

In the real world, his size was intimidating. The men, with whom he worked—with giant egos, big bellies, and even bigger insecurities, were jealous of his looks and build. He was known to be career Army, with time as a Drill Sergeant and five tours in 'Nam. They decided that only one kind of guy insisted on fighting a war that the U.S. simply had to lose. Tre, like so many other returning soldiers, was tagged: whack-job; nut-case; drug addict; baby killer. Gossip branding him as unapproachable and humorless spread fast, as bad and damaging rumors often do. No one had the slightest inclination to find out that people, like everything else in life, can surprise you. In-country, Tre could slough-off this particular brand of stupidity, but now, with everything that was at stake, sloughing-it-off was not an option.

Simply being in the Pentagon building didn't automatically give Tre access to every document stored there. There were levels of access and his was low. Gaining higher access meant remaining at the Pentagon until attaining a higher level clearance. Of course, that would take years and years. Another way was to make friends with someone who already had access to everything. Problem was, after five tours in a place where men dropped like flies, Tre was no longer good at acquiring new friends and his reputation, albeit a false one, wasn't helping matters.

The five caucused. The war was over, but waiting might be what got them all killed. Wrong as it was, it came down to befriending the Army's fiche-keeper. They would concentrate all efforts on Tre befriending one of the men whose destiny it was to help them. It wasn't completely out of the question that they would become genuine friends. If that happened, would it be so outrageous for one friend to ask another friend for help? No, they convinced themselves, not outrageous at all. The hitch and risk was getting an innocent bystander killed for helping-out a friend.

The fish-keeper turned out to be a nobody, named Harvey Bishop. A friendless man, but still, a man with access. A nobody? A friendless man? That was practically a description of Tre. Aside from the four men whose lives were bound to his, he made as many new friends since entering the service as Harvey seemed to have right then. Exactly none. Not a soul in the building wanted a thing to do with either one of them.

Harvey was a civilian who never smiled. He took his job seriously, maybe a little too seriously. His official title was Records Manager—keeper and protector of information, the Army variety. Behind his back, his title was Techno-geek. He was lean, well built, and not half bad looking, but everything else could not have been worse. He had a bad haircut, his eye glasses were hopelessly out of style and his body could use some extra muscle and tone. His ill-fitting suits and shirts were solid polyester, so were the ties. Nothing exactly clashed, but nothing exactly went together either. From day one, he struck Tre as a one man nerd squad, but his access made him the most important soul on earth.

*   *   *   *

Every morning for the first two weeks, Tre arrived early to pass Harvey's office and exchange a few pleasantries—try and break the sound barrier, as it were. Tre made sure the aroma of his home-brewed coffee and freshly baked pastry wafted into Harvey's office. Once or twice, Tre thought he actually saw Harvey salivate. Each morning he extended a cheerful greeting and a big smile. Harvey's answer was always a silent nod.

He seemed perpetually preoccupied and that preoccupation, whatever it was, invariably put him in a sour mood. It made finding his good side no easy task. Tre started thinking of getting thru to Harvey, like the morning runs at Basic—

painful, but not impossible. The challenge was on. The invisible gauntlet had been cast to the ground. Soft sand couldn't get the better of him then and Harvey Bishop would not get the better of him now. Tre would wear him down with friendship—starting with a steaming hot cup of sinfully delicious coffee and one of Molly's fresh muffins.

His story was lame, but he was committed and well armed. He approached Harvey's office, opened the paper bag, fanned the aroma toward the door, and crossed his fingers.

"Say Harvey, you're a coffee drinker?" The silent nod. "I'm such a doofus. I packed both my breakfast and my wife's in the same bag this morning. There'll be some choice words waiting for me, when I get home." Tre rolled his eyes for effect. "The coffee in the break room is awful and the idea of starting my day with that swill…" He pretended to shudder. "Listen, I shouldn't have so much pastry or caffeine and there's no reason to be on Molly's bad side *and* waste the food, so would you be interested in a home-made muffin and a cup of hazelnut coffee?"

Harvey was dumbfounded and gave Tre a blank stare. Not in the four years he'd been in the building did anyone offer him so much as a morning hello, let alone a home-made breakfast.

Tre promised himself that, no matter Harvey's reaction, he would not be put off. *It's like the morning run, just forge ahead.* "After five tours in 'Nam, I just can't throw away perfectly good food." Tre placed the coffee and muffin on Harvey's desk. "Really, you're doing me a huge favor." Then, he left Harvey to enjoy the fruits of another man's kitchen.

Harvey was 4-F and didn't serve. It surprised him that Tre's Vietnam remark, which could have sounded high handed or like bragging, was simply by way of an explanation.

On Tre's way to lunch, he stopped by Harvey's office again. His usual bag lunch, eaten alone in his office, was sitting on the desk—a small carton of milk and something beige between two slices of over-whipped white bread. Ugh! "As long as I screwed up this morning, I'm sure Molly will be interested in what you thought of the muffin. She and my mother use us as Guinea pigs. Sometimes the recipes are great. Sometimes they're science experiments. The trade-off is, every-one who eats gets to put in their two cents." Tre's expression was alive with expectation. "Well?"

"It was good." The answer lacked enthusiasm, but it felt like a two cent comment to Harvey.

"Just good? Huh? Well," Tre shrugged, "I guess we won't see those muffins again. The rule is: only fabulous food makes history, so if it isn't fabulous, it *is* history," he chuckled. "That's entirely too bad. I rather liked mine. Oh, well." Tre shrugged again and started to leave.

The word *we* registered immediately—we, not I. *We* won't see those muffins again. "Wait a minute!" Harvey stopped him. "I guess I didn't understand that you wanted a thorough evaluation or that so much rested on what I thought." He paused a moment remembering the taste and texture of the exquisite muffin. "It would be a shame *never* to eat another one. It *was* rather good, very moist, kind of fluffy, with just enough nuts and…what was the fruit?"

"Cranberries." Tre grinned.

"Yes." Harvey's mouth began to water all over again. "Tell your wife, um Molly, it was delicious."

"Delicious? Really? That's great. Yes!" Tre pumped the air. "Those muffins are in! You have no idea what that evaluation will do for Molly's ego, not to mention helping to get me out of the dog house. Thanks." Tre left the doorway of Harvey's office sounding very grateful, wearing an expression that spoke of relief and the idea that he was making headway in the new friend department. Not exactly a home-run, but Harvey bothered to remember Molly's name. It was first base, definitely first base.

OK, time to draw Harvey out a little further. The next Friday Tre brought in a pie, that Connie sent to the house, armed with paper plates and plastic utensils.

"Harvey, listen, I know you aren't on the payroll as a taster or anything, but you were so great about the muffins that I thought you wouldn't mind giving it another go. My mom is testing new recipes for her shop, and every one of us got a pie. She knows I'd eat the whole thing myself, so it came with instructions. Look!" He displayed the note Connie taped to the lid of the box. It read: *Share and get opinions!* It was signed, *Love, Mom*. "How about it? Are you game?"

Before Harvey could answer or object, the box was open and the aroma of pecan pie filled the small office. "Your mother has a shop?" It was all he could manage without drooling.

"Oh, didn't I mentioned that? Yeah, she's The Pie Lady." Tre offered, in an off-hand manner that said it was no big deal.

"Your mom is The Pie Lady? *The* Pie Lady? She's famous! Those were the greatest pies. My mom used to order them for holidays and special occasions." His mind drifted to a time when the arrival of a Pie Lady pie at his family's door-step was a very big deal.

"Used to? Did my mom's pies fall out of favor with your mom? She'd be devastated to hear that a customer was dissatisfied with—"

"She died last year," Harvey interrupted.

"Gee, man, I'm awfully sorry. Here I am carrying on about pies, when—"

"It's not your fault," Harvey stopped him with a raised hand. "You didn't know."

By then, the pie was sliced and Tre was handing Harvey a plate. He took the other for himself. They sat, forks poised, each waiting for the other to dig-in first. In that long moment, the first sign of a budding friendship appeared. Harvey laughed at how ridiculous they looked, each man terrified of a little piece of pie. Second base.

The following Monday Tre decided to advance their friendship, one step further, by inviting Harvey to lunch. Tre held his breath and prayed he was arriving at Harvey's office before he started eating the disgusting beige whatever-it-was. Relief. It was on the desk, unopened. "Harvey, you did me such a favor with the baked goods that I feel like I owe you. Let me take you to lunch. Really, it's the least I can do."

"That isn't necessary," Harvey's answer was stiff. He didn't even bother to look up.

The cool reception made Tre feel like he was back at square-one…and maybe he was. "Come on," he encouraged. "One good turn deserves another. That's what friends do."

"We aren't friends. We simply work together. I have no interest in being the butt of anyone's joke." Harvey answered Tre's puzzled look. "Do you suppose I'm deaf? I know what people call me behind my back. I was foolish to let down my guard and believe that someone like you—career Army, built like Charles Atlas, would actually want a friend like me. A nerd. *A geek in a polyester suit.*"

"But—," Tre tried to object.

"Please!" Harvey's hands went up, cutting him off. "I came by your office, late, the day you brought in the pie, just to say how much fun it was to be included. I heard you on the phone, talking about me, laughing at me behind my back. Is that *also* what friends do?"

"You've got it all wrong." Tre remembered Molly's call and the argument that ensued when he got home. "You heard half a conversation and probably only the last part of the last half. It really wasn't like that."

"Fine!" Harvey crossed his arms over his chest, in an I'm-from-Missouri posture. "Enlighten me." He extended his hand palm up, commanding Tre to explain the unexplainable. "Go ahead! He said, crossing his arms again. "Tell me what it was *really* like?"

"Listen," Tre started talking fast, "my wife works over at Walter Reed, in the lab, with a zillion unmarried women. They think she can fix them up with soldiers, 'cause I'm in the service and know lots of unmarried guys. They're also fool enough to think that every soldier *wants* to get married, and if they snag one who's a lifer, well," Tre threw his arms up in disgust, "they'll be all set with a big, fat government pension when they're old and grey.

"Of course Molly knew I was going to ask you to try the pie, so she called to see how it went. I told her how we laughed about being taste-testers." He paused, giving Harvey a chance to remember, but he gave no sign of it. "I guess you missed that part. Anyway, she asked me to describe you, which I did…reluctantly. I'm sorry if I sounded harsh or catty. I didn't mean to.

"Molly hooked-up her old roommate, from when they were in the USO, with my friend Carl. Carl and Amy turned out to be a good match, but they already knew each other, already liked each other. They just fell out of touch, kind of like Molly and me, once, but don't let's get started on that story. Now, Molly thinks her true calling in life is match-making and since you're kind of involved with her now, if only in the most distant sort of way, she feels absolutely compelled to find someone for you.

"You don't know my Molly, but when she gets an idea into her head, everybody stand back. You probably heard me tell her to butt out, 'cause, first of all, I hate when she butts into other people's lives uninvited and, second, 'cause I was sure you weren't interested. Not because of what people say, just that you weren't interested in those awful lab women—that swarm of bees—that bag of snakes. I've met a few of them and trust me, the safest thing is to just say no and run, not walk, in the other direction.

"Yeah, OK, I'll admit I said you *look* like a geek in a polyester suit, but I never said you *were* one. Frankly, I don't listen to the gossip of jealous morons. If I did, then I'd also have to believe what they say about me, and I know how much crap it is. I never said there was anything wrong with *you*, just the packaging. Let's face it, the package could use some sprucing-up and I could help you with that…if you're interested."

Making friends with Harvey was supposed to be a means to an end, but, once Tre gave him a chance, he found that he actually liked the guy. He wanted to be real friends and not have Harvey think he was a jerk. The years in 'Nam were spent making almost no friends and praying that the ones he had going in would come out alive. He was lucky. He went in with three, and a total of five tours later, still had the same three plus one more. It was unusual; 'cause no matter how careful you were, how careful your friends were, you could lose one in the blink of an eye. Tre, and his friends, never blinked once.

He reminded himself, daily, that he was not in 'Nam. OK, it wasn't exactly Jaffrey, New Hampshire, where no one ever locked a door, but, for now, Washington, D.C. was home. A friend, old or new, wasn't at all likely to step on a land mine or get his head blown off by a sniper. There was an excellent chance of keeping any friends he made now, for the rest of his life. Making a friend felt good, even if the friendship got started for the wrong reason.

"You could really help me with the packaging?" Harvey finally asked.

"Sure. Nothing to it." Tre snapped his fingers. "My friends and I each spent six months as Drill Sergeants. We could whip you into shape in no time flat. You've got some good raw material and you're not half bad to look at." There was a pregnant pause as they locked eyes. "That's Molly talking. Honestly, she saw you one morning when she dropped me off." Tre quickly added, laughing. "Getting fit will be a lot of work, but you don't suppose I got like this overnight?" Tre struck a body-builder's pose. "We could start this evening by getting you a decent haircut and ordering some new glasses."

"You'd do this for me?" Harvey's eyes narrowed. "Why?"

"Let's just say, everybody has reasons. Besides, what goes around comes around. At least, I like to think it does. Someday, I'll need a favor and you'll help me. All you need to do is let me be a friend and accept my help."

"This one's gonna come back to bite me in the ass, isn't it?" Harvey sounded worried.

Tre preferred not to leave the question hanging in the air, so he made light of it. "Oh, yeah." His Cheshire Cat grin made Harvey worry that he was getting in over his head.

"Aw, jeez!" He grimaced. "And it's gonna hurt, too."

"Uh, huh!" Tre kept smiling.

"How bad?" Harvey furrowed his brow.

"You're tough. I think you can take it."

Tre'd been holding his breath for a month. He finally allowed himself to exhale. His daily prayer for an opening to exchange favors was answered and thank goodness Harvey took the bait. It was a great deal for everyone and when the time came, hopefully their request would feel like a trade, rather than a trap.

That day, the beige *whatever* went into the trash and the new friends headed to lunch thru the nearest exit. That evening, after work, they went into the Avenue B Hair Salon for Men. Next they dropped by Carney's men's clothing store, where Harvey was fitted for a heather grey, gabardine suit and a navy blue pin-stripe.

"Leave them a little big in the shoulders and chest," Tre advise the tailor, when he came out to fit them, "otherwise he'll be replacing them in a few months."

They visited the swank, Eyes Front to order a new pair of glasses, and left McCarthy's Haberdashery with five new shirts and eight new ties. They caught up with Carl, Isaiah, and Poopsie and each man put a deposit on a one year membership at a nearby gym. One, Harvey Bishop began the next Monday sporting some very sore muscles and a completely new look. It was nearly a total transformation—one that secretly both surprised and pleased the very beautiful and sexy Marilyn Costanza.

The new plans for lunch every day? Four former Army Drill Sergeants, all ex-football players, helped Harvey Bishop be all that he could be.

*   *   *   *

"So who's the broad we're working so hard to impress?" Tre asked as he demonstrated forward rows.

"She isn't a broad!" Harvey took umbrage at Tre's remark.

"Harvey, my man, any woman worth having is a broad." Tre assured him and the others agreed. "Take my Molly for example."

Since they began working out, Harvey briefly met Molly and she was absolutely the furthest thing from a broad that he could imagine.

"She might fool you with that sweet face, her delicate and tender heart, great disposition, and nurturing spirit. You might think she's a fragile little flower and…," he gave a shrug, "maybe she is. But, when she means business and you screw with her, size is irrelevant. She has no problem wiping up the entire floor with you, has a wicked sense of humor, will laugh at a dirty joke, and when she laughs,…have mercy. And even after being pregnant with William, she still completely fractures me with that body.

"I must warn you, that if you ever tell her I said she was a broad, I'll deny it to the death, and then I'll have to kill you." Tre flashed his most insincere smile and brightly asked, "OK?"

"Yeah, yeah!" Harvey laughed. "You guys are already killing me!" Then he grunted, lifting a heavy free weight.

"Come on, fess up. Who's the dish?" Carl encouraged.

"Marilyn Costanza." Harvey finally admitted.

"Nice!" Tre gave everyone a knowing smile. "I heard her laugh once. *Very* nice! Shit!" He chastised them. "I bet she likes you exactly the way you are and we're doing all of this for nothing."

"A man can never dress too well or have too many muscles." Harvey struck a pose. "That way, if she tries to get away, I can stop her and look damn good doing it."

"See! Tre was right. She *is* a broad," Poopsie chided, as he lifted three hundred sixty pounds with his back and shoulders, on a squat machine. He did ten quick reps, relieved himself of the weight and gave two thumbs up. "You lucky dog!"

CHAPTER 21

▼

WASHINGTON, D.C.—1972
THE TRADE

What to do on the date was the next big question. Tre recommended dinner and dancing. "I can never figure out why, but any woman I ever met *loves* to dance. Must be in their DNA."

Harvey started taking dance lessons three nights a week. What if Marilyn said yes, when he finally asked her out? He didn't want to embarrass himself. The day finally came and he was floored—she didn't even think about it. It was like she was waiting for him to ask, and though he didn't know it, she was.

Tre coached him with dating small-talk, etc. "Walk with some pride, man! Don't schlump along, like an old fart."

"Schlump? That isn't even a *real* word."

"Of course it's a *real* word!" He demonstrated Harvey's schlumping-along style.

"I do *not* walk like that!" He protested.

Tre folded his arms and dropped his chin, glaring.

"OK...*sometimes,* I walk like that." Harvey shook his head, embarrassed. "So, that's called schlumping, huh?" Tre nodded. "It isn't very attractive."

The day of the night of the date finally and mercifully arrived. Waiting was definitely the worse part. It was pure torture and poor Harvey was a wreck. *Why can't you ask and go the same day,* he thought. Late that afternoon, his boss, Colonel Carmichael, called him into his office and jumped on his last good nerve.

"Bishop, I need this by tomorrow." He handed a folder to Harvey. "Shouldn't take but three or so hours."

"You'll have it before Noon, sir." Harvey's assurance was enthusiastic.

"I'll have it on this desk by 0-800 tomorrow morning." The Colonel sternly assured Harvey.

"Sir, I have plans this evening. Couldn't it possibly wait 'til noon?"

It could, but he was Colonel Robert J. Carmichael and no one, including Harvey Bishop, said 'no' or 'later' to him. He got exactly what he asked for, exactly when he asked for it—no matter that it meant an all-niter or a full weekend of work for someone else. Besides, he enjoyed making the plebes jump and he was used to the little nerd-queer not having a life. Carmichael noted Harvey's radical changed in style—actually looked like a man in man's clothing and, for some reason, it pissed him off.

"On this desk by 0-800," he repeated the deadline, tapping the desktop with his index finger, "and not a second later. Are we clear?"

Harvey worked for the government. He had only as much life as they let him have and it usually wasn't much. "Yes, sir. On your desk by 0-800." He left the Colonel's office feeling pretty much like a man waving good-bye to his future. He stopped by Tre's office, on the way to his own, a dejected look on his face.

"Waste of time all this getting ready. The clothes. The dance lessons. The working out."

"You're not gonna bail? Our reputations as builders of men are on the line."

"Carmichael needs this by 0-800 tomorrow." Harvey limply waved the folder. "He wouldn't take Noon for an answer, so…," his voice trailed off. "At best, it'll take four hours to complete. Even if I start now, I can't possibly finish before 8:00 tonight and I'm supposed to pick up Marilyn at 6:00. I'll have to tell her the date's off."

"You'll do no such thing." This would be the defining moment in their friendship, time to request a favor for a favor. "Remember I said everyone has reasons and that one day I'd want a favor in return for the coaching?"

Harvey nodded like it didn't matter anymore.

"Well, today is that day. I know this is going to look bad, but hear me out. You've been training me to do the same work as you. Right?" Harvey silently agreed. "Um, would you say that, without the clearance, I have the ability to access everything on my own?" Harvey nodded again. "Well, I have a friend in a pickle. Fact is, the soldiers and I are all in the same pickle jar with him. We're

betting that your records hold the answers to our dilemma. We'd look somewhere else, but your records are the place and the information is classified."

"The fiche."

"Yes," Tre admitted. "The fiche. I know how this must look, like, if you were
a woman, I was being nice just to get in your pants. Truth is, at one time, I'd
have done just about anything to be alone with that fiche, but we're friends now,
real friends, and I didn't. I couldn't. I wouldn't have even brought it up now,
except that Carmichael expects that done over-night," he indicated the folder in
Harvey's hand, "and you and I could each use a favor. Tonight you've got the
hottest date in all of the Americas and the soldiers and I are in a bind. You gotta
give Carmichael credit for his perfect Timing. On today of all days, the guy just
had to be a dick-weed. He didn't, by any chance, specifically say you had to do
the work yourself?"

Harvey shook his head, and brightened a little.

"As long as he gets his what he wants, does it matter who prepares it?" Tre
grinned conspiratorially. "Not your fault if he *assumes* you did it. We can both
start now and, later, I'll move into your office, with the door locked, and finish.
All you have to do is stick a do not disturb sign on the door. I'll be quiet as a
mouse, no radio, no whistling, no humming, nothing to let on that I'm not you."
Tre gave Harvey a knowing smile. "No sense rubbing his nose in it. We'll slip
you out a side door, so you can keep your date, then call me when you're on your
way back. I'll meet you at the exit, and let you back in.

"I swear, tonight wasn't my plan. OK, maybe it was my original plan, but that
was then, this is now. I don't use my friends. The new plan was to stay at the
Pentagon until my own clearance was high enough. Carmichael just created an
alternate scenario and provided the opportunity for us to exchange important
favors. Now, the soldiers and I will very gratefully be a few years ahead of schedule. Maybe we should go thank him."

"If I agree and we get caught, we'll lose our jobs, maybe go to jail."

"If we get caught, jail, even Leavenworth, is the least of our worries. Poten-
tially, there's a Pointman on our asses and we suspect he's Brass...and from the
Point."

"A Pointman from the Point? You can't mean *West Point*!" Harvey was incredulous.

"I can and I do." If Tre was going to convince Harvey to help, he would have
to come completely clean. "Not for repeat."

Harvey nodded his agreement.

"Because of some Army asshole—a Brasshole, if you will, almost three hundred men died on what we were told was a routine retrieval mission. Suddenly, there was round-after-round, rockets, grenades, mortars…," Tre's voice trailed off as he remembered that night. "Then it was just over. Before anyone could even scream. Carl and Poopsie and I came away without a scratch, but that wasn't part of the plan. Understand?

"We're fairly certain the Brasshole is looking for us, only he doesn't exactly know who he's looking for. Unfortunately, we have the same problem. We don't know his identity either. Every day, the knot in my gut says he's another inch closer. We have to find whoever it is before he finds us.

"I'm taking a terrible chance saying even this much and I've said almost nothing. It isn't that I don't trust you, but the less you know, the safer you are. If it should somehow get back to this guy that you were poking around, you'd wind up in the same boat with the rest of us…and just as dead. I won't down-play the risk. It could mean your life."

"Picking me for a friend really wasn't a random selection." It was as much a statement as a question.

If Harvey was going to be in, he wanted all-the-way-in, right up to his eye brows. He also wanted every scrap of available information, in case knowing could help him cover any trail that might lead in their direction. Their conversation continued over coffee in Harvey's office, the door shut, *Do Not Disturb* sign already in place.

"Not that I doubt *something* happened, but three hundred men?" Harvey protested. "Are you sure you got the number right? Sure it was three hundred?"

"Yeah." Tre's disappointment was unmistakable. "I boarded the men. Think of the trucks as a Broadway theater—available seats, versus butts in them. It was a sold-out show. The paper on my clip board didn't have names, but there was three hundred hash marks. Three guys returned. You do the math."

"That's a lot of people to erase. It's not so easy to do."

"Didn't say it was easy. In fact, I'm hoping our guy did a lot of explaining and that the Army took notes. As a whole, they're not the brightest bulb in the pack, but I think the guys who had to explain to those even higher up, may have suspected a thing or three, but had no proof and even less inclination to look for it, what with Mei Lei and all of that."

"What do you want from the fiche?"

"A name. Maybe the Army liked someone and there's a record of it."

"No branch of the service keeps records like that. Suspicion of a crime, without evidence, isn't recorded anywhere, not even their personal fiche. If this was a crime, like you say, you're going to need hard evidence."

"So, what *is* in the fiche?"

"Mission details—morning and after-action reports, mission records themselves, casualties, number dead, stuff like that."

"We sure could use the mission record or after action report for two very specific missions. Any in-charge with enough foreknowledge to arrange the ambush of them had to be very involved." Tre took a beat. "Would a clerk write-up a morning report the way our orders read, you know, match what we were told, and then the after-action to reflect what really went down, even though it was different…and name names?"

"Depends who wrote it."

"So it's *possible*?" Tre asked.

"I'll give you a very guarded yes." Harvey shrugged. "I suppose anything's possible. Any leads?"

"The mission dates and a legend made up of clues." Tre repeated the ones that led him to Harvey. "If *fish* is really fiche, and *building five* really is the Pentagon, then, since we're Army, you're one of our fish-keepers. It's why I pushed so hard for us to be friends. Friends help each other and I knew that, one day, I'd need your help. The whole mess makes me look like a heel and a great big jerk, but it can't be helped."

Harvey was all forgiveness and accepted Tre's apology, but he still had questions. "What the hell kind of pusher?"

"No idea. Our interpretation of the legend is based on a story that goes with it, but it's little more than speculation. Nothing in stone, if you know what I mean."

Harvey new exactly what he meant.

"Both of these missions found their way to Cambodia in '68 and both were ambushed," it was more than Tre wanted to reveal. "Charlie knew we were coming, and exactly where to find us. Only the rank had that kind of info. Get it? I wish to god there was another explanation and we've tried eight different ways to find one, but we keep coming back to one ambush meant to cover-up or complete another."

"That sounds rather ominous."

"It is. The first ambush left a survivor. We believe that was an accident, so *whoever* needed a second ambush to eliminate everyone sent to retrieve the contents of the trucks and possibly find the survivor. In other words, complete the job of the first ambush, so that, one way or another, the lone survivor would end up dead and the enemy could keep our technology."

"Jesus Christ! You're talking mass murder in order to aid the enemy. What the hell were you retrieving?"

"They said it was supplies, but it wasn't. The payload, alone, made the first mission mostly covert. The retrieval of it, and from Cambodia..." Tre shook his head. "The men should have been highly trained, Special-Ops guys, not volunteers. I'm telling you, it was a set-up."

*   *   *   *

"I have an interesting story too." Harvey's turn to come clean. "I had a brother...maybe I still do, I don't know. Great guy, except that he thinks he's indestructible. When Brian was in Basic, the Platoon Guide for his Barracks was a real ball-buster, made up his own rules, even decided to follow the example of some former Platoon Guides and made everyone write to somebody every single day. He said he was keeping their tradition alive and quoted them—*Someday, you'll be glad you did it.* Sometimes the letters were novellas. Sometimes they were one line—*the sink drips, the toilet runs, I'm still alive.* Bottom line, we got a letter every day.

"Brian wanted to be Infantry. The Army, in its infinite wisdom, made him a Company Clerk. He still wanted to come home with a chest full of medals and unit citations up to here, so he volunteered for everything, especially, the high risk stuff—all the medal potential.

"By the time Brian arrived in-country, the daily letter writing was such a habit that they kept coming, almost like a war diary. You know how the mail was over there, so some days we'd get no letter, then several all at once. Mother and I didn't like it, but we got used to it. Then there were no letters for about a week. No one ever showed up to say Brian had been killed, but we knew something terrible had happened, and the letters were how we knew. The Army said they needed more proof, but it was more than plenty for us.

"Mother and I called everyone, including our Congressman, but no one would confirm or deny. The Army said they have one of Brian's dog tags, and maybe they do, but they claim he put it around the neck of a dead soldier and walked away. The tag, however they got it, is all the proof they need that my brother's a deserter. I know Brian Joseph Bishop and he's no deserter! Whatever happened to him was terribly inconvenient for the Army. They went on and on about how his company was left without a clerk to type up the fucking morning reports! At this point, it's all about the money. If they declare him MIA, they'll have to shell-out back pay and benefits.

"Brian's last letter said his next mission was volunteer, but that it was also routine. There's no such thing as a routine mission that's volunteer. You know as well as I do that routine and volunteer are exact opposites in the service. I work here, so that, possibly, one day, I can find out what happened to Brian.

"Both of those missions went into Cambodia in '68, but the U.S. wasn't there in '68. So, ask yourself, why were so many men retrieving trucks that weren't supposed to be there in the first place? I think your story picks up where mine leaves off. If so, then my brother was in one of the trucks on the first mission. You were right when you said everybody has reasons. Mine is to find Brian. There are records for everything, every maneuver, every bomb, every can of napalm that got dropped. If you know what you're looking for and where to look, you can find anything."

"Like I said, we have some clues and the date—"

"So do I," Harvey interrupted, "because Brian dated every letter. That's what made them so much like a diary. The last one was either the day before or the exact day he went missing. If our dates line up, we're in this together."

"Hold on a minute." Tre put up both hands, as if to physically stop Harvey in his tracks. "You don't have to be part of this. I'd have left you out entirely, if there was any other way."

"But there isn't...and you know it," Harvey said what Tre was thinking.

"Involvement means an enormous danger factor. If you say no, you're out. No hard feelings. Really. I'll understand," Tre assured him, "and I'll still help you keep tonight's date with Marilyn. It's not a problem."

"Like it or not, I'm in. You want the fiche, you take me with it. It's not a discussion. Look, once there was the two of us, Brian breathed in; I breathed out. If he were—," Harvey couldn't bring himself to finish the thought. "My gut says he's alive, somewhere, and he's the only family I've got. I have to know." Harvey's voice became a whisper, as his chin dropped to his chest. "I have to." Steely determination was etched in his eyes when he looked up. "I need a real answer, good or bad. Understand?"

"Yeah." Tre understood.

"So, what else should I know before we start?"

"Um...where did Brian do Basic?" It was a reluctant question.

"Ft. Dix. Why?"

"Well...," Tre offered a sheepish grin, "...because Carl and I are the Platoon Guides that started the mandatory writing-to-someone-everyday-deal and...I believe that makes today the very someday your brother, if he's alive, will be glad that he did it." Tre turned serious and unbuttoned the cuff of his shirt. "You're smart, read a lot, know things that, maybe, others don't." He shoved up his sleeve. "What do you know about this?"

Harvey blinked to be sure he wasn't seeing things.

"You can stare 'til dooms-day. Still gonna be there when you're done."

Harvey nodded. "Myth says you were marked as a Reweaver, destined to Overlap."

"This mark, and everything that goes with it, is no myth."

Harvey remembered Tre saying there was a reason for everything, even if you didn't like what it was. He wondered, was this the reason he became a fish-keeper—to help Tre and his friends? He paused a long moment, silently wishing that the greater good Time chose Tre for, a greater good that somehow involved him, could have involved Brian as well. "Still, you didn't have to reveal yourself."

"Yeah, I did. This is seriously dangerous business that could end badly. Very badly. This mark only complicates things." Tre's voice didn't betray the tremor in his heart over having drawn an innocent into the fray. "Plus, there was no other way to prove that my purpose in getting to know you wasn't just to be an asshole. If you're in, then you're as entitled as the others to know exactly what you're getting into. Anyway, now you know."

CHAPTER 22

▼

WASHINGTON, D.C.—1972
ST. ELIZABETH'S HOSPITAL

"Hey, Harvey, I'm meeting the soldiers over at St. Elizabeth's. Poopsie's been there all day, trying to console his wife over one of her patients. We're taking her out to dinner to try and cheer her up. If you aren't busy tonight, would you mind being a soldier? Your brother was in the service. For tonight's purpose, that's close enough."

"Sure. I'll be a soldier. What's my rank?" He teased, grabbing his jacket.

"You want a real rank, wise guy? I recommend that you enlist. Otherwise you're a PFC like all the other PFC's that didn't serve."

The sound of snickering came from around the corner.

"What do you mean? Why are they laughing? I thought PFC *was* a rank."

"Oh, it is," Tre agreed, as they headed for the exit. "But, in a case such as yours, it's not Private First Class." He put an arm around Harvey's shoulders and leaned in, conspiratorially, letting him in on the joke, "It's Private Fucking Citizen."

*   *   *   *

Tre was overly silent on the ride to the hospital. A behavior that Harvey had come to know was completely out of character. "What's going on with you?" He asked.

"Like I said, Poopsie's wife, Dorothea, she's really down. She developed this wonderful program for soldiers with psychological injuries. Matter of fact, that's how she met Poopsie, she basically saved his sanity.

"She's got this patient—no name, so no records, either can't or won't speak, hardly eats, sits all day staring into space. She's sure his mind is somewhere else, still trying to get home. The guy looks at her when they're in session, but, with every day that passes in silence, she's afraid she's losing a little more of him.

"A patrol found him wandering around in the jungle; out of uniform, barefoot, tagless, and covered in blood that wasn't his. Aside from some nasty scrapes and bruises, that had been healing for a while, physically, he was fine. He was shipped back to the U.S. and delivered to St. E's, where he's been ever since. The government doesn't even know which branch of the service he was with. Meantime, they're going thru MIA dental records, looking for a match. It's more than a year later and he's still John Doe. The service doctors pretty much gave up on him. It's apparently quite bad.

"Ethan, that's my dad, heard about him from a patient at the Peaceful Center and he offered to send Dorothea. Unfortunately, the guy's in such bad shape, it would be a giant mistake to transport him to Jaffrey." Tre shook his head. "It may never be a good a idea. That's just one of the reasons Poopsie wanted to get stationed here, in D.C. Dorothea can't give up on the poor bastard.

"Of course, the government still considers her program very experimental. There was enormous objection to her even looking at this guy, but, everyone considered him such a lost cause, they decided it wouldn't do any harm to let her take a crack at him. We think the only reason they let her try is that they really want her to fail; 'cause somehow it proves she's just been lucky and the program doesn't work. If she loses this one, it'll be the program's first failure and all the reason the Army Witch-Doctors need to pull the plug on the Peaceful Center's funding. She's taking the whole thing pretty hard."

"Taking her to dinner won't fix that."

"Yeah, but all that soldier-style faith sitting at one table, you know, the faces of people who actually fought and know what the Baby Program can do and that it really does work, couldn't hurt."

*   *   *   *

They entered St. Elizabeth's thru the lobby and were directed to Dorothea's office. They found her in Poopsie's arms. Poopsie motioned for them to come in. Tre stood in the doorway with his arms akimbo, a stern look on his face and barked. "What's the first rule in the Army, Private?"

Dorothea jumped, embarrassed, quickly mopping her tears with a tissue, and snapped to attention, playing Tre's game—in life, everyone was some sort of a soldier. Her rank? The unofficial variety of PFC. "There's no crying in the Army, sir." She gave him a weak salute.

"And what, exactly, were you doing?"

"Eyelash in my eye, sir. Just trying to flood it out with some natural saline." She always offered the same lie when caught crying.

"Were you successful, Private?"

"Not yet, sir."

"See that you get that eyelash out, Private. Can't have people thinking we allow crying in the Army."

"No, sir." She gave him a smart salute, followed by a hug. "Thanks."

Dinner was ordered and eaten without additional tears. The soldiers talked about their work and Dorothea complained about the other Psychiatrists. Everyone was sympathetic. Since her standard protocol wasn't working, she asked for ideas to deal with her new patient.

"You know," Harvey began, "there's this hand clapping, slapping, singing, thing that girls did when we were young. Mother taught it to my brother and me, when we were small. You know how it was, no daughters. Anyway, it combines coordination, vision, and rhythm. The point being that it makes the participants concentrate. If you sing the song, then he wouldn't have to speak. It's worth a try. Maybe you already know it."

"Mirror me and do what I do." He instructed Tre, who was beside him at the table. "Each person holds one hand palm up and the other palm down, then you clap hands with the other person, clap your own hands together—do that twice, then slap hands—do that twice. Then—"

"…then you change hands." She interrupted excitedly. "I know this! It was called the Spades!"

"That's the one!" Harvey pointed at her. "The song is really stupid and it was mostly a girl thing, but it's a lot like Patty-Cake, which babies love, and your guy is sort of a baby. It's a bit more complicated, but provides some fun physical contact. It couldn't hurt to try."

*   *   *   *

The next day, Dorothea had a session with her baby. "Good-morning sweetheart. Did you sleep well?" She asked, even though the night orderly told her that the man had had a restless night. Baby didn't answer. She stood behind his chair and placed her hand on the top of his head and played with his hair. Usually, he ignored her, but today, when she caressed him in that slightly different way, he responded. He took her hand and held it for a second. It was the first sign that he was interested in anything about her. She didn't know if his interest came from the way she touched him, or her hand? Her hand. Harvey's suggestion.

"Would you like to play a hand game with Mommy, sweetheart?" No reaction. Dorothea pulled a chair up in front of him and took a seat. "Let's try. OK?"

He did not pull his hands away when she put them in the correct position. She showed him the movements and made his hands hit hers. At first, he was cooperative, but, ultimately, he dropped his hands into his lap. He leaned in, obviously trying to see her thru the haze of the perpetually glazed look in his eyes. He either did not recognize her or see whoever he was hoping for. He turned away, disappointed.

It was his first reaction. It was encouraging. "Let's try again. Look at Mommy." He allowed her to turn his face back to hers and position his hands again. "It's called The—"

"...Spades," he finished her sentence and looked away again.

"That's right!" She nearly gasped the words as her hand flew to her throat, in a surprised reflex. He spoke! It was only one word, but it was the right word. He hadn't simply talked, he talked *to* her, answered her. She was thrilled beyond words, but kept her cool. "Have you played it before?"

No answer, but he stared at her again, then turned away. He dropped his hands back into his lap. Dorothea saw that he had reached the end of his tether. "You did fine today, honey. We'll try again tomorrow."

Dorothea returned him to his room and virtually ran to her office. Without even so much as 'hello', or any other preamble, she launched into her story, when Tre answered his phone. "You'll never believe what happened. I can hardly control myself. He spoke! He actually spoke! Tell your friend he was right. In fact, tell him he's a frigging genius! It was one word, but it was so fabulous. Baby's first word was 'Spades'."

"Fine and you," Tre answered her excitement with calm humor.

"My god!! Do you realize what this means? I reached him. I reached him!" She repeated herself. "It was the hand game, it worked. I'm going to try again tomorrow. I already called Poopsie, but I still have to call Ethan. Gotta go." The line clicked-off.

Harvey rounded the corner to Tre's office.

"Me? My day? Oh, thanks for asking. Really, I'm having the most marvelous day. First I solved the mystery of the ages and then I single-handedly captured all ten of the ten-most-wanted. Yeah, they were going to publicly honor me this evening, but I said that I was attending my son's school play."

"Who are you talking to?" Harvey asked.

"No one." Tre returned the dead receiver to its cradle. "That *was* Dorothea, twirling around in the middle of a tornado with a side of hurricane, and then she hung up," he sighed. "Not even hello or good-bye. Apparently, your game worked. She said to tell you you're a frigging genius."

"Frigging genius. At last! A rank and I didn't even have to enlist."

"Yeah, yeah! Don't let it go to your head."

Several days later, Poopsie called to invite the soldiers to a celebration. "Wives are included. I guess Dorothea whines with the soldiers, but when she celebrates, she includes the women. Isn't that backward? Aren't we the ones in the Army? It's wrong. It's just not military. There's no friggin' whining in the Army. If I live to be a thousand, I'll never figure that woman out." Then, there was a weird silence.

"You still there or have you turned into your wife—Mrs. hit and hang up?"

"It just struck me that I said *It's just not military*. That's the Colonel's line. Is your father's words escaping your own lips a sign of age or dementia? Don't answer that. Neither one is good. Oh, tell Harvey he's the guest of honor and to bring Marilyn."

Dinner was a riotous celebration with toast after toast made in Harvey's name. He humbly accepted all accolades tossed his way. It was quite late when they left the restaurant.

"I have to stop by the hospital on the way home, to check on my baby." Dorothea told Harvey. "Would you like to see what you helped to accomplish?"

"Are you sure it's OK? I mean, I don't want to be the cause of a set-back. Sure the guy's not too fragile for visitors?"

"He won't even know you're there. He sleeps in a sound-proof observation room."

"If you're sure it's OK, I'd love it."

Poopsie offered to drop Marilyn and Molly at their respective homes and Tre said he would drop Dorothea at the house when they were through at the hospital. Everyone said their good-byes, each hugging Dorothea with enthusiastic congratulations for her progress with the former hopeless case.

*　　*　　*　　*

Tre and Harvey entered the observation room and took seats.

"When the night-light comes on in Joe's room, this panel becomes a two-way mirror. Joe probably isn't his real name, but one of the orderlies called him GI Joe and he responded. Until we figure out who he is, we're calling him Joey."

Dorothea switched on the intercom before she left, so they could hear what was being said in the other room. As she entered, the guys heard her call to her baby in her most soothing Mommy voice. "Joey. It's Mommy. Are you still awake, sweetheart?" The light came on and the form in the bed began to stir.

Harvey helped Dorothea reach him, but he wished he could do more. He made a quick evaluation, figuring his height at around six feet and his weight at about one-sixty. He laughed to himself—*he's awfully big to be thought of as any sort of baby.* Somewhere in the Army's records, was the reason this poor soul was in the condition he was and filed away in St. Louis was his name.

Dorothea approached the bed and the baby took her hand. He tried to make her play the clapping, slapping game. "Not now, honey, it's late. I just wanted to be sure that you're all right, and you are." She reassured him, brushed the hair away from his face and kissed his forehead. She got to the door and turned to look at him. "Good-night, Joey." The form sat up and his shaggy hair tumbled over his eyes. He made several frustrated attempts to push the wayward lock of hair back where it belonged, but it wouldn't stay. "Lay back down, Joey. Go to sleep, sweetheart." Baby obeyed and Dorothea switched-off the light.

She entered the observation room, smiling happily that her baby finally knew who she was and had missed her. There was nothing to prepare her for the scene taking place.

"I was gone two minutes. Two minutes! What the hell happened?" Harvey was hysterical, weeping and laughing and shaking a baffled Tre.

"Don't look at me. All of a sudden he started jumping up an down, like a nut, and then he grabbed me."

Dorothea pried Harvey's fingers from Tre's arms. "Harvey! What happened?" He didn't answer. She snapped her fingers a few times and tried again. "Harvey! Look at me!"

He kept shaking his head, weeping and laughing. Finally, she slapped his face and he looked from her to Tre. He ran out of the observation room, closely followed by Dorothea and Tre. He was trying desperately to open the door to Joey's room.

"For goodness sake, you can't go in there! First of all, it's locked and second of all...," she groped uselessly for an adequate second reason. "Second of all, you can't go in there!"

Harvey ignored her and kept pulling on the door. He eventually gave up in frustration, turned his back to the door and slid to the floor, hanging his head between his knees. He was hyperventilating and shaking his head from side to side. Dorothea got on the floor with him, cradled his head and shoulders in her arms and began to rock him. She looked up at Tre.

"Hey," he shrugged in ignorance. "I already said, *don't look at me*. I was sitting right there and I'm as clueless as you."

They helplessly watched Harvey cling to Dorothea like a life-preserver, tears streaming down his cheeks. After what seemed like an eternity of crying and rocking, Harvey looked up at Tre, his breathing still shallow. He said exactly one word.

"Brian."

At first Tre didn't understand, then he realized it was the one word that could say it all. Dorothea continued rocking and consoling, as Tre explained. It was the most amazing, exciting story she ever heard.

CHAPTER 23

▼

WASHINGTON, D.C.—1972
THE JOY OF VICTORY...

The following day, Dorothea arranged for Joey to have his first visitor. "Good morning, sweetheart. Mommy has a big surprise for you. We are going to comb your hair and get you all dressed up. A guest is coming here, just to see you. He wants to talk and play games and tell you stories. Won't that be fun?"

Dorothea's voice had an odd tenor, which did not escape her baby's notice. As she combed his hair, her hands started to tremble. He took her hands in his and held the palm of the free one to his face. He silently caressed the hand between his own hand and his cheek. When she continued to shake, he pulled her close, gently rocking both of them. "I'm fine, sweetheart. Just a little excited." She reassured him, returning a parental embrace. "I always get excited when company comes over."

She relaxed a little and she said she was fine. Her baby believed her, let go, and smiled. Baby's first smile, she told herself, in fact, it was also baby's first voluntary hug. This was going to be a good day. Twenty minutes later, the front desk buzzed Joey's room, which made Dorothea jump. "Dr. Tilson, your guest has arrived."

She calmed herself before answering. "Thank you Jayne. Please have someone escort him to the solarium. We'll be right there"

"Yes, doctor."

Harvey impatiently paced in front of the bank of windows that overlooked the courtyard. Hand-in-hand, Dorothea and her baby entered the solarium. Harvey stopped dead in his tracks. It was everything he could do not to run over when he saw his brother.

"I know it will be difficult," Dorothea warned, "but you cannot treat him like your brother or even a real man. You cannot! Keep your distance and allow Brian to come to you in his own time. You must treat him like any other baby and babies can't be pounced upon. It frightens them and, frankly, he's frightened enough."

Dorothea motioned Harvey toward a small grouping of chairs at a table in the corner, while she gave her baby one last look. There were two other chairs at the table and Dorothea made her baby take the seat nearest to Harvey. He leaned against his Mommy's side for protection, the way small children do. She wrapped a reassuring her arm around his broad shoulders.

"Honey, this is Harvey. He came here to visit you. Wasn't that nice of him?" The baby was silent and kept his head down like a shy toddler. If this meeting was going to do any good, Dorothea had to get him to look at Harvey. "Guess what, sweetheart! Harvey knows the Spades."

Baby looked up.

"Would you like to play, Joey?" Harvey offered. "Your Mommy said you're very good. I'm afraid I'm a bit rusty, myself, but let's try. OK?"

Harvey put his hands in the proper position and waited for his brother to do the same. "Go ahead, sweetheart. It's OK. Harvey is a friend. That's why he's here, to play with you."

Baby had permission and he took it. Harvey sang the song and the brothers clapped and slapped each other's hands. Harvey increased the speed with each verse of the song, until he missed and laughed. Joey laughed with him.

Baby's first laugh.

It was soon time for lunch and Dorothea invited Harvey to join them in the patient cafeteria. Joey walked between them and, as usual, held his Mommy's hand. Apropos of nothing, he took Harvey's hand as well. It was the first time baby reached out to a stranger. Dorothea told herself, *This is going to be a very good day.* They ate lunch, mostly in silence, but Harvey related snippets about his brother. When lunch was over, Dorothea announced it was nap time. Baby began shaking his head and making a fuss. His eyes watered, as if he would cry any second.

"Come now, Joey" she caressed him, "you take a nap every day." He would not calm down. "Please, Joey, you don't want Harvey to think you can't behave yourself."

Baby's first tantrum, not such a good day after all. He pushed Dorothea's hand away and started to cry—it was breaking Harvey's heart. His brother was alive, but in so much pain. He came to help and now it looked as though Brian was suffering a set-back.

"I'm sorry." Harvey apologized and started to stand. "I should go." Joey grabbed him around the waist and held on for dear life. "Do you want me to stay, Joey?" Baby sniffled and nodded. Dorothea and Harvey exchanged troubled glances. Joey needed to be kept to his schedule, if they were going to keep progress on track, but he would not let Harvey go. What to do? Think, and make it snappy.

"Harvey can stay and visit with Mommy while you have your nap, sweetheart. I promise, he'll be here when you wake up."

Joey held Harvey tighter.

"Jesus, he's squishing me. I forgot how strong he is."

What now? What was left? "Do you want Harvey to take a nap with you, honey? Is that what you want?" Joey immediately let go and the tears instantly evaporated. Baby's first crocodile tears.

There was a second bed in Joey's room, the double bed Dorothea used the first few nights she was with him at St. Elizabeth's. It was always made up, in case of emergencies. She grabbed some clean hospital scrubs for Harvey and Joey put on his pajamas. He snatched a stuffed bear from his own bed and sat on the bed meant for Harvey.

"It looks as though he not only wants to have his nap *with* you but *next* to you. He doesn't have nightmares, so you're OK in the same bed, if you don't mind."

"Fine by me. It's how we napped when we were little."

Harvey climbed in next to the wall. Joey lay next to him, snuggled down with his bear and shouldered Harvey. "Story!"

"I'm afraid I told Joey you were going to tell him stories." She thought for a minute. "You could try some about when the two of you were small."

"If you're sure it won't damage anything, I'm game."

"Maybe start out making them 'Once upon a Time' stories. It will make them remote enough to let him come into the story when he's ready, especially if you mention his real name fairly often," she leaned down to kiss Joey's forehead and hovered just over his face finishing her thought, "you know, Brian this and Brian that."

At her mention of his real name, Joey put an arm around her neck, pulled her toward him, and kissed her cheek. Instead of eyes shrouded in fog, Dorothea was looking into eyes that smiled.

She went to the door, almost in a trance, then turned to Harvey, who was puzzled by the exchange. "He's been here for over a year. Everyone gave up on him, said I was wasting my energy. I'm sure it's the only reason they gave me a chance. There were many firsts today—his first smile, first laugh. That?" she touched her hand to her cheek. "That was baby's first kiss."

*   *   *   *

Although Brian was two years older, today Harvey was the big brother. With Dorothea's help, one day, hopefully soon, their roles would reverse again. Harvey lay next to his brother and told him all the stories he remembered from their childhood. Joey fell asleep to the sound of Harvey's voice, then he dozed-off, himself. At around two-o'clock, Dorothea returned. Harvey had been wide awake for a while. He stopped her from waking Brian.

"What would happen if we tell him who he is?"

"I don't know. The situation never presented itself before."

"He looks at you funny every time you call yourself Mommy, like somewhere in his head he knows you aren't really his mother. Tre explained the Baby Program, and I really do understand, but Brian's the only family I've got left. He was always a stubborn cuss, had to figure everything out on his own, but this…," he paused. "It's different. It's like he almost knows, but can't quite figure it out. What if he never does? I keep waiting?

"I can hardly believe he's alive, let alone right next to me. I need Brian back and he needs to be back. If he understands that we know who he is, maybe it will give him a reason to return. Maybe that's what's been missing all along. He's just floating out there in the nowhere because he has no reason not to. Can we try giving him a reason? Please?"

"I have an idea." Dorothea leaned down and touched Joey's shoulder. "Sweetheart. It's Mommy. Time to get up." He stretched, opened his eyes, then turned toward his visitor relieved. "Harvey is still here, just like I promised."

"Mommy needs to talk to you about something." She sat on the bed next to him. "You know that you are a boy baby. Well, Harvey was a boy baby too. When two boy babies have the same Mommy and Daddy, those boys are called brothers. Do you understand?" Her baby silently blinked at her. "Harvey has a brother, named Brian, who was a soldier in a far away place. One day, he got hurt very badly and somehow he got lost. No one could find him, not even Harvey, and he looked and looked for a very long time. Harvey was very sad."

Tears started to well in baby's eyes and he clutched his bear.

"Brian is the best guy I know," Harvey added, "my best friend. He's smart and strong and resourceful and I miss him very much. Life is very different and sad without him. I really need him back."

"Before you came here, to be with Mommy, you were badly hurt, in a far away place, and were lost for a very long time. You know that Mommy loves you very much and wants you to get well. Harvey came here today to try and help make that happen." The baby called Joey looked from Harvey to Dorothea. "We both want you to be well, so you can go home from the hospital." She cupped his cheek in her hand and looked into his eyes. "Would you like that, Brian?"

It was the first time that she spoke *to* him, instead of *about* him, using his correct name. They waited for a response, but there was none. Dorothea's hand remained on his cheek as she looked at him. Suddenly he grabbed her wrist very tightly, started to pull her hand way, then changed his mind, as though the haze clouding his memory were beginning to lift. He sat up, used her wrist to pull her closer, until they were practically nose-to-nose.

"It's B.J." The words spilled out. "It's B.J." He repeated.

"Brian Joseph." Harvey supplied, sitting up. "It's probably why he responded so well to Joe and Joey. Mother always called us for dinner, using our whole names. Brian Joseph and Harvey—"

"...John." Brian finished and turned toward the male voice. So familiar. "What's going on? Where am I?"

"You are Brian Joseph Bishop." Dorothea said. "You were badly injured while you were a soldier in Vietnam. Do you remember being there, being hurt? You suffered a concussion and memory loss. You're at St. Elizabeth's Hospital, in Washington, D.C. This is your brother, Harvey. Harvey John Bishop."

"I have a brother." He repeated her words like a parrot, making every effort to digest the information and bring himself out of the fog that shrouded his mind for better than a year. Then suddenly...he knew. "I *have* a brother! His name *is* Harvey." Brian looked at the visitor again, with full recognition. "Harvey! Oh, man!" He grabbed him in a great bear hug and buried his face in his shoulder. He held Harvey close, feeling him, as if for the first time.

"Welcome home." Harvey returned the hug with his own firm embrace.

"Mom? Where's mom?"

It was the one question Harvey dreaded, yet knew had to be asked and answered. "She passed away last year. She made me swear never to give up looking until you were found—by either the government or me. They sent you home, but my friend Tre, he helped me find you."

Harvey remembered silently asking why he was attached to Tre and why Brian couldn't be too. He now had answers to both questions. Time attached Harvey to Tre to help him find the *pusher*, and so Tre could accidentally lead him to Brian. It's why Brain couldn't become attached to Tre—he already was, but…

what if he hadn't accepted Tre's extra breakfast
what if he hadn't let Tre explain the overheard phone call
what if he and Tre hadn't become real friends
what if he hadn't been one of 'the soldiers' that night
what if his mother hadn't known the hand game
what if he hadn't suggested it as a possible aid
what if he wasn't interested in the good it did?

What if? What if? He had his brother back, and suddenly the *what ifs* didn't matter. A reason for everything, he reminded himself—that did matter. Spared for a reason, returned for a reason. Tre accidentally helped Harvey find Brian. Did that make Brian another key to Tre's puzzle? It was a question for later.

Brian studied Dorothea. A pretty woman, a concerned face. "Who are you?"

"I'm Dr. Dorothea Tilson. You've been part of my Baby Program these last few months. Since we didn't know who you were, we couldn't even begin to locate your own mother. I didn't know until just now that she passed away. I'm so sorry. At any rate, there was no one else, so, I've been your Mommy."

"I beg your pardon?"

"Each man in the Program has a Mommy to care for him."

He studied her face again. "You kept calling yourself Mommy, but somewhere in the back of my memory, my mother was arguing the point. It was a relentless war of words, first yours then hers." He shook his head. "After everything that happened, I couldn't make myself care enough to correct you. Is that how it works? When I was well enough, I would correct you."

Dorothea nodded. "It would have been the first sign you were returning. Only the memory of your mother's voice made any sense. Your mind was buried under too much rubble to argue with me. If Harvey's idea hadn't worked, frankly, I don't know what I would have done, but I couldn't let them just warehouse you."

"I'm no one to you. Why would you even care?"

Harvey interrupted with Tre's answer. "Let's just say, everyone has reasons."

"Yes." It felt as if, somehow, Harvey had just read her mind and Dorothea gratefully agreed. "Let's just leave it at that."

Brian shrugged and told his story. "The woman, she was so young and sad. One day, enemy rebels invaded, shot-up everything. There was so much blood. The woman, she protected me. She and her baby, they died in my arms. I...," he pressed his fingers to his temples, "...I never even knew their names. Then I was here. You were kind, kept talking to me." He paused. "You gave me a second chance by being my Mommy. Is that right?"

"Yes," was all Dorothea could manage, without breaking Tre's cardinal rule—no crying in the Army, but Brian understood that she managed to pull him out of the abyss.

Brian and Harvey were reunited, but their mother was not alive to share the moment. The mourning of her so fresh for one, a painfully reopened wound for the other. They were nearly lost to each other for good, but now, they could move forward together. It was what their mother would have wanted.

Shirley Bishop carried each them inside of her for nine months, gave them breath and the life they had before this moment. Dorothea Tilson gave them a second change to share that life with each other. The seconds ticked by. "Family hug!" They called out, simultaneously, each tugging on Dorothea, pulling her into their embrace. They made a sandwich of her, squishing her and making her laugh. They had done the same to their own mother, many times.

One year and three months earlier, Brian Joseph Bishop was returned to the United States from South Vietnam. One year and three months later, he was finally home.

CHAPTER 24

▼

COHASSET, MA—1974

Molly and her son, William, arrived at Cohasset Beach for a day of fun and sun. They waited patiently for the only parking space anywhere near the beach. A jittery mother and her nervous teenage son were hastily loading their car, preparing to leave.

"Eric, sweetheart, please hurry!" The mother almost pleaded. The boy hopped in and started to close the car door when William leaned over and honked Molly's horn. He hung out their car window and pointed to the barrier wall.

"You forgot your bag," he shouted.

The boy jumped back out and grabbed the bag. "Thanks, kid," he yelled back, then tossed the bag onto the front seat shaking his head in disgust. How could he have left behind the bag with his brother's precious letters? All they had were his letters. They almost never got to see or talk to him.

The mothers and sons smiled and waved to each other in passing.

Molly began setting up the blanket, cooler, and beach umbrella that she borrowed from her parents' garage.

"Can I go in now? Pleeeease!!" William begged.

"This won't take ten minutes."

"Ten minutes, but that's forever." William pouted and kicked the sand.

Against her better judgment, Molly relented. "You have to promise to stay near the shore line. Don't go in past your knees and stay where I can see you. I'll finish setting up and be right down to join you." She held up both hands, every finger extended. "Give me ten minutes." Molly pulled William's inflatable football out of their beach bag and fastened it around him.

"I don't need the football anymore," he objected. "I'm a good swimmer."

"Yes, I know. You're a wonderful swimmer, in the pool, but this is the ocean. There's no life guard today and there's an undertow. I need you safe."

"Safe isn't any fun. I don't want to wear it," he complained. "How come you don't have to wear one?"

"If they made a football in my size, I'd wear one too." William laughed at his mother's joke. Molly gave William his final instruction before he ran toward the water. "Remember, if you can't see me, then I can't see you, so stay where you can see me."

"I will." He called over his shoulder as he ran toward the water.

Molly shook her head with a smile and planted the beach umbrella into the sand. "Kids! Always in such a hurry."

William played in the surf, picking up shells and stones, and tried skipping them in the ocean. He hadn't kept an eye on his mother and in the ten minutes Molly spent setting up their beach camp, the knee-high waves tugged him some twenty yards down the beach. When he looked up, William realized that his mother was beyond his line of vision.

"If I can't see her, she can't see me." William removed his football, dropping it on the beach, leaving it to go in and out with the surf. He ran toward the waves and little by little, wave by wave, he was pulled out by the undertow.

When Molly finished, she looked to where she last saw William. He was not there. It was a few short minutes, but he was gone. She ran to the shore line, ankle deep in water, calling his name. He did not answer. Molly ran down the beach, then back up. No William.

Twenty feet up the beach, something yellow, dancing in and out at the water's edge, caught Molly's eye. She ran toward it, assuring herself there were a million others exactly the same. She yanked it out of the light surf afraid to look, but did. There, on the underside, in waterproof magic marker was a name—William. She turned back toward the water screaming his name.

*　　　*　　　*　　　*

Tre found himself walking on a sand beach, the air warmed by the summer sun. The whistling in his ears had stopped and the queasy feeling in his gut had passed. He traveled with precious few memories of what he knew was an eventful life. One-by-one, they caught up with him. The first to do so was of a summer day in 1964. He and his friends were swimming at the abandon quarry in Manchester. A group of five or six kids showed up, daring any local to dive from the top of the highest cliff. Tre shook his head, realizing, again, how stupid it had been to take the bet for the few lousy dollars.

"Gotta be a dive," the ring leader said. "No jumping. Shit, anyone could do that."

That wasn't exactly true—anyone could jump, but not just anyone could live to tell about it. When no one accepted the dare, Tre spoke up. "What's the ante?"

"Ten bucks if you live." Their leader waved a ten dollar bill in the air.

"I've got a fiver that says you chicken out before you even reach the top," said another.

"No one else?" Tre looked from one new kid to the next.

"You ain't no Johnny Weissmuller," a third boy said as he reached into his pocket. "I've got a ten spot," he snapped it twice in front of his own face, "says you draw blood."

"Tarzan will climb to top of Escarpment now," he pointed to the ledge above them and beat his chest a few times, like an ape. "Carl, can hold the bets," he said, in his real voice.

"Tre, no!" Carl warned as the bills were shoved into his hand. "I'll give you twenty-five if you *don't* do it."

"You know I can't take *your* money, bud."

"Stu Winslow took a running leap and made it." Their friend, Curtis Johnson, yelled to Tre, when he was about half way up.

"Running leap for wimp!" He called back in Tarzan-English, as he hung from a boulder by one hand. "Tarzan will fly." He used his free arm and tightly cupped hand to demonstrate the arc his dive he would make.

Curtis saluted him when he reached the edge of the cliff. Tre saluted back, surveying the rocks that jutted out directly below. He'd made the same dive dozens of times, but it was on days when the forces were with him and the crystal clear water revealed the shape of the unyielding razors of granite below its surface. Today, the mirror-like plane reflected a cloudless blue sky. His only map for the shape the of boulders below the surface was his memory. If his memory was faulty, rather than gliding to the surface, he'd be floating to it—lifeless. He really would kill himself, if he didn't push out far enough. In the most conservative terms, he had to execute the dive of his life to keep his life and earn twenty-five dollars.

Tre took a deep breath, went into a half squat and curled his toes around the edge of the cliff. His powerful legs propelled him away from the cliff and he executed a perfect swan. His hands broke the water's smooth surface and he entered the safety of water deep enough for a dive. He completed the dive's arc under water, grazing the tops of his feet over a jagged boulder just below the surface, but it so easily could have gone another way. If he penetrated the water a few feet nearer the cliff, his chest would have crashed into the sharp edge instead of his feet simply skimming over it.

That moment crystallized into a memory he would never forget. What were the piddly wagers compared to the value of his life? But his mother needed the money to buy ingredients for a large order she was about to turn down. She was too embarrassed to borrow the front money from her only friend, Fran, Carl's mom, and Tre was too proud to accept Carl's offer of help. The old adage *you have to have money to make money* couldn't have bitten Tre or Connie any harder—its roots firmly planted in their every day reality.

Tre persuaded her to accept the order, promising to get the money, somehow. Fulfilling the order turned out to be instrumental in establishing Connie's reputation, but Tre knew that taking the dare was unnecessarily risky and foolish. As long as the circle on his arm remained unchanged, he would never do anything remotely like it again. His life was marked for something better than death by stupidity.

An undefined panic suddenly seized Tre; urged him to run the beach. The lose texture of the dry sand might have barred his feet from gaining traction or slowed him down, but the fear transported his mind back to Basic. Then, the daily run was something the Army made him do, in sand so dry and soft that his sheer weight made him sink well into it. In the beginning, it frustrated an angry young teen, way too full of testosterone. In the end, the run had made his feet swift and sure, his body quick and agile in combat. For the balance of his career, the morning run was his bonding ritual with his ally—Mother Nature. He was certain she would serve him in this moment, not get the better of him. *Stupid sand cannot beat me, not then, not now.*

He finally stopped running, his chest so tight, his lungs nearly burst with a need for more oxygen. He looked around, recognizing the familiar spot—an empty life guard tower, multi-colored towels lying all around it on the sand. It was his nightmare come true.

Floating out in the water, beyond the swimmers, was an unidentified object. It would not let him look away. He rushed toward the shore, yanking off his shoes as he ran. He dove into the waves, clothes and all, not wasting precious seconds stripping them off. A strong swimmer, since his days at the quarry, he quickly reached the floating object, but it turned out not to be an object. It was a child. Tre rolled him over onto his back. Instant recognition. Not another image from his nightmares, but a blast from the past. Other than the child's brown hair, the boy was the spitting image of himself at five. Tre tread water there, forced a few breaths of air into the boy's lungs, then slipped an arm under the boy's chin, and swam like hell for shore.

*   *   *   *

Molly continued running up the beach, where a man was exiting the water. His dripping wet clothes clung to him. He was carrying something. No, it was someone. He began looking for signs of life in the motionless form.

"Oh, my god! Oh, my god! That's my son! My William!" Molly screamed, as she reached them.

The man continued checking for breath sounds and a heart beat. Nothing. He began administering mouth-to-mouth and CPR. Still nothing, but the man did not give up.

"Hold on, son." In moments of life and death, he always called his soldiers *son*, and old habits die hard. A crowd began to gather and someone called for help. The seconds ticked by as he kept working on the boy, but without response. The man resumed the mouth-to-mouth and CPR. As he pumped on the boy's small chest, he repeated words said to him one tearful night. "Do not go gentle into that good-night."

He offered the same words to many a young soldier, bleeding to death, half a world away from home. Words that, more often than not, saved a life that might otherwise be lost without something, anything, to cling to. He would not let this young life slip away either—not if he could help it. He grabbed the boy by the shoulders and shook his little body, forcing the boy's back, hard, into the sand, finishing the poem, by barking the words like an order. "Rage. Rage against the dying of the light!" Molly said the words with him, but he did not seem to hear her.

He felt for a pulse and listened at the boy's chest again. Nothing. Time and hope were running out, while panic and the memory of a night, on a newly flattened hill in Vietnam, were creeping in. A local man, distraught and anxious, pleaded. "Wife! Baby!" The man's English was poor, but Tre got it that the woman was already in labor. There was no doctor or midwife and there was no one else. "Must come!" The man grabbed at Tre's arm.

Once the baby was in Tre's hands, he smacked her bottom to get her breathing on her own. His panicked and drifting mind said a smack equaled breath and a cheek's a cheek. Without thinking, he slapped the boys face—hard enough to make his mother jump. The moments ticked by, one…two…three…The boy started to cough and spit up sea water. Tre rolled him onto his side, gently rubbing his back, to help the water come up a little easier. Finally, Tre sat back on the sand and heaved a huge sigh of relief.

Molly dropped to her knees, throwing her arms around him. "That was incredible. You knew exactly what to do. You saved my son's life." She kissed his cheek. "How can I ever repay you?"

Something about the embrace was too familiar and made Tre uneasy. "He can save me next time," he patted her back lightly, "and we'll call it even."

By then, an Ambulance arrived and the EMTs took over. Tre and Molly got up from the sand and stepped away to let them do their job. He got a good look at her. For him, she had not changed much. At forty-nine, he bore little resemblance to the young man to whom she bid farewell, on Oahu, but there was something familiar about him and she knew his words. Hers was the face of the only woman he ever loved. His was the face of a stranger.

The EMTs got William onto a stretcher and he asked for the man who saved him. Tre went over. Except for the hair color, the boy was the spitting image of himself as a boy. His imagination wasn't playing tricks on him.

"Those men said you saved me."

"I guess I did. Sorry I slapped you, but I couldn't get your attention. It'll never happen again," he promised, remembering the beatings Jack doled out, like candy. He gently touched the boy's still pink cheek. "Does it hurt?"

"Stings a little, I guess." The boy rubbed it quickly several times. "Not bad though." He flashed Tre an easy smile.

Tre smiled back, absently touching the boy's hair. "What were you doing so far out, all by yourself, without a life preserver?"

"Gettin' wet," William admitted, sheepishly.

"And what were your orders?"

"To wear my football and stay at the shoreline." William was more than a little embarrassed.

"Next time you'll obey your orders, won't you?"

William nodded.

"Orders can keep you alive, soldier. If you listen you live. If you don't, the only thing you *get* is dead. Remember that." It was an instruction from a night so long ago that Tre almost forgot it. What made him repeat those particular words? He was not sure.

William noted a quick flash of light in the big man's eyes as he finished speaking, but he blew it off. "Yeah, sure. I'll remember." He paused. "Mister, Mommy always says nothing's free. How much do you charge for saving someone."

This wasn't just another boy he called *son*, a young man who was really someone else's son. This was his own son, whose life he just saved. When he returned from wherever he was now, he swore to find him, even all grown up, somewhere out there in the world. Tre repeated what he said to Molly.

"You save me next time and we'll call it even." There was another flash in the man's eyes. It distracted William enough to not notice Tre's extended hand. "Deal?"

"Um," William hesitated for a second. "OK. Sure. It's a deal." Father and son shook hands. "I'll save you next time."

"Remember your orders." Tre admonished sternly.

"I will." William repeated the words exactly. "Orders can keep you alive, soldier. If you listen you live, if you don't, the only thing you *get* is dead."

Tre saw a flash in William's eyes. He questioned it, trying to remember seeing it before, then it registered—twice in the field and again in the bar at Xuan Loc. Were he and his son, saving each other's lives by trading words?

"That's what you said. Isn't it, mister?" The question returned Tre to the moment, and he nodded the affirmative. "Say, I don't even know your name."

"Matthew. My name is Matthew."

"I'm William. G'bye Matthew. I'll never forget you."

"Good-bye, son." Tre could hardly get out the words. "I'll never forget you either."

Molly climbed into the ambulance after William's stretcher and blew Tre a kiss with her left hand, mouthing the words *Thank you*. He waved back, but his heart sank when he noted a wedding band on her ring finger. The eerie whistle and queasiness returned and he knew that his allotted time in this place was nearly over. A man had collected Tre's sneakers and was walking over. With all the commotion, he'd nearly forgotten about them.

"Some dad's gonna be plenty grateful when he gets home tonight. He still has a son." The man briskly pumped Tre's arm in congratulations, but he exuded no trace of joy—not on his lips, not in his eyes. "Lucky you happened along when you did." It was almost a question.

"It's the place I was supposed to be," Tre's answer was matter-of-fact.

"Well, you're a real hero, mister."

Some hero, Tre thought. His son and the woman he loved were spending their lives without him and Molly was married. He wondered what kind of hero that made him. He unenthusiastically nodded his head. "Yeah, a real Super-hero," he absently mumbled his disgust, then dusted the sand from his feet, pulled on his shoes, tied them, and began his solitary walk back up the beach, in the direction from which he came.

He checked his arm, desperately hoping to return to his own Time, to resume his search for Molly, the woman he couldn't forget, and now his son. Disappointment. The circle had closed only part way. He plodded along, watching his feet sink into the soft dry sand, his head bowed his head in grief. Would finding Molly and William have to wait? "*Some* lucky dad still has a son." His words were laced with bitterness. An alternate possibility occurred to him, *It's Overlap, maybe I'm the lucky dad.* The old exhilaration of the morning runs returned as he flew up the beach.

✳   ✳   ✳   ✳

The man who retrieved Tre's sneakers watched the woman climb into the ambulance, the EMTs load the stretcher, shut the door, and drive away. The lead that brought him to Cohasset Beach was sketchy at best, and neither this woman nor her boy were the ones he came for. It was another dead end and an enormous waste of both time and money.

He took a quick look around and decided that more than one thing didn't add up. Nearly every man present had long hair, or at least long-ish. Even he let his own hair grow-out, a little, in recent years. The hero had a fresh crew-cut and that was wrong. There was also the matter of Crew-cut's sneakers—chunky soles, with writing in the tread and a big 'N' on the side. He never saw anything like them before. Heavy concentration knitted his brow together. He looked back up the beach for another quick look at the shy hero. He was gone. The man followed the unusual footprints the hero's shoes left in the sand, but they went only so far. The hero, the footprints…simply vanished.

Admittedly, it was an assortment of very small details, but he spent nearly his whole career making decisions based on smaller details than those. He decided that Crew-cut referring to himself as a Super-hero seemed more like a clue than a coincidence. He spent years looking for three men, each one called Super-hero, and he was plenty short on reliable clues for finding them.

It wasn't at all likely that Crew-cut was one of *the* Super-heroes, but his gut said find him and get rid of him anyway. It was just barely possible that eliminating this faux Super-hero would flush-out the real ones. But how do you find a man who disappears the second you aren't looking—especially working alone and from another state?

*   *   *   *

He heard about a guy in the North End who'd vanish anyone for twenty-large, but the guy would need a way to find his prey. *Say, how about the Police*, he asked himself. They had sketch artists—who wouldn't be accommodating, if they knew how he intended to use their drawing. What if he roughed himself up, tore his clothes a little, then went to the Police and reported himself as having been mugged? He could say the guy stole something expensive…at gun-point, then offer to describe the assailant.

He drove around for a while, trying to choose a Police Station. The one in Dorchester was the most likely candidate, lots of muggings in Dorchester. His would be one more, added to what was probably a very long list. Not much the Police could do about his particular mugging, since he was making up the whole thing. With any luck, the report would end up getting lost in the shuffle. When the guy eventually turned up dead, the police would think he got his comeuppance and no one would be the wiser.

CHAPTER 25

▼

DORCHESTER, MA—1974
THE HIT

The man entered the Dorchester Police Station trying to look skittish. He told the Desk Sergeant why he was there. He was directed to the desk of Detective Allan Reynolds.

"I was mugged," he blurted, pretending to be all shook up.

"Anything taken?" The Detective asked.

"A necklace, for my daughter's birthday. The big 2-1," he lied. "It was too expensive to just walk away—three hundred dollars. The guy who jumped me had a gun. I got a really good look at him, though…if you have a sketch artist."

"No sketch artist, but, if you'll have a seat, we can try the Identi-kit. It isn't perfect, but we usually get pretty close."

"What happens then…with the picture, I mean? Do I get one to take with me?" He regretted asking the moment the words left his lips. It sounded as if he wanted a souvenir, but it couldn't be helped; he needed a copy.

"No. We never give composites to victims. We send them around to the other districts and outlying Police stations. We'll let you know, if he's caught."

"Oh." His disappointment was evident. "I see…but you will notify me, if he's ever found?"

"Your address and phone number will be in my report. If he's ever caught, we'll be in touch."

"Right...and it doesn't matter that I'm from out of state?"

"Nah. It's all too common for this kind of thing to happen to tourists."

Reynolds began filling out paperwork, then pulled his Identi-Kit from the metal storage cabinet behind him, set the working parts on his desk, along with a witness interview sheet.

"Have you ever done this before?" The victim shook his head. "I'm going to ask several very specific questions and, from your answers, I'll put together what's called a *first effort composite*. From there, you tell me what's correct and we'll work on what's not."

Using the eight basic questions: sex; race; height; build; age; hair color; hair length and hairstyle, the mugger was identified as a white male, square build, over six feet tall, probably over forty-five, with short, light colored hair, maybe some grey. Reynolds used the Guild-Line Chart, then spun the composite right side up for the victim.

"Are we anywhere close?"

"I guess the head and jaw are the right shape, but the hair was longer on top, more like a regular crew-cut, the lips were thicker, the nose wasn't so turned up and I'm not so sure about the eyes." Reynolds handed over a book of alternate features. The victim began flipping the pages. "This is the hair." He held up the book, touching the picture with the pad of his index finger.

"No, no. If you stop to show me each one, this'll take forever. See how each picture is marked with a number?" The man nodded. "OK, just read the numbers of the parts you think match and I'll pull the transparencies."

Although the man picked out the hair on the first try, he tested each pair of eyes and lips and each nose at least twice. He considered that his problem was that Crew-cut wasn't really a criminal. He was a hero. Maybe a hero wouldn't match any of the features in the kit. Then again, he admitted to himself, he lacked any artistic talent. Maybe he wouldn't recognize the correct features, unless they were in the exact right combination, so, even the correct features would continue to look wrong. More than two hours later, Detective Reynolds' patience worn thin, the man returned to the first pair of eyes and they finally had it.

Reynolds carefully paper-clipped the transparencies together and took them to the copy machine. Meanwhile, the man excused himself to the men's room—the only semi-private place, to ponder the problem of not getting a copy of the composite for himself. He was sure the copies were still running when Reynolds was paged to take a call. The detective would most likely take it at his own desk—

away from the copy machine. He selected that moment to emerge from the restroom. Luck was on his side. The machine was unattended and no one was looking. He took the opportunity to snatch a copy, quickly folded it and slipped it into his pant pocket.

He returned to Reynold's desk as the receiver was being returned to its cradle. The detective retrieved the copies and returned to his desk to conclude their business.

Reynolds examined the finished product. "You sure this is our man?" The victim nodded, trying his best to look shook-up, at the sight of the criminal. "He's a bit old for it, and maybe it's just me, but this guy looks more like a soldier than a mugger." He shrugged, unable to place the face, but the composite sure looked familiar.

Prophetic words, considering the years the victim spent looking for three soldiers. There was no way Crew-cut was the right age to have been a grunt in the field, taking orders from that butinsky Sergeant Major, when he was so old now. The only reason he bothered covering this base was because Crew-cut called himself Super-hero. After spending nearly twenty years skimming money from his wife's trust fund, his pocket was pretty deep, but it would quickly get shallow, if he spent money unnecessarily. But the last thing he could afford was to let Crew-cut live and be wrong.

He left the Police Station and headed for La Trattoria, on Hanover Street, in the North End.

CHAPTER 26

▼

COHASSET, MA—1974

Molly held William's hand the whole way to the hospital, trying to keep both of them calm. She was pretty sure that he was fine, but wanted someone with the initials 'M.D.' after his name to say so. The ambulance arrived at the ER and Molly hopped out first, giving the EMTs plenty of room to remove William's stretcher.

"Mommy!" William's panicky voice called to her.

"I'm right here." She took his hand again, as the stretcher was wheeled inside.

It had been quite a day for the two of them, but Cohasset Community Hospital's ER had seen little activity. A near drowning, although not exactly the stuff of headline news, did put the staff thru their paces. The ER attending listened to William's heart and lungs; took his blood pressure; checked his pulse; and gave him the tongue depressor used to check his throat. A nurse took his temperature—a perfect 98.6. William got to see his chart and everything written on it. The entire experience was very exciting for him. The closest he ever got to being a patient in a hospital was when he was born.

When the examination was completed, William asked his mother, "Mommy, do we know that man…the one that saved me?"

"No, sweetheart. We don't."

"Are you sure? He looked very…" William couldn't find the right word in his five-year-old's vocabulary.

"Familiar?" His mother supplied.

"Yeah! He looked familiar." He said excitedly.

"I thought so too."

"Is he one of daddy's friends?"

"I don't think…" Molly caught herself. There *was* something about the man, the hint of a fading scar on his cheek, the slight wave of his close-cropped hair, his size, his embrace, his words,…the mark on his arm. She saw it when he removed his shirt to wring out the sea water. Maybe not many, but other people had similar marks—two that she knew personally.

The first time Molly ever saw one was on the arm of a big, strong, sexy soldier. The day they parted, she recited the words of Dylan Thomas. She meant them to be a life preserver, something to cling to, if he got hurt. She was young and afraid of saying something so mushy that she'd feel stupid later. She said, in the only way she could back then, that she couldn't bear the idea of him going back to fight and being hurt, or killed. She wanted to grab him to her and never let go, but he was a soldier. He had to go whether she liked it or not, whether he liked it or not.

He took her in his arms and buried his face in her neck. He inhaled her smell, embroidered the feel of her on his mind. She cried. He would not let himself. Then, they said good-bye.

Molly recalled the man on the beach. She already etched him into her memory—his broad shoulders, the still mostly fair hair of his youth with small touches of white, the look on his face, in his deep blue eyes, when they waved good-bye. So sad. She would never forget him or what he did for her that day. When she and William returned home, at the end of the week, she would tell her husband about the man who saved their son. She would confess everything and apologize, from her soul, for poo-pooing and totally disregarding his request to strictly avoid the beach.

"Mommy." Molly was too distracted and the word didn't register. "MOMMY!!" William's voice finally pulled her back.

"Yes, sweetheart."

"Can I do this when I grow up? Work in an emergency room. It's so cool. Look at all the great stuff you get to play with." He held up his tongue depressor and the stethoscope the doctor left on the examination table. "Here." He offered the ear pieces. "Stick 'em in your ears. You can hear my heart."

"William." She tried to keep the tremor out of her voice. "Did the man on the beach you tell you his name?"

"Sure. It was Matthew.
Ohmigod!!

CHAPTER 27

▼

PETERBOROUGH, NH— JANUARY, 1969

As Tre ran the beach, the hold on his heart became tighter. It was evident Time's plan for him was more immediate than another day in the future. He was seized by renewed panic, making what he just experienced seem like nothing by comparison.

Shadows enveloped him as his running feet began striking pavement instead of sand. Above him, a black sky, jammed full of stars, blanketed everything, and he inhaled the smell of what could only be a winter evening in New Hampshire. As his pace slowed, dry, dead leaves and light puffy snow flakes swirled at his feet. Although his clothes were now dry, they were far too tropical for the weather. Tre's exposed skin stung from the frozen air.

He quickly surveyed his surroundings. Marginally familiar stores, on both sides of the quiet commercial street, were closed for the night. The two lane road, which allowed parking on both sides of it, was totally deserted. The vacant parking lanes added to the street's width and, more often than not, turned it into a main drag. It wasn't uncommon for cars, in need of one repair or another, to speed up and down the street.

A beat-up jalopy, sounding very much like it needed a new muffler (among other things), approached an unidentified woman as she plodded slowly on her way. She carried a rather heavy-looking grocery bag, in both arms, oblivious to everything around her, including Tre's footsteps approaching from behind. She never turned around, even as the noisy car got closer.

Tre was already gaining on her, when the engine's roar stopped him dead in his tracks. The woman passed under a street lamp. Her dark winter coat and the back of her closely cut blond hair briefly illuminated. Tre turned toward the car, shrouded in darkness, flanked on both sides by street lamps whose bulbs had gone out. The vehicle was traveling well above the posted limit, quickly closing the distance between itself and the woman. It fishtailed a few times, weaved, and went up on the sidewalk about three hundred yards behind Tre. He hurried toward the woman, panic making him run again. When he reached her, he grabbed her around the middle and propelled both of them into a recessed doorway.

The car continued barreling up the street, swerved onto the sidewalk again, right where the woman had been walking, taking out a wooden bench and several large, terra-cotta, flower pots. The car swerved, trying to miss the next street lamp, but its right front tire drove up the curved base of the lamp pole, causing it to flip over onto the driver's side and continue to roll.

The unlocked passenger door flew open, ejecting the unbelted driver thru it. His body traveled in a giant arc, until it crashed, head first, through the plate glass window of Kane's Hardware, across the street. Glass splintered into a thousand tiny shards and the array of fall merchandise, in the window, came crashing down. Metal trash cans went rolling into the street as rakes and a saw fell from their precarious perches in the display. The car finally came to rest on its tires, dented on all sides, including the roof, its windows shattered.

The woman's paper grocery bag had flown from her arms into the door in the alcove, splattering the contents. Eggs and milk were dripping from her hair and the bag of flour, that burst open, covered her and Tre from head to toe in a white dusty cloud.

"Are you OK?" Tre asked before he got a look at her.

"I don't think anything's broken." She checked herself for broken bones.

"Except your groceries." He picked a few pieces of egg shell and glass milk bottle from the top of her head, her coat and his shirt. "They're smashed to bits."

"Why did you do that?" She asked, baffled.

"That car was headed right for you—would have run you down, if I hadn't grabbed you."

"What car?"

"The one that sounded like an old lawn mower." Tre indicated the smashed and dented Chevy. "Didn't you hear it?"

"I guess my mind was elsewhere."

They locked eyes. His gaze penetrated her.

"Mom?" He asked, disbelieving. It was his second nightmare come true. His mind said it was impossible, but here he was. The woman turned away, clasping a hand over her mouth to stifle a cry. Tre grabbed her by the shoulders and spun her back around. "Mom? Connie Makepeace?" He looked up and read the address painted on the alcove door. 49 Carpenter Boulevard—the entrance to his mother's apartment, next door to The Pie Lady.

"Please!" Her plea was almost a whisper. She tried to escape, but Tre locked an arm around her shoulders and pressed her back tightly to his chest. She felt the strength of every muscle in his body, as she grabbed his forearm trying, unsuccessfully, to pry herself free.

"Mom, don't be afraid. It's Matthew." The woman continued to struggle, frightened more by the man holding her than the car and smashed store window. But he wouldn't let go, wouldn't let her get away. "It's the Overlap. Please, tell me how to prove I'm me and I will." He held tightly, until all of the fight went out of her and she began to relax.

"Your arm."

"And you won't run, if I let go." His cheek was pressed gently against hers.

She shook her head. Tre released her and pushed up the sleeve of his shirt to reveal the light red circle. The large break, that had been there his entire life, was nearly closed; his mission nearly complete. Connie touched it, brushed her thumb over it lightly several times, tried to brush it away, wish it away, will it away, as she did on the day he was born. The mark remained; because it was real. She looked up at him, put her hand on his scared cheek. He remained; because he was real.

"You're my Matthew?"

"Yes."

Tre swept her into his arms and held her tightly to him. Connie quickly considered the touches of grey in his hair, the faint lines of age on his face and clung to him, with every bit of her strength. The Matthew in her arms was older than she was now. He would survive that awful war, a war that was stealing other mother's sons. Her son would return, in one piece, his mind intact. Connie held him closer and cried tears of relief onto his shoulder.

Their exchange had been brief, taking hardly more than a minute, during which no movement or sound came from inside the hardware store. The rumbling of the car, the crashing of it into things, the smashing of glass, and the banging of metal began to draw the curiosity of Carpenter Boulevard residents. Someone called the police. Sirens, in the distance, were screaming toward them from the center of town, as the pair already in the street climbed into the smashed picture window of the hardware store to see if there was anything they could do.

Glass was everywhere and crunched under their shoes. The vehicle's driver had crashed thru the back of the display, taking a direct path toward the register counter and landed on his belly. Connie carefully climbed down from the platform of the display window and into the main body of the store.

"Is he OK?" Tre asked.

"Climb out of the window and cross the street. Do it! Now!"

Ever the soldier, Tre did as he was told, not stopping to ask questions. As the two of them disappeared into the stairway leading to Connie's apartment, people began milling in the street. She covered the switch plate with her hand, to prevent Tre from turning on the light. She closed the door behind them, just as the first Police car arrived.

"What's with the hustle to hide and the black-out?" He whispered.

"Upstairs. Quickly. Quietly," she whispered back.

"But—"

"Move!" Connie cut him off, barking the order.

She left Matthew to drip on a kitchen chair, while she grabbed a pair of knit pants and a sweatshirt from her bedroom, then ran to the bathroom to quickly rinse off the caked and dried food. She emerged a few minutes later, clean, her hair still wet, and went to Matthew's room. She returned with some fresh sweats and a towel and told him to do likewise. Connie waited in the living room. He exited the bathroom finger-combing his closely cropped, damp hair.

"Care to share what that was all about?"

"Sit down." She touched the sofa next to her, pausing to collect her thoughts, wondering where to begin. "Kane's has been running a fall clean-up special; trash cans, rakes, stuff like that. During store hours, they make a display on the sidewalk, then, at closing, they pull it all back inside. They don't exactly put it away, just pull it far enough into the store to lock the door."

"So?"

"So, this week they added ice fishing equipment: lumber, heaters, tools. Someone stuck a barrel with those long handled ice picks, used to chop holes in the ice, between the check-out counter and the window display. You know the ones, hard wood handles, about four feet long, giant steel spike on the end."

"Yeah, and?"

"Some fool put them spike end up and the man from the car landed right on them. It was too dark to see how many pierced his body, but," she paused, "…I'm pretty sure he was dead."

"Wow!" Tre leaned back on the sofa and let out a low whistle.

"You can say that again." Connie leaned back with him. "It was Jack."

*   *   *   *

"He never signed the final divorce papers, so officially, we're still married. You know how he always was with money, spend and spend, even when we didn't have. Well, some things never change. He was in debt up to his eye-balls, owed money everywhere and to everyone…" Connie used a finger to push her nose to one side. "…if you know what I mean.

"The Pie Lady is doing really great." She said proudly. "I've got four employees now. People come from all over, as far away as Boston and Quincy, to buy my pies." Then her mood went somber. "Jack's been calling, asking for money. Of course, I said no. He threatened to go to Ethan, tell him he'd *never* sign the divorce papers. I was at the lawyer's office most of today trying to see if there's anything I can do, but there's nothing. I can't force him to sign and I have no one who can."

Tre gave her a look that said she always had him.

Connie smiled at her son. "You were always there to protect me, Matthew, but the young you is fighting a war, half a world from here." She reminded him. "There's no one else. I couldn't involve my parents and I couldn't tell Ethan. How could I explain?"

"By explaining." He said matter-of-factly.

Connie shook her head. "He'd never understand."

"You don't know that!" Tre's infamous temper boiled over. "Ethan's a terrific guy. He would understand. I know he would."

"I guess you're right, but…" Connie shrugged, not finishing her thought. "Jack threatened to *get me* maybe even get Ethan and you, when you return from the war. I was afraid he'd make good on that threat. It's obvious, now, I had reason to be afraid. I couldn't allow Jack to hurt either one of you. I'd rather die myself.

"I've been a mess these last few weeks, my mind held hostage in that awful place where Ethan and I never get to be together. The whole nasty business was running through my head. I guess that's where I was when you grabbed me. I didn't hear a thing—not you, not even that old car of Jack's. I'm supposed to get married tomorrow. If I go through with it, I'll go to jail for bigamy. If I don't go through with it," she shook her head. "Either way, I lose Ethan again."

"What do you mean *again*?

Connie told him the story of his true ancestry. Matthew thought back to the night his mother was so badly beaten and his handshake with Ethan. He had been right, Ethan Craig was no ordinary guy. Jack might have been the only father he ever knew, but he was not a father by blood.

*   *   *   *

"Does Ethan know?" Connie shook her head. "Well, you have to tell him! He's entitled to know."

"What would I say?" Connie's look was pure terror. "After all these years, everything he missed, everything that's happened, including what happened tonight, no explanation would be adequate. He'd never forgive me. Would you? What if all of a sudden you found out that you had a fully grown son?"

"I'd be fine with it." Tre's mind flashed to William. His situation virtually identical to Ethan's, he'd give nearly anything to know where William and Molly were. "Mom," his tone grew softer, "did it ever occur to you that your silence tore our first hole in Time and marked me for Overlap? You couldn't tell Ethan you were pregnant, so you married Jack, which meant you had to keep my true lineage a secret. Jack beat both of us for years and we never told a soul. Ethan, Carl and I kept quiet about the night he nearly beat you to death. And I end up Overlapping to save you from Jack, again—all because of this killing silence.

"I popped out of the dark. Maybe my sudden appearance is what made Jack swerve—one of Overlap's fortunate accidents. If he kept to his course, and without me to grab you, he'd have hit you instead of the bench and pots. If I hadn't been there to grab you out of the way, you'd be dead now. How fair is that? Oh, Jack would have some bumps and bruises, but he'd be alive.

"There were no other witnesses to what happened on the street tonight. Knowing Jack, he probably would have ditched the car in the quarry or set the thing on fire, then let your accident look like a hit-and-run. He'd have played the estranged, but grieving, husband and gotten everything you worked so hard for. The facts are that I *was* there and he's the one that's dead, and now—," Tre stopped mid-sentence. "Gee, come to think of it, now you don't need those divorce papers. You can be with Ethan, like you should have been from the beginning; because it was meant to be. It makes a full circle of events. Doesn't it make sense?"

It made all of the sense in the world and Connie knew Matthew was right. Silence was always her answer, but it was *never ever* the right one. She remembered reading somewhere that the definition of insanity was repeating the same action over and over, yet expecting a different result. Was she insane to think silence could solve future problems when, so far, it hadn't solved any. Time sent Matthew to personally deliver a wake-up call. She promised to do everything in her power to answer it. "How did you get so wise?"

"Too many years sorting things out under fire. Matthew shrugged, then told Connie about his life—the battles he'd fought and helped win, his medals and honors. He spoke about *his* boys—the ones who looked up to him. He trained them to save the lives of others. They would gladly follow him into any battle.

*   *   *   *

Matthew stood at attention as the new crop of fresh young faces got into formation for the first time. He gave them their first order. "Attention!" They all snapped-to and he began to slowly pace back and forth, in front of them, looking at no one, and measuring his words carefully. "There are two rules of war. The first rule is that soldiers die. The second rule is that no one can do anything about rule number one. Although the first rule is true enough, I greatly dislike and disagree with rule number two.

"That is why you are not soldiers." He always advised them of their status. "What you are is *my* soldiers. Do not be confused into thinking that one of my soldiers is the same as some other soldier. I assure you, they are totally different.

"For the next eight weeks, I will be your mother and father. There is no transferring out, requesting others parents or a pardon from this prison, (he always chuckled here), I mean Basic. You will be trained until you either wish you could beg me to stop, which you cannot, or wish that I'd get it over with and kill you, which I will not. The reason I am so certain neither of those things will happen is that *my* soldiers must conduct themselves by two additional and separate rules of war.

"Rule number one is for me and will aid you in achieving rule number two—there's no whining in the Army. Whining includes crying and begging, so there'll be none of those either. Rule number two—there's no dying. No one dies unless I give my permission and I will *never* give my permission for anyone to do any such thing.

"*Do not go gentle into that good-night. Rage. Rage against the dying of the light.* Dylon Thomas wrote those lines. You will commit them to memory. They sound like three separate statements, but the first is a question, which, when asked, must be answered by the other two. Don't ask how, but some day, those words could save your life.

"The first half of my job is to train you according to these second two rules of war. Your job is to do as you are told, so that my training takes. You will see distant lands, be confronted with hostile fire and, if you follow *my* two rules of war, you will come out alive. That is my pledge.

"Take a moment to look at the man standing next to you, behind you, in front of you." The men hesitated to move a muscle. "Go ahead. I'll wait." He paced, while his charges silently obeyed.

"That man is probably a piece of shit. Someday, he may also be the man fighting next to you or be the one that has your back. You may find yourself in the unfortunate position of having to trust that piece of shit with your life. To the man who is not a piece of shit, don't become one. To the man who knows he is a piece of shit, take a lesson from the men who are not. Remember, someday, that man who is not a piece of shit, but knows that you are, may be the man fighting next to *you* or be the one that has *your* back. Understand this—no man knowingly risks or sacrifices his own life to save the life of a piece of shit.

"The second half of my job is to kick the shit right out of you, while doing the first half of my job. I know every trick there is. You cannot fool me and you will not get away with anything. When you hear criticism, it will be real. When you hear praise, it will also be real. You may have come into Basic a piece of shit, but you will leave here as one of my soldiers." He searched each young face to see that his commitment had sunk in. Once again, he stood before them, this time at attention, and his voice took on a much gentler tone. "Remember, gentlemen, the suit may make the man, but the man makes the uniform." Tre welcomed his new boys with his oft used quote. "Do not go gentle into that good night," he waited for their response.

"Rage. Rage against the dying of the light." It was their first act as a unit.

"Now that we understand each other, any questions?"

A loud and resounding answer rose up from the entire group, as if it were one voice instead of many. "No, Sir!"

*   *   *   *

Tre told Connie about William. "The good news is, somewhere out there in the world, I have a son, whose mother I've loved nearly all of my life. You have a grandson and somewhere way out there—a great-granddaughter. The bad news is, I have no idea where they are or how to find them."

Connie went to the desk in the corner of the room, that served as an office for her growing business. She pulled an envelope from the middle drawer, returned to the sofa and handed it to Matthew. "This came the other day. According to the date on the back, it took six weeks to get here."

Matthew examined the envelope carefully. It had traveled a very long way. "It's addressed to me. Return address says Xuan Loc. The young me was there six weeks ago, and so was the person who wrote this. Why send it here? Why not just talk to me, or give it to me?"

Connie shrugged. Matthew knew it wouldn't be from one of his friends, and the only other people who knew he had leave for his mother's wedding were his new Sergeant and the Clerk who processed the request. He tore open the envelope and read the letter. His face grew pale and his mouth dropped open.

Dear Dad,

I wanted to meet you my whole life and now I have. I know one of the pictures you wear—the one of you and Carl and mom, in Hawaii. She talks about that night, like it happened yesterday, must have told that story a million times. She's always saying how brave you were—a hero. She was more than right.

You said that you tried to find mother, but couldn't. Well, she tried to find you too. She never loved anyone else, never married. I don't know when, or if, this will reach you. I only pray this doesn't end up in a dead letter pile. I may already be born by the time you receive this, but it doesn't matter. What does matter is that you're my dad. Whenever you get it, just please, come get us. Mother and I need you.

Sorry I fudged to get an address, but I'm sure you'll find a way to forgive me. How else could I give you what you wanted so badly and still have you believe me? Tell you I was her son? Tell you that I was your fully grown son on a mission from the future? I'll let you prove it to yourself—in your own handwriting. And just in case you're wondering, Lloyd Cummings' life really was worth saving. In my Time, he's a really great man. I know how hard this is to believe, but you will; you're a Reweaver. So am I.

The letter was signed: *Sergeant Major William Houser.*

Written underneath: Molly Houser
                                385 Brighton Avenue, Apt. 3B
                                Allston, MA

What address? Tre checked the envelope. Tucked into a corner was a scrap a paper. He pulled it out and handed the letter to Connie. "The letter's wrong,"

Tre said when she finished reading. "It says Molly never married, but she had a wedding band."

"Things are changing."

"Changing how?"

"You're floating in Time, about to Overlap yourself. The contents of this letter should be old news, but it's not. The Matthew that arrives tomorrow, must have done something that you didn't. This letter never waited for you, but it's certainly waiting for him."

*   *   *   *

"Remember I said that I had a son?" Connie nodded. "Well, the Overlap is how I know. Time took me to a beach where I saved the life of a small boy. Except for his brown hair, he looked exactly like me when I was little. When I saw Molly, I knew for sure. I promised myself, right then, that I'd find him and her, but I had no way to keep that promise. Now I do. My son, my fully grown son, somewhere in the future from now, gave me a way. Well," he corrected himself, "...he gave the me that arrives here tomorrow a way."

Matthew from the future told his mother all about the boy and the man he became and the Overlap he fulfilled.

"Your son, the man who wrote this letter, did you see a flash of light in his eyes?"

"Now that you mention it, a couple of times. I thought it was my imagination. It happened once with the boy too."

Connie shook her head. "Your time with the boy was your Overlap. If one of you saw something, it should have been him. It happens only when the course of a life can change. Perhaps something that happened before, happened again, something he said or did."

"We said the same words back and forth to each other. I said them, the boy repeated them, then the flash. I couldn't think of what made me say them, but when it was all over, I remembered that my grown son, said those very words in the jungle. Are you saying that those words changing our lives?"

Connie shrugged. "Changing or saving."

"That last time with Houser, I didn't know he was my son, but the letter says he knew I was his father. He asked for an address, in case he found Molly."

"And you saw the flash; because he intended to send this letter. He was just asking for a place to send it. If his Overlap was like every other, that was the thing he accidentally did to change the outcome of your life."

"But why not just tell me who he was?"

"Matthew, you're my son and I love you, but you inherited what is probably Ethan's worse trait. You always had to prove everything to yourself. Your son knew the only person you'd believe was you. That's why he included the scrap of paper."

"But where did he get it?" He examined the scrawl. "It's my handwriting, but I never wrote this." His head began to swim and he pressed his fingers to his pulsing temples.

"Take a deep breath," Connie instructed and Tre did.

"That's the thing that's different. The me that arrives tomorrow asked the bar-tender for paper and something to write with. *He* wrote this and now *I* remember it."

Connie's hand flew to her lips. "This is our story's first *second memory*. When you return to your own Time, the life you and I remember now will be gone. Tell me everything you know. I may need the details to persuade Matthew to go to Molly, so the ring on her finger ends up being yours." Tre did that too.

"Just as my Overlap began, I kept Houser, my grown son, from being run down in a crosswalk. A car and I were each racing toward him. All I knew was that I had to protect him, could be that I saved his life, again. He looked so familiar, but with all the hustle and so many years between seeing him…, but now I'm sure. It *was* him.

"He repeated other words we've been trading thru Time—it's lines from Dylan Thomas. He used them to reach Lloyd Cummings out in the jungle, and me in the street. Molly said them…when we said good-bye. She taught them to our son."

"Matthew, to most people, Overlap is a myth, a word you can look up in the dictionary. But there are others, who are not marked, that know what it really is. Are you in some sort of trouble?" When he had no answer, she asked the question for which she wasn't quite sure she wanted *any* answer. "Are you positive the car was heading for the man in the crosswalk?"

*   *   *   *

"Do you hear the whistle yet?" Connie asked.

"No," he said distractedly.

"Then you're probably here for a while. "Oh, god! What if someone saw us on the street. What if they ask who you are? The wedding is tomorrow. Matthew, I mean, the young you is due to arrive in the morning. Oh, forget about other people, what do I tell *Matthew*?" They thought in silence for a moment. "Anyone asks, you're my cousin, here for the wedding. Same story for Matthew."

"For anyone else, fine, but the truth for Matthew." Tre corrected her. Reluctantly, Connie agreed. Truth and telling it had to be the way, if the future was to be different from the past. "What do you know about the whistle?" Tre gave his mother a stern look. "And I want the whole story…the unabridged version."

"I never wanted you to find out." Connie told him about the night Jack beat her so badly. "You went off to find Jack and Carl stayed with me. Remember?"

Did he remember? There wasn't a thing about that night Tre would ever forget.

"When it was all over, and I was back, Carl said that he and Ethan knew, that they saw the mark when they patched me up. I don't know how, but Ethan knew exactly what was coming and that I shouldn't be alone, and I wasn't. I had Carl that night."

Yes, Carl knew about the mark and their legend and the story that went with it, and he had been there for Connie and Tre was grateful. Tre asked himself how often Carl was there for him, through a lifetime in the service, covering his back—once taking out a sniper, whose rifle was aimed directly at Tre's head. Carl the medic—friend to the end, through thick and thin, sometimes through thin and thin, sticking to him like glue, making sure he stayed alive to complete his mission—whenever that was.

CHAPTER 28

▼

PETERBOROUGH, NH— JANUARY, 1969

It isn't every son who can attend the first wedding of his mother and father and also be the best man. Tre put in for Compassionate Leave and the Army gave him three days. Compared to the risks he took on the Army's behalf, it felt like small potatoes.

On the flight home, he came to realize why the compensation felt so inadequate—it wasn't enough time to find Molly. Finding her should have been easy—just get her address from the USO office, but the guy in the office said he didn't have it and, without his help, finding Molly was next to impossible. No matter how he tried, he couldn't move on—Molly and his increasingly frequent nightmare drawing him to her, were always in his head. Sweet Molly, so terrified and he couldn't help her.

Tre landed at Manchester Airport, in a small four-seater. He traveled in his dress uniform, the medals he earned proudly pinned to his chest. The three other passengers were each dressed in business suits and barely acknowledged his presence. He knew the war was an unpopular subject at home, but had no idea the extent of the animosity felt by those who didn't serve, for those of their countrymen that did.

It was honorable to fight for one's country, to defend her flag and the land it represented. But Tre knew, all too well, that this war was not an honorable one and that the last thing it was about was protecting American soil. It wasn't even about protecting South Vietnamese soil. It was about money and oil and big business and getting rich. The monetary price tag of what was happening in Southeast Asia was reaching into the billions, but Tre knew that the real cost was dead GIs. Everyday guys were killed by booby traps, as a matter of course. Some deployed body piercing spears, attached to pressure activated land mines. The leader was skewered, while the men behind him were exploded into nothingness. Never had a war been so ugly, so horrific, or shamelessly profitable.

Tre waited until the businessmen were inside the tiny airport terminal, to disembark. From the look of them, they were making a bundle from the war, by riding on the backs of people working for crap and hour. They looked as if they might spit on him, given half the chance. He decided not to give them that chance.

Tre entered the building and a lone, older man stood, respectfully, and extended his hand. "You're Matthew Makepeace." It wasn't a question.

Tre saw something unusual in the man's eyes—tremendous sadness and maybe a serving of gratitude, though he couldn't figure why this stranger should be grateful to him. He also saw a marked resemblance between them—their height, build, coloring, the faint remnant of a scar on his cheek. Tre let it go, but an odd sensation shot thru him even before they shook hands. It was very nearly the same sensation as when he shook Houser's hand. He let that go too. But he was forced to ask himself the exact same question—*intuition or some cosmic connection?*

"Your mom asked that I pick you up," he offered, without volunteering who he was and Tre didn't ask. "She's a bit nervous. Complained of butterflies flapping and tap dancing in her belly...and, of course, she's anxious to see you," he added quickly. "If this is your only luggage, let's stow your gear and get going."

Aside from the few prosaic pleasantries, *how was your flight*, and the like, they drove to Keene in relative silence. When the car pulled up in front of Connie's apartment, Tre jumped out, hoisted his gear onto his shoulder, as if it weighed no more than a dish towel, and took the stairs three at a time.

"Mom?" Tre called into the silent apartment. No answer. He stood frozen in the middle of the living room, desperately trying not to relive the moment he called for his mother from the living room of their darkened farm house. He shook himself, banished the awful memory of finding her in a broken heap on the kitchen floor, then looked around. Connie's apartment was beautifully decorated in pale grey with accents of dusty blue and mauve and smelled like a garden of fresh flowers. It bore no resemblance to the shabby, run-down, farmhouse, with its beat-up and musty smelling furniture.

From the corner of his eye, he caught a movement coming from the direction of the room his mother thought of as his. It was Connie, in her wedding dress— a beautiful swirl of ivory chiffon that hit mid-calf. He swept her up into his arms, his cheek pressed tightly against hers, her arms closed around his neck. Connie buried her face in the shoulder of his uniform and they held each other. Connie's cream, satin pumps fell from her dangling feet and hit the thick, grey, carpet with a muffled clunk. Tre finally returned her to terra ferma and she reached her delicate hand up to his cheek.

"My special boy, still waiting to be the hero of someone else's life." It was a statement, because, of course, Connie already knew.

"Yes." He hated talking about his mission, so this was their code, to confirm he was still waiting. Tre was grateful to the man, who picked him up, for delaying his arrival in the doorway to the apartment, allowing mother and son a moment alone. He even cleared his throat, as he came up the stairs.

"Put your shoes on Lucy," he pointed to Connie's bare feet. "Don't want to be late for your own wedding."

They all laughed a bit nervously and, for the time being, Connie introduced her son to the older gentleman as her cousin, Matthew. She had no other plausible explanation to have Tre accept older Matthew as family, until she could really come clean.

"You share your first name."

Older Matthew wagged a corrective finger and his stern look silently reminded her, *The truth for Tre*. Connie offered a sheepish smile, deciding that the addition of, *announcements to be made later*, might square things. They left for the Temple and the Rabbi's chambers.

The ceremony was brief and the guest list short—Ethan's parents, Connie's parents, Carl's parents, Tre and older Matthew. There was a small reception at Ethan's house, where they discussed their plans for the immediate future—to move Ethan into Connie's apartment and turn his entire house into a full clinic. The zoning board had just approved the plan to allow Ethan to extend services that were ordinarily available only in a hospital. It was going to be wonderful for the community and do wonders for his practice. He already bought two file cabinets, which stood like mute, wooden centennials near the side door.

When the party was over Connie, Ethan, Tre, and older Matthew returned to Connie's apartment and changed out of their party duds. They were all relaxing when older Matthew excused himself, pleading a headache.

Tre got everyone's attention. "Mother says there are some announcements. Since I have one too, I might as well go first. I'm going to make the Army my career."

There were sighs and objections from Ethan. He only just found out that he even had a son. Jack had him for eighteen years and abused him. Ethan was not going to sacrifice him to that terrible, bloody war the foreign correspondents brought into his living room every night. Tre did not yet know that Ethan was his father, that revelation was going to be one of Connie's announcements, but he swore he would not lose the opportunity to be a father twice, with the same child.

"I'll be all right and I'll come home in one piece," Tre protested, choosing words that would hopefully ease everyone's mind.

"I know." A thin, thready voice came from Connie.

Her quiet acceptance threw Ethan and Tre off guard, but Ethan found his voice in a hurry. He loved his new wife, loved her nearly his entire life, but he turned on her in that moment.

"You watch the same news I do, that horror show the media broadcasts like entertainment. Boys are coming home without arms and legs, their minds blown to bits by the things they see and are forced to do over there, not to mention the drugs and booze, and it won't be over tomorrow. Oh, no! This *war that isn't a war* is far too profitable to end just yet!" His tone was sarcastic. "It'll be years and billions of more dollars before it's over. In the meantime, we're losing an entire generation of boys and you have no objection to Tre making a career of this thing. All you can say is *you know*, like it's all right with you. The politicians can call it any god damn thing they want, but by me it's still a war, and in war, nobody knows. What do you know that no one else in the world does?"

"I know that he'll be OK."

"And how do you know that?" Ethan demanded.

"Because it already happened and Matthew, the life we had with Jack, it never should have." Both Tre and Ethan fell silent and Connie steeled herself for a possible explosive reaction from Tre. She learned from her tet-a-tet with older Matthew that his famous short fuse hadn't gotten any longer with time. "I was afraid to ruin everyone's life, take Ethan's future away from him by saddling him with a wife and child before he could afford them. I married Jack Makepeace, but Matthew…Ethan is your rightful father. By trying so hard to make things better, I ruined everything, for everyone. It's all my fault. I'm so sorry." Connie's face dropped into her hands and she sobbed.

Ethan and Matthew both went to her, one on each side, wrapping one arm around her, the other around each other. In that moment, in a tiny huddle, their heads touching, they became the family, each of them longed for—offering solid grounding, warmth and protection, casting aside their stubbornness, accusations and flaring tempers.

"But it's fixed now, Connie, we're all together." Ethan tried to console her.

"Yes," Matthew agreed, "we're a family. Nothing can change that." Matthew smiled at Ethan. "Isn't that right, dad?"

"Don't look at me, son. Ask your mother. She seems to know everything." But how did she know, Ethan asked himself and then her. "Connie, what did you mean, *it already happened?*"

"We should include my cousin, I mean Matthew. He can explain this, maybe better than I can."

Tre volunteered to get him, but returned alone, holding an envelope and looking a little pale. "Where did he go? He didn't leave and he wasn't there. Only this." He displayed the envelope. "It was on the bed. It's addressed to me, from Vietnam and it's been opened."

Older Matthew's headache was the feverish queasiness that marked the end of his Overlap. He accomplished everything he was meant to do and was returning to his own Time. The rest was up to Connie—retell the events of the previous night, repeat the story she was told, while trying to convince her son and her new husband that she was not insane.

"He's gone, because he's you, Matthew. That's how I know you'll be OK. You survive every skirmish, every battle and come home. There were no metal plates in his head, no broken bones, no healed over bullet holes. He showed me. There isn't a mark on him, except for the ones Jack put there. Coming here and saving me from Jack, again, is part of your Overlap mission. It happens in your forty-ninth year." Connie recounted the events of the previous night.

All the while Connie was explaining, the phrase, *it already happened*, echoed in Ethan's head. A memory of those words bore into his present like a pesky mosquito. He tried to remember where he heard the words before and, then, he did.

"Ohmigod!" Ethan started pacing the room. "Everything is happening exactly like I heard it would. Christ! The file cabinets! I finished filling them this morning and I stuck Jane Doe at the back of the very last drawer."

"What are you talking about?" Connie asked.

Who's Jane Doe?" Connie and Tre asked in unison.

Ethan told the story of the young girl he met when he was a boy and why he believed her.

"We were both just ten, and couldn't figure out why no one would tell her why you were with Jack. Now I see. It's *because* she was ten that she didn't know. What reason would you have to be with a man that grown-ups wouldn't discuss in front of a ten year-old? You were pregnant and unmarried.

"CeeCee, you sacrificed yourself for no reason. You knew us. We would have found a way to make it work. We could have married right away, then you could have stayed at home to finish your senior year, if you wanted, or gotten a GED, like you did anyway and started your pie business right then and there. The way things are going you could be famous by now."

"I am famous," she corrected, her voice full of pride.

"OK, so you could be more famous. Don't you see? Overlap is what makes the Time-piece the beginning of the story, when she isn't born until the end of it. We have to decode your legend and story, so she'll know exactly how to fix us. That way, we can get it right in the past that is waiting in our future. That legend is the key to figuring everything out, but it's a jumble. Figuring it out is going to take a lot of doing, plus four Reweavers and seven Overlaps. Let's face it," he proffered a crooked smile and a shrug to his new-old family, "we're a mess!"

"How do *you* know all this?" Connie asked.

"The Time-piece told you herself, because *you're* the father." Tre sounded like a narrator. "Tell me you're the father."

"Well, we already know that I'm *your* father. Is that what you mean?" Ethan quizzed him.

"Maybe. My friends and I think we unjumbled the legend, but the father was the one person we couldn't identify. Do you know anything about stones jumping on water?"

Ethan nodded. "The Time-piece, Emily, she taught me to skip a rock, like it was jumping on water. Is that enough to make me the father?"

"Yes. But why did you need the legend and story before anyone else?"

"I needed more time than anyone else. There was no money and I had to plan for medical school. Otherwise, I couldn't have helped Connie after Jack was done with her that night."

"Or Matthew's friend Poopsie," Connie despondently looked at the floor.

"What happened to him?" Concern colored Tre's voice.

"Nothing…yet. But he desperately needs Ethan to be a doctor." Connie wouldn't elaborate. What could she say? Nothing would prepare any of them for what lay in Poopsie's future.

"Have you met Emily?" Ethan asked Tre, hardly containing his excitement. "She's quite a girl."

"No, but let's just say," Tre gave a rye smile, "the kid gets around."

"Who is this Emily to us?" Connie resisted accepting what she knew was true.

"Hold on to your hat," Ethan answered. "She's our great-granddaughter, and Tre, here, is her Pop-op. She said her Pop-op was my child."

His words sunk in and Tre nearly jumped out of his skin. "You mean to say we got it right?" His voice betrayed more than a hint of pride. "So, that's the four Reweavers—Emily, Houser, me, and," Tre looked at his mother, "…and you."

"But…," Connie stopped herself just short of denying it. "I never wanted you to know." She pushed up the sleeve of her shirt, revealing the mark to her son, for the first time.

"There's no way to prove it now, but that mark may be why Jack beat you so badly," Ethan offered. "I don't think it was a coincidence he broke your left arm. He may have been trying to break the connection between you and Time—hurt you in a way no doctor could repair. Only Time and another Reweaver could help you. But Tre wasn't supposed to be home. Remember? Perhaps that's why Joy Evans went into early labor, to give Tre the opportunity to be in the right place at the right Time."

Connie never voluntarily thought about that night, but Jack did seem satisfied when he finally heard the bone in her arm crack. He immediately stopped the beating and left the house, leaving her alone on the floor, perhaps to die. Maybe what Ethan proposed wasn't even possible, but maybe it was. Matthew's unexpected schedule change did put him at home when he should have, or could have, been elsewhere. To a teenager who lived on a farm, an afternoon to himself was a precious commodity. He might have gone to any of a thousand other locations.

Christopher Evans was three now, or was it four? Connie would send a special pie to the Evans home to help celebrate his next birthday. The years had slipped away from her, but it was a date she would never forget. It was Connie's turn to come clean. She told Ethan and Matthew the story of her Overlap in Time.

*   *   *   *

Peterborough, NH—1946

As Connie lay on her kitchen floor, she heard an eerie whistle and her heart began to feel constricted. She thought she must be having a heart attack. Then, from some far and distant place was Ethan's voice, then nothing but the whistle.

Connie found herself wandering the locker lined hallways of what appeared to be a school. A woman, clip-board in hand, was headed straight for her. "Mrs. Perkins! Am I glad to see you! I'm Vice-Principal Claire Barton." The woman extended her hand. "But you should've come to the front office first. The agency called to say you wouldn't be available until noon. I was just on my way to advise the girls they were having a study-hall instead of Home-Ec. If you'll come with me."

A confused Connie was escorted to room D-15 and introduced by the Vice Principal. "Class, this is Mrs. Perkins. She's substituting for Mrs. Henner." Then to Connie. "Everything you need is either in this Fridge or those cabinets. Anything you want to teach the girls is fine with me."

Anything? Which anything? A slightly panicked Connie reminded herself that she'd made at least two pies a day for the last eighteen years. "Class," she nervously announced, "get out rolling pins, flour and butter, while I take attendance." Connie used Mrs. Barton's alphabetical list to call names. The last name was Constance Yellowfeather.

Connie suddenly remembered that day with crystal clarity. She learned she was pregnant the afternoon before and was frantic over what to do. She opted to tell no one, especially Ethan. He was away at college, making the future he planned for so long. She would not take it away from him. His budget was so tight that he could barely afford to come home once a semester. He certainly couldn't afford to, all of a sudden, support an entire family.

Connie got virtually no sleep the night before. When she finally did fall asleep, she woke up in a sweat from her recurring nightmare. She lay her hands on her still flat belly and began to cry. "What am I going to do, little one?" She spoke to her unborn child. "There's a man in Keene who can make you go away until Ethan and I are ready, but you're part of my Ethan...my Ethan. What if you are my only chance to be a mother?" In that moment, there was a slight flutter in the pit of her belly. She swore she would not destroy Ethan's future, even if the consequences were that she would not share that future with him, but she resolved to find a way to keep the baby growing insider her. Even though everyone in town knew she was Ethan's girl, she had made up her mind.

A new boy, named Jack Makepeace, was hanging around school. He wasn't a student, but seemed to pop up wherever Connie was. Jack hung with a group of rowdy boys, before and after school. Heaven only knew what he really did with himself, while she was in class. The rumor was that he inherited his father's chicken farm over in Jaffrey. Inherit. The word made the farm sound like it was worth something.

Jack was a wild kid, with a reputation for favoring fast cars and loose women. He was constantly trying to make eye-contact with her, but she never even returned his smile, let alone considered accepting a date. Connie felt it was a stroke of luck that he was part Native American, plus he wouldn't need much encouragement.

Nearly all of her free time was spent with Ethan. There wasn't enough left over to build truly close relationships with any of her girlfriends. Their conversations revolved around everyday sorts of things, school, movie stars, clothes, boys, homework, and little else. By eliminating the possibility of speaking to either her own parents or Ethan's, she virtually had no one with whom to talk over her situation, and no one to talk her out of her ill-fated plan.

Her mind was so distracted the next day at school that she was grateful for something else to center on, that wasn't too complicated. The substitute teacher for Home-Ec taught the class how to bake a pie with a flaky crust. The lesson stuck and came in mighty handy when she needed a way to earn extra money for her family…for her son. She was always grateful to that substitute and now realized that she was the very woman to whom she was so grateful. It was her destiny—go back in Time, Overlap herself as a teenage girl, and give herself and her son a way out of poverty. Something was missing though, but she couldn't put her finger on what it was.

*   *   *   *

Peterborough, NH—January, 1969

"Mom," Tre hesitated unsure whether to finish asking his question. "You said you are *one* of the ones I am meant to save. Who else?"

Connie hesitated too, but there was only one way. *The truth for Matthew,* older Matthew said. He wanted him to know. "Your son."

"My son? But how did you know about—"

"That envelope...," she indicated the one he was still holding, "...it's a letter, from a person named Houser."

"You opened my mail?" He looked at her in astonishment.

"Not exactly." How do you explain the unexplainable? Like older Matthew said, by just explaining. "Since Matthew, I mean, older Matthew, is you, I gave it to him. *He* opened it, then he gave it to me to read. So, in an unexplainable, twisted sort of way, you opened it. Anyway, the letter, it's from him. From your son."

"You're saying that Houser actually *is* my son?" Matthew could hardly believe his ears, but Connie nodded. Right again. "Houser spared our lives in Cambodia. Carl's and Poopsie's and mine. And the four of us saved another guy named Lloyd Cummings." Tre removed the letter from the envelope and went pale as he read. "My god! Houser really *is* my son, and Molly, my Molly, is his mother. He offered to help me find her, but I said it was a lost cause. This is Molly's address, where I can find her right now. Today. This minute. That's why he sounded so confident, like a guy who already knew, because he did."

"Did you know," Connie smiled, "that if you call Brighton information and your party is listed, they give you the phone number," she snapped her fingers, "just like that?" No one answered. "Well, they do. I called last night." She handed the phone to Tre, then went to her desk and came back with a slip of paper.

"Call her now," they urged, "before you lose your nerve."

"Please!" Tre blustered. "I'm a professional soldier. I have nerves of steel."

"You're more like me than you want to admit—a stubborn wimp." Connie tried to goad him into proving her wrong.

"We'll just see about that, now, won't we?" He dialed the number. "Stubborn wimp in deed!"

The phone on the other end rang. Once...twice. Just before the third ring, an out of breath female voice answered. "Hello?" It was Molly. Tre started to hyperventilate. "Is someone there?" Molly persisted. "Hello!" Again, no answer. "If this is a crank call, you stink at it. I can hear you breathing. Do you have asthma or something? Are you all right?"

"Wimp!" Connie teased, her voice loud enough to be heard on the other end of the line. "Say something for god sake."

"Yes, for god sake, Wimp," Molly agreed with the disembodied female voice. "please say *something*. I ran for the phone, and if you made me run for nothing, I'll be forced to track you down and kill you. None of us wants that, now, do we?" She gave a heavy pregnant sigh, sat on the sofa and put her feet up on the coffee table. "If you have something to say, by all means, please say it. Really. I'm all ears."

What do you say to the woman you know you can't live without and who, in a different life, your prior memory says you looked for, for nearly thirty years. He chose Molly's parting words. "Do not go gentle into that good-night."

"Rage. Rage against the dying of the light." They finished the quote together and then there was a long pause.

"Where are you? I tried to find you, so many times, but I couldn't and no one would help me. Where are you?" Molly repeated.

"New Hampshire, three days Compassionate Leave. It so happens that I may be eligible for three more. We can use them to get married…if you'll have me."

"If you'll have *me*. I've changed since you saw me last." Molly patted her ever widening middle. "You may not want me any more."

"I may not want you any more," he teased, "but I don't want you any less. I want you *and* our baby."

Molly stammered. "But…I never said, 'cause I wasn't really sure…and but, but you…how did you…" And finally a coherent thought. "How long will it take for you to get here?"

"With good directions, just under two hours. I'll explain everything when I get there."

Before Tre left to convince *his Molly* to become *his wife*, he explained the interpretations he and his friends gave to the legend. When he was gone, Connie retold older Matthew's story to Ethan.

"Much as you might think so now," older Matthew said, "the war doesn't last forever. Eventually, we come home, but only Carl, Lloyd, Isaiah, and I can get near Poopsie. He creeps-out everyone else." Tre explained the details. "The head shrinkers walk away shaking their heads. He's fit for battle, but not much else. He needs a special kind of help. Find it for him."

The farm. But in the past that lay in the future they all wanted, Connie wouldn't marry Jack Makepeace and Matthew wouldn't simply inherit it. Ethan and Connie began to develop a plan that would place them there anyway and aid Ethan in finding the right person to help him use it. The story was unfolding in front of them—the one Emily would tell, one day, to help them fix the past. The farm was only one of a thousand details to work out and that Emily would have to learn. Little Emily, not even born yet and destined to become the hero of all of their lives.

CHAPTER 29

▼

JUNE, 1976
TRAITOR

Contrary to his request, and much to his own chagrin, the Army trained Brian Bishop to be a Company Clerk. How very convenient that his training and on-the-job experience made him the perfect candidate for a recently vacated government position—the Army's personnel fiche keeper, in St. Louis. When Brian was ready to leave St. E's, Harvey and the soldiers wrote glowing recommendations for him. The government made an offer and he grabbed it.

*　　　*　　　*　　　*

Their search had been on-going. Each night Harvey and Tre searched the fiche—thousands upon thousands of useless records, one at a time, noting the mention of any Army Brass in ones from Vietnam. Tre was sure there was plenty of Brassholes among them. Anyone over the rank of Sergeant qualified; any one of whom might be some sort of a pusher, but there was never the first notation attaching anyone to their story—neither directly nor indirectly. The list of suspects grew long. Tre knew that meant it was too long. The balance of the story unraveled when looked at correctly. This mess simply wouldn't unraveled and that couldn't be right. There had to be a clue, or clues, they were missing. And the much hoped-for reference to a pusher was probably stuck in the personnel records out in St. Louis. One night Tre and Harvey discussed who in the world it could be.

"It must be someone high ranking," Tre stated the obvious. "No one else had access to troops or moved them around. I'm telling you, it's someone who knew Lloyd and had a grudge." Tre knew a thing or two about the reasons for wanting someone dead. He also knew that one soldier trying to killing another, over some personal dispute, wouldn't be a first. Maybe the quarrel wasn't even with Lloyd, but with his old man. Perhaps the plan was to get the Colonel by killing his kid. That wouldn't be a first either.

"All the clues come from the same source. Without being completely obvious, each identifies the most likely and least likely suspect. But who is that?" He pounded the desk with the side of his fist. "I'm telling you, this guy's right under our fucking noses and not on that damn list." Tre was right, but with no way to narrow it down, it literally still could be almost anyone.

Are Time and technology your friends or your enemies? That's a tough decision. The government eventually decided that microfiche was neither the easiest way to update nor look up records. Although the fiche would always exist as back-up, it was decided to try automating the records for easier access, then cross reference them by mission number and location.

No one knew how long the process would take, or if the project was economically feasible. A Time-study would be conducted using the data from two hundred records. The higher-ups would then decide whether to continue. They didn't care which two hundred records, as long as they were consecutive. As the senior in the department, Harvey was to handle the automation process. He selected the place to start—just beyond where he and Tre were conducting their search.

Tre stopped by Harvey's office to collect him for lunch. "I'm starved! Let's blow." Harvey's fingers continued flying over the keyboard. "Come on, man. Give it a rest."

Harvey's fingers stopped moving, but he sat frozen. Tre knew a problem when he saw one and swiveled Harvey's desk chair around. His eyes were glazed, his breathing uneven.

"Harvey!" Tre gave his face a few light slaps. "Come back from wherever you are."

Shock prevented speech. Harvey was pointing from his computer screen to the fiche reader and back.

He was in the process of entering data from the selected fiche records onto his hard drive. Thus far, all bore dates near to that of the Cambodian field incident—twenty-nine of which ended in disaster. Twelve missions involved Lloyd Cummings own Platoon, seventeen more his entire Company. Those statistics were jarring enough, but add in the missions to set up the beacons, and then retrieve them, and the number of physical casualties and deaths was staggering. There was Brass up the wazoo, heavily involved and names were named. The old list was history. This was their list.

They mailed it to Brian. Brass that high would be Lifers with limitless pages of war history to be transferred and reviewed. They needed the answer to a riddle, so every word was scrutinized for hidden meaning. Although The Freedom of Information Act declassified the material they wanted, they felt better having Brian work surreptitiously.

Wasting time continuing to mail documents or taking a chance that something would get lost in-transit was not an option. What if the wrong someone picked up a fax meant for Harvey or Brian, or reviewed the long distance phone bills for the in-house fax machines? The safest solution was running second phone lines into each of their homes and installing personal fax machines.

Each day, Brian made copies. Each night, he faxed them to Harvey. Living in different time zones meant Harvey didn't receive them until the evening, but given the circumstances, it was the best they could do. Harvey dissected and re-dissected the records, but never found anything that meant anything beyond that the missions were headed-up by the worse strategists in the U.S. Army. Hard to believe that such well trained officers could screw-up that much or that often. Tre didn't call them Brassholes for nothing.

They were about two months into it when, at the appointed time, Harvey got a phone call instead of the usual fax. He thought Brian was in the mood to chat. "Helllllloooo," he answered brightly, though he was exhausted from way too long a day.

Brian's response was three emotionless words. "I found it." He did not need confirmation that the second needle-in-a-hay-stack was in his hand.

Harvey parked himself in front of his machine, impatiently waiting for the pages to print on the curling fax paper. The record literally contained an endless list of awards and honors. Last detail: strategic planning; Covert-Ops; Black-Ops. Harvey'd never heard of Black-Ops. Seemed their man traveled to Cambodia, several times, supposedly as liaison between the U.S. and the Kymer Rouge.

Notations of domestic violence were interspersed throughout the record—many where his wife was treated at Walter Reed. Apparently, he abused her on numerous occasions. On the last occasion, she required emergency surgery and was admitted. Regardless that no charges, military or otherwise, were ever pressed—her husband shoved her down a flight of stairs. Pushed. The last entry was the soldier's retirement at the Army's request. Two of the earliest notations were his home town—Cummings Point, Virginia, and were he attended school—West Point.

Heaped on top of Harvey's long day, the news made his head spin. He poured over the record several times, in the hopes that Brian was mistaken. When he finally picked up the phone, it was late, but everyone agreed. If Brian or Harvey found anything, no matter the hour, they would not delay sharing it. He considered what to say as the phone at the other end started to ring.

The next day Harvey and Tre visited the morgues of all the local newspapers trying to verify what Brian found in the fiche. There was one small article, buried in the middle of a local paper.

"This doesn't line up at all with the stinking fish. It says there was a break-in by some unidentified criminal."

"The paper has a bogus public story." Tre re-explained what Lloyd had shared that night in Xuan Loc. "In the aftermath of the real story, the Army might have let this guy retire on his own, but, according to his service record, *they* retired *him*. That's good news for us; he can be reactivated down the road, anywhere down the road, even if it's only for a Court Martial."

The legend had played-out. The fish-keepers had found the pusher from the Points. They had their man. Unfortunately, they had no proof.

▼

CHAPTER 30

WASHINGTON, D.C.— NOVEMBER 13, 1982
GOING TO THE WALL

Poopsie never fully recovered to be the happy soul he was in Basic. While he could laugh at a ridiculous situation, finally had a life of his own, and no longer cut off people's ears, he was never again the jokester who always had a casual smile. That part was lost somewhere deep inside himself, with shame as his constant companion. No one, not even his mother, could pull him out of that sad dark place of horror and guilt.

*   *   *   *

News of plans for a Vietnam Veteran's Memorial swept the country. Individuals and corporations made donations, families of dead Vets sent checks and children collected pennies from their parents and friends. The country finally came together to finish what technically had ended in 1975. With news of the memorial's unveiling, Dorothea thought there was a glimmer of hope that the Poopsie held hostage inside his pain might really be saved.

She and Tre spoke by phone. "He never had closure. I think he can get it from this memorial. If it's ever going to be completely over, there can't be any ghosts left to haunt him. He sees himself as *the one*. We can go with him and be his *many*, his strength, in case he can't find his own."

*   *   *   *

Poopsie and Dorothea married while he was at The Peaceful Center. Tre took him for a walk and they had a not-so-peaceful conversation. "If you love her, don't be a great big jerk. Don't follow my example. Where will you be if you lose her?" Poopsie didn't budge. "I think you're afraid!" Tre dared, but Poopsie still didn't bite. He switched to the direct approach. "For Pete's sake, our clue is *their wives will be the ones who save them*. Isn't she very busy saving you right now? That legend is our map and we agreed to stick to it. Besides, there's no fighting that fucking legend. I'm telling you, she's the one—not to mention Molly, Carl's Amy, Lloyd's Michelle, and Isaiah's Denise. We feel safe with them; 'cause not a one of them has even ask about The 'Nam. Not ever. Just say I'm wrong and I'll back off.

"She could say no."

"Are you out of your mind? No," Tre raised a hand. "Don't answer that. We already know or we wouldn't have sent you here." They both laughed. "Let me remind you, my friend, the five of us are a collective handful. Who the hell else would put up with us, but the women who save us? Shit, maybe it's even *why* they save us. Look, my parents are already here. Yours can be here in a few hours. Molly and William, Carl, Isaiah, Lloyd, the girls; they're all just short plane rides away. Tell me that Wanda and the Colonel aren't ready for a house full of Little Poopsies. I'm sure Dorothea's parents would love to see her married to someone who loves her. If I volunteer my mother to arrange the whole thing, then will you ask her, butthead?"

In the end, Poopsie asked, 'cause legend or no legend, he simply couldn't resist Dorothea's big brown eyes.

*   *   *   *

"Just get him there, whatever it takes. Break a leg, if you have to. We're losing him again. Everyday, he drifts further and further away and if he goes off the deep end, I'm afraid it'll be for good. The Wall might be our only chance to really get back the whole Poopsie and nothing but the Poopsie."

In her best medical opinion, if not her not-so-objective personal one, Dorothea felt Poopsie's presence for the Wall's unveiling, would either kill him or save him. She prayed very hard for the latter. Tre caucused with Carl and Isaiah, wangled three day passes for himself, Poopsie and Carl, and the FBI gave Isaiah some much needed time off.

A small caravan of cars began the long trip from New England. It grew into a convoy, as each family took their place in the cortege, until it reached its final destination. The *boys* spent the night in a small motel, just outside of D.C., and arrived at Constitution Gardens in dress uniforms—shirts starched and pressed, caps firmly in place. The four silent men, who blended into the background had not seen the monument beforehand and did not know what to expect.

There were others in uniform, both active and retired. Some were in wheel chairs, some with arms and legs missing, some walked with the aid of canes, but no one who wanted to be there hadn't come. A few came to carry signs proclaiming peace for the future, and witness what was, hopefully, the unveiling of the last memorial to America's young, dead soldiers.

Friends saw old friends, men they hadn't seen since the day they left the service, and gave each other silent, bone-crushing hugs—the kind that no matter how close they brought the other man, couldn't possibly bring him close enough. There was silence between them, but when emotions speak in such volumes, words become unnecessary. Some cried—for themselves, for the memories they carried, for the guys who saved their lives, but didn't make it home themselves. And some cried for the sake of the memorial itself, that it marked the death of innocence and more than a few great men.

The drapes dropped from The Wall—a wide V-shaped, black scar in the earth. A collective gasp went up, followed by a hush. The speakers took the podium and, one-by-one, read the 58,132 names inscribed there. It was appropriate for the occasion, appropriate for the dedication. Whatever anyone's personal reason for coming, whatever feelings they carried inside, whatever thoughts they held for the war in general, or even The Wall itself, everyone who saw it, knew that the price of the war was too high—58,132 lives.

If Poopsie was going to break, it would be when the names 'PFC Corey Edward Black' and 'Sergeant Gregory James Smiley' were read. They stood fast and waited as names peeled off the list. All breath was suspended in those moments…and then the moments passed. The two names were read. Poopsie, Colonel Tilson, Tre, Carl, and Isaiah, collectively saluted them. Dorothea took Poopsie's hand and saw the tears standing in his eyes—tears he still could not shed. He cradled her face in big hands, telling her, the only way he could, that he was as right as he was going to get. He kissed her once on each ear.

The final list was read by Lloyd Cummings. He had nothing personal prepared for when he finished, but spoke simply and from his heart. "Even now, there are too many names on The Wall and yet, the list of dead and missing is not complete. Let us never forget the sacrifice they made. Let us never take for granted the life they left for us to enjoy. Let us always be grateful for the lives they saved, by giving up their own. Let us honor every soldier who served, both living and dead. And let us pray that this is the last such sacrifice the youth of America will need to make. Let us promise ourselves that this is the last such monument we will *need* to build."

Lloyd finished and the crowd began to mingle. People went to The Wall and touched the black granite, and soon, for them, it was real. Memories, promises, saved lives, lost friends, united with mirror-like reflections from the shiny surface. Mothers, fathers, and widows, saw reflected memories of what was, and all that was lost so many years before. Sons and daughters saw the reflection of what might have been, but wasn't—simple things like learning to throw a ball or how to dance by standing on their father's feet.

The Craig, Tilson, Summers, Smiley, Houser, Jefferson, and Bishop families made their way down to The Wall, moving en masse, without exchange of words. Wanda Tilson checked one of the directories for the names of PFC Corey Black and Sergeant Gregory Smiley. Panel 51 east, lines 56 and 75. They, each in turn, touched the names, laid paper over them, and scraped pencils across the paper to leave an impression—on the paper and on their hearts. And then, for all of them…it was finally real. The Wall said that others, besides Abernathy Montrose Tilson, knew the sacrifice Greg Smiley and Corey Black each made for their country, but only Poopsie knew how Corey Black had died.

"I have to go," he announced.

"Well, if you're sure." Ethan was concerned for Poopsie's pale color. Their pilgrimage was meant to help, not cause him a heart attack or a stroke. "No one wants to rush you. We can stay as long as you want."

"No. I mean, I need to see the faces of the people who weep for him. I'll never find peace until I tell them what I did."

Ethan and Dorothea locked eyes. "I'm sure we can find out where they live," she offered, taking his hand again. "We can plan a trip and make arrangements to visit."

"No. Not a plan, not another trip. Today, right now…in front of all of you. They live in Arlington, 489 Wentworth Avenue."

The caravan of cars looked almost like a funeral procession, and maybe it was one. Poopsie and Dorothea's car lead the way to the Black home. Some twenty minutes later, a somber Abernathy Montrose Tilson pulled-up in front of a recently painted house, emerged from his car, placed his cap firmly on his head, and made the long silent march up the front walk alone.

A man in his mid-fifties, standing about five-foot-nine, with sad eyes and graying hair, came to the door. A woman, an inch or so shorter than the man, and around the same age, stood behind him. The others exited their vehicles and waited silently at the curb.

"Can I help you, soldier?" The man's voice was full of respect.

"I need to speak with you and your wife, sir? My name is Tilson, Captain Tilson now. I served with Corey in The 'Nam."

The man looked beyond his visitor to the sea of mournful faces, mere yards from his door. "What is this about? What's wrong? Has something happened? Our son is dead, Captain."

"Yes, sir." He stood at full attention, his voice laden with disgrace. "I killed him."

Miranda Black pushed past her husband and lunged for Poopsie. He was prepared for some sort of aftermath to his announcement—screaming, swearing, curses hurled at him and his family. He steadied himself for Miranda Black's impassioned slap across his face, the pounding of her fists against his chest. He could take it. After all, he believed that he deserved it. He was completely unprepared for the reaction he got.

She jumped into his arms and held him to her as she would have held her own son, had he returned to her alive. She pressed her lips to the side of his bare neck and kissed him gently. She whispered in his ear. He whispered something back, firmly shaking his head. As Poopsie held her tightly to him, setting her back on the ground, she said something else. And finally, Poopsie Tilson cried. Deep mournful wales. Miranda Black rocked him in her arms, like an infant.

The Blacks had opted for a private funeral for Corey, rather than a military one. The staff of Jameson's funeral parlor cut and combed his hair, shaved his face, applied enough make-up to make him look like the photograph his father provided, and they undressed him before they put on his uniform—the full dress uniform of the U.S. Army, 101st Infantry, Delta Company.

There was a sudden commotion in the preparation room. Two men ran out the back door and threw-up in the parking lot. The young girl who did the make-up whirled away from the body screaming and ended up in a corner weeping uncontrollably. Her brother was serving in the same area as Corey Black. Everyone saw the bullet hole in his chest and even without an official autopsy, everyone in the room knew exactly what killed him.

What was the whispered exchange between Miranda Black and Poopsie?

"My poor brave boy. I waited all these years to meet you, to thank you. You showed my Corey mercy. Your bullet found its mark. You shot him, but you did not kill him."

"I was there." He shook his head. "There were tears. Dead men don't cry."

"Neither do they bleed," she answered. "No blood exited the bullet hole. He died before you shot him. Maybe it was seconds before, but believe me, it was before. You saw that grotesque mutilation and did the first, best, thing you could think of. You gave Corey what you would have wanted, had you been in his place. You tried to give him the dignity you thought he deserved, but you did not take his life."

Miranda Black let him go, retrieved a handkerchief from the pocket of her dress, wiped her own eyes, then Poopsie's. She reached up and cradled his cheek in the palm of her hand. Poopsie took it in both of his and kissed it. George Black stepped forward, starring at Poopsie. Inwardly, he acknowledged the bravery it took to remain in the service after that horrible *war that wasn't a war*, the guts it took to do the right thing for his son, even though it was too late and the Army would never approve. And, more than anything, the balls it took to appear at their door-step and admit what he'd done. But, George had something to say and would not be satisfied until it was said.

"I'd like to give you exactly what you deserve for what you did," he said, his face and voice unyielding as cement, holding in the tears that stung the back of his eyes. "I'd like to...," his voice caught.

"Please, sir. If you want to hit me, curse me, throw me off your property...it's not less than I deserve." Poopsie hung his head.

"*I'll* be the judge of what you deserve." George regained his composure, and stabbed himself in the chest, several times, with his thumb. "And what you deserve is...," his voice caught again and Poopsie looked up to take whatever it was. "...you deserve the salute I would have given to my son. I'd like very much if you'd let me give it to you now."

The enemy, not Poopsie, had ended Corey Black's life. He had lived with the guilt for so long, that he could hardly believe it was true. But with this new knowledge, the heavy yokes of guilt and shame lifted from his shoulders. He could leave this place knowing that Miranda and George Black did not hate him or blame him, and had, in fact, been waiting these many years just to thank him. They would have done so sooner, but no one, not even the Army, could reveal who made that final, merciful gesture to Corey.

The Black family couldn't bring themselves to attend the morning's dedication. Poopsie's arrival on their doorstep now made it possible for them to go to The Wall, see it, touch the place where their son's name was etched into granite, visible, forever, to all who came to the memorial. Now, they could leave the red rose of love that would let someone, anyone, everyone, know that Corey Black died for his country and left behind people who loved him.

One-by-one, each member of the caravan stepped forward. Poopsie remained to make the introductions. At last, a small boy, who had been holding the hand of the woman introduced as Dorothea Tilson, looked up at her excitedly, whispered something George and Miranda could not hear, then ran toward them.

"It's my turn now," he said proudly. "Mommy says, last place is saved for the most important one. That's me."

George and Miranda crouched down on their haunches, to be eye-to-eye with him. "Well, well, well." George tried to be as serious as the boy. "Just what makes you the most important one?"

He had no idea what was coming.

"I was born with soldiers inside me." The boy began, touching his chest with great earnest. "One got hurt in a bad place called The 'Nam. My daddy and my uncle Greg tried to help him. They failed. The other soldier *is* my Uncle Greg. He was so sad about what happened to the first soldier that Uncle Greg hurt himself." The boy looked at the ground sadly, shaking his head back and forth. "They died in that bad place.

"Sometimes they make a scary rumbly in my chest." He looked back at Miranda and George. "If I talk to them, tell them they're safe inside me, the rumbly gets quieter, but it doesn't go away. There was a really bad rumbly this morning, but even when I said the soldiers were safe, the rumbly didn't get quiet.

"Then we went to The Wall and special people read a really long list of all of the people who didn't come home. After, we looked in the book of names and found the soldiers inside me. We put paper over their names and rubbed pencils on them, to take them with us. These are them," he pulled two crumpled scraps of papers out of his pocket and handed them to George, "...the soldiers. Each of us kissed them good-bye, then we came here. Since I'm the most important one, I went last. When I kissed Uncle Greg good-bye, the rumbly totally stopped. Mommy says, it stopped forever. I think she's right."

George and Miranda read the names that had been transferred to the bits of paper.

"But what's *your* name, young man?" George asked. "You haven't told us who *you* are."

"Oh! Didn't I? I was supposed to." He looked from the Blacks up at Poopsie, who shook his head. "I'm Greg, sir." The boy stuck out his small hand to shake with George and gave him an enormous, friendly smile. "Gregory Corey Tilson."

Miranda and George Black were beyond words. George finally let go of his own tears and gave Greg's hand a firm shake. It made the boy feel very grown up, for being only five. Then, Miranda took his face in her hands and kissed him on both cheeks.

"That's my mom," Greg turned his head toward his mother and pointed to Dorothea, "and this is my dad." He looked up proudly at Poopsie, took his father's big hand in both of his small ones and gave the Blacks a serious look. "He's a very brave soldier."

"Yes." George agreed, looking at Poopsie and got up from his still crouched position. "He *is* a very brave soldier."

"Would you mind if we write to you, Gregory Corey Tilson?" Miranda asked. "If you write back, that'd make us pen-pals. Would you like that?"

"You mean my own mail, with my name on it, with stamps and everything?"

Miranda nodded. "With stamps and everything."

"Boy, would I!" Greg beamed. The Blacks hadn't asked anyone else to be pen-pals. *Boy-oh-boy, Mommy was right!* He told himself. *Last place is saved for the most important one.*

After the hugging and tears were concluded, the Craigs, Tilsons, Summers, Smileys, Housers, Jeffersons, and Bishops piled back into their cars. As ignitions turned-over, Poopsie's real healing finally began. The caravan began the long drive that would end when the last car was parked in the driveway of a small-town, New England farmhouse.

$$*\qquad*\qquad*\qquad*$$

At The Wall's unveiling, standing among the other soldiers, in green fatigues, was a solitary older figure with craggy lined skin and steely eyes, the brim of his cap pulled way down to hide his face. He strolled, head down, among the clusters of visitors, never making direct eye-contact with anyone. He was listening intently to bits of conversations, taking quick side glances, seeking two familiar faces he never found. He listened with only half an ear as the names were read, but paid careful attention to Lloyd Cummings' personal remarks.

As always, Lloyd kept them general, and didn't mention any names beyond the ones from his portion of the list; not even the four who risked their own lives to save his. In fact, he never gave them individual thanks. But this day, in particular, was for remembrance and dedication not special congratulations. Lloyd spoke of lives lost and saved, of gratefulness, of sacrifice and honor, of promises.

The story of Lloyd's service in Vietnam was well known—five tours, where he earned nearly every citation and award issued and was a hero, many times over. He was considered a modern day hero for what he accomplished in Washington. The old soldier didn't think much of Lloyd's supposed good works. How could anyone think of such a bleeding heart as a hero? The credo, *there are losses in war*, suited the old soldier much better.

The old soldier was a veteran of so many wars he'd stopped counting. He knew that Lloyd's flowery words were so much crap and nothing. There would always be a war somewhere in the world, young men would die fighting it, and other men would feel it necessary to uselessly honor them with bronze and stone.

He remembered being a young boy, begging and going to military school, which meant he had been a soldier nearly his entire life. Soldiering taught him two things—only the strong survive; and the small, the weak, didn't deserve to live. He could spot a weakling at a thousand paces. With his service to his country ended, his self imposed mission was to eliminate one weakling at a time, along with those who protected them.

He waited years for his current prey to slip-up, but, so far, that hadn't happened. He looked for them everywhere. They were never anywhere. He hoped they would appear at The Wall on this day, but that hadn't happened either. He hoped to catch a modest salute across Constitution Gardens. There wasn't one. Nor was there silent eye contact or a surreptitious wink. The trip had largely been a waste, but there was still the contents of The Wall. He might get lucky and find some crumb of assistance. It was a simple matter of patience...and he was a very patient man.

He stood in line while family after family and friends and buddies each took their turn looking up the location of the names of the dead—panel number, line number. Finally it was his turn. He scanned the pages. Not only was the needle-in-a-haystack not there, it was never anywhere he looked and he looked everywhere.

During the last fifteen years of his professional career, he found and silently destroyed many. Two of his latest targets were real. The remaining four, though one had a name, were like phantoms. He hired private detectives, even asset searchers to invade IRS records, but they always came up empty. It was impossible, but somehow, that name had no record of any kind. No Service or Social Security number, no disability or death benefits, no physicals, no Basic, and most especially no fiche.

Even when the government disavowed all knowledge of a soldier, when every record on him disappeared, including dental records from back home, there was always the damn fiche. The government never destroyed that. Good or bad, the fiche was forever. If that soldier existed, there would be records somewhere, and where there was one, the others would not be far away. But in that moment, for the life of him, he didn't understand how any of them, let alone all of them, simply dropped off the face of the earth.

CHAPTER 31

▼

WASHINGTON, D.C.— JANUARY, 1983

Tre and Harvey sat at the bar of the Wet Whistle Pub. They each ordered a scotch-rocks and, metaphorically speaking, began crying in their beer. They had found the correct missions and the man responsible for their disastrous conclusions. But, without any sort of tangible proof, something beyond the word of a man who spent time in a mental health facility, and two obscure mission records, they were in the exact same boat as before—a boat going nowhere. And they'd been sitting in that boat for a good, long time.

The bartender served their drinks and stepped away, picked up a dish towel and began polishing bar glasses. He was beyond tired of hearing guys go on-and-on about their time in *The 'Nam*, when they either never served or, like himself, were stationed so far to the rear that they virtually saw no sort of combat at all. It was revolting. But something about the look of the men made him keep half an ear on their conversation.

"There's got to be proof somewhere! There just has to!" Tre drank his scotch in one quick swig, then banged his glass on the bar in utter frustration. "Without it, we have the same nothing as before. We're this close!" There was half an inch between his index finger and thumb. "We can't allow Fred and Ginger to be written-off as bad leadership, when the SOB's responsible! Someone's gotta make him pay!"

They were attempting to have a private conversation, *soto voce*, but the bar tender had ears like a bat and heard every word. His mind said, the tall one was the real thing, maybe the shorter one was too, and somehow, they knew about Fred Astair and Ginger Rogers. The terrified voice of one of Ginger's young Sergeants was with him every moment of his life, forever repeating the three words he didn't have enough rank to act upon himself. *Request...immediate...extraction.*

The bartender walked over. "You guys need a refill."

"No, we're good," Harvey answered amiably, looking up.

"It wasn't a question." The bartender's response was brusque, his eyes lit with a strange fire Harvey'd never seen before, his features more like stone than flesh and blood. He set a third glass on the counter, poured each of them another scotch-rocks, and one straight-up for himself. He lifted the glass to his lips and scanned their faces over its rim without drinking. "You serve in The 'Nam?"

"Me, yes. Him, no," Tre answered for both of them.

"See any action?"

"Some," was Tre's hesitant reply.

So, the tall guy was the real thing—one word answers to questions about the war. It was a good policy. Tell nothing, unless you're asked, and even then. Besides, what could you say? It was worthless and too many died?

"What was your M.O.S.?" (Military Operations Specialty).

"Artillery. You?"

"Unofficially, I was Step-'N-Fetch-It to an asshole. Mostly I was his clerk and got to work in his quarters. Pretty plush by in-country standards. His bunker had an air conditioner and an actual wooden floor. We had steak, cold beer, even ice cream. On the surface, it looked like a cushy little job—no action and I'd get to come home in one piece. My folks were delirious about my post. I guess I was too, at first. By day two, in-country, it was obvious I was in fuckin' purgatory." He shook his head in self-loathing. "How many different ways can a guy be wrong about the same fuckin' thing?" It was a rhetorical question, for which he already had the answer.

"I can't hardly remember typing up an after action report that didn't include a high number of casualties and so many dead...," his voice trailed off. "But who was I gonna tell? And without going public, what the hell reason could I give for requesting a transfer? So, I kept my mouth shut and typed my little reports."

The bartender exhibited all the signs of having seen the uglier side of war, but there was something else. Every Vet Tre ever met, who saw action, was a little twitchy—even he would never allow himself to be seated with his back to a door. This guy wasn't just twitchy, he was spooked and periodically looked over his shoulder for something or someone that wasn't there. He looked like he needed a few good nights' sleep, maybe more than a few. Tre looked at him skeptically. "You headed somewhere with this, buddy?"

"It's Benny. Benny Walker."

"OK. Benny, you headed somewhere with this?"

"I've been sitting on something for better'n a decade, but there was no one to go to; no one I was sure would listen or believe me; no one who wouldn't toss what I have into the circular file, then disappear me over it. I don't sleep much. I'm afraid going near my family will put them in danger. I got no life and no friends. I can't keep a regular job, so, the owner of the pub, Robertson, he lets me tend bar. The guy's a Vet himself, so he mostly understands…and he pays in cash. No trail. I usually tune everyone out, then you guys walk in. I don't even know what made me eaves drop. Can't remember the last time I cared enough to do that. You want my official M.O.S.?"

Tre and Harvey sat wide-eyed, nodding.

"Radio operator, at the rear—Fire Base…Sierra…Echo…X-ray."

CHAPTER 32

▼

CUMMINGS POINT, VA—
JANUARY, 1983

When Lloyd left the service, he severed all direct contact with his friends—it was too risky. As a Senator, living life in the public eye, getting piece after piece of unpopular legislation passed, anyone could have tapped his phone and his life. No calls and no mail, until something real was found…and could be proved.

Lloyd's lawyer, Irwin Cohen, became the go-between. He was visible, approachable, did good works for the community, and, with quiet help from the Saunders Foundation, established battered women's shelters, before it was popular. He was also attached to one of the most prestigious law firms in the D.C. area. It was decided best that Harvey, not a Super-hero, initiate contact and a meeting was scheduled.

*   *   *   *

Like their mothers, Jean and Juliet, Lloyd and Irwin had been good friends since childhood, but as of the night Lloyd and Junior found their mother half dead at the bottom of the front stairs, their lives became irrevocably intertwined. Lloyd paced a rut in the terrazzo of Walter Reed's waiting room, but once word came that Jean would survive, he and Junior exited the hospital without so much as a word to anyone, and found a pay phone on the street.

Senior finals at Yale had ended a week or so earlier and Irwin was home on break. Lloyd called, impatient, as the phone on the other end rang. The words of the strange, young girl—*You'll need to put these in a safe place until you find a lawyer you can trust*, bounced around his head. He was leaving for Basic. His next destination was Vietnam. No telling what might happen to him there. He was in no mood to waste time looking for what he could build himself. Without preamble, he spoke the second Irwin answered.

"I need a lawyer I can trust." Lloyd demanded.

Irwin recognized the restive voice. "What can I do to help?"

"Go to law school and pass the Bar."

CHAPTER 33

▼

CUMMINGS POINT, VA

Late November, 1968

Lloyd came home on a one week Convalescent Leave, shortly after the Cambodian field incident. It was a terrible risk to travel alone—be separated from the others, even for a short period, but there was no other option. He requested a meeting with Henry Simpson and Toller Donahue, the owners and senior partners of Simpson & Donahue, Attorneys-at-Law. The Cummings name and the money behind it, the Saunders millions, were well known in and around the Point and the money had a very loud voice. Being the one in charge of that money meant Simpson and Donahue took the meeting. Lloyd requested a young, aggressive attorney to handle all matters for his family and the Foundation. He wanted Irwin Cohen, who just passed the Bar.

"We have several more experienced attorneys here on staff," Henry Simpson answered first. "I'm sure that any one of them can handle anything you or the Foundation need done."

When Henry and Toller received Lloyd's request for a meeting, they knew the Saunders Foundation was in need of legal representation. It was common knowledge that Jean Cummings handled every aspect of administering The Foundation herself, but disappeared several years previous, but not before transferring control of all the Saunders money to Lloyd. As he had not yet reached the age of majority, every cent was put into trust and, for the time being, invested in U.S. Treasury Bonds, due to mature in two more years. Everything else—the work, the endowments and scholarships, came to a grinding halt and, most especially, no one was generating any fees.

The fact was, the partners decided they would act on behalf of the Saunders family, divide the work and pocket all of the billable hours themselves, should the opportunity present itself. It was simply a matter of directing the conversation toward that end. Adding another attorney to the payroll and/or taking a percentage of the money generated by administering the Saunders Foundation, was not in the cards. Not as far as they were concerned. When Lloyd shook his head and made a face that said some unknown was unacceptable, Simpson and Donahue had their opening.

"If it would create a higher confidence level, Toller and I will personally handle all legal representation on your family's behalf."

Each blink of Simpson's eyes made Lloyd envision cartoon dollar signs registering fees. He wondered how many billable hours could be charged-out for investigating a Pointman, or pretending to, and then get the necessary proof to press charges. Beyond not trusting Simpson or Donahue, they were each in their fifties. It was imperative to have someone in place who was young. It was even more crucial they know how to keep silent.

Irwin was in need of a post, and not above taking a hand-up from a friend in a high and influential place. He was also nearly family and his stake in The Saunders Foundation was personal—his Law School career was purchased with a Foundation scholarship. He was forever mindful that, should the whereabouts of Jean and Junior Cummings come to light, it might be certain death for all of them—Irwin and his mother included. Lloyd's plans were in place—a premature death for any of them did not figure into the equation.

"Irwin Cohen is the man I want, but if he isn't the man for you, then he's not the man for you."

A look of quiet victory crossed their faces and did not escape Lloyd's notice. "I'm so glad we were able to come to an..." Toller paused, overly gracious, "an understanding.

Lloyd understood their position all right—*greed and anti-semitism*. "I thought, surely you would be interested in associating yourselves with The Saunders Foundation, but if the answer is no, then, it's no. It won't be easy, but I'm sure I'll eventually persuade Mr. Cohen to open his own firm to handle the management of The Foundation and my own extensive, personal, legal work. Of course, there will be occasions when he'll require knowledgeable co-council. Such a shame that co-council won't come from your firm. Good day, gentlemen."

*   *   *   *

December, 1983

Fast forward to 1983. Enter the Northeast corner office of Simpson & Donahue, Attorneys-at-Law—the office of Irwin Cohen, youngest man to make partner in the firm's long history. Harvey explained what they found. Irwin contacted the principals to apprise them of the change in their situation. Each was crushed, but not surprised.

Irwin located their man through the VA. He lived in a small apartment and lead a spartan life. A private detective followed him and got a handle on his daily routine. He arrived at a tiny office in the city by 5:00 AM, stayed till eleven, worked-out at a nearby gym, ate a quick basic lunch, practiced at a firing range, then returned to the office, which he did not leave until 5:30 PM. He left his apartment so early that the FBI was forced to go outside standard procedure and arrest him at his office rather than his home.

Irwin presented their findings to the Army Board of Inquiry—Criminal Investigation Division, and the Grand Jury. He advised both bodies of their suspect's whereabouts and schedule.

The Judge issued an arrest warrant. Isaiah Jefferson and two star General, Warren Hollander, went to prefer charges. Isaiah read the list of criminal charges, General Hollander those involving the military. Their man was handcuffed, arms behind his back, and removed from his office, without incident or resistance. Although Isaiah advised against it, Lloyd and the soldiers insisted on witnessing the final chapter of their nightmare.

When he saw them waiting on the sidewalk with Lloyd, he knew they had to be the famed Super-heroes—the focus of his decade-long search. Invisible blinders kept him from seeing anything but his own mission—finding them. It never occurred to him that they might be looking for him. He picked the moment he passed them on the sidewalk to squirm away from his escorts and run up into Lloyd's face screaming.

"Where's my wife?"

Lloyd returned the favor. "She's nothing but a punching bag to you. Why do you care where she is?"

"Why isn't your business!" He snapped.

"That may be," Lloyd's face was flame red, but his voice was dead calm, "but the hundreds of American soldiers who died for nothing because of you. They are. If I had been among them, you'd have gotten away with mass murder."

"That *was* my plan," his voice was indignant.

"You mean to say that you had them slaughtered; because you wanted me dead?" Lloyd was incredulous.

"If you must know!" He defiantly stuck out his chin. "There are losses in every war."

"War didn't kill those boys, you did, trying to kill me. Why would you do such a thing?"

"There's a punishment for every crime."

"Since when is preserving someone's life a crime?"

"Since the life wasn't yours to preserve. Anyone that can't protect themselves, doesn't deserve to live. The collateral damage couldn't be helped," he added indifferently.

"Collateral damage! You unbelievable son-of-a-bitch! Those boys were America's young, her future." Lloyd tried to slug him, but Carl and Poopsie anticipated the moment and interceded. The adrenaline coursing thru Lloyd's body was nearly as strong as both of them combined and they were so preoccupied with holding him back they failed to notice Tre's blood come to a boil. His fist connected with the man's jaw. When he fell backward to the ground, Tre kicked him in the ribs, hard.

"That's for Phil Baker." Tre spit on him. "Rot in Hell!"

General Hollander pushed Tre several steps back. "That'll do!"

Before the man could respond, Isaiah did. "I advise you to say no more. Remember...," he produced the recording device he promised would tape everything that was said and it was visibly running, "...anything you say now can, and will, be used against you in a court of law." The man heeded the warning. "Take him away," Isaiah told the others on his team.

*   *   *   *

The legend was correct, the fish-keepers found the pusher. The Army had retired him which entitled them to return him to active duty, if only for the purpose of a Court Martial. Everyone involved was grateful and relieved it had worked out that way. A just punishment would finally be meted-out. There was more than enough evidence to take to trial and get a conviction.

Five big men, who spent fifteen years protecting each other with silence, wordlessly stood side-by-side, and watched the FBI's shiny, black, unmarked car drive away—Colonel Walter Bristol Cummings, Sr., in its back seat.

CHAPTER 34

▼

BOSTON, MA—1996
THE RETURN

"Pop-op!" The baby cried excitedly, reaching for the motionless man in the bed. "Pop-op!" She squirmed.

"Sweetheart, please be still." The woman holding her objected and the baby settled down.

"It's OK. Give her to me." The doctor took the baby into his arms and held her near enough to the patient to touch him. "Do you have something to say, honey?"

"Pop-op, come home!" She demanded. "Come home!" The baby laid her small hand on his cheek and the man in the bed roused at the little girl's touch.

His eyes fluttered open as he heard his own groggy voice ask, "Who's making that infernal racket?"

The doctor lifted the baby back up and rested her weight on his hip.

"Pop-op home!" She baby squealed with delight and clapped her hands together.

"Are you OK soldier?" The doctor asked.

Although his eyes refused to focus and it was too soon to have any second memory, the terrible pain in his left leg said the Overlap was over. He was back in his own Time. "Who wants to know?" The answer from the blurry image would confirm whether he had been successful. Tre nearly held his breath.

"Houser, sir. Special assignment. William Houser-Craig, at your service, dad." He offered a quick salute. "I believe you saved my life out there on the street. I owe you."

Tre pressed his eyelids tightly closed, knowing there was only one response. "You save me next time, and we'll call it even." Finally able to relax, he took a deep breath. Second memories, of their altered life, began taking their rightful place and would remain.

"I believe this is yours," William reached into the pocket of his Army issue pants—the ones he always wore to work, instead of scrubs. He extracted the item Eric Walters retrieved from the gutter on their scavenger hunt and let the artifact extend to its full length. Well, it wasn't *exactly* the one that they found. That necklace was Army issue. This was a shiny replica of the ancient dog-tags the Army let him keep, when he retired into quiet obscurity.

The two old tags listed his name, service number, religion, blood type, gas mask size and branch of the service and served several functions. They were basic ID and the thin pieces of metal would have spoken for him, in case he could not speak for himself. While on active duty, the long chain hung around Tre's neck; the short one was stuffed inside his left boot. Together, the chains could be used to mark Time—in the event he was taken prisoner. The short one could be used alone, as an impromptu toe-tag—in the event he was killed.

The necklace William returned was a three hundred sixty-five bead, white-gold chain with two small, shiny, rectangles both hanging from it. Its fifty-two bead partner hung uselessly thru the hole of one of the tags; because, now, there was very little risk of the swift and urgent need for a toe-tag. These tags were an expression of thanks for years of dedication and teaching.

Tre's hand closed around the necklace. His second memory expanded to include two sets of similar tags, received the night of his and Carl's and Poopsie's retirement party. Each man's son offered his father a sharp salute and a small box from their current crop of *boys*. Each man returned the salute, then opened his box. Three former soldiers were left without words for their emotions.

The rest of that particular second memory said he removed the old tags from his neck and stuck them into his pant pocket. At home, after the party, he placed them in the small gift box lined with cotton, taped it shut, and never planned to open it again. The Army's tags would spend the remainder of his life in that box, tucked in the back of a dresser drawer.

*   *   *   *

They had been in the service exactly thirty years. The Army was the only life they knew. It was the life which allowed them to save so many lives, their own included. They saw active and fought for other people's freedom in many parts of the globe. They worked with the Delta Force during the Iran Hostage Rescue. They were there in Liberia helping to protect the U.S. Embassy. They landed on Greneda along with the Eighty-Second Airborne. They were part of the ground forces that went into Panama. They saw the oil fires and smoke of Dessert Storm. They went into Somalia. They were part of the forces that went into Haiti to act as police, when the Haitian police were starving and beating people, and they stayed until the politicians got things straightened out.

"We didn't know what to get you, sirs," the spokesperson said, "but it had to be something meaningful. These were Molly's idea," he turned to her and offered a smile, which she returned. "She said the best part of her life was spent with you guys as soldiers and even now that you're retiring, she'll always love the soldier in you, and without it, she would have lost everything."

The three retiring Colonels gave each other knowing looks.

"I knew better than to pry and ask what that meant," he continued, "but was certain you, sirs, would understand."

Tre now remembered each wife stepping forward, removing the gift from its box and placing the shiny, new chain around her husband's neck. As the three men leaned forward, to receive them, Molly, Dorothea, and Amy began reciting the quote that laced all of their lives together thru Time. It was the few lines Molly borrowed from Dylan Thomas all those years ago and gave to Tre on a night she had nothing else to offer to protect his life. Every man in the room knew it, so very well.

"Do not go gentle into that goodnight," their wives began.

The room erupted as their boys finished it, cheering. "Rage! Rage against the dying of the light!"

*   *   *   *

An unfamiliar man stepped forward and William moved aside. The man took a pen-light from the pocket of his hospital coat and examined Tre's eyes. "Do you know what happened?"

"A car and I had a difference of opinion over who had the right of way."

"I guess that's one way to look at it," the man gave a light chuckle. "Do you know what year it is?"

"I was hoping for 1996." It was almost a question.

"Very good. You've got a busted leg, but, all things considered, you're in pretty good shape. You'll be on crutches for a while, but I'll go out on a limb and say you're going to be just fine," the doctor announced.

William sidled up to the doctor and rested a hand on his shoulder, as if they were very good friends. "I guess introductions are in order. Dr. Eric Walters, this is my dad." The two men shook hands.

"It's good to finally meet you, sir." Eric said warmly, and as if he had been waiting to do so for a very long time.

"He's been looking after you since the accident," William explained. "He passed the story to me and supplied the needles and antibiotic for Lloyd."

"But, who told *you*? Who *are* you?" Tre couldn't comprehend.

"This is an amazing family, chock full of little heroes." He smiled at the toddler in William's arms and kissed her cheek. In return she reached around his neck and hugged him tightly, like *they* were very old friends…or maybe future friends, in the past. Tre could hardly believe it, but he understood who the little girl was.

"In another life, everyone called me Junior," the doctor confessed. "Walter Bristol Cummings, Junior. Lloyd is my brother. After the night the old man beat our mother so badly, Lloyd arranged for her and me to get new lives. The old goat's such a squirelly old bastard, we knew that, if we went with the obvious, we could hide in plain sight. I took Lloyd's middle name for my new first name, then we turned Walter into Walters, and here we are. In fact, here we all *really* are. Everyone, that is, except Lloyd and Michelle." He looked at his watch. "Their plane landed half an hour ago and he's due here any minute. You know how it is when you're famous," he grinned, "everyone wants an interview.

"Lloyd called earlier, to remind me that today was the day. That's how I was here almost immediately after you were hit, just in time to tell William what he needed to know…and do. Now that you're back, and once Lloyd and Michelle get here, we might consider this night our first official Anniversary, so to speak."

Everyone in the room agreed. The night was something to be celebrated annually.

Molly! Where was she? If William and Junior were here, Molly would be too. There she was, standing beside William with her hand on his arm. His Molly, standing so close he could touch her. How had he lived five minutes without her, let alone nearly thirty years?

"Those foolish boys nearly killed you. We were all so worried, frantic with worry." She flew into his arms.

He couldn't believe he was actually holding her, breathing in the smell of her—Dove soap and Molly. He totally forgot his resolve never to allow anyone, or anything, to make him cry again and a tear ran down his cheek into Molly's hair.

Now that the flood gates were opened, his head swam with thousands of second memories of their life together. Wonderful memories of growing up with his rightful family—a family where Ethan Craig, not Jack Makepeace, was his father, from the beginning. A family where he wasn't the often beaten Matthew Martin Makepeace (AKA Tre), but Ethan Matthew Craig—The Third. It was a life where Coach's nick-name for him started out being just that—*The Third*, but soon decided it sounded too much like *The Turd*, so he eventually opted for the Italian for three. Everyone, except his mother, had called him Tre ever since.

He touched his face, trying to feel the thickened scar that had been a constant reminder of Jack's most severe beating, more than forty years earlier. It was gone, like it was never there, along with *nearly* all of the memory of the whoopin' that put it there. He suspected the scar on his back was, likewise, gone.

One second memory said that in this life, there was no compassionate leave to attend Connie and Ethan's wedding, since they were married before he was born. He did, however, elect to come home between tours and was picked up by a man, later introduced as Connie's cousin. William's letter about Molly was waiting for him on his bed. He now understood that Connie's cousin was himself, still hanging around after saving his mother from a speeding car, a drunken Jack Makepeace behind the wheel—killed after being ejected from the car as it flipped over.

Tre now remembered speeding to Brighton, Massachusetts, on that same January afternoon, in 1969, to persuade Molly to be his wife. He recalled not having to try too hard. Later that same night, Molly went into labor and he was in the delivery room when William was born. The sensation of the nurse putting his son into his arms, to hold for the first time, the clearest memory of all.

He remembered receiving letters from Molly—one about the night William had colic so bad that she walked the floor with him 'til 3:00 AM, and how he had the nerve to puke all over her, then immediately fall asleep. Tre remembered laughing when he pictured it. And he remembered not laughing after hearing about William's near drowning and the man who saved him. He remembered teaching William to ride a bike, Little League, his graduation from Medical

School, and the day he married K-K-K-Katie, who never minded that he and her father sang that corny old song at every family gathering. Most of the time, she sang along. After all, she was the only one in the family with a theme song.

Finally added to Tre's list of second memories was the day Katie gave birth. Tre and Katie's dad entered the hospital lobby together, shortly after the baby was born, escorted each other to the elevator, did their own rendition of Chip and Dale's "Oh, no, I insist, after you" routine, then marched arm-in-arm, up the hallway of the maternity ward, humming Katie's theme song. By the time they reached the door to her room, they were skipping and singing like children, "K-K-K-Katie, beautiful Katie. She's the only g-g-g-girl that I adore. And when the m-m-m-moon shines over the cow shed, she'll be waiting for me at the k-k-k-kitchen door." They left a wake of laughter behind them.

"Have you decided on a name?" Katie's father asked.

"The jury's still out," she said, tenderly cuddling her daughter. "William and I can't agree. What names do you and two like?" The men gazed at the little girl, took the quickest beat, then answered in unison, "I like Emily."

In this life, things were significantly different. Tre hadn't spent his life with no family of his own and no Molly to love him. All of the people he had ever cared about were here—in this room and waiting outside to get in. This was the life he heard about for years and now they were all getting to live it. The old life was beginning to feel like a bad dream. Emily saw to that. She would do for all of them, and set in stone, what they had not been able to do for themselves.

"Where's my girl?" Tre asked Emily, reaching for her.

"Pop-op!" The little girl reached for him, wriggling out of her fathers arms and into Tre's. She could never get enough of him. She covered his face with dozens of little kisses, then wiped away the remnants of his tear with her tiny hand. "Don't cry," she said soothingly, then climbed onto his chest, put her head on his shoulder and hugged him tightly. "Pop-op home!"

"Yes." Tre held her close and rested his huge hand on the back of her head. "I'm home." It was late. It had been a long day for everyone and they were all exhausted. Emily yawned, snuggled down, closed her eyes, and promptly fall asleep.

$$* \qquad * \qquad * \qquad *$$

The police arrived, after the car and bicycle accident, and took a full report. At first, they thought the car was stolen from some out-of-town renter, who wouldn't know it was missing until morning. They'd find themselves financially responsible for the cost of the car and utility pole. IDs said the joy-riders were each under seventeen and would have been booked as careless juveniles, except the IDs turned out to be phony and the Police dug deeper.

The plate was run thru the Registry of Motor Vehicles. It, and the car, belonged to the Logan Airport lot of Easy Car Rental. It had been rented by a company, called Sones Management, and was delivered to a specifically requested parking space in the garage of the Ritz Hotel. Sones Management had been hired by a dummy corporation and it soon became obvious there was more going on than originally met the eye. The police summoned the Lieutenant in charge of the Traffic Division of accident reconstruction. He was already on his way.

He hated this shit—pulling extra shifts, at night. His extra shift had ended and was supposed to have been the last of his overtime. He already changed out of his uniform into street clothes and was almost home when his beeper went off, calling him back to the job. Fine! He drove into the hospital parking garage reminding himself why he wanted the extra duty in the first place—big anniversary coming up and he promised his wife that this was the year they would finally take that cruise. He was running out of time to put the money together, so he took all the extra duty the Department offered him. So, now there'd be a few extra dollars to blow in the ship's casino.

He located the responding officers in the Emergency Room. They advised him that the vehicle was already checked for contraband—no drugs, no alcohol. The boys were definitely on *something*, maybe coke or pills, but the car itself was clean.

The Lieutenant checked the vehicle himself. There wasn't much, not even skid marks. His well trained eye said it was a total and would be towed to the impound lot in Dorchester. Inside, the air-bags had deployed and the only personal items were half a pack of cigarettes, and a disposable lighter. He took all the necessary photographs, then sat on the car's front passenger seat making notes. Something sticking out of the closed glove box, caught his eye—the corner of a piece of paper. It practically screamed his name.

He popped open the glove box to find a Police composite. Most of them were unremarkable, but he remembered this one. He should. He built it more than twenty years earlier, when he was still a Detective. The transfer to Traffic Division came at his own request, a short time afterward. He enjoyed being a Detective, but too many cases went unsolved when their trails went cold. The Accident Reconstruction Unit of the Traffic Division provided the opportunity to close more cases, and he liked closure. He never considered the transfer a step down;

just a different kind of Detective work. Through the years, he kept active files, for each composite he made, where the case remained unsolved, and periodically reviewed them. His own habits had turned the image in his hand into an old friend.

Why did these kids have one of his antique composite? How did they get it? The better question was; where did they get it? And why did he continue to feel that he knew the guy…from somewhere? He smoothed the crumpled paper, folded it and tucked it into the inside pocket of his jacket.

What the fuck was going on? He reentered the hospital and spoke to the officer who was finishing the paperwork on the pedestrian the kids had hit. The guy was going to be OK, but the family was pressing charges. At the very least, there were the matters of failure to stop for a pedestrian and driving negligently, not to mention the DUI. The boys might be underage, but something weird was going on. They would be questioned down at the station, maybe even booked.

The Lieutenant was directed to ICU. He wanted to speak to the pedestrian, if he was up to it. There were so many anxious relatives in the room that the Detective was one among the many waiting in the hall for a turn to see him. He approached four older women in a huddle. Two were salt and pepper brunettes, one was black, and they were each trying to console a still pretty blond with short-cropped hair.

"Excuse me, ladies," he pulled out his hip badge, "I'm Lieutenant Allan Reynolds, Boston P.D. Could I have a moment?"

The blond, visibly agitated, looked anxiously in the direction of the pedestrian's room.

"Another time, if you don't mind," Fran Summers spoke up.

"We're waiting to see Connie's son," Jean Walters added.

"That's why I'm here, about the accident."

"Accident, my ass!" Connie harumfed. "Worthless trash with a driver's license. License to kill, is more like it. He's tall like a tree, shoulders out to here." Connie showed him. "What? He isn't big enough? They couldn't see him?"

"Yes, Ma'am," the Lieutenant's voice was respectful. Tall like a tree? Shoulders out to here? That's where he knew him! Biggest son-of-a-bitch he ever knew up close. In a flash, the paper he retrieved from the glove box was unfolded, the image examined again. The face *was* someone he knew, but older and that's how he got side-tracked.

"Do not go gentle into that good-night," he half mumbled the words.

"Rage. Rage against the dying of the light," the four ladies finished. "It's Dylan Thomas," Connie stated the obvious.

He handed the crumpled and creased composite to Connie, and asked the four ladies to look at it. "Do any of you know this man?"

"Where did you get this?"

"Do you know this man?" He asked Connie again.

"This is an old drawing of my son." Connie had a strange panicky look. The composite contained the scar on Tre's cheek, the one he no longer had. She was right all those years ago. Someone *was* looking for him.

"This is your son!" He poked the paper. "This is the man who was run-down?" Dismayed, he poked the paper again. "*This* man? You're sure?"

"She knows her own son, when she sees him, Lieutenant," Carrie Jefferson assured him.

Reynolds snatched back the paper and stared at the face, in disbelief. His mind replayed the mother's words. *This is an old drawing of my son.* OK, the paper was a little yellow and beat-up, but how did she know the picture itself was old? It was a crappy little detail, but The Police Force paid him to zero in on crappy little details exactly like that one.

He allowed his mind to drift back over the years and remember that the weird guy, who said he was mugged, but didn't really look like it, asked for a copy of the composite. Did he manage to take one when no one was looking? Was that why he came to the police station in the first place; he needed a tool?

Without thinking, Reynolds barged his way into the victim's room, braced himself at the doorway, the composite flapping in his hand. He looked from the composite, to the man in the bed, then back to the composite. Same man, same age—but not the same age as the day he built it, twenty-something years ago. What the…?

"May I help you?" Eric placed himself firmly in front of the intruder, trying to block his path. They worked too hard and waited too long to screw-up now. He wasn't taking any chances. Keep to the original plan—no one saw Tre until he saw them and found out who they were and what they wanted.

"No!" Reynolds shoved Eric aside, muscling his way into the room.

The child sleeping on Tre's chest was their future. "Emily!" He warned, losing his balance, falling backward into the wall.

In a blink, Emily was on the bed, Tre's body providing a protective shield for hers. The man stepped to the foot of the bed and froze, as if rooted to the spot. Taking no chances either, Isaiah, Carl and Poopsie strong-armed him, but he made no move toward anyone and no attempt to extract himself. It was as if he didn't notice anyone else, beside himself and Tre, was in the room.

They locked eyes. "You Craig?" His voice was firm and demanding without also being ominous. "Sergeant Craig?"

Something about the man's face or his stance told the soldiers that this stranger was not the unknown menace that was lurking in the shadows, and he called Tre *Sergeant Craig*, like he knew him. They each asked themselves, *does he know him?*

"It's Colonel, now," Tre offered, a fraction less tense. "U.S. Army, retired, but yes, I'm Matthew Craig." His eyes lingered. "And you are…"

"Lieutenant Allan Reynolds, Boston P.D." Isaiah, Carl and Poopsie let go, so he could flash his hip badge. "I passed thru Dix in '69. You?"

"I was a Drill Sergeant there in '69."

"Yeah, my Drill Sergeant," he informed the assembled crowd. "And your little *Welcome to Basic* speech? It saved my life. It's all these years later and I still never forgot it, or you."

Everyone in the waiting room forgot the hospital's rules and crowded into Tre's room to hear Reynolds weird story.

When the last morning run of Basic was over, on his way into his own barracks, the Drill Sergeant stripped-off his sweaty, short-sleeved t-shirt. There was a broken circular mark on his left arm. Reynolds never saw anything like it, not before or since. He convinced himself it was just a birth mark or a tattoo. Over the years, he'd heard tales of such marks and Overlap. The stories were entertaining enough, but he never believed any of them…until 'Nam.

"My Company was out on patrol and I got hit pretty bad—lost a lot of blood. They said I was in shock, that my mind was adrift in the quagmire of The 'Nam. Your speech kept repeating in my head—saying I needed your permission to die. You weren't there to give it, so my only option was to keep repeating the Dylan Thomas and live…so I did. The guy who had my back got me out."

After he didn't die on that fateful patrol, Alan Reynolds never again questioned the mark's meaning or needed any convincing that Overlap was real. He was living proof that the unremarkable words and deeds of a Reweaver could remarkably change the outcome of someone else's life. In that moment, in the ICU of Boston Memorial Hospital, he was already a believer and had been for years.

He finished, by explaining about the composite. "The guy was kinda hinky, if you know what I mean. Claimed he was mugged and the thief, I mean you, got away with an expensive necklace. I never spent so long on one mugg. I built this from a transparency kit, no less. Thank god we're on the computer now. Even then I said the guy looked more like a soldier than a mugger." He displayed the composite. "Don't you just love it when you're right!" Then he addressed only Tre, again as if they were the only two people in the room. "Man, some guy's been hunting you down for over twenty years. And somehow, he knew what you'd look like twenty years later. Coincidence?"

"You believe in coincidence?" Tre asked.

"No," his answer was firm. "No I don't."

"In that case..." Tre told the Lieutenant his own story.

✳   ✳   ✳   ✳

"You know, the station could have leased those Identi-kits, but they bought them, and," he beamed, proud of himself, "I'm a pack-rat. I never throw the first thing away. My old kit's still in my storage cabinet. Mary, that's my wife, she's always after me about keeping stuff I don't use anymore. Looks like it finally paid-off. I've still got a pretty good memory for faces and I bet I could build a composite of the guy that had me build the one of you. If I can, and I can lift some good prints off of the kit he used, maybe we can get to the bottom of this."

The trail was poorly covered—20K didn't go as far as it used to. With the help of a reliable snitch, a low-life named Hurney, that Reynolds knew from his days as a detective, the car and the boys in it were traced back to one, Colonel Walter Bristol Cummings, Sr., serving Time at Leavenworth Prison for crimes against the U.S. government. Tre's *accident* had been a hired hit—bought and paid for twenty-one years earlier. A new charge would be brought against the Colonel. Conspiracy to commit murder.

CHAPTER 35

▼

BROOKLINE, MA—2011
EPILOGUE

*　　　*　　　*　　　*

For most of her life, Connie felt that something in her past was wrong, or missing, but she was never able to put her finger on exactly what. As of tonight, she would discover that it was not some*thing*, but some*one*. Someone was missing.

*　　　*　　　*　　　*

Connie awoke in the middle of the night, holding Emily in her arms. A second memory of them falling asleep on the couch together, held fast to a previous memory of being a frightened teenager in Home-Ec class. She was seventeen, and crazy with worry. The day before, she learned that she was pregnant.

Vice-Principal Barton had just introduced a substitute, Connie knew was herself, and she was about to teach the class how to bake a pie. That was old news. Now there was a second memory of the Vice-Principal returning, a moment later, with a student in tow—a girl in a candy-striper uniform. That was new news. The girl was assigned to the only work-station with one student that day…the one where Connie was getting out supplies. That student was the girl in her arms—her Emily, so determined that Connie should believe her. Her voice was low enough that no one else heard, but she was direct and relentless. ﹐

"I can't allow you to screw-up all of our lives! Pop-op needs you and Popi to be together from the beginning." Emily wasn't getting thru. "You must protect him." Connie's hands instinctively flew to her belly, to shield her unborn child. "Everyone's depending on me and I'm depending on *you*. This is the moment of change!" Emily smacked the counter. I'm here to help you." She pushed up her left sleeve. "Let me. You must believe me."

The girl's face was nearly a carbon copy of Horace Yellowfeather—his mouth, his eyes, his fair hair. The mark of the Time-piece said she was responsible for traveling to the beginning, to secure the future. There would be consequences, if she failed. Pure stubbornness was all that made Connie doubt her. She could hardly believe her own words. "Why should I?"

"Because it already happened—all of it; the pies, your nightmare, the Overlaps, everything. Call Ethan tonight. Ask him where he learned to skip a rock. I taught him. Ask him who Jane Doe is. It's you, eighteen years from now. And ask how he got the money for College and Medical School. I told him how. Give me your word that you won't do anything stupid until you speak to Popi, I mean Ethan. It's a simple phone call and Papa Horace said you could. Please, say you'll do it! It's one day."

Connie's mind was already made up. She refused to ruin everything Ethan worked so hard for. On the other hand, the girl was right. It was only one day. One phone call. Jack Makepeace would still be there tomorrow. It couldn't hurt to ask Ethan about the things Emily said. Long distance calls were expensive, but her father said she could call once per semester. How did she know that? How did she know her father's name?

"If you know so much, *you* fix everything."

"If I could, I would, but a Reweaver, even a Time-piece, is merely a messenger. I can't change the outcome of things in this Time. Only you can do that. The story's been passed from daughter to daughter, which makes you the key, now. Learn to bake a pie, then go home, call Ethan, and tell everything. Every everything! Just don't wait twenty years to do it this time." As an after thought, Emily added. "And stay away from Jack; he's nothing but trouble."

Connie's voice was little more than a whisper. "How did you know about Jack?"

"Because you made sure I knew. I know this story inside-out." Emily grabbed Connie's left arm and pushed up the sleeve of her blouse. "I know about this mark and that you hide it under sleeves, like it's something to be ashamed of. Don't be ashamed, CeeCee. Be scared and brave. It's not brave, if you're *not* scared. You and I and Pop-op and dad, Time marked all of us. That nightmare you keep having? Choose Jack and he'll make it real for you. You can't really want the scars that go with his beating." Connie's look was pure disbelief; Jack didn't seem like the violent type. "Fine! Doesn't Mrs. Perkins look familiar? She should. She's you. You Overlap the night Jack nearly beats the life out of you to and come here, to teach yourself how to bake a pie.

"One day, you and the others will teach me everything I'll need to know today, *including* how to bake a pie. Remember that! Teach me everything. Tell me *everything*." It sounded like an order; because it was. "The pies are your gift. Which way will you use it? Choose Jack and you'll need it to pull you and Pop-op out of his sewer. Unchoose him and it will persuade the fish-keepers to help us. Make your choice, CeeCee. Popi…or Jack."

"OK," Connie relented. "I'll call Ethan tonight. You have my word." Emily sighed with relief and hugged her—her word was as good as a fact, not just a way to make Emily stop.

"Thank you," she whispered. "Thank you, for all of us." Emily finally smiled. "Now, how about the two of make that pie."

Once their pie was in the oven, Connie finally asked. "Do we do this often?"

"It's our Anniversary specialty." A flash of light sparkled in Emily's eyes, as she picked up the sponge to begin washing their utensils. "Anniversary—with a capital 'A'."

It was the best class Connie ever had—the most fun and their pie was the best one in the class. Emily told Connie the entire story.

"Mrs. Perkins-you won't come over and volunteer the information, but if you *ask*, she'll tell you anything you want to know. I'll go with you, if you want the moral support."

✳   ✳   ✳   ✳

It was late the night Connie called Ethan. He was beyond weary, and bleary-eyed from so many hours of study. He could hardly think, let alone carry on an intelligent conversation, but the sound of Connie's voice revived him a bit. He sat on the floor, next to the phone-desk in the hall, and rested his head against the side of it. Connie asked Emily's questions. He reluctantly confirmed the answers he knew she already had. When they were done, she divulged that she was pregnant. He got so excited that he bumped his head on the edge of the desk, when he jumped up from the floor. They were married during the Christmas break.

Ethan knew Connie Yellowfeather well enough to know she already decided what to do about the baby. Calling, and voluntarily telling him, was not it. He loved her more than anything, but she was the single most stubborn and frustrating woman he ever met. Someone had to have persuaded her to call him at B.U. Ethan hoped that someone was Emily. He remembered how she promised to do everything possible. Was it possible she saved Connie from herself? The more he thought about it, the more he thought Emily could do almost anything. She was his hero. One day he would tell her so.

*   *   *   *

Emily opened her eyes. She was clutching Connie.
"Is it over?"
Connie pulled Emily close. "Yes. It's over."
"Did we do it?" Emily held her breath.
"*You* did it." Connie kissed Emily's cheek.
Was it true? Emily looked at Connie in amazement. Something was different. Emily finally realized what it was and knew that Connie was right. They held each other in the comforting quiet and allowed their minds to relax. Second memories began taking their rightful places.
Connie now remembered convincing Ethan to purchase the Makepeace farm. They moved to Jaffrey the June before Matthew's freshman year of high school. Living on the farm was a huge adjustment and a tremendous amount of work. But Connie knew the importance of owning it, even though it would not become The Peaceful Center for many years.
The farm house was in pretty rough shape, nearly condemned, and required complete renovations, but they managed to live in it throughout the process. Connie handled that project, the incubator and egg collecting. Matthew and their handyman, Chris Wilson, took care of the coops, the chickens, mowing, and the cows. Ethan,…well Ethan had enough to do just being a doctor, although he liked chopping fire wood.
With the encouragement of Carl Summers, the boy from the next farm over, Matthew joined several after-school sports teams—baseball, basketball and football. The boys became close friends, virtually overnight. (Making up for lost Time.) Connie and Carl's mother, Fran, began calling them the Corsican Brothers. If one got a bruise, they were certain the other felt it. The boys helped each other with chores and homework, and spent many an evening listening to Connie tell her story, while they ate her delicious pies.

*   *   *   *

Connie was home, alone, the day Jack Makepeace let himself in thru the kitchen door. "Heck, I'da asked more for the place, if I'da knew it could be fixed up so nice," he startled her.

Connie sprang from her chair at the breakfast table, yelping, as she turned to face the intruder. Her hand flew to her throat. Her heart pounded in her chest. "What do you want?" Jack closed the distance between them and Connie understood exactly what he wanted. She took a few steps backward.

"You was some looker back in High School and ya ain't half bad even now."

Connie tried to step back again, but she was already at the wall. Jack leaned on it, with outstretched arms, blocking her path in every direction, preventing any chance of escape.

"Everyone said you was the Doc's girl, but I always thought that we could be really fine together, if you'da gimme a chance." He leaned in closer. "I always wished we coulda…you know," his words hung in the air.

Connie's adrenaline started to flow—fright with no chance of flight. Her head reeling, she stood up to him anyway (at least verbally). "No, I don't know. And I don't care to know."

"Kinda late to be playin' the virgin. Ain't it? *You* know you like it and *I* know you like it."

"I beg your pardon!" This couldn't be happening. The man she deliberately spent years avoiding, simply waltzed into her home and talked to her like he owned it…and her. She chose Ethan. Emily swore it would change the outcome, but it looked as though the nightmare of this moment was going to happen anyway.

"This is a small town," Jack's voice snatched Connie from her thoughts, "everybody knows everything about everybody. A kid that big ain't no preemie. You was knocked-up when the Doc married you and you didn't get that way from hating it. How many were there before the Doc come along? The kid's big like the Doc, but I bet one of your pies, the kid ain't even his."

Jack's face was uncomfortably close. "Get away from me!" She tried to push him back.

"Come on!" He ignored the protest. "A little free and loose, right here on the kitchen floor. You know you want me. Don't fight it." He dragged the back of his dirty fingers across her cheek and she shuddered.

"Don't touch me!" Connie slapped his face, hard.

His hand flew to his cheek and rubbed the hand print she left behind. "So you like it rough. Excellent!" Jack leaned in, pinning her to the wall with his body. "I can do rough." His voice became husky. "I *like* rough."

Connie tried to push him away again, but it only proved to make him mad. Jack smacked her across the mouth. She kicked and punched, but Jack was bigger and, even drunk, he was stronger. He got in another good hit. She touched her lip. Blood. He began to unbuckle his belt.

From out of nowhere came the sound of Matthew's voice. "Mom! You here?"

"In the kitchen!" Connie cried. "Come quickly, Matthew. Hurry!"

The panic in her voice put wings on his feet and, in a blink, his bulk filled the kitchen doorway. "What are *you* doing here?" He immediately recognized the sleazy man who sold them the farm and didn't like how close he was to Connie. Matthew saw her bloody lip and his blue eyes went black with menace. "She's no match for a *big man* like you," he said facetiously, striding toward them. "Let's, you and me, take it outside," Matthew invited with a malicious smile. "It would be my pleasure."

Jack took several steps back. "No need to get excited over a misunderstanding."

"Really?" Matthew stepped closer, looming over Jack. "Well, let's just see. You dropped by, uninvited, to a property that's no longer yours, and, finding the property occupied, invited yourself to a nice big helping of the lady of the house." He indicated Jack's half unbuckled belt. "That about do it?"

"You don't know that's what happened! She asked for it," he snapped. "She wanted it."

"So, you were minding your own business when she dragged you in, off the street, so she could slap your face?" Jack's hand flew to his still stinging cheek, covering Connie's hand print. "You'll never convince me she ask for the bloody lip? Get out!" Matthew ordered.

Jack made no move to leave. "People around here know this place as The *Makepeace* Farm." He defiantly stuck out his chin. "*I'm* Makepeace." He stabbed himself in the chest with his thumb. "I can come here whenever I like."

"Not any more." Matthew's calm voice didn't betray the anger boiling inside him, but his eyes grew more threatening. "People can call this property any damn thing they want, but as of four years ago, you gave up all rights to set foot on it. We live here now and you're not welcome."

Matthew grew tired of the pointless banter. He couldn't wish the man far enough away from their home or away from his mother. He grabbed Jack by the front of his shirt, dragging the struggling man behind him like a squirming bag of live trash, and headed for the front door. He tossed Jack out onto the porch with such force that he rolled down the front steps. He landed on the freshly paved walkway and struck the back of his head. He touched the now tender spot, then checked his fingers. Blood.

"You know," Matthew warned, "we're doing all sorts of new construction on the farm." He made a hand gesture indicating the entire property. "Anything could happen to a person on a work-site…not all of them good, if you get me. A man might have a nasty accident, maybe take a spill, and hit his head on something. A friendless man could be missing for a very long time, before anyone even knew to look for him. Someone like yourself, for instance, wouldn't want to vanish 'cause he was stupid, now, would he? Be smart!" Matthew instructed. "Leave, and don't come anywhere near here, or her, again." He slammed the door firmly behind him.

Matthew looked at his mother with left over fear. "I don't care how small a town this is and I don't care what everyone else does. You're calling a locksmith, first thing tomorrow, and getting locks for every one of these damn doors and windows. And we're using them! Understand?" Connie nodded. "That guy has no reason to hurt you, but from the look of things…" Matthew shook his head. "We're not taking any chances he'll come back to finish what he started."

"Oh, Matthew!" Connie ran to him—so big, so strong, so solid. "I wasn't expecting you for hours."

He pulled Connie close. "Mrs. Coach went into labor and practice was canceled. You've been so great, handling your pie business and working with the builder, I decided to hear about the new baby tomorrow. Since I had the opportunity, I thought it'd be a nice surprise to come home early to help you."

The fact was, nothing could have delayed his coming home on that particular day. The last five nights in a row, his nightmares provided more and more detail, until nothing was left to the imagination. His gut said go home. His gut was seldom wrong. His mind replayed the nightmare again—he arrived after the beating was over. And the scariest bit was that, somehow, Jack Makepeace was not only Connie's husband, but his father. He was glad the actual event and his life were different from the nightmare.

The nightmares were too short and frightening to analyze. In retrospect, he understood they were the reality from a different outcome—one where that awful man with the bad teeth, who stunk from booze and tobacco spent years beating his mother and him. A cold shiver ran thru him. In this life, the nightmare was a warning that, at that exact and uncertain moment—the moment of change, his mother needed him. Nothing could have kept him from her. If practice had not been a canceled, he would have skipped it—even if it meant getting kicked off the team.

"I hate to think what would have happened, if you hadn't shown up exactly when you did." Connie cringed at a flash of a previous memory—the outcome in her nightmare. A decision, made nearly nineteen years earlier, started a chain reaction that changed the outcome of her altercation with Jack Makepeace. Yes, she had chosen him, but Emily gave her the strength to unchose him. That being the case, this was not one of so many days that he beat her. Nor could he simply walk into her home and start smacking her around. Some conversation, such as it was, was required, followed by a bit of an argument, and a struggle—in other words, a delay. And exactly enough time for Matthew to get home.

"Then forget it." Matthew issued a direct order. It was not a point for discussion. "Let the whole thing go! I was here and you don't ever need to think about that awful man again." He pulled her closer.

"Ouch!" Connie touched her lip. It was swollen. She tipped up her chin, for Matthew to get a better look. "Do I look like a prize fighter?"

"Oh sure," he teased, "I'm always confusing you with Joe Frazier." He made her laugh and the lip started bleeding again. "Way-to-go, slugger." He gave her a pretend punch in the arm.

"No, really? How bad is it?"

He crooked a finger under Connie's chin and turned her head from left to right, to examine the injury. "Not so bad, but I think dad should look at it."

"We have no way to get there. Ethan took the car this morning and it's his late night."

"I'll call Carl. Since he got his own wheels, he jumps at any opportunity to drive anywhere, for anything." Carl drove the three of them to Ethan's clinic in Keene.

Ethan thought Connie was overly preoccupied with the prospect of a scar. He kept assuring her that no visible mark would remain. As he applied a butterfly bandage and ice to her lip, his mind ran to the Jane Doe file, which lived at the back of the last drawer of his file cabinets, stuck in the metal slider, behind the Zs. It sat untouched for years. He mentally reviewed the photos, that served as a silent warning, and understood. One showed Jack had split Connie's lip out onto her face. The split required stitches and would leave behind a permanent reminder. A visible scar. Ethan was relieved not to be taking those ghastly pictures of his beautiful Connie. He was equally relieved not to be remaking that horrid file.

The truth made Connie chose *me*, he reminded himself. A different outcome. He shook off all memory of the folder.

Many years before, Emily explained how Overlap worked, how Time's mark would gift Connie with the recurring dreams of a Reweaver. If Emily's second trip was fully successful, Connie's ugly nightmares would change from a foretelling of reality into a warning with a clear message—Jack was coming to inflict a beating. The horror of it, even as a nightmare, made her thrash about in her sleep, screaming bloody-blue-murder.

No matter what Ethan did, Connie's eyes remained tightly shut, until Matthew appeared in their room. No sooner was he close enough to grab, than she clutched both of them to her, and held on with a strength she didn't possess in everyday life. Only when the nightmare released her did her eyes finally open. It was as if she were both surprised and relieved, like she expected someone else. Ethan concluded it was the *who* in the dream—the same *who* she would have had in the alternate outcome, the *who* named Jack.

Their terrified looks made Connie apologize—allegedly for waking them, for unnecessarily scaring them. But Ethan knew it was for ever allowing the other outcome, even if that alternate life no longer existed.

Matthew's also had nightmares that came with cruel regularity. On the nights Connie didn't wake the house, Matthew did. As a result, their family was perpetually exhausted, but Ethan didn't care about the lost sleep. He was too grateful to Time for providing the nightmares that forced his son to arrive in time to prevent a beating Connie never deserved. Not in either life.

By later that night, the swelling in Connie's lip was nearly gone. She lay in Ethan's arms when her belly got queasy anyway; she broke out in a feverish sweat anyway; she went limp anyway; Overlapped anyway. It was like Emily said— *what is meant to be, must be.*

Emily needed a piece of information that only Connie would know. Choosing Jack was it. Knowing is what made Connie believe and call Ethan at school and confess everything. He wasn't required to like it, and he didn't, but he finally understood why some things can't change, why some things *shouldn't* change.

✳   ✳   ✳   ✳

Jack was a pretty common name when they were young, but in all of their years together, Connie never mentioned anyone named Jack—not as a friend or even a passing acquaintance, that is, until she wanted to own the farm so badly.

Connie discovered the farm was for sale and had the idea it would be a great place to live. Now that it was so obvious, Ethan blamed himself for not knowing that *farm* Jack was *the* Jack. If he had figured it out, he was convinced he would not have bought the farm. Then his memory replayed Emily's young voice again. *That which is meant to be, must be. You can't stop it and you can't change it. Only our choices can change and that's what can change an outcome. If we are successful, something as simple as a matter of Timing will probably cause the change we want.*

Ethan and Emily had skipped stones, so they could share the most chilling evidence of the alternate outcome, the Jane Doe file. It was concrete proof that Overlap was real and forced Ethan to accept two undeniable facts. One—as of the moment Connie gave him the opportunity to be Matthew's father, the original outcome was gone forever, which turned the file into so much old paper and photographs, that Emily would find on the day she cleaned out his cabinets. (He had a lot of years to figure that one out.) And two, there was no preventing Connie and Jack's altercation at the farm. One way or another, it would happen.

Living in the outcome where Connie married Ethan instead of Jack meant that *when* Matthew found his mother, became the lone factor that was up for grabs. It was during that small window of opportunity that he and Carl might have gone to the hospital with the rest of the team, might have stopped for a soda on the way home, done any of a dozen things, gone to any of a dozen places, and arrived after Jack was done. They could have, but they didn't. Emily was right. The single changeable factor *was* a simple matter of Timing.

＊   ＊   ＊   ＊

Once they were assembling the pies, Connie heard the deafening silence between herself and Emily. In a moment, Emily would make her request again.

"Please tell the story," Emily's voice broke the quiet.

"When will you stop making me tell that old fable?"

"When I get tired of it, I guess, and it isn't a fable, CeeCee. It's our story and it was real…once."

"But it's changed now and won't ever change back. No one but your dad and Pop-op and the two of us remember the old way. To the others it's just a story."

"But they believe it."

Connie had to agree.

"Sometimes, I can hardly believe it all happened."

"You don't have the luxury of *disbelieving*, Emily" Connie gently admonished. "It was not a dream and you were there for most of it, helping the rest of us, along. Where would all of us be, right now, without you?"

"Right where we are, but the price of getting here…," Emily shook her head, "…nothing should have so high a price."

Emily's part in the story that chased her family and their friends half way around the world, was significant. She and the story had protected them. Now, the story was transformed. The life everyone remembered was forever altered. Nothing and no one could ever change it back. Thank goodness!

Beginning with this particular day, their story's last circular mark had closed. Time was satisfied and the story was over. Well, except for the chapters they would write after today.

Isaiah kept the promise he made to himself the morning he accepted that five friends really were spared by a girl, not even born yet. He expected that if Tre's mother would eventually tell Emily the story, they should contact the girl thru Connie. Everyone agreed and, together, they did the one thing they could do.

Yesterday was Emily's sixteenth birthday. Among the gifts Connie and Ethan gave her was an old and yellowing envelope with one end torn off. It bore no stamp and the return address: 'Xuan Loc'. Inside the precious paper sleeve were two letters.

The first was addressed to Connie:

Dear CeeCee,

Please forgive the informality and, although you have not met most of us yet, five big men have two requests of you. First, when Emily is old enough, please strongly recommend that she become a candy-striper and to continue until they say she is too old. It is imperative that she have the uniform. Without it, she will not be able to slip into Walter Reed, unnoticed, to remove Jean Cummings medical records and give them to Lloyd and Junior when they meet on Cummings Point Beach. A small bonfire is a pleasant way to pass the time, while she waits for them.

Second, please use the enclosed money to purchase our present for Emily's Sweet sixteen. We want for her to have something called a D-V-D and the machine to play it. In the future, a D-V-D is some sort of a movie you can purchase and view in your home. We can't tell you where to find it, or how much it and the gizmo required to play it will cost, but hopefully this will be enough to cover the expense. The title to find is 'Bounce'. You can start looking for it sometime in the year 2001. Please put them away until the morning of her birthday. Say that the givers of the gift wish for her to watch it as soon as it is opened.

The letter was signed, *With Love, The Soldiers*.

It was the second such envelope to arrive from Xuan Loc, in as many days. The first was addressed to Matthew. Connie put that one into the middle drawer of her desk, where it waited, until he Overlapped, to be opened.

This one was addressed to Connie. Thinking it was from Matthew, she hastily tore off the envelope's narrow end and removed its contents. As she unfolded the pages, five pieces of large denomination paper money floated to the floor. When she bent down to pick them up, she saw that each bill was inscribed with love by the man who gave it.

Connie read her own letter first. She was shocked that each boy had so much money to spare, until she remembered one of Matthew's earlier letters. Given where they were stationed, Army food was either in very short supply, or not provide at all. The Army called it *rations unavailable*. The men were compensated with extra pay, meant to procure food from any local vendor. Those serving in that god-forsaken place knew how accurate the descriptor, *rations unavailable*, was. Even locally, more often than not, there was no food to be had. Such was the case at the writing of their letter. They couldn't eat the money, so it served them no useful purpose. Getting Emily what she needed, to secure their collective future, would. Each man pitched in his full month's food allowance; one hundred dollars.

The second letter was to Emily. Connie read that too. It overflowed with warm affection.

Dearest Emily,

Happy Sweet sixteen, honey! As we pen this letter, you are not yet born and we do not know each other, but one day that will change. On that day, perhaps none but you, will remember what happened in the life we leave behind, what you did for us, or that we owe you our thanks and our lives. This letter will take care of that; because it will remain even though, for four of us, the memory of writing it will probably vanish.

Five big men love you and pray this letter helps you do what must be done and be more brave than you are scared. Please know that although you have <u>believed</u> for years that it is <u>us</u>, we <u>know</u> that <u>you</u> are the one who is just like Gwyneth—so brave— because Ben is right, Sweetheart, it's not brave, if you're not scared. Now, go watch your movie.

The letter closed: *"With deepest love, admiration, and respect, to the extraordinary girl who is truly the hero of all of our lives"*. Beneath that were listed five names:

Isaiah Thomas Jefferson

Abernathy Montrose Tilson
Carl Gary Summers
Lloyd Eric Cummings
Pop-op

Isaiah was right, the letters helped Emily accomplish what had to be done and made her frightening task a little less scary. If they retained no memory that she did anything at all, they would never be able to tell her that they *knew* she saved their lives. So, they also managed to do the impossible. They thanked her in advance for what she did on their behalf, in a future that was set in stone, by her, *before* she was born. Beyond everything else, they told her that they loved her.

Connie couldn't bring herself to spend the precious food money on Emily's gifts. Instead, she used her own money and gave the five old bills to Emily, along with the letters and boxes, the morning she turned Sweet-Sixteen. Emily tucked the money into the pocket of her candy-striper uniform and thought about what to do with it while she watched a D-V-D on her new player. While she waited on the beach for Lloyd and Junior Cummings to show up, she re-examined the paper bills, touching the names inscribed on them. She originally intended to return them thru Lloyd, but ultimately decided there was a better way.

Someone fortuitously left a pen inside the manila folder, containing Jean Cummings medical records. Emily scribbled a note on the inside cover—*See you at the Anniversary. One hundred will be waiting for each of you.* Lloyd and Junior didn't find the message until the mystery girl was long gone. As Lloyd lay in a hospital bed in Xuan Loc, discussing the meaning behind the story with the four men who became his new brothers, he didn't think enough about it to consider it worth mentioning.

There was something few people knew about Isaiah. He was exactly like his white brothers, in that unanswered questions plagued him. Tre often said, every question had one, even if you didn't like what it was. Isaiah wanted to know what pulled him together with the Super-heroes and Lloyd. When the boys came home from 'Nam and before beginning his training with the FBI, Isaiah had an after dinner sit-down, one-on-one, with his mother.

"Mama, do you find it peculiar that I have white friends?"

"I was wonderin' when you'd get around to that." Her voice was gentle, yet concerned. "It isn't common, Isaiah. Aside from Craig Boatman, you never even call the boys you knew before you enlisted. With Craig living way up in Boston now, baby, you haven't any friends that are your own kind. I can't remember the last time you and Craig got together, I mean, in person.

"OK, you met these white fellas in the middle of that horrible war, and some-times a war chooses your friends for you, but you're home now, baby. It's a puz-zle why you're still so close to them."

Isaiah was loath to reveal that something besides the war chose these four par-ticular friends. Associating with anyone besides the other big men, let alone an in-person reunion with Craig, was so dangerous it was out of the question. Any sort of explanation, about Craig having saved his life by getting drunk with him...well, he couldn't even tell Craig about that. For the time being, the only way to maintain any sort of relationship with Craig, (and he fully intended to do so), had to be conducted through the U.S. Postal Service or the telephone wires of Ma Bell. The five already agreed, silent and together.

"Did you ever have a close friend, that was white?" Isaiah asked.

"Me? No," Carrie Jefferson answered quickly, then paused. "Well, now that I think about it, I might have spoken too soon. When I was little, maybe around six or seven, my mama worked for this white family. They was real nice to her."

"They *were very* nice to her." Isaiah gently corrected her grammar.

"They *were very* nice to her," Carrie graciously accepted the correction, "and to me too. In the summer, some days, I went with mama, just to keep her com-pany. Once, it was a hot, hot day and the mama of the family, she give me a nickel for a ice cream."

"*Gave* me a nickel for *an* ice cream, mama," Isaiah gently corrected her again.

"Fine." She gave Isaiah her patience-wearing-thin smile and peered at him over the rim of her coffee cup. "She *gave* me a nickel for *an* ice cream. How nice that my evening coffee comes with a complimentary grammar lesson."

Isaiah's embarrassed smile said she could finish without further interruption.

"That family wasn't rich and, that mama, she didn't have to do that, but she scooted me out the door with a smile sayin', *enjoy the ice cream mommela.* She said that means 'little one'. I took my nickel and skipped all the way into town, dreamin' about the wonderful frozen cream. I was so happy when I opened the door to the ice cream parlor, but the man at the counter..." She paused, trying very hard *not* to remember how badly his words stung. "He told me to get out and called me a name. *I can pay,* I said. But it was 1938, before Martin Luther King, before Rosa Parks, before any of it, and he didn't care that my money was the same color as everyone else's." She shook her head. "I just left.

"A few minutes later, the little girl of the family come up the street. Her mama *gave* her two nickels—one for *an* ice cream and another for a movie. There I was, cryin' like a big baby, sittin' at the curb with my feet in the gutter, feelin' just like trash. That little girl sat down next to me and put her feet in the gutter beside mine. She nudged me with her shoulder, *He wouldn't serve you, would he?* My heart hurt so bad, I couldn't even talk. All I could do was shake my head. She put her arm around my shoulders and said, *I'll be right back.* Then, she got up and went inside.

Soon, she was nudging the screen door open with her foot. She stood in the doorway holding two cones. *Just like us,* she said, *one's chocolate, one's vanilla.* She smiled at me and said to pick the one I wanted, then she turned her head to speak to the man at the counter, but her smile was already gone. *She's just a little girl and she had the money. She never hurt you. Did it make you feel like a big man to hurt her? I feel dirty spending my treat money in here, but it's hot and she wanted ice cream. Believe me, I won't do it again.* Then she spoke to his customers. *The rest of you are just as bad. You kept silent while he treated someone that way. How would you feel if it had been you…or your child? Y'all should be ashamed, every last one of you.* She stepped away and let the screen door bang shut behind her.

"She couldn't have been more than six years old herself, but she tore those adults into tiny little pieces—never even raised her voice. She invited me to walk down to the park with her and I went. We sat ourselves under a tree, and talked, and laughed, and pretty soon it didn't matter what the man in the ice cream parlor thought. That little girl thought I *wasn't* trash. I didn't have the opportunity for the fine education your daddy and I got for you, baby, but just the same," her voice filled with pride, "I like to think she was right."

Isaiah took his mother's hand in his. "She *was* right, mama. She's still right."

Carrie smiled at her son. "I tried to give her my nickel, but she wouldn't take it. She said, *Someday you'll do me a favor and we'll be even.* She spent her movie money on *an* ice cream for me." The years slipped away and she resolutely nodded her head. "She was a real nice girl. Real nice. I guess you might say *she* was the closest I ever got to having a white friend, and I suppose I still owe her that favor too. Her family moved away soon after that. Her papa got himself a good job, someplace way north…Vermont or New Hampshire. I never saw her again."

"Would you like to?"

"Well sure, baby, but that'd be like wishing for the moon."

"Mama, do recall the girl's name?" Isaiah was confident he already knew the answer.

Carrie scrunched up her forehead, searching her memory, then grinned, delighted that such a fond memory had not been lost. "Matter of fact, I do. The mama was a real proper lady and her daughter was this little tom-boy, always had a skinned knee or two, but she was a real daddy's girl and he gave her a pet name.

The mama never called her anything Constance, but the daddy, the daddy always called her CeeCee."

Isaiah got up from his chair and led his mother to the living room window. He stood behind her, wrapped an arm around her shoulders. "See that?" He pointed to the bright lunar beacon that lit up the evening sky. "Tonight it's yours."

Carrie gave him a puzzled look. Isaiah decided his mother deserved to know that the long-standing favor she owed would be repaid by her son and Isaiah finally had an answer to his question. He never said, one way or the other, if he liked the answer he got.

Benny Walker's contribution can't be undervalued. He bore silent witness to an endless list of crimes against the U.S. government and its soldiers and was wise enough to do something about it. Credit Benny's dad for a shove in the right direction—*go with your gut and you'll always end up doing the right thing.*

From day-one, much, that shouldn't have been, was wrong with every mission Benny wrote up. His gut said make an extra carbon of each report and save it. Benny listened. During the final days of his tour, more than the usual fuck-up went wrong with the last two missions. He decided their rogue and out of place names was no coincidence. Fred and Ginger went together in every way, like the real Ginger's feet in her custom-made dancing shoes.

Of course, let's not forget his mother's contribution—that incredible recorder. Together, the copies and the tape provided all the physical evidence necessary to press charges against Colonel Cummings and, when all was said and done, get a conviction.

Last but not least, was Lloyd's big interview—the one he could not cancel. It was nearly 9:00 PM when another bit of land-mark legislation was finally passed, with press conference to follow. One persistent news-hound, named John Andrews, always had two questions for Lloyd. The first was relevant to his current activities, the second never changed. *Senator, won't you share the names of the Super-heroes?*

Lloyd's answer to the second question also never changed. *No, John, but thank you for asking.*

In a final attempt to get a different answer, Mr. Andrews altered his second question. *"When you were in the service, Senator, real men had to have carried you out of the jungle. You aren't still asking everyone to believe mythical Super-heroes did it?"*

In Boston, this night was quickly becoming one they would celebrate annually, but it was still not *quite* over. Lloyd thought of the remarkable, quick-acting men that carried him out of Cambodia, and the pledge they made to each other—silent and together, until it's *really* over. *"John, those men were soldiers, just doing their jobs. Actually, each was the polar opposite of a Super-hero."*

"But Senator, the polar opposite of a Super-hero is...an ordinary hero."

"Thank-you. I couldn't have put it better myself." Lloyd left the podium marveling at the ordinary heroes that peopled his world, not the least of whom was his own wife, Michelle, who spent years keeping his mother and brother hidden and safe. Because of Michelle, Junior received the education and future that Lloyd needed him to have—medical. She never once questioned why.

Michelle arrived at the Capital, just as Lloyd's interview began. When it was over, she took his hand and allowed him to help her into the limo, which whisked them off to Dulles. Lloyd sat back and thought how every question had an answer. The question that continued to plague Lloyd was why a strange girl on a deserted beach looked at his brother and him as if she already knew them, already loved them? He came to realize it was because she already did. Lloyd and Michelle boarded a plane bound for Boston's Logan International and took their seats, in first class. The flight attendant greeted them, "Good evening senator. Mrs. Cummings. Would either of you care for Champaign?" They each took a glass. Lloyd smiled at his wife and thought about their amazing life together, their daughter Katherine Jean (K-K-K-Katie to all in their family), and how heroes came in such an assortment of unexpected shapes and sizes.

Along with every other explanation that was due, were the few unanswered questions that remained. The meaning of a long ago message in a manila folder was just one of them. Among the bits of paper Emily planned to show the assembled crowd, to prove that Overlap was real, were five, rather ratty looking, one hundred dollar bills. In a far away place, on the other side of the world, the war-ravaged hands of five big men had each crumpled one of the bills in frustration, then shoved it into the pocket of his Army issue trousers, cursing the fact that the money was useless. Later, in a hospital in a ceaselessly humid jungle, the muggy bills were retrieved from those same pockets, then scrolled with the love and smeared signatures of five ordinary guys—the five big men who, all of her life, were Emily's heroes.

Outcomes were now as Time wanted them to be all along, but they did not change because everyone had chosen the primrose path. Rather, they traveled via dangerously uncertain ground, over unstable and rocky terrain. But the path, however precarious a road, had brought them all to a good life—one filled to the brim with each other.

Time's messengers would never forget the slippery-slope that was the path to this life and how one false step, by any of them, could have spelled doom for all of them. Only they would keep the memory of how destiny changed nothing…and nearly everything. With the final Overlap complete, only the Reweavers would remember how all of their lives were twisted together into the life that they were promised, over and over, had already happened.

Tonight's Anniversary (with a capital 'A') is the tightest link they all have to each other. Everyone will be fascinated by the old tale and each will share their part of the narrative as it now exists; because they are each a small part of it. As of this day, the old story will feel like hearing a fairy tale, but each Reweaver knows it is more like a nightmare. It should be hard for everyone to believe, but it won't be; because Overlap is real and the proof of it, the letters, notes, and photographs, tucked away for years and years, cannot be denied.

Connie's mental replay came to an end. Over the years, there were occasions when she questioned her own resolve to keep a long ago promise to an extraordinary young girl—defy the silence and tell the *whole* story as often as necessary. Today, working beside her granddaughter, creating the simple pies that were the only remnant of their alternate life, there was no doubt in her mind. The promise would be kept.

Connie began telling the story…

0-595-28862-6

adsworkroom@aol.c